A BRAMBLEBERRY SUMMER

RAEANNE THAYNE

THE RANCHER'S SUMMER SECRET

CHRISTINE RIMMER

MILLS & BOON

First Published in Great Britain 2021
by Mills & Boon, an imprint of HarperCollins*Publishers* Ltd
1 London Bridge Street, London, SE1 9GF

www.harpercollins.co.uk

HarperCollins*Publishers*
1st Floor, Watermarque Building,
Ringsend Road, Dublin 4, Ireland

A Brambleberry Summer © 2021 RaeAnne Thayne LLC
The Rancher's Summer Secret © 2021 Harlequin Books S.A.

Special thanks and acknowledgement are given to Christine Rimmer for her contribution to the *Montana Mavericks: The Real Cowboys of Bronco Heights* series.

ISBN: 978-0-263-29980-9

0621

MIX
Paper from
responsible sources
FSC™ C007454

This book is produced from independently certified FSC™ paper to ensure responsible forest management.

For more information visit: www.harpercollins.co.uk/green

Printed and bound in Spain
by CPI, Barcelona

A BRAMBLEBERRY SUMMER

RAEANNE THAYNE

To all the readers who have asked me to write Rosa's story over the years.

CHAPTER ONE

SUMMER SATURDAYS IN a busy tourist town like Cannon Beach, Oregon, were not for the faint of heart.

As always, the sidewalk outside Rosa Galvez's gift shop, By-The-Wind, was packed with tourists. Kids in swimming suits. Parents with sunburned noses, their arms loaded with buckets and towels and umbrellas. And, her favorite, older people arm in arm, enjoying an afternoon of browsing through the local stores.

The long, wide stretch of beach that gave the town its name was only a half block from her store, which meant she had a nonstop view of the action, both in front of her store and farther down the beach.

One could never grow bored watching the kites, the recumbent bicycles, the children building sandcastles.

Some hardy souls were even swimming in the shallows, though Rosa always considered it entirely too cold. Maybe her childhood in Honduras had left her too warm-blooded.

Instead, she was busy working the cash register at her gift shop while her newest employee and dear friend, Jen Ryan, rearranged a display of tiny hand-carved lighthouses an artist in Lincoln City had crafted for her.

Nearby, Jen's six-year-old daughter, Addie, giggled at something in the small children's area Rosa had created, complete with a miniature kitchen and dollhouse. The children's area worked beautifully to keep little hands away from the more breakable items in the store while their parents browsed.

While she finished ringing up a cute handmade teapot for her customer, she kept a watchful eye on Jen. This was only her second day working in the store, though she and Addie had been in town for a few weeks. She still seemed anxious, and was constantly looking toward the door as if she expected something horrible to burst through at any moment.

Rosa hoped that with time her friend would lose that skittish air, the impression she gave off that at the slightest provocation, she would grab her child and bolt out the door of the shop.

How could Rosa blame her, after everything Jen had been through? It was a wonder she could even go out in public. All things considered, she was doing remarkably well and seemed to be settling into life here in Cannon Beach. Having her living at Brambleberry House was a joy.

She finished carefully wrapping the customer's teapot in bubble wrap so it would be safe in whatever corner of luggage it was stuffed into.

"There you are," Rosa said, handing over the bag. "Thank you for shopping at By-The-Wind."

"Thank *you*. This is such an adorable shop. We've

been to every store in town and you have the best merchandise. Authentic and charming souvenirs. I'll definitely be back before we leave town."

"I am very glad to hear this." She smiled and waved the woman and her husband on their way. She was replenishing her supply of bubble wrap under the counter when the front-door chimes rang out again.

She happened to be looking in Jen's direction and didn't miss the way her friend's features tensed with fear and then visibly relaxed when a woman came in, trailed by a young teenager.

Rosa's day, already good, immediately brightened even further, as if the sun had just come out from behind the clouds.

"Look who it is," she exclaimed. "Two of my favorite people!"

"*Hola*, Rosa," the girl said, beaming brightly at her with a mouth full of braces.

"Hello, my dear." Her friend Carrie Abbott brushed her cheek against Rosa's.

"What a wonderful surprise. How may I help you? Are you looking for a gift for someone? I have some gorgeous new purses in and also some fantastic jewelry from an artisan in Yachats you might like."

"Where's the jewelry?" Like a little magpie, Bella was instantly drawn to anything shiny.

Rosa showed her the new display and they spent a moment looking over the hand-beaded pieces.

"Ooh. Those turquoise starburst earrings are gorgeous! How much are they?"

She named an amount that had the girl's shoul-

ders slumping. "I better not. I'm saving for an elec-
tric scooter."

"You know, that's the markup amount. I can probably drop the price by ten dollars."

Bella looked tempted. "I'm babysitting this weekend. If they're still for sale, I'll come back and get
them."

"I'll set them aside until you can get back in," Rosa
promised, which earned her another braces-filled
smile.

"You're too tempting!" Carrie said, shaking her
head. "I could blow my entire mad-money budget in
here. Believe it or not, we didn't come in to buy earrings, no matter how lovely they are."

"Is there something else I can help you find? You
should try the new soaps from Astrid Larsen."

Carrie laughed. "Stop. We're not supposed to be
shopping! I came in because I need to talk to you."

Against her will, Rosa's gaze shifted to Bella and
then back to the girl's mother. "Oh?" she said, hoping
her voice sounded casual.

Carrie leaned against the counter. "Yes. How are
you, first of all? I haven't talked to you in forever."

Carrie did not usually drop in just to chat. What
was this about? She looked back toward Bella, who
was holding the turquoise earrings up to her ears and
looking in the mirror of the display.

"I have been good." She smiled. "Summer is always
such a busy time here but I am glad for the tourists.
Otherwise, I would not be able to keep the store open.
And how are you?"

"Good. Busy, too. Bella is going in a hundred different directions, between babysitting and softball and her music lessons."

Such a normal, happy childhood. It warmed her heart. "Oh, that is nice."

"Did I tell you, we have tickets to the theater in Portland next month?" Bella said. "It's a traveling Broadway production of *Hamilton*. And then we're driving down the coast to San Francisco. I cannot *wait*!"

Rosa hid a smile. Bella had only mentioned the upcoming trip about a hundred times since spring, when she and her parents had first started talking about it. "That will be wonderful for you."

"Other than that, everything is pretty good," Carrie said. "Well, okay. I do have one small problem I was hoping you might be able to help us out with."

"Of course. What can I do?"

"Don't answer so quickly. It's a huge favor."

Carrie had to know Rosa would do anything for her. Theirs was that kind of friendship.

"I was wondering if you've found a tenant to sublease your empty apartment until fall, when your renters come back."

Rosa lived on the top floor of a sprawling old Victorian, Brambleberry House. She managed the property for her aunt and her aunt's friend, Sage Benedetto Spencer.

Right now, Jen lived in the second-floor apartment, but the older couple who had been renting the furnished ground-floor apartment for the past year had moved to Texas temporarily to help with an ill family member.

"It is still empty for now."

She didn't have the energy to go the vacation-rental route, with new people constantly coming in and out.

Carrie's features brightened. "Oh, yay! Would you consider renting it for the next month or so?"

Rosa frowned. "Why would you need a place to rent? Are you doing something to your house?"

Carrie and her husband lived in a very nice cottage about a mile from Brambleberry House. She had recently remodeled the kitchen but perhaps she was thinking about doing the bathrooms.

"Not for me," Carrie assured her. "For Wyatt and Logan."

Rosa tensed at the mention of Carrie's brother and his young son. While the boy was adorable, seven years old and cheerful as could be, his father was another matter.

Wyatt Townsend was a detective for the Cannon Beach Police Department and always seemed to look at her as if she was up to something illegal.

That was surely her imagination. She had done nothing to make him suspicious of her.

"I thought he was staying with you while his home is being repaired."

"He is. And I would be fine with him living with us until the work is done, but everything is taking so much longer than he expected. It has been a nightmare of wrangling with the insurance and trying to find subcontractors to do the work."

Wyatt's small bungalow had been damaged in a fire about a month earlier, believed to have been caused by faulty wiring. It had been a small miracle that neither he nor his son had been home at the time and that a neighbor had smelled the smoke and called the fire department before widespread damage.

Rosa knew from Carrie that the fire damage still meant he had to renovate several rooms and had been living with his sister and her husband while the work was being completed.

"That must be hard for Wyatt."

"I know. And after everything they have both been through the past three years, they didn't need one more thing. But he's doing his best to rebuild."

Rosa certainly knew what it mean to rebuild a life.

"The work will take at least another month."

"That long?"

"Yes. And to be honest, I think Wyatt is a little tired of sleeping on the sofa in my family room with his leg hanging over the edge. Since the insurance company will cover rent for the next few months, he said last night he was thinking about looking around for somewhere to stay temporarily. He even brought up the idea of renting a camp trailer and parking it in his driveway until the repairs are done. I immediately thought of your empty apartment and thought that would be so much better for him and Logan, if it's still available."

The apartment was available. But did she really want Wyatt Townsend there? Rosa glanced over at Jen, who was talking to Addie in a low voice.

She could not forget about Jen. In the other woman's situation, how would she feel about having a police detective moving downstairs?

"I know it's a huge ask. You probably have a waiting list as long as my arm for an apartment in that great location."

Rosa shook her head. "I have not really put it on the market, to be honest. I have been too busy and also I know the Smiths want to move back if they can at the end of the summer, after June's mother heals from her broken hip."

That still did not mean she wanted to rent it to Wyatt and his son. She could not even say she had a compelling reason not to, other than her own unease.

The man made her so nervous. It did not help that he was extraordinarily good-looking.

He always seemed to be looking at her as if he knew she had secrets and wouldn't rest until he figured them out.

That wouldn't bother her, as she did not usually have much to do with him. Except she *did* have secrets. So many secrets. And he was the last man in town she wanted to figure them out.

She should just say no. She could tell Carrie she had decided to paint it while it was empty or put in new flooring or something.

That wasn't completely a lie. She had talked to Anna and Sage about making a few cosmetic improvements to the apartment over the summer, but had not made any solid plans. Even if she had, none of them was urgent.

The apartment was in good condition and would be an ideal solution for Wyatt and his son while repairs continued on their house.

She had to let him stay there. How could she possibly say no to Carrie? She owed her so very much.

What would Jen think? Maybe she would find comfort in knowing a big, strong police detective lived downstairs. Their own built-in security.

"Yes. Okay. He can stay there, if he wants to."

"He will," Carrie assured her, looking thrilled. "I should mention that he has a dog. He's the cutest little thing and no trouble at all."

Rosa was not so sure about that. She had seen Wyatt and Logan walking the dog on the beach a few times when she had been walking her own dog, Fiona. Their beagle mix, while adorable, seemed as energetic as Logan.

"It should be fine. The Smiths had a little dog, too. The ground-floor apartment has a dog door out to the fenced area of the lawn. Fiona will enjoy the company."

"Oh, how perfect. It's even better than I thought. I can't thank you enough!"

"He probably will want to take a look at it before he makes any decisions. And we need to talk about rent."

She told her what the Smiths had been paying per month and Carrie's eyes widened.

"Are you kidding? That's totally a bargain around here, especially in the summer. I know the insurance company was going to pay much more than that. I'm sure it will be fantastic. You are the best."

Carrie and Bella left the store a few moments later, with Bella promising to come back so she could pay for the earrings.

As soon as the door closed behind them, Rosa slumped against the jewelry counter. What had she done?

She did *not* want Wyatt Townsend living anywhere close to her. The man looked too deeply, saw too much.

Ah, well. She would simply work a little harder to hide her secrets. She had plenty of practice.

"Sorry. Run that by me again. You did what?"

Wyatt gazed at his sister in shock. She lifted her chin, somehow managing to look embarrassed and defiant at the same time. "You heard me. I talked to Rosa Galvez about you moving into her empty apartment at Brambleberry House."

He adored his older sister and owed her more than he could ever repay for the help she had given him the last three years, since Tori had died. But she had a bad habit of trying to run his life for him.

It was his own fault. He knew what Carrie was like, how she jumped on a single comment and ran with it. He should never have mentioned to her that he was thinking about renting an apartment until the fire renovations were done. He should have simply found one and told her about it later.

"When I mentioned I was thinking about moving out, I didn't mean for you to go apartment hunting right away for me."

"I know. When you said that, I remembered Rosa had an empty apartment. As far as I'm concerned, you can stay on my family-room couch forever, but I thought a three-bedroom apartment would be better than a little camp trailer for a grown man and an active seven-year-old."

Wyatt could not disagree. In truth, he had made a few inquiries himself that day, and had discovered most of the available rental homes were unavailable all summer and those that were left were out of his price range.

What else did he expect? Cannon Beach was a popular tourist destination. Some of the short-term rentals had been booked out years in advance.

He did not mind living with his sister, brother-in-law and niece. He loved Carrie's family and Logan did, as well. But as the battle with his insurance company dragged on about doing repairs to his bungalow, he had been feeling increasingly intrusive in their lives.

Carrie was already helping him with his son. She didn't need to have them taking up every available inch of her living space with their stuff.

"The apartment at Brambleberry House is perfect! You can move in right now, it's fully furnished and available all summer."

"Why? I would have thought Rosa would want to rent it out on a longer lease."

"The couple who have been living there are supposed to be coming back in a few months. I don't think Rosa is very thrilled about having vacation renters in and out all summer."

"What makes you think having Logan and me downstairs would be better for her?"

"She knows you two. You're friends."

He was not sure he would go that far. Rosa hardly talked to him whenever they were at any kind of social event around town. He almost thought she went out of her way to avoid him, though he was not sure what he might have done to offend her.

"She said it was fine and that you can move in anytime. Today, if you want to. Isn't that wonderful?"

Again, Wyatt wasn't sure *wonderful* was the word he would use. This would only be a temporary resting place until the repairs were completed on their house.

On the other hand, it would be better for Logan than Wyatt's crazy camp-trailer idea. He couldn't deny that.

Poor kid. His world had been nothing but upheaval the past three years, though Wyatt had tried to do his best to give him a stable home life after Tori died.

Wyatt had been working as a police officer in Seattle when his wife went into cardiac arrest from a congenital heart condition none of them had known about. Logan had been four.

Numb with shock at losing his thirty-year-old, athletic, otherwise healthy wife, he had come home to Cannon Beach, where his sister lived, and taken a job with the local police department.

He hadn't known what else to do. His parents had wanted to help but both were busy professionals with demanding careers and little free time to devote to a grieving boy. Carrie had love and time in abundance, and she had urged him to move here, with a slower pace and fewer major crimes than the big city.

The move had been good for both of them. Wyatt liked his job as a detective on the Cannon Beach police force. He was busy enough that he was never bored but he was also not totally overwhelmed.

He worked on a couple of drug task forces and the SWAT team, which had only been called out a handful of times during his tenure here, all for domestic situations.

The move had been even better for Logan. He loved spending time with his aunt, uncle and older cousin, Bella. He had a wide circle of friends and a budding interest in marine biology.

Wyatt loved seeing his son thrive and knew Carrie and her family were a huge part of that. Logan spent as much time at her house as he did their own.

During the past month, both of them had spent more than enough time with Carrie and her family, since they were living there.

Another month and they could move back to his house, he hoped.

Wyatt counted his blessings that his bungalow hadn't been a complete loss. Fire crews had responded quickly and had been able to save most of the house except the kitchen, where the fire had started, probably from old, faulty wiring. The main living area had also been burned. Even so, all the rooms had suffered water and smoke damage.

Dealing with the renovations was a tedious job, filled with paperwork, phone calls and aggravation, but Wyatt could definitely see the light at the end of the tunnel.

"What do you think?" Carrie looked apprehensive but excited. "Don't you think it's a fabulous idea? Brambleberry House is so close, you can easily drop off Logan when you need me to watch him."

Location definitely was a plus. Carrie's house and Rosa's were only a few blocks apart. Brambleberry House was also positioned about halfway between his house and his sister's, which would be convenient when he was overseeing the repairs.

Wyatt knew there were many advantages to moving into an apartment at Brambleberry House. Wouldn't it be good to have their own space again? Somewhere he could walk around in his underwear once in a while if he needed to grab a pair of jeans out of the dryer, without having to worry about his sister or his niece walking in on him?

"It could work," he said, not quite willing to jump a hundred percent behind the idea. "Are you sure Rosa is okay with it?"

"Totally great." Carrie gave a bright smile that somehow had a tinge of falseness to it. What wasn't she telling him? Did Rosa Galvez really want to rent the apartment or had Carrie somehow manipulated her into doing it?

He wouldn't put it past his sister. She had a way of persuading people to her way of thinking.

Wyatt's cop instincts told him there was more to Rosa Galvez than one could see on the surface. She had secrets, but then most people did.

The bottom line was, he was not interested in digging into her secrets. She could keep them.

As long as she obeyed the law, he was not going to pry into her business. Rosa could have all the secrets she wanted. It was nothing to him.

So why, then, was he so apprehensive about moving into Brambleberry House?

He did not have a rational reason to say no. It really did make sense to have their own place. It would be better for Logan, which was the only thing that mattered, really.

It was only a month, maybe two at the most. Wyatt would survive his unease around her.

"Are you sure the apartment is affordable?"

"Absolutely. She told me how much she's charging and you won't find anything else nearly as nice in that price range. It's well within your budget. And I forgot to mention, the apartment already has a dog door for Hank and a fenced area in the yard."

That would be another plus. Logan's beagle mix was gregarious, energetic and usually adorable, but Carrie's two ragdoll cats were not fans of the dog. They would be more than glad to have Hank out of their territory.

"It sounds ideal," he said, finally surrendering to the inevitable. "Thanks for looking into it for us."

"As I said, the apartment is ready immediately. You can stay there tonight, if you want."

He blinked. How had things progressed so quickly from him merely mentioning the night before that he was thinking about moving out to his sister handling all the details and basically shoving him out the door today?

He could think of no good reason to wait and forced a smile. "Great. I'll start packing everything up and we can head over as soon as Logan gets home from day camp."

Carrie's face lit up. "You can at least wait for dinner. I imagine Rosa is probably working until six or seven, anyway."

"Right."

"I think you're going to love it. Rosa is so nice and she has a new tenant, Jen Ryan, who has a little girl who is a bit younger than Logan. Rosa has a wonderful dog, Fiona, who is more human than dog, if you ask me. I'm sure Hank will love her."

At the sound of his name, Wyatt's beagle mix jumped up from the floor, grabbed a ball and plopped it at Wyatt's feet. He picked it up and tossed it down the hall. Hank scrambled after it, much to the disdain of one of the ragdolls, who was sprawled out in a patch of sunlight.

He had seen Rosa on the beach, walking a gorgeous Irish setter. They were hard to miss, the lovely woman and her elegant dog.

Rosa was hard to miss anywhere. She was the sort of woman who drew attention, only in part because of her beautiful features and warm dark eyes.

She exuded warmth and friendliness, at least with everyone else in town. With Wyatt, she seemed watchful and reserved.

That didn't matter, he supposed. She was kind enough to let him live in her apartment for the next month. He didn't need her to be his best friend.

CHAPTER TWO

NOW THAT THE deed was done, Rosa was having second, third and fourth thoughts about Wyatt Townsend moving in downstairs.

Why had she ever thought this would work?

That evening as she pulled weeds in the backyard after leaving the store, she had to fight all her instincts that were urging her to call up Carrie right now and tell her she had made a mistake. The apartment was no longer available.

"There is no law against changing your mind, is there?" she asked out loud to Fiona, who was lying in the grass nearby, watching butterflies dance amid the climbing roses.

The dog gave her a curious look then turned back to her business, leaving Rosa to sigh. She yanked harder at a stubborn weed that had driven deep roots into the ground.

She would do nothing. She had given her word and could not back out now. Integrity, keeping her word, was important. She had learned that first from her own mother and then from her adopted parents.

Lauren and Daniel Galvez were two of the most honorable people she knew. They would never think of reneging on a promise and she couldn't, either.

Yes, Wyatt made her extremely nervous. She did not want him moving in downstairs. But she had given her word to his sister. End of story.

Because of that, she would be gracious and welcoming to him and to his sweet son.

Thinking about Logan left her feeling a little bit better about the decision. He was a very adorable boy, with good manners and a ready smile.

It was not the boy's fault that Wyatt made her so nervous.

She had almost talked herself into at least accepting the new status quo, when an SUV pulled up to the house a half hour later.

Fiona lifted her head to sniff the air, then rose and hurried over to the vehicle to greet the newcomers.

Rosa climbed to her feet a little more slowly, pulled off her gloves and swiped at her hair before she headed for the vehicle. She might be accepting of her new tenants, but summoning the same kind of enthusiasm her dog showed so readily would be a stretch.

When Rosa reached the vehicle, Logan was opening the back door and jumping to the ground, his little dog close behind.

Fiona barked a greeting, then leaned in to sniff the newcomer, tail wagging. The Townsends' dog sniffed back, and a moment later, the two were circling each other with joy.

At least Fiona was happy to have them here.

"Hello, Logan," Rosa said.

"Hi." The boy beamed at her, showing off a gap in his teeth that she found adorable.

"Guess what?" he said. "We're moving into your house! Dad says we can stay here until our house is done and I'll have my own bedroom and won't have to sleep in Aunt Carrie's sewing room anymore."

"This is so wonderful, no?" She smiled down at him, trying not to pay any attention to his father walking around the vehicle, looking big and serious and intimidating.

"What is the name of your dog?"

"This is Hank. Don't worry. He's nice."

"I never doubted it for a minute," she assured him. "Hello, Hank."

She reached down to pet the dog, who responded by rolling over to have his belly scratched. Rosa loved him immediately.

"This is Fiona. She is also very nice."

Logan grinned and petted Fiona's long red coat.

Wouldn't it be lovely if she only had to deal with the boy and the dog? Unfortunately, the boy had a father. She had to say something to Wyatt, at least. Bracing herself, she lifted her attention from the two dogs and the boy, and faced the man who always looked as if he could see through her skin and bones into her heart, and was not convinced he liked what he saw.

She drew in a deep breath and forced a smile. "Hello. Welcome to Brambleberry House."

He nodded, always so serious. "Thank you for allowing us to stay here until our house is repaired. It's very kind of you."

She shrugged. "The apartment was empty. Houses are meant to be lived in. Brambleberry House in particular seems a little sad without people, especially children."

She immediately regretted her words, especially when Wyatt raised a skeptical eyebrow.

"Your house seems sad."

Logan giggled. "Houses can't be sad. They're just houses."

She shrugged. "This is no ordinary house. I think you will find that after you have been here a few nights. Come. I will show you your apartment."

She did not wait for a response, but simply walked up the front steps and into the entryway.

"There are three levels of the house with three apartments, one taking up each level. We share the foyer. We try to keep the outside door locked for the security of our residents. I will give you the code, as well as the key."

She was even more vigilant about that right now for Jen's sake.

Wyatt nodded. "Makes sense."

"Your apartment has a separate key. It is on the ground floor. I live on the top floor. If you have any questions or problems, you can find me there or at the store."

"My sister told me you have another new tenant on the second floor."

Rosa's protective instincts flared. "This is true. Her

name is Jen Ryan. She lives there with her daughter, Addie, who is six."

"I don't believe I know her."

It was one thing for Wyatt to look at *her* with suspicion. She could not let him turn his police detective's scrutiny toward Jen.

"Jen and Addie only moved here a short time ago from Utah. She is a friend of mine from university."

"Ah. That must be why her name doesn't ring a bell. What brought her to Cannon Beach?"

Rosa's hackles rose. Jen did not need all these questions. It would not do for Wyatt to become too curious. "She works for me. She was looking for a change and I needed someone to help me at the gift store."

He nodded. "Guess I haven't been in for a while or I might have met her already."

He hadn't been in ever, as far as she could remember. But then, Wyatt Townsend was not the sort to buy shell wind chimes or lighthouse-shaped knickknacks.

"I can introduce you after I show you your apartment, if you would like."

"Sure."

Better to get their introduction out of the way. With luck, Wyatt could then forget about Jen.

She would have to send a text to Jen to warn her before showing up at her door with a police detective.

She had already told the other woman about the new tenant moving in. As she had expected, Jen had been both apprehensive and relieved, for a complex mix of reasons.

"This house is big," Logan exclaimed, looking up at

the grand entry stairway, one of Rosa's favorite parts of Brambleberry House.

She smiled, in full agreement. "Yes. Each apartment has at least two bedrooms and two bathrooms. And each has a lovely view of the ocean."

She unlocked the first-floor apartment and swung open the door. Immediately, the sweet scent of freesia drifted through the air.

It wasn't unusual to smell flowers at random places in the house. She knew her aunt Anna and Sage Spencer believed the ghost of the previous owner still walked the halls.

Abigail Dandridge had died a decade ago and left the house jointly to Anna and Sage. She had been dear friends to them and also had left Anna By-The-Wind, the gift shop in town that Rosa was a part owner of and now running.

All the old-timers in town still remembered Abigail with fondness. Hardly a week went by when someone did not come into the shop with a memory of Abigail.

Rosa wished she could have known her. She also wanted to be the sort of person whom people remembered with such fondness.

She wasn't sure she believed the stories that Abigail still lingered in the home she had loved and she was also quite certain a no-nonsense police officer like Wyatt Townsend would never believe a benevolent spirit drifted through the place.

She couldn't deny that scent of freesia, though, which had no logical explanation.

Ignoring it for now, she let them inside the apartment.

"This apartment is the largest in the house. It has three bedrooms and a very nice sunroom. The master bedroom and the kitchen face the ocean. The other two bedrooms each have a view of the garden."

"Oh, I like this place." Logan ran into the sunroom, which had an entire wall made of glass.

"That looks like a great place to read a book on a stormy afternoon."

"Yeah. Maybe you can read me more of *The Hobbit*," Logan said.

"Sure thing."

Wyatt smiled down at his son with a softness Rosa had not seen before. Instead of looking stern and foreboding, he looked younger and far more handsome.

A little shiver of awareness blossomed in her stomach. She swallowed, taken completely off guard.

No. No, no, *no*. She did not want to be attracted to this man. It was nothing personal against Wyatt Townsend. She wasn't interested in romance at all. Okay, it was a *little* personal. She especially didn't want to suddenly find herself attracted to a police detective who was trained to be suspicious of people.

She let out a slow breath. This was ridiculous. He was her tenant and her friend's brother. That was all. She was not attracted to him. She would simply not allow it.

She had too much to worry about right now, keeping Jen safe. She did not have time to be distracted by a gruff detective, no matter how sweetly he smiled at his adorable son.

"The laundry room is off the kitchen there. You can

control the temperature of your apartment independently of the other two units in the house. The control is in the hallway. The garbage trucks, they come on Monday. This apartment has a dog door so that Hank can go out into the fenced area of the yard during the day if he needs."

"That will be handy."

"The garden is for all the guests to use at any time. We have a swing in the tree that Logan might enjoy. I know that Addie does. We also have direct access to the beach, but I ask that you keep the gate locked for security reasons. It is the same code as the front door, which I have written on the paper for you, and your key will also open it."

"Got it."

"Do you have any questions?"

"I have a question," Logan said. "Can Hank and me play with your dog sometime?"

She smiled. "Of course. Anytime. She comes to the store with me most of the time during the day, but when we are home, she would love to play with you."

She looked up to find Wyatt watching her with an expression she could not read. It still made her nervous.

"If you think of any other questions, my phone number is there on the desk."

"Got it. Thank you again. We'll try not to be any trouble for you."

His features were stern once more, making her wish suddenly that he would smile at her as he smiled at his son.

"Yes. We don't like trouble here at Brambleberry House. I would hate to have to call the *policia* on you."

Logan's eyes went big. "My dad is the *policia*!"

She smiled at him. "I know. I was only teasing. Do you have things I could help you carry in?"

"Not much. A couple of suitcases. Logan and I can get them."

"Only that?"

"We're traveling pretty light these days. A lot of our things were damaged in the fire by the smoke and by the water from the fire hoses."

She needed the reminder that they had been through difficult things the past few months. It was a small sacrifice to offer a home to them, which she could easily do.

She could also be kind and gracious to them, despite her personal misgivings about having Wyatt in her space.

"I am sorry for that. If there is anything else you need, please let me know."

"Carrie said you have dishes and pots and pans and things."

"Yes. The apartment is fully furnished."

"That will be handy. Thanks."

His poor little boy. First, he lost his mother, then he lost his house to a fire. She wanted to cuddle him close and make everything all better.

"What about food? You will need to get groceries."

"Carrie sent along some meals I only have to thaw and heat for the first few days. We'll head to the grocery store this evening to pick up some staples after we unload our things. Most of the time, we eat pretty simply, don't we, Logan?"

The boy nodded. "Except Aunt Carrie says we go out to eat too much and I need more vegetables." He gave Rosa a conspiratorial look. "I don't really like vegetables."

"Yes, but you must eat them, anyway, if you want to be strong and healthy when you grow up. My mother used to tell me 'Rosa, if you eat enough vegetables, soon they will taste like candy.' They never did, but I still like vegetables."

He laughed, as she'd hoped, and Rosa felt a little pang. She loved children but didn't expect she would ever have any of her own, for a wide variety of reasons.

"Your mother sounds funny."

"She was. She always tried to make me laugh, even when things sometimes felt very dark."

She missed her mother deeply. The older she got, the more Rosa realized how many sacrifices Maria Elena made on her behalf. She had never been hungry, even though she knew her mother barely made a living cleaning homes for some of the more well-off people in their village. Her mother had always insisted she work hard at school so she could have a brighter future.

She pushed away the memories of her childhood. Her first fifteen years sometimes seemed a lifetime ago, as if they had happened to someone else.

"Oh," she said, suddenly remembering. "I wanted you to meet Jen and Addie, who live upstairs from you."

"All right."

"Let me check if she can meet you."

She quickly sent a text to her friend. After a longer-than-usual pause, Jen replied that she and Addie would come down to the foyer.

"She said she would meet us outside your door," she explained to Wyatt.

"Okay."

"You will like Addie, Logan. Maybe you will make a new friend."

"Maybe."

Life could be filled with so much pain sometimes, Rosa thought as they walked out into the hall to wait for Jen. Each of the inhabitants of Brambleberry House had walked a hard road.

At least for now, they had a safe place to rest, a beautiful home set on the seashore surrounded by flowers, one that might contain a friendly spirit who could not seem to leave.

As Wyatt waited for his upstairs neighbor to come down to meet him and Logan, he couldn't shake the feeling that this was too good to be true.

The apartment was perfect for their needs, with a good-size bedroom for Logan and a very nice en suite for him, as well as an extra room he could use for an office if he needed.

It was actually bigger than their little house and certainly had a bigger yard for Logan to play in.

Brambleberry House would be an ideal temporary home for them while the construction crew repaired the fire damage at his place.

He still had misgivings but Rosa had been welcoming enough. She was certainly kind to Logan, if still distant toward Wyatt.

He followed her into the foyer, with its sweeping staircase and elegant chandelier, to find a woman walking down with a young girl's hand clutched tightly in hers.

She had brown hair pulled back into a tight ponytail and quite striking blue eyes with shadows under them.

"Jen, here are the new tenants I was telling you about," Rosa said in her melodious, accented voice. "This is Wyatt Townsend and his son, Logan. Wyatt is a police officer in Cannon Beach and Logan is seven years old, starting second grade when the summer is over."

"Hello."

She was soft-spoken and didn't meet his gaze directly.

Just what he needed. Another woman here who had secrets.

"Pleasure to meet you." He purposely kept his voice calm, neutral, as he did when he walked into a situation where a witness or a suspect might be prone to bolt.

He didn't miss the way Rosa placed her body slightly in front of her friend's, as if to protect her. He had a feeling Jen didn't miss it, either.

From him? Did Rosa really think he posed a threat to either of them?

The little girl seemed to have none of her mother's skittishness. She stepped forward with a big smile. "Hi. My name is Addie and I'm six years old."

"Hi, Addie." Wyatt was happy to see she seemed well-adjusted and friendly. Whatever was going on with her mother hadn't impacted her yet.

"Hi," she said to Logan, who hadn't said anything yet. "My name is Addie."

"I know. I heard you before."

"What's your name?"

"Logan. I'm seven." His son spoke with a tinge of superiority over his advanced age that made Wyatt hide a smile.

He caught Rosa's gaze and didn't miss her surprised look. What? Did she think he never smiled?

Addie pointed behind them. "Is that your dog?"

Wyatt turned to find Hank plopped in the doorway as if he owned the place.

"Yep," Logan answered. "His name is Hank."

"Will he bite?"

"Only if you bite him first," Logan said, which made Addie giggle.

"I'm not going to bite a dog! That would be gross."

"You can pet him, if you want."

She plopped onto the ground and Hank, predictably, rolled over to have his belly scratched. The dog was shameless for affection.

"I don't have a dog, I have a cat. Her name is Lucy. She's old," Addie explained. "Sometimes I pretend that Fi is my dog."

"Who is Fi?" Logan looked confused.

"Fiona," Rosa explained. "My dog, remember? Sometimes we call her Fi. And you can pretend all you want, darling."

"I will," the girl said cheerfully.

"How are you enjoying Cannon Beach so far?" Wyatt asked Jen Ryan.

She focused her attention somewhere over his shoulder, still not meeting his gaze.

"I like it here. The people are friendly, for the most part, and the scenery is amazing."

"Rosa said you came from Utah. I've got friends there. What part?"

He wasn't surprised when his innocent-seeming question made both Rosa and Jen tense. As he suspected, she was in some kind of trouble. Was she running from an abusive relationship or a custody problem? Or something else?

The two women looked at each other for a moment then Jen gave a smile that looked forced. "A small town in Utah, near the Idaho border. No one has ever heard of it."

She answered in such an offhand manner, he knew she was being deliberately evasive.

He wanted to ask her what town in Utah, but suspected she would shut down fast if he asked.

He also didn't want to raise the wrath of Rosa Galvez. Not when she was doing him a big favor by letting him stay here.

Anyway, Jen Ryan was only a neighbor. Not a suspect.

She probably had very legit reasons to be cautious of strangers.

Sometimes he needed to remind himself to separate the detective from the man. They would be sharing this house for the next month, but likely would not see much of each other, anyway. Did he really need to know the poor woman's life story?

"Rosa says you are a police detective."

"Yes."

"I see."

She didn't sound thrilled at the confirmation. He couldn't help feeling a little defensive. He was passionate about his job, protecting and serving, and tried to do it with compassion and dedication toward all.

"It was nice to meet you," she said, though he suspected she was lying. "I hope you're comfortable here."

"Thank you."

"Come on, Addie."

The girl protested a little but still took her mother's hand and the two of them went back up the stairs again. Addie sent a smile over her shoulder all the way up the stairs at Logan and Hank and her pretend dog, Fiona.

That one would be a little heartbreaker when she grew up. He could tell she already knew how to charm people.

He turned back to Rosa in time to see her watching Jen with a worried expression. When she felt his gaze, she quickly wiped it away.

"There. Now everyone knows everyone else living in the house."

"Yes." One big not-so-happy family. "We'll just grab our things and settle in."

She nodded. "Be sure to contact me if you have any questions."

"Thank you."

"Good night, then. Come on, Fiona. We have tools to put away."

She walked outside in the fading sunlight and he and Logan followed her to grab their suitcases and the few boxes of belongings he had brought from his sister's house.

When they returned from the last trip outside, Logan collapsed onto the comfortable-looking couch. "I like this place. It feels nice."

Logan was the reason he was here. Wyatt was grateful for the reminder. He and his son needed their own place until the house was ready. It was only a short time, and then they could get back to their real life.

Yes, he might be uncomfortably attracted to Rosa Galvez, but he wasn't about to make the mistake of acting on that attraction.

No matter how tempting.

CHAPTER THREE

THE BUSY SUMMER season and her responsibilities at By-The-Wind, combined with her volunteer activities, meant Rosa only saw her new tenants in passing for several days after they moved in.

Even when she didn't actively see them, she was aware of them. Knowing that Wyatt was living two floors below her, she couldn't seem to stop imagining him walking around the house at night. Taking a shower, sprawling out on the big king-size bed wearing next to nothing...

Her entirely too vivid imagination annoyed her severely. When she would catch her mind dwelling on him, she would quickly jerk away her attention and make herself think about something boring, like taking inventory or meeting with her tax accountant. Anything to keep her mind off the attractive man who lived downstairs.

She wasn't sure how she would make it through an entire month or more of this.

Rosa was trying hard to remember that Wyatt and Logan were guests in the house. A month wasn't long, especially during the busy tourist season, when the store was so busy she didn't have much free time, anyway.

She could endure having them there, even if their stay dragged into two months, especially as it was one small way she could work on repaying her vast debt to his sister.

Nearly a week after Wyatt and Logan moved in, Rosa sat in her spare bedroom at the desk she had pulled beneath the window overlooking the Pacific, wishing for rain. For the last few days, the weather seemed as unsettled as she felt. The days had been overcast, brooding like a petulant teenager.

Outside, the ocean seethed and churned, restless in the random moonbeams that found their way through the gathering clouds.

Perhaps a storm would blow through and wash away the unseasonable heat that seemed to have settled over the area.

Brambleberry House did not have air conditioning, as summers here along the coast were mild. The nights usually turned cooler, but until the sun went down, her apartment on the third floor of the old house could be stultifying.

Rosa spent most of her evenings working in the garden. She missed Sonia Davis, the woman who had lived on the second floor until two Christmases earlier, when her estranged husband had come to fetch her, and Rosa had learned her tenant had been living under an assumed name.

Rosa's thumb wasn't nearly as green as Sonia's, and

her friend now lived happily with her husband in Haven Point, Idaho. The gardens didn't look as good as they had under Sonia's care, but Rosa did her best.

To her delight, Jen and Addie joined her most evenings. She enjoyed both the company and the help, and was thrilled to see Jen becoming more at ease here in Cannon Beach.

Her friend was settling in. She seemed more comfortable at the gift shop, as well, no longer looking as if she wanted to escape every time a man walked in.

Rosa felt good about her progress. She had wondered if encouraging Jen and her daughter to leave behind their life in Utah was the best decision. Seeing her friend begin to relax into her new life gave her hope that she had been right.

Rain suddenly clicked against the window and she looked up from her laptop. Finally! Perhaps a storm would at last blow away the heat.

Unable to resist, she opened the window more and leaned down to watch the storm roll in.

Lightning arced across the sky, followed closely by a low rumble of thunder. In the blast of light, she could see the sea, dark and tumultuous.

Rosa loved a good storm. They probably should frighten her, especially after some of the intense storms she had experienced in Honduras, but she always found them invigorating. Refreshing in their own way.

She gave up work and decided to relax with a book. The only thing better than a storm was curling up with a good book while she enjoyed it from a safe shelter.

Books had saved her when she first came to the

United States. She had always loved to read, but the book selection had been limited in their village.

Once she had moved in with Daniel and Lauren, she had free rein at the town library in Moose Springs and at the school library. Books helped her learn English. Like most other girls her age, she had fallen in love with Harry Potter. Lauren had been wise enough to buy her both the Spanish and the English versions. Rosa would read both at the same time, comparing the words and the sentences to help with her word fluency and her grammar construction.

She still reread the books often. Once in a while she would read the Spanish version so that she didn't lose touch with the language of her heart, but mostly she read in English.

She was currently reading a cozy mystery by one of her favorite authors. She settled into her favorite reading spot, a wide armchair in the corner of her bedroom, and was deep into the story when she was distracted by a sudden banging from outside.

The sound stopped as abruptly as it started. She sank back down and picked up her book again, then she heard it once more.

With a sigh, she set aside the book. If only she had a landlord she could call. Unfortunately, things that banged in the night were *her* responsibility.

She had a feeling she knew what the trouble was. The door on the garden shed wasn't latching tightly. She had noticed it the last time she had mowed the lawn.

If she wasn't mistaken, that was the door to the shed blowing open, then banging shut.

Lightning flashed again, and in that burst of light, she could see she was right. The garden shed door was wide open.

As much as she didn't want to go out into the rain, she couldn't let the banging continue all night, for her tenants' sake, as well as to protect the contents of the shed.

Rosa threw on her rain boots and coat and found a flashlight, then hurried down the stairs.

When she reached the bottom step, the door to the ground-floor apartment swung open suddenly. Startled, she almost stumbled but caught herself just in time.

Wyatt stood there, silhouetted by the light coming from inside the apartment. He looked rumbled and gorgeous, his hair messy as if he had been dozing.

He was wearing jeans and a T-shirt, and was barefoot. Through the open doorway, she could see a television on inside with a baseball game playing.

Logan was nowhere in sight, which led her to believe he must be sleeping.

Her mouth felt dry suddenly and Rosa had to grip the railing of the stairs to keep her balance.

Ridiculous. What was *wrong* with her?

"Sounds like trouble out there."

She nodded. "Nothing major. I believe it is the door to the garden shed. It is not latching the way it should."

"You're not going out in that, are you? Some of those lightning strikes seem close. That's nothing to mess around with."

"I know. But I cannot let it bang all night to disturb everyone."

He gave her a long look, then nodded. "Give me a moment to throw on some shoes, then I'll come with you."

"That is not necessary," she protested. "I can wedge it closed with a rock if I can't fix it."

"Wait. I'll only be a minute."

She really could handle it by herself, but didn't want to be rude so she waited. A few moments later, he returned wearing tennis shoes and a raincoat with a Cannon Beach Police Department logo.

Together they walked out of the house. The temperature had cooled down considerably. Rosa shivered a little at the wet wind that blew through the porch.

Her eagle-eyed neighbor didn't miss her reaction. "I can handle this, if you want to stay here on the porch, where it's dry."

She shook her head. "*You* should stay here where it's dry. Taking care of the house is my responsibility."

"Fine. We'll both go."

She pulled up her hood and hurried down the steps toward the garden shed.

When they reached it, she was grateful for his help. The door was heavy and the wind made it hard to move. She wasn't sure she could have wrestled it on her own.

"I don't think you're going to be able to fix the latch tonight. Where's the rock you were talking about so we can keep it closed until the weather is a little better?"

"I will have to find something."

Lightning flashed again, followed almost immediately by thunder. It was one thing to enjoy the storm from the comfort of her easy chair. It was something else to be out in the middle of it, with the wind whipping raindrops hard at her face.

She fumbled to turn on the light inside the shed. Wyatt joined her in the small space and she was instantly aware of him. He smelled delicious, some sort of masculine scent that reminded her of the mountains around Moose Gulch, covered in sagebrush and pine.

His gaze landed on a heavy concrete block. "That should do it for now."

He reached down to pick it up and brushed against her. Rosa quickly took a step back, though there wasn't much room to escape.

He didn't appear to notice, much to her relief.

He left the shed again. She took a moment to draw a steadying breath, then turned to follow him. As she reached to turn the light off, her hand caught on something sharp inside.

Pain sliced through her and she couldn't help her gasp.

"What is it?"

"Nothing," she said. "Only a scratch. I am fine."

In another lightning flash, she saw he looked doubtful but he didn't argue with her.

He muscled the door shut, then wedged the concrete block in front of it.

"That should do it, barring a hurricane tonight." He raised his voice to be heard over the storm.

"Let us hope we do not have a hurricane. I had enough of those when I was a girl."

He gave her an interested look but didn't ask questions. Another lightning bolt lit up the sky, followed by the loudest thunder yet, a rumble that seemed to shake the little garden shed.

"That one was too close." Wyatt frowned. "We need to get to shelter. We're too exposed here."

He led the way to the closest entry to the house, the door to his sunroom.

This was one of her favorite parts about Brambleberry House. If she was ever tempted to leave her third-floor sanctuary, it would be to move to this floor so that she could have the sunroom, with the glorious view of the ocean.

Rosa could spend all day every day here. She would probably put in a bed so she could sleep here on long summer nights with the sound of the sea and the breeze blowing through.

She liked the idea of it but the reality probably would not be as appealing. She would feel too exposed here. Anyone could walk up from the beach, climb over the beach gate and break a window to get in.

She would have no defenses.

That was the reason she had not given this apartment to Jen, though both had come vacant at the same time and this apartment was larger. Jen needed to feel safe, above all else.

Security wasn't an issue for Wyatt. Something told Rosa the man could take care of himself in all situations.

"Now," he said when they were inside, "let's take a look at your hand."

Rosa tensed, suddenly aware of how cozy this sunroom was in the middle of a storm.

She should not have come in here with him. Not when she was fighting this unwanted attraction.

"It is fine. I only need to put a bandage on it. I can take care of it upstairs."

Wyatt frowned. "It's your right hand, which is always harder to bandage for someone who is right-handed. Let me take a look."

How had he noticed she was right-handed? Something told her Wyatt was a man who did not miss much.

He flipped on the light inside the sunroom and held out his hand. Unless she wanted to run through the apartment and up two flights of stairs in her awkward rain boots, she had no choice but to show him the wound.

The cut on her palm was about two inches long, shallow but bloody.

Rosa felt her knees go weak at the sight of those streaks of red. To her great embarrassment, the sight of blood always left her feeling as if she would faint.

Her mother used to be a healer of sorts and people would come to their small house for care. Maria Elena had even delivered a few babies.

Rosa had never liked seeing blood or having to help her mother clean it up. It was a weakness she despised in herself, but one she couldn't seem to help.

"Sit down and I'll go grab my first-aid kit. Normally, I keep one in the kitchen but it burned up in the fire. Lucky for you, I've got another one out in my vehicle."

Was she lucky? Rosa would have liked to argue but she was trying too hard not to look at the blood dripping off her hand.

After he left, she tried to focus instead on the storm still rumbling around them.

He and Logan had already left a mark on this room. It was obviously well-used. A couple of children's chapter books were stacked on the table and she could see some small trucks on the floor.

Wyatt returned a moment later with a red case. "Come into the kitchen, where we can wash off the blood. I should have had you do that while I was getting the first-aid kit. Sorry. I wasn't thinking."

She followed him, trying to come up with the words to tell him again that she could take care of her very minor injury on her own.

No words would come to her other than the truth— that she was afraid to let him touch her.

Since she couldn't tell him that, of course, she followed him into the kitchen.

Here, again, he and Logan had made the space their own. A couple of art-class projects had been stuck with magnets to the refrigerator and homework was spread out on the table.

Hank, his cute little dog, wandered into the room and stretched in a dog-yoga pose as Wyatt pulled a few paper towels off the roll.

"Come over here by the sink."

Keeping her gaze fixed away from the cut, she followed him. He turned on the sink and ran his hand under it for a few moments to gauge the temperature, then carefully gripped her hand and guided it under.

Rosa held her breath. Why did he have to smell so good?

He turned her hand this way and that to rinse off the blood. "I don't think you need stitches. It's fairly shallow."

"That is what I thought also."

"We can clean it off pretty well and I think I have a bandage big enough to cover it."

She didn't see any point in arguing with him when he was trying to help her. "Thank you."

Why did her voice sound so breathy and soft? She had to hope he did not notice.

Lightning flashed again outside, followed almost immediately by a loud clap of thunder. She managed to swallow her instinctive gasp.

"How does Logan sleep through such a noise?"

He smiled softly and she felt those nerves sizzle inside her again.

"He can sleep through just about anything. It's a talent I wish I shared."

"I, as well." She was unable to resist smiling back. He seemed a different person when talking about his son, much more open and approachable.

He looked at her for a moment, then seemed to jerk his attention back to her hand.

He patted it dry with a bit of gauze from the first-aid kit. "I didn't see what you scratched your hand on out there."

"A nail, I think. I am not sure. I will have to look more closely in the daylight."

He nodded. "Any idea when your last tetanus shot was? If it was a nail, it might be rusty. This is the coast, after all. Everything rusts."

"I had the shot only a few years ago after I stepped on a rock at the beach and needed a few stitches."

It was a good thing she had been with friends that time. Her foot had bled so much, she probably would have been too light-headed to walk to her car.

"Good news, then. You shouldn't need a second shot. I'm just going to put a little first-aid cream on it. If it doesn't start to heal in a few days, you will probably want to see your doctor."

"Yes. I will do that."

She missed having Melissa Fielding living in this apartment. Melissa was a nurse and was great at patching up scrapes and cuts. Now she was happily married to Eli Sanderson, who was a doctor in town. Eli was a wonderful stepfather to Melissa's daughter, Skye, and they had a new baby of their own, Thomas.

Wyatt squeezed out the antibiotic cream on the bandage before sticking it onto her skin.

"That is smart."

"A little trick my mother taught me."

"She sounds like a very wise woman."

He smiled a little and she again had to order her nerves to behave. "She is. She's a judge in Portland. That's where Carrie and I grew up."

"I thought your mother was friends with Abigail." She frowned a little, trying to make the connection.

"She was, sort of. It was really our grandmother who was best friends with Abigail. My mother grew up here, in a house not far from Brambleberry House. Her parents lived there until they died several years ago. I can remember visiting Abigail a few times, back in the days when the house was all one unit, with no apartments."

The curtains suddenly fluttered and Hank, who had just settled down on the kitchen rug, rose again to sniff at the air. Rosa could swear she suddenly smelled freesia.

"Do you smell that?"

He sniffed. "What?"

"Flowers."

He raised an eyebrow. "I smell vanilla and berries. It's making me hungry."

She could feel herself flush and was grateful he probably could not tell with her brown skin. That was her shampoo, probably.

"I thought I smelled freesia. That was Abigail's signature scent."

"Why would it still smell like her?"

"My aunt and her friend who own the house think Abigail still wanders through the house. Do not worry. If she is here, she is a kind spirit, I think."

"Do you buy that?"

"Not really. Sometimes I must wonder, though."

He seemed to take the news of a ghost in stride. "I suppose I'm a big skeptic. I haven't noticed anything in the time we've been living here."

"Did you not see Hank standing in the corner, looking at nothing? Fiona sometimes does that. She makes me wonder what she can see that I cannot."

"I hadn't really noticed."

She studied him. "Would you mind if Abigail were still hanging about?"

"Not really. I remember her as being very kind when I was a boy. She always gave me butterscotch candy."

He smiled a little at the memory.

"As long as she doesn't watch me while I sleep, we should get along fine."

Rosa had a hard enough time not thinking about him sleeping a few floors below her. She didn't need another reason to picture it.

"I do not know if you can tell a ghost she is not welcome in your bedroom."

He smiled. It wasn't a huge smile and certainly not anything as overt as laughter. She still found it enormously appealing.

She wanted to stare at his mouth, will his lips to lift again into a smile as heat soaked through her.

After an awkward moment, she forced herself to look away. She slid her hand back and pressed it into her stomach against the silly butterflies dancing there.

"I should go," she said. "Thank you for your help with the door and with this."

She raised her hand and, as if she had waved a magic wand, another bolt of lightning lit up the kitchen and an instant later the lights flickered and went out.

"Oh, dear," she exclaimed. "I was afraid of this happening."

"It would not be a storm along the coast without some kind of power outage."

He went to the window of the living area that faced out to the street. "I don't see any lights on in the whole neighborhood. It looks like the power is out everywhere."

Rosa knew that was not unusual. Electricity often went out during big storms in the area.

She knew there was nothing to fear. Still, she could feel herself begin to panic. Full darkness always did that to her. It reminded her too much of hiding in the back of a pickup truck, afraid she would not see another day.

"Where is my flashlight? Did I leave it in your sunroom?" She looked around the dark kitchen, as if she could summon it with her will, and tried not to panic.

He must have sensed some of her unease. Wyatt reached out a comforting hand and rested it briefly on her arm. Heat radiated from where he touched her and she wanted to lean into his warmth and solid strength.

"I'll find it. Stay here. I don't want you to hurt yourself again."

She leaned against the kitchen sink, breathing deeply and ordering herself to be calm.

A moment later, he returned with her flashlight on, pointed to the ground so he didn't shine it in her eyes.

"Here you are."

"Thank you."

She felt silly at her overreaction, wishing for a different past that wasn't filled with moments of fear and pain.

"Thank you again for your help. Good night."

She turned to leave and somehow wasn't surprised when he followed closely behind her.

"I'll walk you up the stairs to your place."

She shook her head slightly. "That is really not necessary. I can find my way. I am up and down these stairs all the time."

"Maybe so. But not in the dark. I would hate for you to fall on my watch."

She didn't want to argue with him. Not when he was being so helpful. She gave an inward sigh as she headed for the apartment door and out to the main foyer.

Wyatt followed her up one flight of stairs. When she saw Jen's door, Rosa immediately felt guilty. She had been so busy trying not to become stupid over Wyatt Townsend, she had not given a thought to her friend and how nervous Jen and Addie might be in the dark.

She was a terrible friend. The worst.

She paused outside the door and turned to face him. "I should probably check on Jen and Addie."

"They might be asleep."

"I do not believe so. I saw lights on inside earlier, when we were out by the shed. She might be nervous with the power outage."

"Good idea."

She knocked softly on the door. "Jen? This is Rosa. Are you all right?"

A moment later the door opened. Jen held a candle in one hand and a flashlight in the other.

Rosa couldn't see her face well, but her blue eyes seemed huge in the dim light.

"Everything is fine here," Jen said. "Thank you for checking." She suddenly noticed Wyatt and seemed to freeze. "Oh. I thought you were alone."

Rosa shook her head. "Wyatt helped me fix the

banging door on the garden shed and now he seems to think I need his help or I will fall down the stairs."

"How nice of him to help you." Jen smiled a little, though her anxiety still seemed palpable. "Quite a storm, isn't it?"

"Yes. But do not worry. The power should be back on soon. I see you have a flashlight. Do you need anything else?"

"Only for the power to come back on." Jen's gaze shifted down the stairs behind them, as if she expected someone else to come racing up any moment.

Oh, the poor thing. She had been through so very much. Rosa's heart broke all over again for her.

She knew very well what it felt like to be so afraid of what might be lurking around every dark corner. Rosa had seen plenty of real boogeymen in her life and knew that reality could be worse than any horror movie.

That was a long time ago, she reminded herself. A world away from this beautiful house, which might or might not contain a friendly spirit who smelled like flowers.

She tried to give Jen a reassuring smile. "It should not be long," she repeated. "But if you need anything at all—even company—you know where to find me. In fact, if you would like, you and Addie could sleep in my guestroom."

Jen looked up the stairs as if tempted by the idea, then shook her head. "We should be all right. It's only a storm. But thank you."

Impulsively, Rosa reached out and hugged the other

woman, sensing Jen needed reassurance as much as Rosa did.

"Good night, my friend. Everything will be better in the morning. That is what my mother always told me."

"I might have to hold you to that."

Jen waved at them both then closed the door. Rosa could hear the sound of the dead bolt locking. Good. Jen could not be too careful.

She and Wyatt continued up the final flight of stairs. She had not locked her door when she'd left in such a hurry. Behind it, she could hear Fiona whining.

She hurried to open it and was met with a warm, worried dog, who came bounding out to lick her hand.

"I'm here. Safe and sound, darling. Were you worried about me? I am so sorry I left you."

She rubbed her dog until Fi settled down enough to go over to investigate Wyatt.

He reached an absent hand down to pet her. Here on her apartment landing in the dim light of the flashlight, a quiet intimacy seemed to swirl between them.

She wanted to kiss him.

The urge came over her, fiercely undeniable.

She *had* to deny it. She should get that crazy thought out of her head immediately. Wyatt wasn't the man for her and he never would be.

It was hard to remember that now, here in this cozy nook with the rain pounding against the glass and his scent swirling around her.

"What is your neighbor downstairs running from?"

Rosa tensed, all thought of kissing him gone in her instant defensiveness over Jen.

"What makes you say that?"

"I've been in law enforcement for a long time. I can tell when someone is scared of something. Jen is frightened, isn't she?"

She could not betray her friend's confidence. If Jen wanted Wyatt to know what had happened to her over the past year, she would have to be the one to tell him.

"I cannot tell you this."

"Can't? Or won't?"

"What is the difference? She is my friend. Her business is her business."

"Just like your secrets are your own?"

What did he know about her secrets? Rosa felt panic flare. Carrie would not have told him what she knew, would she?

No. She could not believe that. Carrie had agreed never to tell anyone the things she knew about Rosa's past and she trusted her friend completely.

"Everyone has secrets, do they not? Some they share with those they trust, some they prefer to keep to themselves."

He was quiet for a long moment. "I hope you know that if you ever want to share yours, you can trust me."

She trusted very few people. And she certainly wasn't going to trust Wyatt, who was only a temporary tenant.

"If I had any secrets, I might do that. But I don't. I'm a completely open book."

She tried for a breezy smile but could tell he wasn't at all convinced. In fact, he looked slightly disappointed.

She tried to ignore her guilt and opted to change the

subject instead. "The lightning seems to have stopped for now. I am sure the power will be back on soon."

"No doubt."

"Thank you again for coming to my rescue. Good night. Be careful going back down the stairs."

"I will do that. Good night."

He studied her, his features unreadable in the dim light of her flashlight. He looked as if he wanted to say something else. Instead, he shook his head slightly.

"Good night."

As he turned to go back down the stairs, the masculine scent of him swirled toward her. She felt that sudden wild urge to kiss him again but ignored it. Instead, she went into her darkened apartment, her dog at her heels, and firmly closed the door behind her, wishing she could close the door to her thoughts as easily.

CHAPTER FOUR

HE DIDN'T WANT THIS.

As Wyatt returned down the stairs at Brambleberry House, his own flashlight illuminating the way ahead of him, his thoughts were tangled and dark.

He didn't want to be attracted to Rosa but couldn't seem to shake her image. The high cheekbones, the warm, dark eyes, the mouth that looked soft and delicious.

He had wanted to taste that mouth, with a hunger he hadn't known for a long time.

He didn't want it. He wasn't ready. He didn't know if he ever would be.

Tori had been the love of his life. His childhood sweetheart. He had loved her fiercely and wholeheartedly.

She had been funny and smart, a little acerbic sometimes but kind. A dedicated school guidance counselor, she had loved her students, their home, their family.

He had fully expected they would have a lifetime together. Her death, especially coming out of nowhere, had shattered Wyatt's entire world. For the last three years, he had done his best to glue back together the pieces, for Logan's sake.

He thought he had done a pretty good job for his son. He knew Logan missed his mother. How could he not? Tori left a huge hole to fill. But by moving to Cannon Beach, Wyatt had made sure Logan had his aunt Carrie to fill in some of those gaps. She was there with hugs at the end of the school day, she baked him cookies and she helped him with his homework.

His son was happy. That was the most important thing.

As for Wyatt, he knew he couldn't stay in this odd limbo forever.

For the first two years, he had been in a daze just trying to survive with work and being a single father. About six months ago, he had started dating a little here and there, mostly going out to lunch or coffee while Logan was in school.

Those experiences had been such a bust that he had decided he wasn't ready to move on.

Maybe he would never be ready.

He would be okay with that, though he knew Tori wouldn't have wanted him to be alone forever.

He kept recalling a conversation between them when they were driving home from some event or other, just a month before her death. Almost as if she'd had some instinctive premonition, Tori had brought up what should happen if one of them died.

He worked in law enforcement, was at much higher risk for a premature death, so he had assumed she had been thinking about what she would do if *he* died.

They both said they wanted the other one to move on and find happiness again. She had been insistent about it, actually, saying she would hate thinking about him being lonely and would haunt him forever if he didn't find another woman.

Maybe she and Abigail were in cahoots. The thought made him smile a little, imagining a couple of ghostly matchmakers, scheming in the background.

Now that the raw pain of losing Tori had faded to a quiet, steady ache, Wyatt knew he should probably start thinking about the rest of his life.

He wasn't ready, though. The past three years had been so hard, he didn't know if he could ever risk his heart again—and there was no point in even thinking about it in connection to someone like Rosa Galvez, who didn't seem to like him very much.

Rosa had secrets. He had known that for some time. She always seemed evasive and tense whenever he was around, especially on the rare occasions he was wearing his badge.

Maybe she didn't like the police. He knew there were plenty of people in that camp, for some very justifiable reasons.

She could keep her secrets. They were none of his business. He was living in her house for only a short time and then he and Logan would be back in their own home, away from a woman who smelled like vanilla and berries and made him ache for things he wasn't ready to want again.

A major fraud investigation kept him busy over the next week and Wyatt didn't see much of his lovely landlady or his intriguing, skittish neighbor on the second floor. He was grateful, he told himself. At least about the former. He didn't need any more temptation in the form of Rosa Galvez.

He had decided it was easier all around to pretend his attraction to her was only a figment of his imagination.

By the Friday of the week after the storm, Fourth of July weekend, he was looking forward to extended time with Logan. He had the weekend off and he and his son had a whole list of fun things to do before he had to go back to work on Monday—fishing, going for a bike ride and picking out new furniture for Logan's room in their house.

Right now, his focus was dinner. Wyatt hadn't given any thought to what to fix and Hank was running around in circles after spending all day cooped up.

He decided to solve both problems at the same time. "Why don't we take him for a walk down the beach and grab some dinner at the taco truck?"

"Tacos!" Logan exclaimed joyfully, setting down the controller of his device.

After Wyatt changed out of his shirt and tie and into casual weekend attire, they hooked up Hank's leash—a tricky undertaking while the dog jumped around with excitement.

Neither Rosa nor Jen and her daughter were out in the large yard of Brambleberry House as he and Logan walked through the garden toward the beach gate at the back of the property.

The early evening was beautiful, the air scented with the flowers blooming all around them.

Though it was still a few hours from sunset, the sun had begun to slide toward the water, coloring the clouds orange as it went.

The beach was crowded with weekend visitors. Everybody seemed in a good mood, which was one of the benefits of working in a town frequented by tourists.

"What did you do at camp today?" he asked Logan as they walked across the sand. With Carrie's help, Wyatt had been lucky enough to find a place for his son in one of the most popular science day camps in town.

"Tons of stuff. We went tide pooling and I saw about a zillion starfish and a cool purple anemone. And when we had free time, I played on the slide with my friend Carlos, mostly."

"Do I know Carlos?"

"He just moved here and he's my age. He likes *Star Wars*, just like me."

Logan went on to enumerate the many wonderful qualities of his new friend as they walked a few blocks along the packed sand toward the parking lot just above the beach, where their favorite taco truck usually parked.

"And after lunch and free time, we did another art project, the one I showed you. And then you came to get me to go home."

"Sounds like a fun-packed day."

"Yeah," Logan said cheerfully just as they turned up toward the taco truck.

"There it is. Yay. I'm starving!"

Seven-year-old boys always seemed to be starving.

"Are you going to get the usual? A soft chicken taco and a churro?"

"Yes!"

The taco truck was busy, as usual. The food here was fresh and invariably delicious. He and Logan joined the queue and were talking about some of the things they planned to do that weekend when Logan's face suddenly brightened.

"Look who's here! Hi, Rosa. Hi, Fiona. Hank, look. It's your friend Fiona!"

Hank sidled up to greet Fiona with enthusiastic sniffing, as if they hadn't seen each other for months, while Wyatt tried to calm the ridiculous acceleration of his heartbeat.

He had not been able to stop thinking about Rosa since the night of the storm.

She beamed at his son but avoided meeting his gaze. Was it deliberate or accidental?

"¡Buenas, Logan! ¿Cómo estás?"

"I don't know what that means."

"It means 'good evening. How are you?'"

"How do I say I'm good?"

"You can say soy bueno or just bueno."

"Bueno," Logan said, parroting her. "¿Cómo estás?"

She smiled. "Soy buena."

Wyatt had to again fight the urge to kiss her, right there in front of everyone in line.

"This is our favorite taco truck," Logan told her. "Do you like tacos, too? Oh, yeah. You probably do because you speak Spanish."

He winced at his son's cultural misassumption but

Rosa didn't seem offended. "Except I am from a country called Honduras and these are tacos from Mexico. I like them very much, though. The owner is also my friend."

They reached the order window at that moment and the owner in question, Jose Herrera, ignored Wyatt for a moment to greet Rosa in Spanish.

Wyatt had taken high-school Spanish and had tried to work on his language skills over the years. Unfortunately, he still understood best when Spanish speakers spoke slowly, which didn't happen often in general conversation.

He had no idea what the guy said. Whatever it was, it made Rosa laugh. She answered him in rapid-fire Spanish, which sparked a belly laugh in Herrera.

"Go ahead and order," Wyatt said to her.

"You were here first."

"We're still trying to decide," he lied.

She gave her order then stepped aside for him and Logan to do the same.

"Don't forget my churro," Logan instructed.

"How could I?" Wyatt smiled at his son.

When he finished, the three of them moved together to one of the open picnic tables set around the truck that overlooked the beach.

"And how are you, Señor Logan?" Rosa asked.

"Señor means 'mister.' We learned that in school."

"You are correct."

"I am fine. I like living in your house. It's friendly."

She smiled with warm delight. "I am so happy you think so. Some houses, they are cold. Brambleberry

House is not that way. When you step inside, you feel like you are home."

"And it always smells good, too. Like flowers," Logan said.

Rosa met Wyatt's gaze with an expressive eyebrow, as if to say *See? I told you.*

"Aren't we lucky to live in such a nice place with beautiful flower gardens that smell so good?" Wyatt replied blandly.

"How is your house coming along?"

Was she in a hurry to get rid of them? No. Rosa had been nothing but accommodating.

"We're making progress. They're painting soon, then we need to do the finish carpentry."

"That *is* progress. You will be home before you know it, back in your own bedroom. Your dog will like that, yes?"

He loved listening to her talk, completely entranced by her slight accent and unique phrasing. Okay, the truth was, he was completely entranced by *her*. She could read a lawn-mower instruction manual and he would find her fascinating.

"I think so far he's having fun being friends with Fiona," Logan said.

The two dogs did seem pretty enamored of each other. Hank hadn't been around a lot of other dogs and it was good to see him getting along well with the Irish setter.

Rosa smiled at his son. "Fiona can be a charmer. She is quite hard to resist."

That made two of them. Wyatt sighed. This had to

stop. He didn't want this attraction. Even after a short time, he still hadn't come to terms with his growing interest in his landlady.

Seeing her again here in the July sunshine, bright and vibrant and lovely, only intensified the ache that had been growing since the night of the storm.

He pursed his lips, determined not to think about that. "How is Jen settling in, living in Cannon Beach?"

He had only seen the second-floor tenant in passing a few times. She still seemed as anxious and uncomfortable around him as before.

"Good, as far as I know. She and Addie seem content for now."

Something told him that was a new state of affairs. He didn't know what the woman was going through but was glad at least that she was finding peace here.

"We bumped into Addie and Jen at the grocery store the other night. Jen seems a little uncomfortable around me."

If he hoped Rosa might take the bait and tell him what was going on with Jen, he was doomed to disappointment. She quickly changed the subject away from her friend.

"I'm sure I don't know why. Logan, did I see you walking past my store window today with a bucket?"

"I don't know. Maybe. My day camp went tidepooling."

"Oh, I love doing that at low tide. What did you see?"

"About a zillion sea stars and some anemone and a sea cucumber. Only it's not the kind you can eat."

"How wonderful. Is it not fun to see what can be found beneath the water?"

"Yeah. It's like another whole world," Logan said. He started regaling Rosa with a few stories of interesting things he had seen during previous tide-pooling trips.

"My teacher said you can sometimes go snorkeling and be right in the water looking at some different habitats. That would be fun, don't you think?"

"Yes. Very fun. Maybe your father should take you to Hawaii. Or to my country, Honduras."

Logan's face lit up. "Can we go, Dad? And can Rosa come with us?"

Wyatt cleared his throat, his mind suddenly full of images of warm tropical nights and soft, flower-scented breezes.

"That would be fun. But Rosa has a busy job here. She probably wouldn't have time."

Logan seemed unconcerned. "Maybe we could go with Aunt Carrie, Uncle Joe and Bella. That would be fun, too."

Not as fun as Hawaii or Honduras with Rosa, but, of course, Wyatt couldn't say that. To his relief, a moment later Logan's attention was diverted from snorkeling and travel when he saw another friend from school ride up to the taco truck along with her parents on bikes.

"There's my friend Sadie," he announced. "I need to tell her something."

He handed the leash to Wyatt and hurried over to talk to his friend. Wyatt realized that left him alone at the table to make conversation with Rosa.

"What part of Honduras are you from?"

He didn't miss the way she tensed a little, then seemed to force herself to relax. "A small fishing village near the coast. I left when I was a teenager."

"How did you go from a small village in Honduras to living at Brambleberry House and running a gift shop on the Oregon coast?"

She shrugged. "A long story. The short version is that *mi Tia* Anna is part owner of the house, along with her friend Sage. Anna and her husband live in Portland while Sage and her family spend most of their time in California. Anna needed someone to run the gift shop for her. I have a retail marketing degree and was working a job I didn't enjoy that much in Park City."

"Utah?"

"Yes. Have you been there?"

"No. I'm not much of a skier. My parents used to take us to Mount Hood when I was a kid. I never really enjoyed it."

She smiled a little. "I do not ski, either. It seems a silly pastime to me."

"I guess some people like the thrill. You're not an adrenaline junkie?"

"No. Not me. I have had enough adventure for a lifetime, thank you."

He wanted to pursue that line of questioning but didn't have a chance as Logan and their food arrived at the picnic table at the same time.

They had never really made a conscious decision to eat together, but it somehow felt natural, especially as their dogs were nestled together and had become fast friends.

What happened to Hank's restlessness? Wyatt wondered. Right now, the dog did not look like he wanted to move.

The food was as good as always, the chicken flavorful and the salsa spicy.

He spent a moment helping Logan get situated, then turned his attention back to Rosa. "So you were saying you lived in Utah but you don't like to ski. And that you have had enough adventure and aren't an adrenaline junkie."

She took a drink of the *horchata* she had ordered. "Utah is beautiful year-round. In the summertime, I do like to hike in the mountains and mountain-bike with my parents and *primos*. Cousins," she explained at Logan's quizzical look."

"I have one *primo*. Cousin. Her name is Bella."

Rosa smiled at him. "I know your cousin very well."

"You sound like you are close to your family," Wyatt said.

"Oh, yes. Very. My family is wonderful. My parents, Daniel and Lauren Galvez, are the most kind people you will ever meet. Daniel is in law enforcement, as well. He is the sheriff of our county."

"Is that right?" He found the information rather disheartening. If she had law-enforcement members in her own family, his occupation wasn't likely to be the reason she was so distrustful of Wyatt.

"Yes. Everyone loves him in Moose Springs and

the towns nearby. And my mother, she is the doctor in town."

"The only one?"

"It is not a very big town. Some people go to Park City when they need specialists, but Lauren is the best doctor in the whole world."

She spoke of her parents by their first names, which made him wonder at the relationship.

"Is she also from Honduras?"

He wasn't surprised when her jaw tensed at the question. "No. She is from Moose Springs. Daniel, as well. They adopted me when I came to this country."

He wanted to pursue that line of questioning but reminded himself this was a casual encounter over tacos, not an interrogation. She had the right to her privacy. This was obviously a touchy subject for her and he didn't want to make her uncomfortable.

"So. What do you think of your taco?" she asked Logan.

"Muy delicioso," he said with a grin. "That means 'very delicious.' I learned that from my friend Carlos. That's what he says every day at lunch."

"That is the perfect thing to say about the tacos here. They are definitely *muy delicioso.*"

She and Logan spent a few more minutes comparing ways to gush about their meals, leaving Wyatt to wonder what made Rosa so uncomfortable when she talked about her past.

What was she hiding? She did not like to talk about herself, which he found unusual. In his line of work, he had learned that most law-abiding people loved talking about themselves and their lives. With a few well-aimed questions, Wyatt usually could find out anything he wanted to know.

People who had things to hide, however, learned techniques to evade those kinds of questions.

Her secrets were not his business, he reminded himself. She was a private person and there was certainly no law against that.

He would be smart to remember that her history was her own. He wasn't entitled to know, especially when their only relationship was that of landlady and tenant.

CHAPTER FIVE

THE MAN WAS entirely too curious.

It didn't help that she couldn't seem to keep her usual defensive techniques in place when he looked at her out of those blue eyes. She forgot about protecting herself, about concealing the parts of her life she preferred to forget. She forgot everything, lost in the totally ridiculous urge to lean across the picnic table and press her mouth against his. Anything to stop his questions.

Wouldn't that go over well? She could just imagine how he would react. It almost made her wish she had the nerve to try it.

To her relief, he seemed to give up his interrogation as they finished dinner. He sat back and let her and Logan chatter about Logan's friends, his day camp and the very cool dinosaur bones he saw at a museum in Portland with his aunt Carrie.

He was really an adorable boy, filled with life and energy. He loved *Star Wars*, Legos, his dog and his father, not necessarily in that order.

She enjoyed their company immensely, especially once Wyatt stopped digging into her life.

"Good choice on dinner, kiddo," he said with a warm smile to his son.

Seeing him with Logan was like glimpsing a different person. He was more lighthearted, and certainly more approachable. He had smiled more during dinner than she had seen in all the time she had known him.

The Townsend men were both extremely hard to resist.

"That was so yummy," Logan said as he balled up the wrapper of his taco and returned it to the tray. "Thanks, Dad."

"I didn't do much except pay for it, but you're welcome. You should tell Jose how much you enjoyed it."

At that moment, the taco-truck owner was delivering another tray to a nearby table so Logan jumped up and hurried over to him.

"*Gracias* for the taco. It was *muy delicioso*."

Jose, bald head gleaming in the fading sunlight, beamed down at the boy with delight. "You are welcome. You come back anytime."

He fist-bumped Logan, who skipped as he hurried back to their table.

"That was very nice of you," Rosa said. "People like to feel appreciated."

"My dad taught me we should always tell people thank you for things they do. Sometimes we might be the only ones all day who say it to them."

Rosa had to smile at that. Her gaze met Wyatt's and she found him watching her out of those unreadable blue eyes again.

"That is probably true. Then I must say thank you for sharing dinner with me. I enjoyed it very much."

"So did I," Logan said.

"As did I," Wyatt said to her surprise.

He rose and took her trash and his to the garbage can and dumped it, then returned to the table. "Are you walking back to Brambleberry House?"

"Yes."

"We're headed that way, too. We can walk together, if you want."

Did she? A smart woman would tell him she only just remembered an errand she needed to run at one of the little shops close to the taco truck. Spending more time with Wyatt and Logan was definitely dangerous to her peace of mind.

She couldn't think of anything she needed at any of the touristy places in this area of town, anyway.

"Sure. It makes sense as we are going the same place."

Fiona jumped up from her spot beside Hank, almost as if she had been following the conversation and knew it was time to go.

Sometimes Rosa thought the dog had to be the smartest animal in the world.

As if on cue, Hank jumped up as well, then sat on his haunches and looked pointedly at his owner, as if to tell him he was ready to leave, too.

"I'll take Hank," Logan said and picked up the leash. He led the way, still chattering, as they headed along the sand toward Brambleberry House.

"Looks like it's going to be another gorgeous sunset." Wyatt looked out across the water at the clouds fanning out across the sky in shades of apricot and plum.

"Lovely."

It was the sort of beautiful, vibrant summer evening meant to be spent with a special someone.

Too bad she didn't have a special someone.

Rosa sighed. She hadn't dated anyone seriously since she moved to Cannon Beach four years earlier.

She really should go out on a date or two. All of her friends were constantly trying to set her up, but lately it all seemed like so much bother. Maybe that would distract her from this unwanted and inconvenient attraction to Wyatt.

Rosa was not a nun or anything. She dated, when she found someone worthy of her time, though it was rather depressing to realize she hadn't dated anyone seriously in a long time. Not since college, really?

For two years, she had been very close to a fellow business major whose parents had emigrated from Peru. She and Santos had talked about returning to South America to open a string of restaurants.

As far as she knew, he might have even done that. They had lost track of each other after graduation and she rarely thought of him anymore.

Santos and the few other serious relationships she'd had had taught her that sex could be beautiful and meaningful with someone she cared about.

She was happy with her life. She was running a successful business, she lived in a beautiful home and she loved the surroundings in Cannon Beach. She had good friends here and back in Utah and loved her volunteer work for the local women's shelter.

Okay, maybe she was sometimes lonely at night. Maybe she sometimes wished she could have someone to cuddle with, to talk to at the end of the day, to share her hopes and dreams.

Fiona was lovely but talking to her had its limitations since she couldn't respond.

At the same time, she was not sure she was ready for the inherent risks of trusting her heart to someone.

She had told no one else about the things that had happened to her. Not even Santos or the few other men she had dated seriously had known the entire truth. She had told them bits and pieces, but not everything.

Maybe that was why those relationships had withered and died without progressing to the next level, because she had never completely trusted them to know.

She certainly wasn't about to spill her life story to Wyatt, as much as she enjoyed the company of him and his son.

The walk back to the house passed quickly, mostly because Logan dominated the conversation. He pointed out a kite he liked, told her about riding a bike along the hard-packed sand near the water, went into a long story about the time he and his dad took a charter out to see whales up near Astoria.

"Sorry about Logan," Wyatt said in a low voice when the boy was distracted by something he saw on the sand and ran ahead with Hank to investigate. "He's in a chatty mood tonight. Some days I wish I could find a pause button for a minute."

She smiled. "I do not mind. I love listening to him. Your son is terrific."

"Agreed," he said gruffly. "He's the best seven-year-old I know, even if he does tend to show off a little in front of pretty women."

Rosa felt flustered and didn't know how to answer that. Fortunately, they had reached the beach gate at Brambleberry House.

She punched in the code and the door swung open. As they walked through the back garden, she suddenly saw a strange car in the driveway, a small late-model bright red SUV she didn't recognize.

Rosa tensed, worrying instantly for Jen. She was reaching for her phone to check in with the woman when two females hurried around the side of the house. She recognized them instantly—Carrie and Bella—and shoved her phone back into her pocket.

She smiled and waved, happy at the unexpected visit even as she could feel the usual mix of joy and tension settle over her.

"Hi!" Bella called out to all of them, waving vigorously.

"Hi, Bella," Logan shouted, then beamed toward Rosa. "That's my cousin, Bella, and her mom."

"It is good to see them," Rosa said.

As they moved toward each other, she thought she saw Carrie look between her and Wyatt with a surprised sort of look, as if she wouldn't have expected to see them walking up from the beach together.

"There you are! We rang both your doorbells but nobody answered."

"We bumped into each other while we were grabbing dinner and walked back together," Rosa said quickly, so that his sister didn't get the wrong idea about the two of them.

"We got tacos at the food truck."

"Oh, I love that place," Bella gushed. "My friends and I like to stop there after school. I love their churros."

"Me, too," Logan declared, as if the cinnamon and sugar still dusting his clothes wasn't enough of a giveaway.

Rosa had to smile. She thought she saw Carrie give her a speculative sort of look but couldn't be certain.

"I came by to show off my new wheels," her friend said. "What do you think?"

"Let's take a look," Wyatt said.

They moved toward the driveway and the small red SUV.

"Nice," Wyatt said, walking around the vehicle to check it out.

"I like your new car," Logan said. "It's pretty."

"Thank you, dear." Carrie beamed at him.

"And guess what?" Bella's voice vibrated with excitement. "We're keeping Mom's old car and when I start learning how to drive, I get to practice in that one."

Driving. Bella would be driving in only a few more years. How was it possible that she had grown so much?

"There's plenty of time for that," Wyatt said, looking alarmed.

"Not really. In less than two years, I'll be old enough to get my learner's permit. I'll be driving around town before you know it."

"Good luck with that," Wyatt said to his sister.

"I know. I remember Dad teaching me how to drive. It was a nightmare. And I believe you wrecked a car or two in your day."

"You wrecked cars, Uncle Wyatt?" Bella looked at him wide-eyed and so did his son.

Wyatt gave his sister a rueful look. "One. And it wasn't my fault. A guy T-boned me in an intersection. He got the citation."

"In that case, I'm sorry I impugned your driving credentials," Carrie said.

He shrugged. "I will confess that in the past, I might have had a propensity to drive too fast. Good thing I can do that legally now, with lights and sirens going."

He tapped Bella lightly on the head. "But remember, I'm a highly trained officer of the law. You should always stay within the legal speed limit."

Bella giggled. "What about you, Rosa. Where did you learn to drive? Here or in Honduras?"

She always felt strange talking about her childhood life with Bella and Carrie. "Here. My father taught me when I was in high school. He and my mother were tired of driving me to after-school activities all the time. We had many ranch roads in Utah, where they live, so we practiced for hours until I could feel comfortable behind the wheel."

That was one more gift Lauren and Daniel had given her. Independence. They had wanted her to have all the skills she would need to make a success of her life. She knew they were proud of what she had done and how far she had come. At the same time, she knew Lauren especially worried about her love life.

What would Lauren think about Wyatt? Rosa could guess. She would probably adore him—first because he was in law enforcement like Daniel and second because he was a good man who loved his child.

She would be over the moon if she had any idea how Rosa couldn't seem to stop thinking about him.

She didn't plan to tell either of them about her new tenant. Her parents and siblings were coming to town just before Labor Day, but Logan and Wyatt would be back in their own home by then. She would have to tell them nothing.

Oddly, the thought of the Townsends moving out left her feeling slightly depressed.

"When I get my learner's permit," Bella said, "I'm going to need a lot of practice time. Rosa, maybe you and Uncle Wyatt can help and give my mom and dad a break so they don't always have to ride with me."

Rosa couldn't find words for a few seconds, she was so honored that Bella would even consider allowing her to help her learn how to drive.

"I would enjoy that," she said, her voice a little ragged.

"It's a deal," Wyatt said. "It will be good practice for when I have to teach this kiddo how to drive."

Would she be here when Bella was learning how to drive? Rosa wasn't sure. She had never intended to stay in Cannon Beach for long, but once she had moved here, it had been hard to drag herself away. Now that she was a part owner of the gift store, it became even more difficult.

She didn't like thinking about leaving all the friends she had made here, but perhaps she would one day find it inevitable.

"Showing off my car wasn't the only reason we dropped by. I know you have the weekend off. Joe and I were thinking of grilling steaks and then watching the fireworks on Sunday. We would love to have you. Rosa, you're invited as well. And your friend Jen, if she would like to come."

Rosa wasn't sure if she was ready to have another social outing with the irresistible Townsend men. On the other hand, how could she refuse an invitation from Carrie?

At her hesitation, Carrie made a face. "I know it's rude to just drop in with an invitation two days beforehand. I should have planned better. Please don't worry if you already have plans. But if you can come, we will eat at about seven thirty."

"I do not have plans," she said. In truth, she had been so busy at work, she had not given the holiday weekend much thought.

She could handle a few hours in Wyatt's company. She would simply spend the evening talking with Carrie and Bella.

"Dinner would be nice. What should I bring?"

"Yourself. That's the main thing. But if you want to bring a salad or a fruit plate, that's always good."

She nodded. "Yes. I can do that."

"Oh, lovely. We will see you Sunday, then. Now we're

off to take this beauty for a drive down the coast. With me behind the wheel, of course," she assured them, which made Bella moan in mock disappointment.

A moment later, she stood beside Wyatt and watched the little red SUV back out of the driveway.

"Your sister. She is wonderful."

Rosa could not even put into words her deep gratitude toward Carrie.

"She is pretty terrific. Our mom had breast cancer when I was in high school and Carrie basically stepped in to take care of all of us while Mom was having treatment. She was a young bride herself but that didn't stop her."

"That is wonderful. My mother died of breast cancer when I was fourteen."

She wasn't sure why she told him that. It was another part of her past she didn't usually share.

He gave her a sympathetic look. "I'm sorry. That's a hard loss for a teenager."

She had been so frightened after her mother died. She had no one to share her pain except a few of her mother's friends.

They had been as poor as Rosa and her mother and couldn't help her survive when they were barely subsisting. She had known she was on her own from the moment her mother had died.

That cold truth had led her to making some terrible decisions, with consequences she could never have imagined.

"Hey, Dad, can I show Rosa what I built out of Legos this week?"

Wyatt shook his head. "We've taken up her whole evening. I'm sure she has things to do."

Rosa did have things to do, always. Most small-business owners never really stopped working, even if it was only the constantly turning wheels of their subconscious.

But at the disappointed look on Logan's face, she smiled at the boy. "I do have things to do tonight but I would love to see your creation first."

She could tell Wyatt wasn't particularly pleased at her answer. Why not? Was he in a hurry to get rid of her? Too bad. He could survive a few more moments of her company, for his son's sake.

Wyatt unlocked the front door. As she stood in the entryway waiting for him to open his apartment, Rosa smelled the distinctive scent of flowers that had no logical reason to be there.

Hank sniffed the air and so did Fiona. They both went to the bottom of the stairs, wagging their tails.

Apparently, Abigail was active tonight. Rosa rolled her eyes at her own imagination. She did not believe in ghosts, benevolent or otherwise. If she did, she would never be able to sleep for all the ghosts haunting her.

The dogs followed them as they went into the ground-floor apartment.

"My room is back here," Logan said. He grabbed Rosa's hand and tugged her in the direction of his space.

A *Star Wars* blanket covered the bed and toys were scattered around the room. It made her happy to see the signs a child lived there, and somehow she had the feeling it would have made Abigail happy, too.

"It's over here. This was the biggest set I've ever made. It had over two hundred pieces! I wasn't sure I could do it but my dad helped me."

He showed her a complicated-looking brick master-piece, which she recognized as a spacecraft from one of the *Star Wars* movies, though she couldn't have said for sure which one.

It warmed her heart to think about the boy and his father working together on the project.

"How wonderful. It must have taken you a long time."

"Not really. It's not that hard if you follow the pic-ture directions. My friend Carlos got one, too, and he was able to put it together and Carlos can't even read in English very much."

"Can't he?"

"He's getting better." Logan looked as if he didn't want to disrespect his friend. "Anyway, he hasn't been here very long, only a few months. He told me he speaks Spanish at home all the time. I want to learn Spanish so I can talk to him better but I don't know very many words."

His eyes suddenly grew wide. "Hey. You speak Spanish *and* English. You could teach me."

"Me?" Rosa was so shocked at the suggestion that she didn't quite know how to respond.

"Rosa is very busy with her store," Wyatt said from the doorway. "We don't need to bother her. You and

I can keep reading the books and practicing with the language app on my phone."

How could she be anything but charmed at the idea of Wyatt and his son trying to learn Spanish together so Logan could talk to his friend?

"I would not mind practicing with you when I can," she said quickly. "I should tell you that I have been speaking mostly English almost as long as I spoke only Spanish, so some of my vocabulary might be a little rusty."

"Oh, yay! Thanks, Rosa. *Gracias*."

"*De nada*. I am usually home after six most nights. You can come knock on my door and if I'm home, we can practice a little in the evening."

"Cool! Thanks!"

To her shock, her gave her a quick, impulsive hug. Her arms went around him and she closed her eyes for a moment, grateful for this tender mercy.

When she opened her eyes, she found Wyatt watching her with a strange look in his eyes.

"Okay. Bath time. Tell Rosa good-night, then go find your pajamas and underwear. The clean ones are still in the dryer."

"How do I say 'good night' again?"

"*Buenas noches*. Or sometimes just *buenas*."

He repeated the words, then hurried off to find his pajamas.

"Thanks for your patience with us," Wyatt said in a low voice after the boy had left.

"I do not mind. He is a sweet boy. I enjoy his company."

And yours, she wanted to add. *Even when I know I should not.*

"If you don't really have time to practice Spanish with him, don't worry about it. He'll probably forget by tomorrow morning."

She frowned. "I will not forget. I promised to help him and I would not make a promise I did not intend to keep."

He looked down at her, that odd light in his eyes again. "An admirable quality in a person."

She was not admirable. At all. If he knew her better, he would know that.

"I meant what I said. I will be happy to help him. Send him up any evening he is free or even outside when I am working in the yard. I do not know if I would be a good teacher, but I will do my best."

"I'm sure you will be great," he said. "I just don't want my son to bother you."

"He is never a bother. I will enjoy it."

"Thank you, then. He will probably learn faster from a native speaker than any app could teach him."

"I will do my best," she said again. "Now if you will excuse me, I must go."

She really needed to leave soon, before she did something foolish like throw herself into his arms.

"Good night," she said, edging toward the door.

"Buenas noches," he replied, with a credible pronunciation. "I guess I'll see you on Sunday at Carrie's house."

Oh. Right. She had almost forgotten the invitation. "Yes. I guess so."

"We could always walk over together."

What would Carrie think if the two of them came together to her dinner party? Rosa suspected his sister was already getting the wrong idea about them after seeing them together tonight.

Still, it made sense. It would be silly to drive when the house was so close. "All right. Come, Fiona," she called.

Her dog rose from the rug, where she was cuddled with Hank, and gave the little dog a sorrowful look, then followed Rosa up the stairs to her apartment.

Something seemed to have shifted between her and Wyatt during this evening spent together, but she couldn't have said exactly what.

He was attracted to her.

She wasn't sure how she knew that but she did. Maybe that look in his eyes as he had watched his son hug her… Touched, surprised…hungry.

She was imagining things. Wyatt Townsend was certainly not hungry for her.

If he was, it was only because he didn't know the truth. All the secrets of her past, which she had pushed into the deep corners of herself, where no one else could see.

CHAPTER SIX

SUMMER EVENINGS ALONG the Oregon coast could be magical, especially when they were clear, with no sign of coastal fog.

As they walked the short distance between Brambleberry House and his sister's place on Sunday, the air smelled of the sea, mingled with pine and cedar and the flowers that seemed to grow in abundance this time of year, spilling out of flower baskets and brightening gardens.

Independence Day turned out to be perfect. He and Logan had spent the morning fishing in their favorite spot along the nearby river. Even though the fishing was a bust and they didn't catch anything big enough to keep, Logan still had a great time.

Afterward, they had gone on a hike at one of their favorite trails in Ecola State Park and then had spent the afternoon playing in the sand.

He wouldn't be surprised if Logan fell asleep early.

Of course, he wasn't anywhere close to sleeping now. He was having too much fun quizzing Rosa about the Spanish word for everything they passed.

"How do you say *mailbox*?" Logan asked, pointing to a row of them across the road.

"Buzón."

"And *house* is *casa*, right?"

"Yes. Very good. And we are walking. *Estamos caminando.*"

"Yes. To my aunt Carrie's *casa*."

She smiled down at him, looking bright and lovely in the golden evening light. To himself, Wyatt could admit that the main reason the evening seemed particularly beautiful had to do with the woman he was walking beside.

"Excellent," she said. "You and Carlos will be jabbering up a storm in Spanish before you know it."

"I think his English will always be better than my Spanish."

"But you are trying to learn for your friend. That is the important thing. It was very hard for me when I came to this country and could not always find the words I wanted. I am grateful I had very patient family and friends to help me."

He had to wonder again at her story. She had said her mother died when she was fourteen, which meant she had probably come here by herself. But what were the circumstances that had led to her being adopted by a family in Utah?

None of his business, he reminded himself. She was his landlady, nothing more, though it was hard to remember that on an evening like this, especially when his son slipped his hand in hers, as if it was the most natural thing in the world.

Rosa looked down at Logan and their joined hands with an expression of astonishment, and then one of wonder, that touched Wyatt deeply.

"How do you say *whale*?" Logan asked when they passed a house that had a little whale-shaped bench out front.

"Ballena."

"What about *tree*?"

"Arborio."

"How about *library*?"

"Biblioteca."

Rosa never seemed to lose her patience with the constant barrage of questions. He could only guess how relieved she must have been when they reached Carrie and Joe's house a short time later.

"Now you tell me. What was *door* again?" she asked him as they approached the porch.

"Puerta."

"No. *Puerto. Puerta* means *port.*"

"It's so confusing!"

"English is far more confusing," she said with a laugh. "Try figuring out the difference between *there*, *they're* and *their.*"

"I guess."

"You are doing great. We will keep practicing."

His son was already enamored with Rosa. They had practiced together the night before while Rosa was working in the small vegetable garden at the house. Wyatt had come out ahead in the arrangement, as she had sent Logan back to their apartment with a bowl of fresh green beans and another of raspberries, his favorite.

He always felt a little weird just walking into his sister's house, even though he had been living there only a few weeks earlier. He usually preferred to ring the doorbell, but this time he didn't have to. Bella opened the door before they could and grinned at them. "I saw you all walking up. *Hola.*"

"Hola." Rosa's features softened. "That's a very cute shirt. Is it new?"

Bella twirled around to show off her patriotic red, white and blue polka-dotted T-shirt. "Yeah. I picked it up this afternoon on clearance. It was super cheap."

"I like it very much," Rosa said.

"I'm going with some friends to watch the fireworks in Manzanita."

He thought he saw disappointment flash in Rosa's dark eyes before she quickly concealed it. "Oh. That will be fun for you."

"I'm going to go play on the swings," Logan announced, then headed out to the elaborate play area in the backyard.

"I'll take these into the kitchen," Wyatt said, lifting the woven bag that contained the bowl of Rosa's salad, the one he had insisted on taking from her when they met up outside Brambleberry House for the walk here.

He found his sister in the kitchen slicing tomatoes. He kissed her cheek and she smiled. "You're here. Oh, and Rosa's here, too. You came together."

"Yes," Rosa said. "It was such a beautiful evening for a walk. I made a fruit salad with strawberries from my garden."

"Oh, yum. How is your garden this year? I've had

so much trouble with my flowers. I think I have some kind of bug."

"They are good," Rosa replied. "Not as lovely as when Sonia was here to take care of them but I do my best with it."

"I miss Sonia," Carrie said. "I guess we should call her Elizabeth now."

Rosa nodded. "I will always think of her as Sonia, I am afraid."

Wyatt knew the story of Rosa's previous tenant. For several years, she had lived in Cannon Beach as Sonia Davis but a year earlier, she had admitted her real name was Elizabeth Hamilton. For many complicated reasons, she had been living under a different name during her time here, until her husband showed up out of the blue one day to take her back to their hometown. It had been the talk of Cannon Beach for weeks.

Rosa had been good friends with her tenant and Carrie had told him how astonished she had been at the revelation that the woman she thought she knew had so many secrets.

"How is Sonia Elizabeth?" Carrie asked, the name some of the woman's friends had taken to calling her. "Do you ever talk to her?"

"Oh, yes. We speak often," Rosa said. "I texted her the other day to ask her a question about a plant I didn't recognize and we did a video call so she could take a better look at it. She seemed happy. Her children are happy. She said she isn't having seizures much anymore and she and her husband are even talking about taking in a foster child with the idea of adopting."

Carrie looked thrilled at the news. "Oh, that's lovely. Do you know, I was thinking about Sonia the other day. I bumped into Melissa and Eli and Skye at the grocery store. Do you see them much?"

Melissa Fielding Sanderson had been another tenant of Brambleberry House. She had married a doctor, Eli Sanderson, whom Wyatt had known when he used to visit his grandmother here during his childhood.

"Oh, yes," Rosa answered. "We still meet for lunch or dinner about once a month. She's very busy with the new baby."

"Thomas is such a sweetheart," Bella said. "I watched him last week when Melissa had a test."

Melissa, a registered nurse, was studying to be a nurse practitioner and juggled school with being a mother and working at the clinic with her husband and father-in-law. Somehow she made it all work.

"What time is Jaycee's mom picking you up?" Carrie asked her daughter.

"Not until eight."

"Then you probably have time to eat with us. Why don't you and Rosa start carrying things out to the patio? We thought it would be nice to eat outside and take advantage of the gorgeous weather. Bell, you can take the plates and silverware and Rosa can take these salads."

Rosa looked delighted, which Wyatt thought was odd. Maybe she was just happy to have a task.

"Yes. That is a wonderful idea. I am happy to help."

She picked up the fruit salad she had brought and the green salad Carrie had just finished preparing, then carried them through the back door to the patio. Bella joined her, arms laden with plates and the little basket full of silverware Carrie used for outdoor entertaining. As they opened the door, Wyatt caught the delicious scent of sizzling steak.

"What can I do?"

"I think that is it for now." Carrie paused, then gave him a meaningful look. "Rosa is lovely, isn't she?"

Oh, no. He knew where this was going. Carrie seemed to think it was her job now to find him dates. She was always trying to set him up with women she knew, despite his repeated attempts to convince her he was perfectly happy and not interested in dating right now.

He gave her a stern look, though he feared it would do no good. Carrie wasn't great at taking hints.

"Yes. She's lovely."

"Inside and out," his sister said, then gave a careful look to make sure she and Bella were busy setting the patio table.

"You know, so many people could have let what she has been through turn them bitter and angry. Not Rosa. I think it's only made her stronger and more empathetic to everyone."

Wyatt frowned. "What has she been through?"

Carrie gave him a vague look. "Oh, you know. Life in general. Coming here when she was young. Losing her mother when she was just a girl."

What else did she know about Rosa's background? He wanted to push, but then had to remind himself that he was already becoming too entangled in her world.

The more he learned about her, the harder it was becoming to fight off this attraction.

Bella came back into the kitchen as he was wrestling against his curiosity to know everything he could about the intriguing Rosa Galvez.

"What else can we take out?" she asked. "Also, Dad is asking for a platter for the steaks."

Carrie pulled one out of the cabinet above the refrigerator and handed it to Bella, who immediately headed back outside with it.

"I only meant to say that Rosa is a lovely woman," she said when they were alone again. "When you're ready to start thinking about dating again, she would be an excellent choice."

Wyatt shifted, vowing to do his best that evening to keep his sister from figuring out that he was already fiercely drawn to Rosa. Once she realized that, Carrie would never give up trying to push them together.

"What if I'm never ready?"

"Oh, don't say that." His sister looked anguished. "You are a young, healthy man. You can't spend the rest of your life alone, for your sake or for Logan's. You know Tori would never have wanted that."

Yes. He knew. That conversation with her had been running through his head more and more often. But a hypothetical discussion with his wife when he still thought they would have the rest of their lives together was one thing. The reality of letting someone else into his heart was something else entirely.

He was tired of being alone, though. Maybe there had been a few nights lately when he had thought it might be lovely to have someone in his life again. Someone to make him laugh, to help him not take himself so seriously, to remind him that life was a beautiful, complex mix of joy and hardship.

Even if he was ready to move on, he sensed that Rosa wasn't that person. She was wonderful with Logan but it was clear she didn't trust *him*.

Just as well. Since he *wasn't* ready, there was no point in dwelling on the issue, especially on a sweet summer night.

Rosa always loved spending time with the Abbotts. Joe and Carrie were deeply in love, even after being married more than twenty years. They held hands often, they touched all the time and they kissed at random moments.

And Bella. Being around the girl was a unique experience, like constantly walking a razor wire between joy and pain.

At dinner, Bella wanted to tell Rosa all about a boy she liked named Charlie, who might or might not be going to the same place in the nearby town to watch the fireworks.

"I really like him but I'm not allowed to date until I'm sixteen. That's not fair, is it?"

Rosa looked over to where Carrie was talking to Joe and Wyatt. She did *not* want to interject herself into a dispute between Bella and her parents over rules.

"I think that your parents have your best interests at heart. You should listen to them."

Bella clearly did not welcome that answer. "It's not

like we're going to go somewhere and make out. We're watching fireworks with about a billion other people."

Rosa did not want to come across as a boring old woman but she also felt compelled to offer some advice. Bella looked on her as an older sister of sorts, just the person who *should* be giving counsel.

"You should stay with your friend and her parents, especially since they are giving you a ride."

"I know. I would never ditch my friends over a boy, no matter how cute he is."

"What cute boy are you talking about?" Carrie asked, overhearing her daughter's words.

Bella looked as if she didn't want to answer her mother but she finally sighed. "Charlie. He texted me to tell me he might be going to the fireworks."

Carrie looked vaguely alarmed. "You didn't tell me that."

"Because I knew you would blow everything out of proportion. We're not going together. I might not even see him there."

She gave Rosa an annoyed look, as if it was *her* fault Carrie had overheard their conversation.

"I don't even know if I like him that much," Bella said. "You don't have to make a big deal about it."

"I just want you to be careful. You have plenty of time for boyfriends," her mother said.

"I know. I told you he's not my boyfriend. I like him a little but that's all. I need to go find my portable phone charger. Jaycee's going to be here any minute."

"Don't forget to take a hoodie. It's going to be much colder once the sun goes all the way down."

"I know." Bella hurried off to her room and Rosa had to fight the urge to go after her and warn her again not to leave her friends.

"I hope I can make it through these teenage years," Carrie said, shaking her head.

"You can."

"All this talk of boys and learning to drive. She's growing up, isn't she?"

Rosa nodded, that bittersweet joy a heavy weight in her heart.

CHAPTER SEVEN

THE BARBECUE WAS one of the most delightful evenings Wyatt had experienced in a while. He always enjoyed hanging out with his sister and considered his brother-in-law one of his closest friends. But having Rosa there, listening to her laugh with Carrie and Bella, tease Joe and trade corny jokes with Logan, somehow turned the night magical.

He tried to tell himself he was simply savoring the delight of good food and family. That didn't explain how the stars seemed to sparkle more brightly and the air smelled more sweet.

"Everything was delicious," he said to Carrie. "That cherry pie was divine. Did you try a new recipe?"

She shook her head. "No. I'm using the same one Grandma always made. She got it from Abigail Dandridge, actually. The cherries are just extra delicious this year, I think."

"That must be it."

"Looks like somebody is out for the count," Joe said, gesturing to their outdoor sofa, where Logan had curled up a little while ago.

Wyatt followed his gaze and found his son sound asleep under the blanket Carrie had brought out for him earlier, after the sun had gone down and the evening had turned chilly.

He wasn't completely surprised. Their day had been filled with activity and fun.

Love for his son washed over him. Logan was the greatest gift.

"Good thing he can sleep anywhere."

"He is very lucky," Rosa said. "Some nights, I cannot even sleep in my comfortable bed with cool sheets and soft music playing."

What was keeping her up at night? Did she also ache for something she didn't have?

"We're watching Logan for you tomorrow and you said you're going into work early, right?" Carrie asked.

He made a face. "Yeah. Sorry about that."

"You know it's no problem at all. But I've got a great idea. Why don't you just let Logan stay over here for the night? He can sleep in and so can we, since tomorrow is the official holiday and we don't have a single thing planned."

That did make sense, though Wyatt didn't like spending even a night away from his son.

"Are you sure?"

"Yes. If you want the truth, I would rather sleep in tomorrow, since I imagine we will be up late worrying until Bella gets home safely."

Rosa looked concerned. "I am sure she will be fine. Bella is a smart girl and she is with her friend Jaycee and Jaycee's parents. They will make sure she does not get into any trouble."

"Parents always worry. It's what we do." Carrie shrugged. "Intellectually, I know Bella will be fine. I'll still probably stay up, which means I'll be doubly glad not to have to get up at six a.m., when you come to drop off Logan."

"I didn't bring any clothes for him."

"He has as many clothes here as he probably does at Brambleberry House. We have everything he should need. Swimsuits, shorts and sweatshirts. Even extra socks. It will be great."

Seriously, what would he have done without his sister and her family over the last three years, when they had stepped in after Tori died to help him raise his son?

"That does seem like a good solution, then. I'll carry him into the guest room."

"Afraid we're going to leave him out here on the patio to sleep?" Joe teased.

Wyatt smiled. "He probably wouldn't care. The thing is, Logan would never even notice if it started raining."

Only after he and Rosa had helped clean up and he had carried a still-sleeping Logan and tucked him into the sewing room daybed did Wyatt realize one significant issue he had overlooked.

If his son stayed here, that meant he and Rosa would be walking home alone together.

He frowned, suddenly suspicious. Carrie had been awfully quick to suggest that Logan stay the night, hadn't she? Were her reasons really about convenience and sleeping in the next day, or was she trying to do some behind-the-scenes matchmaking again?

He gave his sister a swift look, remembering that conversation in the kitchen.

Her reasons didn't matter. The deed was done. He and Rosa were walking back to Brambleberry House together and he could do nothing about it.

A short time later, they left the house, with Rosa carrying the bag with the bowl she had brought, now empty and washed.

Why had he thought it was a good idea to walk here earlier? If he had driven, they could have been home in two minutes.

The walk wasn't far, only a few blocks, but there was an intimacy to walking alone with Rosa that left him uncomfortable.

He hadn't noticed it at all on the walk to Carrie's house, probably because Logan had kept up a constant chatter. His son had provided a much-needed buffer.

"The night turned a little cooler, didn't it? That came on suddenly."

She had brought a sweater, which she had put on earlier. Even so, she shivered a little.

"Yes. And it looks as if the fog they've been talking about is finally moving in."

Tendrils of coastal fog stretched up from the beach, winding through the houses. It added to the strange, restless mood stealing over him like the fog creeping up the street.

He put it down to leaving his son back at his sister's

house. Surely that's what it was, not anything to do with his growing feelings for Rosa.

"You were right—Logan can sleep through anything. I would not have believed it but he did not even open his eyes when you carried him to bed. Will he wake up confused in a strange place?"

"I don't think so. He's spent the better part of the past two months sleeping there, except for the few weeks we've been at Brambleberry House. He's probably as comfortable there as he is in his own bed. I, on the other hand, probably won't sleep at all."

She gave him a sideways look. "Why is that?"

He shrugged, wishing he hadn't said anything. "When I don't have Logan nearby, I feel like part of me is missing."

She looked touched. "He is a very sweet boy."

"You've been very kind to help him learn Spanish for his friend. I know you're busy. Please let me know if it becomes too much of a burden."

"Impossible," she declared. "I am always happy to speak Spanish with someone. Sometimes I worry I will forget the language of my birth."

He suddenly remembered the conversation he'd had with his sister about her. What had she been through, the reasons Carrie said she deserved to be happy?

"That fog is growing more thick. I hope it goes out again in the morning so the weather stays good for the rest of the holiday weekend. It is a busy time for my store."

"Don't you have better business if it starts to rain? I would have thought fewer people would want to sit at the beach when it's raining, so they're more inclined to go shopping instead."

"Sometimes. Or sometimes they decide since it's raining to take a drive down the coast to Lincoln City, or even farther down to some of the other lighthouses like Heceta Head."

"The police department is busy whether it's raining or not. It seems like holiday weekends always bring out the worst in people."

"Do you like your job as a detective?" she asked as they turned onto the Brambleberry House road.

The question took him by surprise. Not many people asked him that. He pondered for a moment before answering, wanting to be as honest as possible.

"I like when I have the chance to help people. That doesn't always happen. The past few years have made me question my job choices. I've seen a lot of injustice and been frustrated by it. Attitudes are changing, I think. It's just taking longer than it should. At the end of the day, I hope I can say I've worked for victims and for justice."

She said nothing for several long moments. When she spoke, her voice was low. "I will always be grateful for the *policia*. My father is the sheriff and he saved my life and the lives of my friends."

She turned onto the walk of Brambleberry House as if her words hadn't landed between them like an errant firework.

After his first moment of shock, he quickly caught up with her. "How did he do that?"

In the moonlight, she looked as if she regretted saying anything at all. "It is a long story, and not a very nice one. I do not like to talk about it."

Wyatt wanted to point out that she had been the one to bring it up. He had the odd feeling Rosa wanted to tell him about her past, but was afraid of his reaction.

"Well, if you ever decide you're willing to share your story with me, I like to think I'm a pretty good listener."

"I have noticed this. That is probably a help in your line of work, when you are fighting crime."

"I hope so."

He knew he had to get up early for his shift the next morning, yet he didn't want the evening to end.

To his vast relief, she didn't seem in a hurry to go to inside, either. She stood looking at the big, graceful old house in the moonlight. It was mostly in darkness except for a light in the shared entry and two lights glowing on the second floor.

In the wispy coastal fog, it looked mysterious, intriguing, though not nearly as interesting as the people who lived inside.

"Looks like our neighbor is home."

Wyatt didn't miss the way Rosa looked protectively toward the second floor, where a shadow moved across the closed curtain.

"Yes. I think she and Addie planned a quiet evening."

"She doesn't go out much, I've noticed."

"Have you?"

As he expected, she didn't take the bait, so he came

right out and asked the question he had been wondering since he moved in.

"What is Jen's story? You can tell me, you know."

In the moonlight, he saw Rosa's features tighten. "I don't know what you mean."

She did. She knew perfectly well. "Why does she seem so nervous around me?"

"Nervous?"

"Yeah. She has allowed her little girl to play with Logan a few times, but Jen herself clearly goes out of her way to avoid me. I'm not sure she's ever looked me in the eye."

Rosa looked away herself. "Maybe she does not like policemen."

"Is she in some kind of trouble? Do you know?"

"Why would you ask that?" Her innocent-sounding question didn't fool him at all. She knew exactly what was going on with Jen.

"I can't help her if nobody will tell me what's going on," he pointed out mildly. He didn't want to intrude, but he was an officer of the law and his job was to protect and serve. That included those who shared the same house with him.

"She has work at the store and she has a safe place to live. That is good for now." She paused. "But thank you for being concerned for her."

"I'm here to help, if you or she ever want to tell me what's going on."

She nodded slowly. "I will tell her this."

"You know I'm one of the good guys, right? At least I try to be."

She gave him a long look in the moonlight. "Yes. I know. I would not have let you move in if I did not think that."

Her words made him feel as if he had passed some kind of test he had no idea he'd been taking.

He was suddenly glad that Carrie had encouraged him to take this apartment for the month, grateful for summer nights and lovely women.

Again, he felt an overwhelming urge to kiss her, this woman with secrets who was filled with so much compassion for those around her.

She didn't trust him. He looked at the house, hating the idea of his empty apartment and his empty bed and the loneliness that had been such a part of his life since Tori died.

"I should probably go in."

"Yes. You are working early tomorrow."

He nodded. "Thank you for the lovely evening. I enjoyed the walk home. I think maybe I've forgotten how much I enjoy talking with a woman."

She gazed at him, eyes wide. In the dim light of the moon, he saw her swallow and her gaze seemed to slide to his mouth.

The scent of her, sweet and feminine, with hints of vanilla and berries, drifted to him. He wanted to close his eyes and inhale her inside him.

"I am glad I could remind you of this," she finally said.

He knew he should walk away, turn around and go into the house, to that empty apartment and the even emptier bed. He couldn't seem to make his muscles cooperate. The pull of her was too strong and he had no tools to withstand this slow, aching desire churning through his blood.

"I would like to kiss you right now."

As soon as he heard the words, he wanted to call them back, but it was far too late. They danced between them like petals on the breeze.

He thought she would turn and walk away since he couldn't seem to do it. Instead, she only gazed up at him out of those soft brown eyes he wanted to sink into.

"Would you?" she finally asked, her voice soft and her accent more pronounced than usual.

"Yes. Would you mind?"

After a brief hesitation, as if she was debating with herself, she shook her head slightly.

That was all the encouragement he needed. He lowered his mouth to hers, his heart beating so loudly in his ears it almost drowned out the ever-present sound of the ocean.

If he had forgotten how much peace he could find talking with a woman, he had *really* forgotten how much he loved to kiss a woman in the moonlight.

Her mouth tasted of strawberries and cream, and her lips trembled slightly. She must have set down the bag she had been carrying because one hand grasped his shirtfront and the other slid around his neck.

It was the perfect moment, the perfect kiss. He had no other way to describe it. A light breeze stirred the air around them, the ocean murmured nearby and the moonlight played on her features.

He wanted to stay right here, with his heart pounding and her mouth soft and sweet and generously responding to his kiss.

Here, he could focus only on the perfection of this moment. Not on the pain of the past or the mysteries that surrounded her or all the reasons they could never have anything but this kiss.

CHAPTER EIGHT

IN HER SECRET DREAMS, Rosa had wondered before what it would be like to kiss Wyatt. Having him live downstairs from her these last few weeks had only increased her attraction to the man, so, of course, she would wonder.

She had suspected kissing him would be an unforgettable experience.

She had not expected it to knock her legs out from under her.

Rosa closed her eyes, her heart pounding as his mouth explored hers.

Now, as he kissed her, she could admit that she had been attracted to him for a long time. Long before he had moved to Brambleberry House, she had been nervous around him. She had told herself it was because of his position with the police department. Now she could admit it was because of the man himself.

His kiss staggered her.

Why? She had kissed other men, of course. Not counting the awful time in her youth that she didn't like to think about, she had had boyfriends.

She wanted to think she had a healthy relationship

now with men, with sex, especially after the counseling her parents had insisted on.

She didn't blame all men for what had happened to her.

Even so, Rosa was fully aware that she usually gravitated toward a different sort of man. Someone who was not as masculine as Wyatt.

Those kind of men were the safer bet, she realized now. They didn't threaten her. She always had held most of the control in every other situation.

Not with Wyatt. Kissing him felt like being caught in a riptide, as if she were whirling and spinning from forces beyond her control.

Sometimes when she saw the intensity between Lauren and Daniel, or her aunt Anna and Harry, Rosa wondered if she had something fundamental broken inside her.

She had assumed that the scars she bore so deeply inside made it impossible for her to feel that kind of passion.

Kissing Wyatt in this moment made her question every single one of those foolish assumptions.

She could want, with a searing intensity that left her breathless.

She wanted to drag him to the dewy grass and kiss him for hours. And more. She wanted more with him.

And then what?

Cold, hard reality seemed to push through the dreamy haze that surrounded her.

After this kiss, then what? Try as she might, she couldn't envision a scenario where she and Wyatt could have anything but a few wild kisses. Where they could live happily ever after.

He was a police detective and she was…herself. A product of what had happened to her and the choices that had led her here to this moment.

They could never be together, so what was the point in setting herself up for more pain?

She drew in a breath, willing her hunger to subside. When she thought she had herself under control enough that she could think straight again, she slid her mouth away, cooled by the night air that swirled around them. After another inhalation, she made herself take a slight step back.

She couldn't see him clearly, but she could tell he had been as caught up in the kiss as she was.

He gazed down at her, his eyes slightly unfocused and his hair messy from her fingers. He looked so delicious, she had a hard time not stepping straight back into his arms.

She had to say something, but all the words seemed tangled up inside her like fishing line discarded on the beach, a jumble of Spanish and English that made no sense, even to her.

She finally swallowed hard and forced a smile.

"That was a surprise."

He continued to look down at her, his face so close she could see each distinct long eyelash and the fine network of lines etched into the corners of his eyes.

He released a long breath. "Yes. It was."

"I thought you meant a little good-night kiss like a friend would give a friend."

"That was substantially more, wasn't it?"

She could feel the imprint of his mouth on hers, could still taste him on her tongue—the wine and mint, the strawberries and cream from the dessert his sister had made. She shivered a little, wishing she could lean in for another kiss.

"Indeed." She hated this awkwardness between them, especially after the closeness they had shared on the walk from his sister's house. She shook her head.

"I'm sorry if I turned the kiss into more than you wanted."

"You didn't. That is the problem. I want, though I know I should not."

He gave a slightly raw-sounding laugh, as if startled by her honesty. "Same. I want. And I know I should not. What are we going to do about that?"

Rosa spent a delicious moment imagining what she would like to do. She wanted to drag him up two flights of stairs to her cozy bedroom under the eaves and spend the entire night exploring all his muscles and hard edges.

That was impossible, for a hundred reasons. The biggest one was right now at the house they had come from.

"I don't know what you will do, but I will go inside, take a soak in the tub and try to focus on something else."

A muscle worked along his jawline as if he was trying to keep himself from responding. He finally nodded. "I suppose that's for the best."

Rosa managed a smile, trying to pretend she wasn't

fighting with everything inside her to keep from doing what she longed to do—tug him back into her arms and kiss him again until they both forgot all the shoulds and should nots.

"Good night to you, Wyatt. I enjoyed the evening… and the kiss."

"Rosa…" he began, but she didn't wait to hear what he said. She hurried up the steps, unlocked the front door with hands that trembled and rushed up to her apartment.

As she took the stairs quickly, she thought she felt an odd cold spot on the stairs and had the strangest feeling that the house or its inhabitants were disappointed in her.

She and Wyatt had decided not to take the dogs with them because of Carrie's spoiled and rather unfriendly cats. Inside the apartment, Fiona rose to greet her, giving her an unblinking stare, as if she knew exactly what Rosa had just been doing in the moonlight with their downstairs neighbor.

"Not you, too."

Fi snorted as if she had plenty to say but only regretted that she did not have the words.

"What do you want me to do?" she said aloud to her dog. "You know I cannot invite the man up. He is a police officer. He would not be interested in me, if he knew the truth."

Fiona whined. She needed to go out, but Rosa wasn't eager to go down the stairs again and risk meeting up with Wyatt. Her dog's needs came first, though.

"Don't be like that," she said as she hooked up Fi's

leash. "You know it is true. I have too many secrets I cannot tell him."

The dog didn't look convinced.

"I cannot," Rosa insisted. "You know I cannot. They are not only my secrets. I cannot tell him."

Wyatt was a good man, A decent, honorable man, she thought as she walked down the stairs again and outside into the moonlight. To her relief, she didn't see any sign of him.

He reminded her so much of Daniel, who would always be her hero for rescuing her in her darkest moment.

She loved her adopted father dearly so she supposed it was only natural that she would be so fiercely drawn to a man who had all of Daniel's best qualities.

"It doesn't matter," she said. She didn't feel foolish carrying on this conversation with her dog. Fiona was the best possible confidante, who listened to all her inner thoughts and only judged a little.

She didn't tell the dog that she suspected she might be falling for Wyatt, though she knew he would never feel the same. Not if he knew the truth.

She knew he was still grieving for his wife. Even if the two of them shared a few kisses, she knew Wyatt wasn't in a good place for anything more.

She wanted things to be different. If only they were both free of their pasts and had met under other circumstances. But she knew she wouldn't have been the same person without all that had happened to her and she thought the same of Wyatt.

She would not kiss him again. What would be the point? Nothing could come of it and she would only end up with more pain.

With the Oregon coast in full tourist season, Rosa didn't have time to think about that kiss more than about two or three dozen times a day at random moments.

Over the next week, she made several day trips out of town to the central coast and to Portland to pick up inventory from some of their vendors.

Today she was busy revamping her window display a week after Independence Day, adding in the new products she had collected to feature, while Jen worked the cash register and assisted customers.

Rosa was thrilled at the change in her friend. Jen had come so far over the past few weeks. She was far more relaxed with the customers. She smiled and chatted easily and seemed to have lost that haunted look she used to wear at random moments.

"Thank you. Come back again. We have new inventory all the time," she told the final customer at her register. A few other browsers were looking at their selection of T-shirts, but they didn't seem in any hurry so Rosa left the window to walk over to Jen and check on her.

"How are things going?" she asked.

"Great. Really good." Jen smiled, looking far more like the woman Rosa remembered from their college days together. "It's hard to be in a bad mood when the weather is so glorious, isn't it?"

They really had been blessed with unusually sunny weather. It was good now, but made her worry about forest fires later in the season.

"You seem to be more comfortable with the customers."

"I am enjoying the work, but to tell you the truth, I'm starting to miss teaching. This is the time of year when I would usually start thinking about my classroom decorations for the next school year and working on lesson plans."

Jen had been a third-grade teacher in Utah and had loved her career. That was one of the things that angered Rosa the most, that her friend had been forced to leave all that she loved in order to escape.

"I can understand that."

"I was actually wondering if I could take a day off tomorrow. I know it's short notice."

"Of course," Rosa said immediately. "I can rearrange the schedule. If I cannot find anyone to cover for you, I will work myself. That should not be a problem, especially now that the holiday weekend is over."

"Thank you. You won't believe this but I already have a job interview lined up!"

"Oh, that's wonderful!"

Rosa knew Jen had recently finished the process to certify her Utah teaching license in Oregon and that she had started applying in the area.

"The first school I contacted called me today and want to talk to me tomorrow. It's at Addie's school, which would be ideal."

"Oh, that is so exciting. Of course, you can have the day off. Or more than that, if you need it."

"To be honest, I'm not sure if I should apply. If I found a job, I would have to quit working here before the tourist season is over in September."

Rosa waved a hand. "Don't worry about that for a moment. I have temporary seasonal workers who have asked for more hours, so I can give them your shifts if you get a new teaching contract. I'm just happy that you like it enough here in Oregon to think about staying for a while."

Jen hugged her and Rosa was happy to note that she had started to gain weight again and seemed to have lost that frail, hunted look.

"It's all because of you," Jen said. "I can't thank you enough for all you've done since I moved here. Giving me this job, a place to live. You have been amazing."

Rosa was only happy she had been in a position to offer help.

"I have been grateful to have you and Addie here. You would have a job here at the store as long as you want, but it would be wonderful for you to return to teaching. You were made to be a teacher."

The T-shirt customers came over to ask a question, distracting them from further conversation. The door opened and more customers entered, so Rosa moved to help them.

A constant flow of traffic moved in and out of the store over the next few hours and she was too busy to have another chance to talk to her friend about her interview.

Finally, things seemed to slow near the end of Jen's shift. One of the other seasonal workers, Carol Hardesty, came in a little early for her own shift and Rosa was about to tell Jen to take off for the day when she suddenly heard a loud crash.

Rosa jerked up her head, instantly alert, to find Jen staring out the window, the shards of a broken coaster scattered at her feet.

Fortunately, it was a fairly inexpensive one in a design that hadn't been particularly attractive, anyway.

"Is everything okay?" she asked, when Jen continued to stare out the window.

Her words seemed to jolt the woman back to her senses. Jen looked down at the mess, a dawning look of horror on her features.

"Oh, no. I'm so sorry."

Rosa moved quickly to her. "You look frightened. Are you all right? Has something happened?"

"Yes. No. I don't know. I just… I thought I saw…"

"A ghost?" Carol hurried up with a broom and dustpan and started sweeping in her no-nonsense way. "We get those here in Cannon Beach. Once, I swear I saw a man all wrapped up in bandages walking around the side of Highway 101. When I slowed down to see if he needed help, he was completely gone. Spooky!"

"Yes. It must have been…something like that."

Jen looked like a ghost herself with her suddenly pale features.

"And the really creepy part is," Carol went on, "when I mentioned it to a few people, I found out Bandage Man is kind of a legend around here. There was even a stretch of the old highway called Bandage Man Road. Weird, right?"

Jen hardly seemed to hear her, still staring out the window.

"You need to sit down for a minute."

"Yes," Carol urged. "I've got this mess and I'll handle any customers. Don't worry about a thing."

Rosa guided a numb Jen to the back room she used as an office, which was also where most of the employees took their breaks. Jen sagged into a chair and Rosa crouched beside her, holding her hand.

"Who did you see? Was it the man you fear?"

Jen shook her head. "Not him. But maybe a friend of his. I can't be sure. I only caught a glimpse of him through the window, but I think he was looking at me as if he knew me."

Her panic was only too familiar to Rosa. She knew just how it felt to be hunted. The memories crowded into her mind but she pushed him away.

This was not about her. This was about Jen and her fear and the man who had made her life hell for months.

Rosa did not offer platitudes because she knew how useless they could be.

"What do you need? Do you want me to call the police? You know you can trust Wyatt. Detective Townsend. He is a good man."

For a moment, Jen looked as if she would consider doing just that, then she shook her head. "What would I say? That I think I might have seen a man who might be friends with a man who scares me but who has never actually touched me? He will think I'm crazy."

"He will not think you are crazy." Rosa did not know how she knew this so completely, but she had no doubt that Wyatt would take Jen's concerns seriously. "Stalking is against the law in Oregon, just as it was in Utah. I believe Wyatt will help you. He will want to know what you think you saw."

Again, Jen looked tempted. Rosa even pulled out her phone, but her friend finally shook her head firmly. "I'm imagining things. I'm sure of it. It was only a man who looked like someone from our town. I don't want to bring Wyatt in."

"You know he will help."

"Yes. If there was anything he could do, but there's not. I cannot run from shadows for the rest of my life. Aaron would have no reason to know I'm here. He doesn't know one of my dearest friends lives here. I never mentioned you to him. And if it was his friend, he couldn't possibly recognize me. I don't look the same. I've lost thirty pounds, my hair is shorter and a different color. I have contacts now instead of glasses. He would have no reason to even connect Jen Ryan with the woman he knew as Jenna Haynes."

Rosa was still not convinced. She had heard the fear, the sheer terror in Jenna's voice when Rosa had called her. She thought it would just be a regular phone call to wish her a happy birthday. Instead, Jenna had spewed out such a story of horror that Rosa had been physically sick to her stomach.

"You must come here," she had told her college friend firmly in that phone call. "I have an empty apartment right now. Just bring Addie and come tonight."

"I can't drag you into this," Jen had replied through her tears. "You've been through enough."

"That is why I have to help you. You are my friend. I cannot let you live in fear if you do not have to. Come to Oregon, where this man does not know anyone. You will be safe here."

Jen had been desperate enough to escape her situation that she had finally agreed, leaving in the middle of the night with only their clothes.

She was finally beginning to relax and enjoy her life again. Rosa hated to think of her living in fear again.

"Please. Consider talking to Wyatt," she said now. "He knows something is wrong. He asked me about it the other night. You know he is a good man. He will do what he can to keep you safe."

"I'll think about it," Jen finally said. Color had returned and she seemed to be breathing more easily, Rosa was glad to see.

"Give me a moment and I will give you a ride home."

Worried that the man stalking her had put a trace on her vehicle, Jen had traded her car in the Boise area for an older model sedan that had seen better days. It was currently in the shop, where it had been for several days.

Jen shook her head. "No. Thank you, though. I would rather walk."

"Are you sure?"

"It's less than a mile and I can pick up Addie on the way. The walk will clear my head."

"Are you sure?"

Jen nodded. Her features grew soft. "I meant what

I said earlier. I cannot thank you enough for all you've done for me. You've given me hope that someday soon I will stop looking over my shoulder. I wish there was some way I could repay you."

"You have, a hundred times. I love seeing you take back your life. You and Addie deserve everything wonderful I know is in store for you."

Jen smiled, though traces of panic still lingered in her eyes. As soon as she left, Rosa almost picked up her phone and called Wyatt herself, but she decided against it. Jenna's story was her own. She had her reasons for keeping it to herself.

Rosa, who had plenty of secrets of her own, could not fault her for that, even though she knew Wyatt was the kind of man who would do everything he could to keep Jenna and Addie safe.

CHAPTER NINE

AFTER LEAVING CAROL and another of her part-time workers to close the store, Rosa returned to Brambleberry House tired, but in a strange, restless mood. She needed to bake something. The urge did not hit her very often, but when it did, she tried to go with it.

Baking reminded her of her mother. Maria Elena had been an amazing baker who used to make delicious delicacies she would sometimes sell in the market. Anything to make a few lempiras.

Rosa still liked making the treats of her childhood, but today she was feeling more like good old-fashioned chocolate-chip cookies, a treat she had come to love as a teenager.

She was just taking the first batch out of the oven when her phone rang. For a moment, she thought about ignoring it. Hardly anyone ever reached out to her with a phone call anymore, unless there was some kind of trouble. It might be Lauren, though, who still liked to have long chats on the phone since they couldn't connect as often in person.

Without looking at the caller ID, she tapped her

earbud to answer the call as she slid the tray of cook-ies onto the cooling rack and put the next tray into the oven.

"Buenas," she said, distracted.

"Hello?" a male voice replied. "Is this Rosa Galvez?"

Her heartbeat accelerated as she recognized Wyatt.

Oh, this was so stupid. They had shared one kiss. Granted, it had been earthshaking for her, but that did not explain why she became weak in the knees, simply knowing he was on the other end of a telephone call.

She was tempted for a moment to tell him "no, wrong number," and disconnect the call. That would be childish, though. What was the point of hiding from the reality that she was falling for a completely inap-propriate man?

"Si. Yes. This is Rosa."

"Hola, Rosa. This is Wyatt Townsend. From down-stairs."

As if she knew any other Wyatt Townsends who could make her head spin. "Yes. I know. Is everything all right?"

He sighed. "Not really. I have a little problem and was wondering if I could ask for your help."

The word shocked her. Wyatt was not the sort of man who could ask for help easily. "Of course. What do you need?"

"I just got called to cover an emergency and Carrie, Joe and Bella have gone to Portland. They're leaving for San Francisco from there. I'm in a bind and need someone to watch Logan for a few hours."

"Of course," she said instantly. "Fiona and I would

be glad to help you. I can be down in ten minutes, as soon as I take some cookies out of the oven."

"You don't have to come down. I can bring him upstairs to you. He's used to sleeping on the couch."

"Don't be silly. He would be more comfortable in his own bed. We will be there in ten minutes."

She had more dough, but decided she could put it in the refrigerator for now and later freeze it for another day.

"Thank you. I appreciate that. Hopefully I won't be gone past midnight."

"Even if you are, I won't mind," she assured him. "I'll be down soon."

While she waited for the timer, she gathered her laptop and a small knitting project she had been working on. She also waited for the first batch of cookies to cool enough before transferring them to a plate to take downstairs with her. As soon as the timer went off, she turned off her oven, pulled out the cookie tray and transferred the cookies to another cooling rack, then headed down the stairs with Fiona following close behind her.

Wyatt opened the door before she could knock, as if he had been watching for her.

"I'm really sorry about this."

"Please do not apologize. I'm happy to do it."

"Logan is already in bed. He'll be sorry he missed you."

She was disappointed that she wouldn't have a chance to hang out with the sweet boy and teach him more Spanish words. She would have enjoyed reading him a story and tucking him in.

"Too bad. I brought him some cookies. Ah, well. He can have one when he wakes up."

"If I don't eat them all first. They look delicious."

He smiled and she had to remind herself she was here to watch his child, not to moon over the boy's father.

She did her best to ignore how fiercely she wanted to kiss him again. It helped to focus on the gleaming badge he was wearing over the pocket of his sports coat, which reminded her of all the differences between them.

"Anything special I need to know or do?"

"Not really. Since the fire, Logan does have the occasional nightmare. If he has one, you only have to stay close and help talk him through it until he falls back asleep."

"Oh, *pobrecito*," she exclaimed.

His eyes seemed to soften. "Yeah. He's been through a few things. The nightmares are not as frequent as they were right after the fire. He probably won't even wake up but I wanted to warn you, just in case."

"Got it."

"Thank you again."

"Do not worry about things here. Go take care of what you have to do. I will be here. And take a cookie with you."

He grabbed one with a smile that left her feeling slightly light-headed. She told herself it was because she had only eaten a warm cookie for dinner.

After he left, she was again struck by how Wyatt and Logan had settled into the space. A video-game controller sat on the coffee table, along with a trio of plastic dinosaurs and several early-reader chapter books.

The house smelled like Wyatt, that combination of scents she couldn't pinpoint. She only knew it reminded her of walking through a forest after a rainstorm.

A light was on next to the easy chair in the sunroom. She wandered in and found a mystery novel with a bookmark halfway through on the side table. A small bowl of popcorn sat next to it.

Rosa's own limited detective skills told her he must have been reading and enjoying a snack when he got the call from work. She liked thinking about him here, enjoying the sound of the ocean in the night through the screens.

While Fiona found a comfortable spot on the rug next to Hank, Rosa continued on her tour. She briefly went to the room she knew Logan used and opened the door a crack to check on him.

The boy was sleeping soundly, sprawled across the bed with a shoebox that looked like it contained treasures tucked nearby.

She fought the urge to go to him, to smooth away the hair falling into his eyes.

The night of the storm, Wyatt had said Logan was a sound sleeper, but she still didn't want to run the risk of waking him and having him be confused at finding her here and not his father.

She did, however, take a moment to adjust the blanket more solidly over his shoulders.

Oh, he was dear boy. Just looking at him made her smile. He looked a great deal like his father, but his lighter coloring and the shape of his nose must have come from his mother's side.

Rosa had to wonder about the woman. She had seen a picture of them all together at Carrie and Joe's house. She had been pretty, blonde, delicate-looking.

Carrie had told her Tori Townsend had been a talented artist and writer, in addition to a school guidance counselor. Though she had been a runner who regularly worked out, she had tragically died of a previously undiagnosed heart condition at a shockingly young age.

Logan must grieve for her terribly, she thought. *Both of them must.* It made her heart ache, thinking of this sweet boy growing up without his mother.

At least he had a father who doted on him and an aunt, uncle and cousin who showered love and affection on him, as well.

After she had assured herself Logan was sleeping comfortably, she returned to the living area. It felt strange to be here in Wyatt's space without him. She wasn't quite sure what to do with herself.

She finally turned on the audiobook she was listening to through her ear pods and picked up her knitting. While the dogs slept tangled together at her feet, she worked and listened to the audiobook above the sound of the wind in the trees and the ever-present song of the ocean.

The chair was comfortable and her day had been

long. Soon she gave in to the inevitable and closed her eyes, thinking she would only doze for a moment.

She had a dream she was running. It was cold, bitterly cold, and she was barefoot. She was so afraid, not only for herself. She had nowhere to go and the winter snow blew past her and through her. So cold. Always so cold. She had been used to sunshine and heat and could never seem to warm up here.

Everything hurt. Her face, her arms, her stomach where she had been kicked and beaten. She needed help but didn't know where to go.

And then she saw him. A police officer. She thought at first it was Daniel but as he came closer she saw it was Wyatt, looking down at her with concern.

"What happened? Why are you running?"

She shook her head, too afraid to tell him. What would he think if he knew? He would never look at her the same way.

"It does not matter," she told the dream Wyatt. "I must keep running. If I don't, they will find me."

"Who?"

"The ghosts," she told him. Tears were running down her face. She could feel them dripping down her cheeks and reached to brush one away but it dried before she could touch it.

"I will protect you. I'm with the *policia*. Just like Daniel. Trust me, Rosa. Trust me. Trust me."

As she watched, the fear still coursing through her with every heartbeat, his image grew more and more faint until he completely disappeared, leaving her alone again.

* * *

She awoke with gritty eyes, a dry mouth and the unsettling sensation that she was not alone.

Rosa blinked for a moment in the darkness, not sure exactly where she was. Not her bedroom in Brambleberry House. She would remember that. Not her room at her parents' home in Utah, either.

A man was there, she suddenly realized. She could see the outline of him in the darkness. She struggled up, tangled in yarn, as instinctive fear and dark memories crowded through her, leaving little room for rational thought.

She had to escape. Run. Hide.

A hand was suddenly on her arm. "Easy. It's okay. It's me."

The voice, calm and measured, seemed to pierce her sudden panic. She knew that voice. Wyatt Townsend.

Was this still part of her nightmare?

Not a nightmare. She blinked a little more as the room came into focus and her consciousness seemed to calibrate again. Right. She had been watching his son for him while he went out to a crime scene and she must have fallen asleep.

Rosa drew in a deep, shuddering breath, embarrassed that she had given in to unreasonable panic for a moment. She thought she had come too far for that.

"You startled me."

"I'm sorry. I didn't mean to. I was just debating if you would be more annoyed with me for waking you or for letting you sleep here until the morning."

"I am not annoyed with you," she assured him.

"I was having a bad dream. I am glad you woke me from it."

"Do you mind if I turn on the lamp?"

She probably looked horrible, with her hair tangled and her eyes shadowed. She carefully reached a hand up to her cheek and was relieved when she didn't feel any moisture. The tears must have only been in her dream.

"It's fine. Go ahead."

He did, and that's when she saw the fatigue in his eyes. This was more than physical, she realized instinctively. Something was very wrong. She wasn't sure how she knew but there was an energy that seemed to be seething around him. Something dark and sad.

"What is it?" She could not resist asking, though she wasn't sure she wanted to know the answer. "What has happened?"

He released a sigh that sounded heavy and tired. "It was a long, difficult night. That's all."

Whatever he had been dealing with seemed to have impacted him deeply.

She had seen that look before on her adopted father's face when he would return from a bad crime scene or accident. He would walk in the door and go immediately to Lauren, wherever she was, and would hold her tightly, as if she was his only safe haven in a terrible storm. She would hold him, comfort him, help him put the pieces of his soul back together before she sent him out again to help someone else.

She could not do that for Wyatt and it made her sad, suddenly. She was no one's safe haven.

"How can I help? Can I make you some tea?"

As soon as she made the offer, she thought it was silly to have even suggested it, but for some reason she thought something warm and comforting might be exactly what he needed to ease the turmoil.

He gave a ragged sound that wasn't quite a laugh. "I don't have any tea. And before you say you've got some upstairs and it will only take you a moment to run and get it, I'll tell you thank you but no. I probably need sleep more than anything. And maybe one of your cookies, but I might save those for breakfast."

"Are you certain? I don't mind going to get tea."

He shook his head. "No. You have done more than enough. I'm sorry I kept you so late."

"What time is it?"

"Nearly two. I thought I would be back long before now but the case was…more complicated than I expected."

"I do not mind. I was glad to help."

"I'm deeply grateful to you for staying with Logan. Let's get you back home so you can at least spend a few hours in your own bed."

She rose, again fighting the urge to go to him, wrap her arms around his waist and let him lean on her for a moment.

"Did everything go okay with Logan?" he asked. "No nightmares?"

She'd had one but hadn't heard a peep out of the boy. "Yes. Just fine. I checked on him when I first arrived and he was sleeping soundly. He doesn't keep the blanket on, though, does he?"

"Not usually. Sometimes I go in three or four times a night to fix it. He rolls around like he's doing gymnastics in his sleep. Once when we went camping, I actually woke up with bruises on my rib cage from him kicking me in his sleep."

He was a good father who adored his child. She could picture him checking on the boy and making sure he was warm in the night. It touched her heart.

"I cannot thank you enough for coming down at the last minute and helping out. None of our usual babysitters were available. With Carrie and Joe out of town, I didn't know what else to do."

"I really did not mind. I was honored that you would ask. Please do not hesitate to ask me again."

"If I do, I'll try not to keep you up until the early hours of the morning."

She shrugged and slung her bag over her shoulder. "I slept more soundly here than I probably would have at home. Please do not worry."

He smiled a little at that, but she could tell his eyes were still hollowed. What had happened?

"Do you have everything? Can I carry something?"

She wanted to roll her eyes when she realized he really did intend to walk her upstairs. "I have told you before, it is only two flights of stairs. I think I will be fine by myself. Get some rest."

"I need to move a little bit after tonight."

She nodded, understanding that sentiment. After that terrible time, she had needed to take long walks with Lauren, finding peace and comfort and a sort of meditation in the rhythm and the movement.

"Do you…want to talk about what happened tonight?" she finally asked.

"You don't want to hear. It was ugly."

She couldn't help it. She rested a hand on his arm. "I am sorry, whatever it was," she said quietly. "I can tell you are upset. If you were not, if you did not care and did not let the ugly touch you, then you would not be the good man you are."

He gazed down at her hand, his features tortured. After a moment, he made a sound of distress, then he folded her into his arms and held on tight.

"Why are people so horrible to each other?" he said, his voice sounding raw and strained.

She had no answer. What could she say? It was the question that had haunted her for fifteen years. One she was quite certain she would never be able to answer.

She only held him tightly, as she had seen Lauren do for Daniel, and tried to give him a little of her strength. She wanted to whisper that she would not let him go, no matter what, but, of course, she could not say that. How foolish to think that she, Rosa Vallejo Galvez, could protect anyone from the storm.

"Sometimes they are horrible," she agreed finally. "I do not know why. I wish I did. But more often people are good. They try to help where they can. I try to focus on the helpers instead."

They stood in the front room of his apartment, holding each other as emotions seemed to pour out of him. He didn't make a sound, but every once in a while, she could feel his shoulders shake as if it was taking everything inside him to keep from breaking down.

"Most of the time, I'm fine," he finally said, his voice still strained. "I like to think I can handle just about anything. But this one was hard. So hard."

"Tell me," she murmured.

"It was a murder-suicide. A domestic. A father who had lost a custody fight because of drug use and mental illness. Instead of accepting the court ruling or trying to fix his problems so he could have visitation, he decided that if he couldn't have his son, the mother wouldn't, either. He shot the boy and then shot himself. The kid was only five. A kindergartener. Younger than Logan."

At the despair in his voice, her heart cracked apart. She could only imagine how excruciating it must have been for Wyatt, who did everything possible to make his son's world better, to witness this kind of a crime scene.

Aching for him, she could do nothing but tighten her arms around him. "I'm so very, very sorry," she murmured.

He clung to her for a long time, there in the apartment, and she felt invisible threads between them tighten. Finally, he eased away, looking embarrassed.

"I'm sorry. I didn't mean to lose it like that. I'm… not sure why I did."

She suspected he had no one to share this kind of pain with since his wife died, which made her heart ache all over again.

"You hold too much inside," she said softly. "It cannot be easy, what you deal with every day."

"Yeah. Sometimes." He studied her, his expression intense. "This helped. More than I can ever tell you."

"I am glad. So glad. If you have another bad night, you know where to find me. Everyone needs someone to hold them when the world seems dark and hard."

"Thank you."

"You are welcome, Wyatt."

Something flashed in his gaze, something hungry and fierce. "I love the way you say my name."

All of the breath seemed to leave her in a whoosh. She swallowed as an answering heat prickled across her skin. "I do not say it in any way that is special."

"It is. It's unlike the way anyone else says it. Don't get me wrong. You speak beautiful, fluent English. I wish I could speak Spanish as well as you speak English. But sometimes your native language comes through on certain words."

The heat seemed to spread across her chest and down her arms. "I am sorry."

"No. Don't ever apologize. I like it."

He looked embarrassed that he had said anything, even as the first hint of a smile lifted the edges of his mouth.

He liked the way she said his name. She couldn't hear anything different in her pronunciation, but she wasn't going to argue.

"Wyatt," she repeated with a smile. "If it makes some of the sadness leave from your eyes a little, I will say it again. Wyatt. Wyatt. Wyatt."

His smile widened, becoming almost full-fledged for a brief moment, and Rosa could feel those invisible threads go taut.

After a moment, his smile faded. "What am I going to do about you?" he murmured.

She swallowed again. A smart woman would leave this apartment right now, would turn and hurry up the stairs to the safety of her own place. "There is nothing to do. We are friends. Friends help each other. They lean on each other when they need help."

He gazed down at her, his expression one of both hunger and need. "Do friends think about kissing each other all the damn time?"

CHAPTER TEN

WYATT KNEW HE shouldn't have said the words.

As soon as they were out, he wanted a do-over. Not because they weren't true. God knows, they were. He thought about Rosa Galvez constantly. Since the last time they had kissed, thoughts of her seemed to pop into his head all the time. She was like a bright, beautiful flower bringing happiness to everyone around her.

He was no exception. Thinking about her made him smile. Since he was thinking about her all the time, he was also smiling more than he had done in years. He knew it was becoming a problem when even other police officers had remarked on it.

Not that he really had anything to smile about. He and Rosa could not be together. Yeah, they had shared a brief, intense embrace. But that was the end of it.

If he could only get his brain to get with the program, he would be fine. But every single time he thought about her, he thought about kissing her. And every time he thought about kissing her, he tried to remind himself of all the reasons why it was not a good idea for him to kiss her again.

None of that stopped him from yearning. He wanted Rosa Galvez in his arms, in his bed, in his life.

In some ways, Wyatt felt as if he had been living in a state of suspended animation for the past three years, as if he had been frozen, like some glitch on one of Logan's video games, while the world went on around him.

It wasn't a good place, but it wasn't really terrible, either. He could still enjoy time with his son, with his sister and her family, with his friends.

He handled his day-to-day responsibilities, cared for Logan, managed to do a good job of clearing his caseload. But whenever he thought about what the future might hold for him, all he could see was a vast, empty void.

Nothing had been able to yank him out of that emptiness. Even when his house caught fire, he hadn't really been devastated, only annoyed at the inconvenience.

His own reaction had begun to trouble him. People had told him that a house fire was one of the most traumatic things that could happen to a person, but Wyatt had merely shrugged and moved into problem-solving mode. Where they would live, what he might change about the house as he was having crews work on the renovations.

Even something as dramatic as being displaced hadn't really bothered him.

He could see now that his reaction had been a self-protective mechanism. After Tori's shocking death and the vast grief that had consumed him, he had slipped into some kind of place where he did not let anything touch him deeply.

Now he felt as if kissing Rosa had somehow kicked him in the gut, jolting him off his axis—that safe, bland existence—and into a world where everything seemed more intense.

A few months ago, he would have felt sad about the crime scene he had dealt with earlier, but it wouldn't have left him feeling shattered.

He was beginning to feel things more deeply and wasn't at all sure he liked it. A big part of him wanted to go back to the safety of his inertia.

If kissing her once could jerk him into this weird place, maybe kissing her a second time would help set things back the way they were before.

Even as he thought it, he knew kissing her again was a stupid idea. That did not stop him from reaching for her, pulling her into his arms again and lowering his mouth to hers.

She made a small, surprised sound, but didn't pull away. If she had, he would have stopped instantly. Instead, her arms went around his neck again and she pressed against him. She kissed him back, her mouth soft, sweet, delicious.

As she parted her lips and touched him tentatively with her tongue, he went a little crazy, all the raw emotions of the evening consolidating into one, his wild need for Rosa Galvez.

He deepened the kiss, his mouth firm and demanding on hers. He had to be closer to her. To touch her, to feel her against him.

She said his name again with that sweet little ac-cented pronunciation, this time in a voice that was throaty and aroused.

He wanted to absorb it inside him.

He wanted to lose himself inside *her*.

His body ached with it, suddenly, the need he had shoved down for so long. He wanted to make love to Rosa Galvez right here in his living room. To capture her gasps and sighs with his mouth, to see her shatter apart in his arms.

Her breasts were pressed against him and he wanted more. He wanted to see her, to taste her. He reached be-neath the hem of her shirt, to the warm, sweet-smelling skin beneath.

She shivered. The movement rippled over his fin-gers and brought him to his senses.

What the hell was wrong with him?

This woman had just spent hours sleeping in his easy chair to help him with his son and he repaid her by groping her in his front room?

He couldn't seem to catch his breath, but he did his best as he dropped his arms from around her.

She was breathing hard, too, her hair loose from the messy bun she had been wearing. She gazed at him out of eyes that looked huge and impossibly dark.

She had been so sweet to him, so comforting and warm when he needed it most. He had been at the low-est point he could remember in a long time and she had held him and lifted him out of it. In return, he had let his hunger for her overwhelm all his common sense.

"I'm sorry," he said, his voice ragged. "I don't know what happened there."

"Do not apologize." Her voice wobbled a little bit.

"Are you…okay? I didn't hurt you, did I?"

Her gaze narrowed, as if he had offended her somehow. "You only kissed me. I am not like some glass figure in my store falling off the shelf. I cannot be broken by a kiss, Wyatt."

There was his name again. It seemed to slide under his skin, burrowing somewhere in his chest.

What was he going to do about her?

Nothing, he told himself again. He just had to suck it up and forget about the way her kisses made him feel alive for the first time in years.

"I'll walk you upstairs."

She didn't argue, much to his relief. She only turned away, gathered her things and called to Fiona, then she and her dog hurried up the stairs.

Wyatt caught up with them on the second landing. The dog seemed to give him a baleful look, but he thought maybe that was just a trick of the low lighting out here in the stairway.

At her apartment, Rosa unlocked the door and opened it. "Good night."

Before he could thank her again for helping him out with Logan, she slipped inside and closed the door firmly behind her.

Wyatt stood for a moment, staring at the beautiful woodwork on the door, a match to his own two floors below.

That was as clear a dismissal as he could imagine. She had literally shut the door in his face.

He couldn't blame her. It was now nearly three and he knew she had to open the store early the next day, just as he had another shift.

He turned and headed down the stairs. He gripped the railing and told himself the shakiness in his legs was only exhaustion.

Something told him it was more than that. That kiss had just about knocked his legs right out from under him.

He was falling for her.

The reality of it seemed to hit him out of nowhere and he nearly stumbled down the last few steps as if the fabled ghost of Brambleberry House had given him a hard shove.

No. He couldn't be falling for Rosa. Or for anyone else, for that matter.

He didn't *want* to fall in love again. He had been through that with Tori. Once was enough, thanks all the same. These feelings growing inside him were only attraction, not love. Big difference.

Yes, he liked her. She was sweet, compassionate, kind. And, okay, he thought about her all the time. That wasn't love. Infatuation, maybe.

He wouldn't let it be love.

The next day, Rosa was deadheading flowers in one of the gardens when Jen drove up in her rickety car, now running but not exactly smoothly. It shimmied a little as it idled, then she turned off the engine.

Rosa waved and Jen and Addie walked over.

"Hello, there," Rosa said. "How did the interviews go?"

"Good. Great, actually. The school offered me a job on the spot."

"Oh, that's terrific! We should celebrate. Have you eaten?"

"Yes. Sorry. Addie wanted a Happy Meal today."

"No problem. Maybe we can celebrate later. I have a bottle I've been saving for something special."

"It's a deal, as long as it goes with your famous chocolate-chip cookies."

Rosa had to smile. She had taken a plate down before she headed to the store and left them outside Jen's front door.

"Can we help you with the gardening?"

"Yes. Of course. That would be great. Thank you."

Addie frowned. "Why are you pulling all the flowers, Rosa? That's naughty. My mommy says I can't pick the flowers or they die."

She smiled, charmed by the girl even as she felt a little ache in her heart. "I am not picking *all* the flowers. Only the ones that have finished blooming and have started to die. This way the flower plant has more energy to make new blossoms. You can help, if you want to. You just pop off the flower if it's brown or the petals have come off and put it in the bucket there."

"I can do that!"

Addie began the task, humming a little as she worked, which made Rosa smile.

"I have a confession," Jen said after a few moments.

"After my interview, I probably could have come in and worked this afternoon. Instead, I picked up Addie from day care early and we played hooky for most of the afternoon."

"Good for you," Rosa said, feeling a twinge of envy. "Did you do something fun?"

"Yes. It was wonderful. We made a huge sandcastle and then played in the water a bit, then took a hike around the state park near Arch Cape."

"Oh, I love that area. It is so beautiful and green, like walking through a movie, with all the ferns and moss."

"Yes. Addie thought it looked like a fairy land."

Oh, Addie was cute. She had such an innocent sweetness about her. Rosa hoped she could keep it forever.

"So," Jen said after a moment. "You and Detective Gorgeous. Is that a thing now?"

Rosa, yanking out a nasty weed that had dug its roots in deep, almost lost her balance.

She could feel her face grow hot. "Why would you say such a thing?"

"I *might* have heard two people going up the stairs together in the early hours of the morning."

Rosa could only be grateful they had kissed in his apartment and not in the stairway for her friend to overhear.

"So are you two…dating or something?"

She had a sudden fervent wish that she could say yes. The idea of doing something as ordinary and sweet as dating Wyatt seemed wonderful but completely out of reach.

"No. We are not dating. Only friends." *Who kiss each other as if we can't get enough*, she wanted to add, but, of course, she couldn't say that to Jen.

"He needed someone to watch his son last night while he went out on an emergency police call. His sister is out of town and he did not have anyone else to ask. It was an easy thing for me to help him."

Jen made a face. "Too bad. I was thinking how cute you two would be together. And it's obvious his son likes you."

Rosa could feel herself flush. She was coming to adore both Townsend males, entirely too much. "I am not interested in dating anyone right now." *No matter how gorgeous.*

Jen nodded and carefully plucked away at a rose that had bloomed past its prime. "I totally understand that and feel the same way. I'm not sure I'll ever date again."

Her emphatic tone made Rosa sad. Jen had so much love inside her to give. It was a shame that one bad experience had soured her so much on men.

"Your husband, he was a good man, yes?" Jen and her husband had met after college and Rosa had only met him at their wedding, and the few times they had socialized afterward, before she moved to Oregon.

"Oh, yes," Jen said softly. "Ryan was wonderful. After he died, I never thought I would find anyone again."

She plucked harder at the rose bush. "I wish I hadn't ever entertained the idea of dating again. I obviously don't pick well."

Rosa frowned. "You did well with your husband.

Nothing else that happened to you is your fault. I wish I could help you see that. You had no way of knowing things would turn out like they have."

"That's what I tell myself," Jen said quietly. "Most of the time I believe it. In the middle of the night when I think about everything, it's harder to convince myself."

"You did nothing wrong," Rosa repeated in a low voice so that Addie didn't overhear. "You went on three dates with this man then tried to stop dating him when you began to see warning signs. You had no way of knowing he would become obsessive."

Jen sighed. "I still wish I could go back and do everything over again. I wish I had said no the very first time he asked me out."

"I know. I am sorry."

Rosa became angry all over again every time she thought about how one man's arrogance and refusal to accept rejection had forced Jen to flee her life and live in fear.

She was so glad her friend seemed to be trying to put the past behind her and make plans for the future.

"And while I don't think I am the best judge of character right now and don't seem to pick well for myself, I do like Detective Townsend. He seems very kind and he is a wonderful father."

Rosa could not disagree. She felt a little ache in her heart at the reminder that she and Wyatt could not be together. Soon, he and his son would be moving out of Brambleberry House.

"He is a good man and, I think, cares very much about helping people."

She paused, compelled to press the situation. "He would help you, you know. You should tell him what is going on."

"I don't know about that."

"I do. Wyatt is a man you can trust. While he is living here, he can look around for anything unusual. Like having security on site."

"I suppose it is a little like that."

Rosa nodded. "That is one of the reasons I agreed to let him move in. I was worried about you and thought it might make you more comfortable to know he is only downstairs."

Jen gave her a sidelong look. "You mean it wasn't because of those beautiful blue eyes?" she teased.

Rosa flushed and tried to pretend she was inordinately fascinated with clipping back a climbing vine. "Does he have blue eyes? I do not believe I had noticed."

Jen snorted a little, which made Rosa smile. She was happy to be a subject of teasing if it could bring a smile to Jen's face.

"You said you're not interested in dating. Why is that?"

"I date," Rosa protested. "I went out three weeks ago to a concert down in Lincoln City."

"With a seventy-five-year-old widower who had an extra ticket."

"Mr. Harris is very sweet. And also lonely, since he lost his wife."

"You know you don't have to take care of everyone else in town. You should save a little of your energy for going after what you want."

If only it could be that easy. She knew what she wanted. She also knew she could not have it.

She didn't have a chance to answer before a vehicle pulled into the driveway. She stood up, suddenly breathless when she recognized Wyatt's SUV. She had not seen him since that emotional, passionate kiss the night before and wasn't sure how to act around him.

He climbed out, and a moment later opened the back door for his son, who hopped out and raced over to them.

"Logan! Hi, Logan!" Addie made a beeline for the boy, who waved at her.

"Hi, Addie. Your hands are muddy."

"I'm picking flowers. Rosa said I could, to help the other flowers grow better."

"Remember, you should only pick the flowers when a grown-up tells you it's okay," Jen said.

She looked momentarily worried, as if afraid Addie would wander through the entire beautiful gardens of the house pulling up the flowers willy-nilly.

"I want to help pick flowers. Can I?" Logan asked Rosa.

"You will have to ask your father if he does not mind."

The father in question drew nearer and she felt tension and awareness stretch between them. He gave her a wary smile, as if he didn't quite know how to act this evening, either. Seeing his unease helped her relax a little.

Yes, they had shared an intense, emotional kiss. That didn't mean things had to be awkward between them.

"Can I pick flowers?" Logan asked Wyatt. "Rosa said it's okay."

"We are taking away the dead and dying flowers to make room for new growth," she told him.

"I want to help, too," Logan said.

"Fine with me. As long as you do what Rosa says."

"Not a bad philosophy for life in general," Jen said, which made Rosa roll her eyes. She wasn't handling her own life so perfectly right now. Not when she was in danger of making a fool of herself over Wyatt.

"Is there something I can do to help?" Wyatt asked. "Were you trying to hang this bird feeder?"

She followed his gaze to the feeder she had left near the sidewalk.

"Yes. It fell down during the wind we had the other night. I was going to get the ladder and hang it back up."

"That would be a good job for Logan and me. Let me put our groceries away and I'll be right back out to do that for you."

"I'm sure you have enough to do at your house. You don't need to help me with my chores."

"Hanging a birdhouse is the least I can do after you pinch-hit for me last night with Logan."

To Rosa's dismay, she felt her face heat again. Oh, she was grateful her blushes were not very noticeable. She felt as red as those roses.

She couldn't seem to help it, especially when all she could think about was being in his arms the night before, his mouth on hers, and the way he had clung to her.

Something seemed to have shifted between them, as if they had crossed some sort of emotional line.

She, Jen and the children continued clearing out the flower garden and moved to another one outside the bay window of Logan's room.

A few moments later, Wyatt came out of the house. He had changed out of his work slacks, jacket and tie into jeans and a T-shirt that seemed to highlight his strong chest and broad shoulders.

"Is the ladder in the shed?" he asked.

"Yes. It should be open."

"Come help me, Logan. You, too, Addie. This might be a job for three of us."

She watched them go to the shed and a moment later Wyatt emerged carrying the ladder mostly by himself, with each of the children holding tightly to it as if they were actually bearing some of the weight, which she knew they were not.

"He's really great with kids," Jen murmured.

Maybe so. That didn't make him great for *Rosa*.

It did not take him long to rehang the birdhouse in the tree she pointed out. While she would have liked to hang it higher up on the tree, on a more stable branch, she knew she would not be able to refill the feeder easily without pulling out a ladder each time.

After Wyatt and his little crew returned the ladder to the shed, they came back out and she set them to work helping her clear out the rest of the weeds and dead blossoms in the garden.

Her back was beginning to ache from the repetitive motion, but Rosa would not have traded this moment for anything. There was something so peaceful in working together on a summer evening with the air sweet from the scent of flowers and the sun beginning to slide into the ocean.

"So how did you two meet?" Wyatt asked them.

"College," Jen replied promptly. "We were assigned as roommates our very first day and became best friends after that."

Both of them had been apprehensive first-year college students. Rosa had been quite certain she was in over her head. She had only been speaking English for three years. She hadn't known how she would make it through college classes. But Jen had instantly taken her under her wing with kindness and support.

She owed her a huge debt that she knew she could never repay.

"Here you are, living as roommates again, of a sort," Wyatt said casually.

"Yes," Jen answered. "Isn't it funny how life works sometimes? I was looking for a change and Rosa had an empty apartment. It worked out for both of us."

Wyatt looked at the children, now playing happily on the tree swing. "What about Addie's father? Is he in the picture?"

Jen gazed down at the flowers, grief washing across her features. "Unfortunately, no. He died two years ago of cancer. Melanoma."

"I'm sorry," Wyatt said gently.

He knew what it was to lose someone, too, Rosa thought. In fact, the two of them would be perfect for each other. So why did the idea of them together make her heart hurt?

Jen sighed and rose to face him. "I might as well tell you, Jen Ryan is not really my name."

Rosa held her breath, shocked that her friend had blurted the truth out of nowhere like that. She could tell Wyatt was shocked, as well, though he did his best to hide it.

"Isn't it?"

"Well, it's not wholly a lie. My name is Jenna Michelle Haynes. Ryan was my late husband's name."

He studied her. "Are you using his name for your surname now as some kind of homage?"

"No." She looked at Rosa as if asking for help, then straightened her shoulders and faced Wyatt. Rosa could see her hands clenching and unclenching with nerves. "Actually, if you want the truth, I'm hiding from a man."

CHAPTER ELEVEN

WYATT STARED, SHOCKED that she had told him, though not really by what she said.

He had suspected as much, judging by her nervous behavior and the way Rosa was so protective of her. He just didn't know the details.

He suddenly felt as protective of her as Rosa did. Who would want to hurt this fragile woman and her darling little girl?

He immediately went into police mode. "Who is he? Can you tell me? And what did he do to make you so afraid?"

She sighed and looked at the children, who were laughing in the fading sunshine as Logan pushed Addie on the swings. The scene seemed innocent and sweet, completely incongruous to anything ugly and terrifying.

She swallowed hard and couldn't seem to find the words until Rosa moved closer, placing a supportive arm through hers. Jen gave her a look of gratitude before facing him again.

"His name is Aaron Barker. He's also a police officer in the small Utah town where I was living after my husband died. He… We went out three times. Three dates. That's all."

Rosa squeezed her arm and Jen gripped her hand. One of the hardest parts of his job was making people relive their worst moments. It never seemed to get easier. He didn't want to make her rehash all the details, but he couldn't help her if he didn't know what had happened.

She seemed to sense that because after a moment, she went on. "Aaron was very nice at first. Showering me with affection, gifts, food. Sending flowers to the school where I taught. I was flattered. I was lonely and—and I liked him. But then he started pushing me too hard, already talking about marriage. After three dates."

She shook her head. "I finally had to tell him he was moving too fast for me and that I didn't think I was ready to start dating again."

Her voice seemed to trail off and she shivered a little, though the evening was warm. He didn't like the direction this story was taking. It had to be grim to send her fleeing from her home to Oregon.

"What happened?"

"He wouldn't take no for an answer. He kept asking me out, kept bringing me gifts. I finally had to be firm and tell him we weren't a good match and I wasn't going to change my mind. I thought he understood, but then he started driving past in his squad car at all hours of the day and night. He kept calling and texting, sometimes dozens of times a day. I had to turn my phone off. I went out to dinner one day with another teacher, a coworker and friend who happens to be a man. Nothing romantic, just friends, but that night Aaron sent me a long, vitriolic email, calling me a whore, saying if he couldn't have me, no one could, and all kinds of other terrifying things. I knew he must have been watching me."

"Why didn't you report him to the police?"

"I tried but this was a small town. The police chief was his uncle, who wouldn't listen to me. He wouldn't even take my complaint. I tried to go to the county sheriff's department but they said it was a personnel issue for our town's police department. I think they just didn't want to bother and didn't want to upset Aaron's uncle."

Again, Wyatt had to fight down his anger. He knew how insular small-town police departments and their surrounding jurisdictions sometimes could be. Often, police officers for one agency didn't want to get other agency police officers in trouble.

He had also been involved in stalking investigations and knew just how difficult the perpetrators could be to prosecute. Most laws were weak and ineffective, leaving the victim virtually powerless to stop what could be years of torture.

"This went on for months," Jen said. "I can't explain how emotionally draining it was to be always afraid."

Rosa made a small sound, her features distressed. He sensed she was upset for her friend but had to wonder if there was something else behind her reaction. Why wouldn't she tell him her secrets, like Jen was finally doing?

"I understand," Wyatt said quietly. "I have worked

these kinds of cases before. I know how tough they can be on the victims."

"Aaron was relentless. Completely relentless. I changed my number, my email, closed down my social-media accounts, but he would find a new way to reach me. He…started making threats. Veiled at first and then more overt. When he mentioned Addie in one of his messages, I quit my teaching job and moved closer to my sister, about an hour away, but the night after I moved, my tires were slashed. Somehow he found me anyway."

So things had taken an even uglier turn. Wyatt wasn't surprised.

"How did you end up here?"

"Rosa happened to reach out to me out of the blue, right in the middle of everything. We hadn't talked in a while and she was just checking up on me. Calling to wish me a happy birthday. I didn't want to tell her, but everything just gushed out and I finally told her everything that had been going on."

She squeezed Rosa's arm. "I don't know what I would have done without her. I was telling her that tonight. She invited me to come stay with her here for a while. She offered me a job and an apartment. It seemed perfect, and honestly, I didn't know what else to do."

"I only wish I had known earlier what was happening to you," Rosa said, looking guilty. "I should have called you sooner."

"Don't ever think that. You reached out right when I was at my lowest point and offered me a chance to escape."

Jen turned back to Wyatt. "I packed up what we had and drove as far as Boise. Maybe I watch too much *Dateline*, but I traded my car on the spot at a used-car lot, in case Aaron had put some kind of tracker on my vehicle, then I drove here."

"That was smart."

"I don't know about that. I had a nice little late-model SUV with four-wheel drive that was great for the Utah winters. Now I've got a junker. It was probably the best swap the dealer ever made. But it got us here to Brambleberry House, where I have felt safe for the first time in months."

"I am so glad," Rosa said.

"I can't tell you how nice it has been not to constantly look over my shoulder."

"Do you think he's given up?" Wyatt hated to ask but didn't have a choice.

Her expression twisted with distress. "I want to think so. I hope so. But I don't know. I don't know how to find out without possibly revealing my new location."

"He was obsessed," Rosa said, placing a protective arm around her friend. "Jenna is only telling you a small portion of the things this man has done to her."

Wyatt hoped the man had given up, though he worried that by fleeing, she had only stoked his unhealthy obsession.

Moving several states away might not be enough to escape a determined stalker, especially not one with law-enforcement experience.

"Thank you for telling me this. I know it wasn't

easy, but you've done the right thing. I'll do what I can to help you. You said his name is Aaron Barker?"

"That's right."

"Do you have a picture or description?"

"Yes. I can email you a picture and also link you to his social media."

"Texting me is better. He might have hacked into your email."

"He's done that before but I changed my account and password."

That might not be the deterrent she hoped. Someone determined enough could find ways around just about anything.

"Once you get me a picture of him and a description, I'll pass it around to other officers in the local PD and sheriff's department so we can be on the lookout. You're in Cannon Beach now and we take care of our own."

"Thank you." Jen looked overwhelmed to have someone else on her side. He understood. Victims of stalking could feel so isolated and alone, certain no one else would understand or even believe them and that their ordeal would never end.

"You're welcome."

He glanced at Rosa and found her looking at him with such warmth and approval that he couldn't seem to look away.

Addie came running over, with Logan close behind.

"Mommy," she said, tugging on Jen's shirt, "I have to go to the bathroom."

Jen gave her a distracted look then seemed to

sharpen her focus on her child. "Right. The door is locked. I'll get it for you."

She turned back to Wyatt. "Thank you," she said again. "I'll get you that picture."

"That's the best thing you can do right now."

"I'm glad I told you. Rosa was right."

She gave Rosa a look he couldn't quite interpret, but one that left him feeling as if he had missed something significant, and then Jen grabbed her daughter's hand and hurried for the house.

After she left, Wyatt turned to Rosa and found her looking at him with that same expression of warmth and approval.

"What were you right about?" he asked.

She shrugged. "I told her she could trust you. That you would help her if you could."

If she believed that, why wouldn't she trust him herself?

He could not ask. "I don't know how much I can do. I hope she's right, that he has lost interest."

"But you do not think so."

He couldn't lie. "If the man was willing to break the law to hack into her emails and completely disrupt her life to that extent, I can't see him giving up easily. I think he will keep searching until he finds her."

"What can we do?"

"Not a great deal unless he does something overt. I'm sorry."

"I feel so helpless."

"I know. It's a terrible feeling. I'll do a little internet sleuthing and see what I can dig up on the guy without coming right out and contacting his department. I don't want to run the risk of him getting wind that a detective in Oregon is looking into him, or that will certainly clue him in that she's here. Meanwhile, I'll circulate the picture around here when she gives me one and we will keep our eyes open."

It didn't sound like much, even to Wyatt. He hated that he couldn't do more. If this Aaron Barker was obsessed enough about Jenna and Addie, he would figure out a way to find them.

"Why can't some men take no for an answer?" she asked quietly.

He gave her a searching look but she quickly shifted her gaze away.

"It usually has to do with power and control. And some men just can't accept rejection."

"She has already been through so much, losing the man she loved with all her heart. It is not fair."

"No. It's not. I hate when any man hurts or threatens a woman, but I especially hate when he's in law enforcement."

"Thank you for believing her. That was the most important thing. Everyone else she told thought she was making it up to get attention or to get this man in trouble."

"You believed her."

"I know fear when I see it," Rosa said simply. "She is afraid or she would not have taken her daughter away from her family and her friends."

Something told him Rosa knew plenty about fear,

as well. He wanted to press her to tell him but held his tongue.

"Have you had dinner?" he asked instead. "We were about to order takeout from the Thai place in town. Buying you dinner is the least I can do for your help last night."

She looked shocked by the invitation. For a moment, he thought she was about to say yes. She looked at Logan, who was now digging in the dirt nearby, with a softness in her eyes that touched him deeply.

After a moment, she looked back at Wyatt, her expression shielded again.

"No, thank you."

He wasn't expecting the outright rejection and didn't know what to say for a few seconds. "If you don't like Thai food, there's a good Indian place with fabulous curry that just opened on the other side of town. I've heard they deliver, too. Or we can hit up the trusty taco truck down the beach."

"I like Thai food," she said, her voice low.

He gazed at her, confused. Was it *him* she didn't like? "Have you already eaten, then?"

She shook her head. "No. I'm not really hungry and I have much work to do tonight."

"We can help you after we grab dinner," he suggested.

After a moment, she sighed, looking distressed again. "I...think it is best if we do not spend a great deal of time together."

"Why not?" He was either being particularly dense or she was being obtuse. "I thought we were friends. That's what you said last night."

"Yes. And then you kissed me and I forgot about being friends and…wanted more."

He felt his face heat up. He could be such an idiot sometimes. Did he really think they could go back to a casual friendship after he had basically had a breakdown in her arms the night before, and then kissed her with all the pent-up loneliness and need inside him?

"Neither of us is looking for romance right now," Rosa went on, deliberately looking away from him. "I know this. But when you kiss me, I forget."

He did, too. When he kissed her, when he felt her arms around him and her soft mouth under his and the curves he longed to explore, Wyatt wanted to forget everything and get lost in the wonder and magic of holding her.

Rosa was right. Neither of them was looking for romance. The more time they spent together, the harder it was becoming for him to remember that.

It would be better to keep their distance until his house was fixed, when he and Logan would move out. Once things were back to normal and he didn't run the risk of bumping into her every time he came home, they would be able to go back to their regular lives.

No more moonlit kisses on the stairway, no more quiet talks on the front porch of Brambleberry House.

Just him and his son and his work.

The future seemed to stretch out ahead of him, gray as a January day.

What if he was beginning to want more?

CHAPTER TWELVE

A WEEK LATER, he stood at his sister's kitchen sink, helping Carrie thread vegetables onto skewers for the grill.

"Thanks for having us for dinner. I've been so busy, I haven't had much time to cook and I think Logan is getting a little tired of the taco truck for dinner."

Carrie laughed. "Surely not. Who could be tired of that?"

He impaled a yellow squash on the metal skewer, followed by a mushroom and then a slice of onion. "I feel like I haven't seen you since the Fourth. Tell me all about your trip."

After taking Bella to the concert in Portland a week earlier, Joe and Carrie had driven down to San Francisco for a few days with her.

"It was fun. We did all the touristy things. Alcatraz, riding a cable car, going to Fisherman's Wharf. And, of course, shopping. You can't visit San Francisco without spending too much money. We bought some cute school clothes for the new year."

He needed to start thinking about the new school year. Logan would be starting second grade. Wyatt still had a hard time believing he was that old.

He was finishing the last of the skewers while Carrie did some shrimp and some chicken when the doorbell rang.

"Are you expecting someone else?"

His sister somehow managed to look coy. "Sounds like Bella is getting it. That will be Rosa."

He nearly impaled his finger instead of a mushroom. "Rosa is coming to dinner, as well?"

He had been trying to stay away from her the past week, at her request. How the hell was he supposed to do that when his sister invited them both over for dinner?

"Yes. I happened to drop into her store today and mentioned Joe was going to grill tonight, and we had plenty. She seemed a little down and I thought it might cheer her up a bit. I hope you don't mind."

Why was she down? He wanted to rush out and ask if she was all right but made himself stay put.

"And you didn't think to tell me until now that she was coming?"

"Does it matter?"

Yes. Most certainly. He would have refused Carrie's last-minute invitation if he had known the dinner party included a woman who had specifically told him they should avoid spending more time together.

"I just wish you had told me."

Carrie made a face. "I'm sorry. I just thought one more person for dinner wouldn't make a difference."

He frowned. This was the second time in only a few weeks that Carrie had invited them both over for a meal at the same time. That couldn't be a coincidence, could it? She had already mentioned she thought he should think about dating her friend.

Did his sister suspect he was beginning to have feelings for Rosa?

If Carrie had any idea about the attraction that simmered between them, Wyatt knew she wouldn't hesitate to do whatever she could to push them together as much as possible. She wouldn't be subtle about it, either.

He wanted to say something but before he could, Rosa and Bella came into the kitchen, Bella chattering a mile a minute about their trip.

Rosa didn't seem to notice him at first. She was listening intently to Bella's story about the ghost tour they went on, and smiling at the girl's animation.

The two of them shared similar coloring. The same dark hair and dark eyes. With their heads together like that, they looked as if they could be sisters, catching up after a long time away.

He frowned suddenly as a crazy thought flitted across his brain. No. Impossible. He pushed it away just as Rosa lifted her head and caught sight of him.

Her eyes widened with shock. "Oh. Wyatt. Hello. I did not know you would be here."

If she had known, he had a feeling she would have refused his sister's invitation. Well, they were both here. Might as well make the best of it.

"Hi," he answered, just as Logan came in from the family room, where he had been playing a video game with Joe.

He, at least, looked thrilled about the other dinner guest.

"Rosa! Hi, Rosa!" he exclaimed. He rushed to her and wrapped his arms around her waist as if he hadn't seen her for months.

It had only been a few nights ago when he had gone up to her apartment for another Spanish lesson and had come back down naming every single kind of fruit they had in their house in Spanish.

"Buenas," she said to him. "How are you tonight?"

"I'm good. Guess what? We're having *piña* and *fresas* tonight."

"Delicious. Pineapple and strawberries. My favorite."

"I didn't know strawberries were *fresas*. I don't think I learned that in Spanish class last year. How did you know?" Bella asked.

"Rosa's teaching me Spanish so I can talk better to my friend Carlos."

Carrie beamed at them and gave Wyatt a significant look. Yeah. She was definitely matchmaking, despite the way he had basically told her to stand down the last time.

He was going to have to do whatever he could to deflect any of Carrie's efforts in that department.

To his relief, his sister was not overtly obvious over dinner, though she did suggest he and Rosa take a look at how her climbing roses were growing, something they both managed to avoid by changing the subject.

Having his sister and her family there, along with Logan, helped make things a little less awkward between them, but he still couldn't help remembering his hurt when she had told him they should avoid being together.

The food was good, at least. Carrie had a great marinade he always enjoyed and Joe was a whiz at the grill. Really, any time Wyatt didn't have to cook, he was happy.

Rosa was too busy talking to Bella and Logan to seem bothered by his presence.

After they ate, Rosa was the first to stand up. "Thank you for dinner, but things were so chaotic as I was leaving work that I am afraid I was not thinking. I just remembered I left some invoices I need to pay tonight on my desk. I would not want to leave them there overnight. Will you excuse me?"

Carrie made a face. "You're not staying for dessert? It's homemade vanilla ice cream that Bella helped me make this afternoon."

Rosa gave a vague smile. "It sounds very good but I really do need to go. Thank you, though."

She hugged both females and Logan, then waved to Wyatt and Joe before hurrying away.

After she left, some of the sparkle seemed to go out of the evening. Wyatt knew he wasn't the only one who felt it.

She was definitely trying to avoid him. He could only hope that everyone else didn't guess that her reasons for leaving so abruptly had anything to do with him.

"I'll have ice cream," Logan said.

"Same here," Bella said. "It's delicious."

He had to agree. It *was* delicious. But all that frozen,

creamy sweetness still couldn't remove the sour taste in his mouth.

"Dinner was great," he said after everyone had finished dessert. "Logan, let's help with dishes."

His son groaned a little but stood up to help clear away plates and carry them back inside the house.

When the dishwasher was loaded, Bella asked if she and Logan could take Hank for a walk before Wyatt left with the dog for home. He almost said no but was in no hurry to return to the tension of Brambleberry House.

"Sure. I can wait a little longer."

Logan was staying the night again with his aunt and uncle because Wyatt had an early meeting.

Joe got a phone call from his parents, who lived in Arizona, and excused himself to talk to them for a few moments, leaving Wyatt alone with Carrie.

"How's the house coming?" Carrie asked after her husband left the room.

"Almost there, I'm happy to report. We should be able to move back in another few weeks."

"That seems fast. But living at Brambleberry House worked out well, didn't it?"

A week ago, he would have said yes. "It's been fine. Logan has enjoyed having his own room again. It's a lovely old house and our apartment is roomier than our actual house."

"I'm glad. And your neighbors are nice, both of them. I like Jen and Rosa."

That was another area of frustration. He hadn't been able to make much progress in Jen's situation, other than to alert the department and do a little online sleuthing. Aaron Barker seemed to be a good cop, from what he could find out. He had no black marks on his reputation that Wyatt could find after a cursory search.

At least nothing suspicious seemed to have happened since Jen had told him about her stalker. He had been extra vigilant but hadn't learned anything new.

"Rosa is lovely, isn't she?" Carrie said in a casual voice that did not fool him for an instant.

He finally voiced the suspicion that had been nagging at him since he discovered Rosa had also been invited to dinner.

"I don't suppose there's any chance you're trying to push Rosa and me together, even after I told you not to, is there?"

"Me? Would I do that? Don't be silly." She gave him a shocked sort of look but he knew his sister well enough to see past it easily. She would do that kind of thing in a heartbeat, if she thought he might have the slightest interest in Rosa.

"Are you sure? This is the second time you've invited us both to dinner. Come to think of it, you seemed pretty determined that I move into her empty apartment at Brambleberry House."

"Only because it was the perfect solution when you yourself talked about moving out! I was only trying to help. As for dinner, it just so happens she is my dear friend and you are my brother. I like spending time visiting with each of you. I can't help it if sometimes those visits overlap."

"Can't you?"

"I didn't realize it would be a problem," she said

rather stiffly. "I thought you and Rosa were friends. Logan is always talking about how she's teaching him Spanish and how much he loves her dog and how you go out for tacos together."

He frowned. "That was one time, when we bumped into each other at the taco stand. Rosa and I are friends. That's all. Neither one of us is in the market for a relationship right now. I told you that."

"But you two are perfect for each other!"

Wyatt felt that little tug on his heart again, remembering how Rosa had held him during his moment of despair over the ugly crime scene he had just left, generously offering him a comfort and peace he had desperately needed.

He was beginning to think Carrie was right, at least on one side of the equation. Rosa was perfect for him. Smart, sweet, kind. He loved how warm she was with Logan and how compassionate and protective she was for her friend.

None of that mattered. Not when she had made it clear she wanted nothing to do with him except friendship.

"It's not going to happen. Get it out of your head, please. I would hate for you to make things awkward between us."

Carrie looked deeply disappointed. "It's just that I love her, you know? I want her to be happy. I want *you* to be happy. Why shouldn't you be happy together? I guess I just thought…after everything she's been through, she deserved a wonderful guy like you."

He frowned. "That's the second time you've made

reference to something in her past. What do you know? What has she been through?"

Carrie immediately looked away, but not before he saw guilt flash in her eyes. "Life can be hard for people trying to make it in a new country. She came here with nothing. She didn't even speak the language well. How fortunate she was to find her adoptive family, Anna Galvez's brother and his wife."

There was something else here. Something he couldn't quite put his finger on. A suspicion had begun to take root but it was one he didn't even dare ask his sister.

What if he was wrong?

Meantime, he had to do what he could to divert Carrie's attention and prevent her from meddling further between the two of them.

"Rosa is an extraordinary woman. I agree. But I'm not looking for anybody, no matter how extraordinary. Got that?"

She looked as if she wanted to argue, but to his relief, she finally sighed. "Fine. I won't invite you both to dinner, unless it's a party that includes a bunch of other people."

Would he be able to handle even that much? Right now, he wasn't sure. At least he would be moving away from Brambleberry House within the next few weeks. When he wasn't living downstairs from her, perhaps he could stop dreaming about her and wishing he could hold her again.

CHAPTER THIRTEEN

IT WAS FULLY dark when Rosa returned to Brambleberry House after stopping at By-The-Wind and running the bills to the post-office drop box.

She hadn't been lying about the invoices. She really had forgotten them, though mailing them certainly could have waited until the next day. That had been sheer fiction, an excuse to escape the tension between her and Wyatt.

She always loved spending time with the Abbotts. Carrie was invariably warm and kind and Joe treated her like a beloved younger sister.

And then there was Bella, full of energy and fun and enthusiasm for life. Her mood always seemed to rub off on Rosa, leaving her happier than when she had arrived.

This time, though, Rosa couldn't shake a deep sense of melancholy.

She knew the reason. Because Wyatt and Logan had been there. Spending time with them was beginning to make her ache deep inside.

She knew she was setting herself up for heartbreak. She could sense it hovering, just out of sight.

She was falling for them. Both of them.

Logan was impossible to resist. His sweet personality and eagerness to learn touched something deep inside of her. She would be so sad when he was no longer a regular part of her life.

And Wyatt. She brushed a lock of hair from her eyes. It was very possible that Wyatt was the most wonderful man she had ever met. She wanted to wrap her arms around him and not let go.

She could not, though. Rosa knew she could not have what she wanted.

She knew people who spent their entire lives wanting something other than what they had. Rosa tried not to be that person.

As a girl growing up with little in the way of material things, she had become used to that feeling of lack. Mostly, she had learned to ignore it, instead finding happiness with what she *did* have.

She was part owner in a business she loved running, she lived in a beautiful house at the seaside, she had cherished friends and a loving family. Most of the time, those things were enough.

Once in a while, though, like on moonlit summer nights, she caught glimpses of the future she might have had if not for a few foolish choices, and it made her heart ache.

Rosa sighed, a sad sound that seemed to echo in the emptiness of her apartment. Fiona nudged at her leg, resting her chin on Rosa's knee and gazing at her out of eyes that seemed filled with empathy.

Sometimes the dog seemed to sense her emotions keenly and offered exactly the right thing to lift her mood.

"You want to go for a walk, don't you?"

Fiona wagged her tail wildly in agreement. Rosa sighed again. She had let her dog out when she first came home a short time earlier, but apparently that was not enough for her, especially when the work day had been so hectic and she hadn't had time to take her on a walk.

Rosa was tired and not really in the mood for a nighttime walk. Part of being a responsible pet owner, though, was doing what she didn't always feel like doing when it was in the best interest of her beloved Fi.

"Okay. Let's find your leash."

Fiona scampered to the hook by the door of the apartment, where Rosa kept all the tools necessary for a walk. A hoodie, Fi's leash, a flashlight, treats and waste bags.

A few moments later, she headed down the steps. They had just reached the bottom when the door to Wyatt's apartment suddenly opened.

She gave a little gasp of surprise when he and Hank came out, the cute little dog all but straining on the leash.

"Oh," Rosa exclaimed. "You startled me."

Wyatt made a face. "Sorry. Hank was in a mood and nothing seemed to be settling him down. I was just going to take him on a quick walk. Are you coming or going?"

"Going. Fiona was in the same mood as Hank."

"Maybe they're talking to each other through the pipes."

Despite her lingering melancholy, Rosa had to smile a little at that idea. Fiona was smart enough that she could probably figure out a way to communicate to other dogs inside the house.

She looked behind him. "Where is Logan?"

"He's sleeping over at Carrie's again. I've got an early meeting tomorrow so they offered to keep him after dinner so I don't have to drag him out of bed so early."

"That is nice of them. Your sister is very kind."

"Truth. She is the best. I would have been lost without her after Tori died. Totally lost. She and Joe have been amazing, basically stepping in to help me parent Logan."

The dogs seemed delighted to see each other, sniffing like crazy with their tails wagging a hundred miles an hour.

She knew it was impossible, but Rosa still could not shake the suspicion that somehow her dog had manipulated events exactly this way, so that she and Wyatt would meet in the entryway of the house.

He opened the door and they both walked out into the evening, lit by a full moon that made her flashlight superfluous.

"Want to walk together?" he asked after a moment.

His suggestion surprised her so much that she did not know how to answer for a moment. Intellectually, she knew she was supposed to be maintaining a careful distance between them. She did not want to fall any harder for him.

How could she say no, though? Especially when she knew her time with him was so fleeting?

"That makes sense, doesn't it?"

"Which direction were you going? To the beach?"

Usually she liked to stick to the paths with streetlights and some traffic when she was walking late at night. Since Wyatt was with her, that wasn't necessary.

"Yes. Let's walk on the beach. The water always calls me."

They walked through the gardens, the air sweet with the scent of flowers and herbs. He opened the gate for her and she and Fiona went first down the path to the sand.

The moon was bright and full, casting a pearly blue light on everything. She certainly did not need her flashlight.

They walked mostly in silence for the first few moments, content to let the sounds of the waves fill the void. Despite everything between them, it was a comfortable silence.

She was the first to break it. "You said at dinner that your house is almost finished. Is everything going the way you like?"

"Yes. We had a few issues early on. It's an old house with electrical issues, which is what started the fire in the first place. I want to make sure everything is exactly right. I think I have been getting on the electrician's nerves a little, but we're getting there."

He gave her a sidelong look. "I'm sure you'll be

glad when everything is finished so we can get out of your way."

"You are not in my way," she protested. It wasn't exactly the truth. He was very much in the way of her thoughts constantly. "You know you can stay as long as you need."

"I know. Thank you for that."

"I am sure you are more than ready to be back in your house."

He shrugged. "I suppose."

"You do not sound convinced."

"It's just a house, you know? I bought it after Tori died, when I knew I needed help and the best thing would be to move near Carrie and Joe. That one was available and it was close but it's never really felt like a home."

She had not been to his house and couldn't offer an opinion, but she had to wonder if the house needed a woman's touch.

She did not want to think about any other woman going in and decorating his house with warm, comfortable touches. She wanted to be the one turning his house into a home.

She pushed away the thought.

"You had many changes in a short time. That can be hard for anyone."

"I guess."

They walked in silence for a few more moments, stopping only when Hank lifted his leg against a tuft of grass.

"Carrie said something tonight that made me curious." He spoke slowly, as if choosing his words with care.

"Oh?"

"Something about you. She implied you had a tough time after you came to the United States. It made me wonder again how you came to be adopted after you arrived. That seems unusual. You were a teenager, right?"

Rosa tensed, remembering that horrible time in her life, full of fear and darkness and things she did not like to think about.

"Yes. Fifteen."

"And you didn't have family here or back in Honduras who could have helped you?"

Her heart seemed to squeeze at the memory of her dear mother, who had tried so hard to give Rosa a better life. She gripped Fiona's leash. The dog, who had been cavorting with Hank, suddenly returned to her side as if sensing Rosa's distress.

"No."

"How did you get here?"

That was a long and twisted story.

"I told you my mother died. I had no money and no family. A friend of my mother's told me I could find work at a factory in the city. She helped me find a place to live with some other girls and gave me a little money."

"That's nice."

"Yes. But then some men came to the factory telling us they knew of many jobs we could do across the border. I was afraid and didn't want to, but other girls, my friends, said yes. Then I…had some trouble with my boss at the factory and he fired me."

She thought of how innocent she had been in those days. Her mother had tried to shelter her when she was alive. As a result, Rosa knew little about the world or how to protect herself from men who wanted to take advantage of her. First her boss, then those offering riches and jobs in a new world. She had been monumentally naive, had thought maybe she would be working in another factory in the United States, one that paid better.

She had been so very wrong.

She was not going to tell any of that to Wyatt.

"What did you do then?"

"I came here and shortly after, I met Daniel and Lauren and they took me in and helped me go to school and then become a citizen," she said quickly.

He gave her a searching look through the darkness, as if he knew full well there had to be more to her story. She lifted her chin and continued walking, pretending that Fiona had led her a little ahead of him and Hank.

She didn't want him to press her about this. If he did, she would have to turn around and go back to the house without him. To her relief, he seemed to know she had told him all she was going to about that time.

"They must be very kind people."

She seized gratefully on his words. "The best. I told you Daniel is a sheriff in Utah and Lauren is a doctor. I was very lucky they found me."

She knew it was more than luck. It was a miracle.

She had prayed to the Virgin and to her own mother that someone would help her, that she could find some light in the darkness. And then, literally, a light had found her hiding in the back of a pickup truck in the middle of a January storm. She had been beaten and bloodied, and had been semiconscious when Daniel and Lauren had found her. They had pulled her from that pickup truck and had saved her. An answer to her prayers.

They had stood by her then as she had spoken out against those who had hurt her. And they had stood by her later when she had to make the most difficult decision of her life.

"Carrie talked about how much courage it must have taken you to make your way in a new country."

Rosa loved her country and her people. People from Honduras called themselves and each other *Catrachos*, a name that had come to mean resilience and solidarity.

She would always consider herself part *Catracha* but this was her home now.

If her mother had not died, she might have stayed and built a happy life there. She probably would have married young and would have had several children by now.

After Daniel and Lauren rescued her, she had been able to get an education that would have been completely out of reach to her in that small, poor village.

"Courage? No. I had nothing there after my mother died. And here I had a family. People who loved me and wanted the best for me. That was everything to me. It still is."

* * *

Wyatt could not doubt the quiet sincerity in her voice. She loved the people who had taken her in.

He was suddenly deeply grateful for them, too. He would have loved the chance to have met them in person to tell them so.

They walked in silence for a few more moments, heading back toward Brambleberry House, which stood like a beacon above the beach a short distance away.

He could tell Rosa did not like talking about this. Her body language conveyed tension. He should let it go now. Her secrets were none of his business, but since she had told him this much, perhaps she would trust him and tell him the rest of it.

"You said you were fifteen when you came here?"

"Yes," she said, her voice clipped.

How had she even made it across several borders? And what about the men who had promised her work in the United States?

He wasn't stupid. He could guess what kind of work they wanted from her and it made him sick to his stomach. Sex trafficking was a huge problem, especially among young girls smuggled in from other countries.

Was that what Daniel and Lauren had rescued her from?

He couldn't seem to find the words to ask. Or to ask her how she had escaped. He was quite sure he would not like the answer.

How was it possible? She was the most loving and giving person he knew, kind to everyone. How could she have emerged from something so ugly to become the person he was falling for?

Maybe he was wrong. He truly hoped he was wrong.

"You could have found yourself in all kinds of danger at that young age."

"Yes."

She said nothing more, only looked ahead at her dog and at the house, now only a hundred feet away.

He thought again of his suspicions earlier that evening at dinner. He was beginning to think they might not be far-fetched, after all.

"I think my sister is right," he said quietly when they reached the beach gate to the house. "You are a remarkable person, Rosa Galvez."

Her face was a blur in the moonlight as she gazed at him, her eyes dark shadows. She shook her head. "I am not. Lauren and Daniel, who reached out to me when I was afraid and vulnerable, they are the remarkable ones."

Tenderness swirled through him. She was amazing and he was falling hard for her. Learning more details about what she had endured and overcome, including the things she hadn't yet shared with him, only intensified his growing feelings.

"We will have to agree to disagree on that one," he finally said. "Every time I'm with you, I find something else to admire."

"Don't," she said sharply. "You don't know."

"I know I think about you all the time. I can't seem to stop."

"You shouldn't."

"I know that. Believe me, I know. But you're in my head now."

And in my heart, he thought, but wasn't quite ready to share that with her yet.

"May I kiss you again?"

Because of what he suspected had happened to her, it became more important than ever to ask permission first and not just take what he wanted.

He thought she would refuse at first, that she would turn into the house. After a long moment, she lifted her face to his.

"Yes," she murmured, almost as if she couldn't help herself.

This kiss was tender, gentle, a mere brush of his mouth against hers.

All the feelings he had been fighting seemed to shimmer to the surface. He could tell himself all he wanted that he was not ready to care for someone again. He could tell everyone else the same story. That did not make it true.

He had already fallen. Somehow Rosa Galvez, with her kindness and her empathy and her determination to do the right thing, had reached into the bleak darkness where he had been existing and ripped away the heavy curtains to let sunshine flood in again.

He was not sure yet how he felt about that. Some part of him wanted to stay frozen in his sadness. He had loved Tori with all his heart. Their marriage had not been perfect—he wasn't sure any healthy marriage could be completely without differences—but she had been a great mother and a wonderful wife.

Wyatt wasn't sure he was ready to risk his heart again.

But maybe he didn't have a choice. Maybe he had already fallen.

He wrapped his arms around her tightly, wanting to protect her from all the darkness in the world. She made a small sound and nestled against him, as if searching for warmth and safety.

"I lied to my sister," he said, long moments later.

He felt her smile against his mouth. "For shame, Detective Townsend. How did you lie to Carrie?"

He brushed a strand of hair away from her face. "She admitted after you left that she invited us both to dinner because she has some wild idea of matchmaking."

Instead of continuing to smile, as he thought she would, Rosa suddenly looked distressed.

Her eyes widened and her hands slipped away from around his neck. "Oh, no."

He nodded. "I told her to get that idea out of her head. I told her we were only friends and would never be anything more than that."

She stepped away. "You told her the truth. That is not a lie. We *are* friends."

"But we're more than that, aren't we?"

She folded her hands together, her mouth trembling a little. "No. What you said to her is the truth. We are friends. Only that."

"You can really say that after that kiss?"

"Sharing a few kisses does not make us lovers, Wyatt. Surely you see this."

He wasn't sure why she was so upset but she was all but wringing her hands.

"This thing between us is not exactly your average friendship, either. You have to admit that. I have lots of friends and I don't stay up nights thinking about kissing them."

She made a small, upset sound and reached for her dog's leash.

"We cannot do this anymore, Wyatt. You must see that. I was wrong to let you kiss me. To—to kiss you back. I should have stopped you."

She started moving toward the house. He gazed after her, hurt at her abrupt dismissal of what had felt like an emotional, beautiful moment between them.

He knew she had felt it, as well. Rosa was not the sort of woman who would kiss someone with so much sweetness and eagerness without at least some feeling behind it.

He quickly caught up with her just as she pushed open the beach gate and walked into the Brambleberry House gardens.

"Why are you so determined to push me away? What aren't you telling me?"

"Nothing. I told you before—I am not looking for this in my life right now."

"I wasn't, either, but I think it's found us. I care about you, Rosa. Very much. For the first time since Tori died, I want to spend time with a woman. And I might be crazy but I suspect you wouldn't kiss me if you didn't have similar feelings for me. Am I wrong?"

She was silent for a moment. When she faced him,

her chin was up again and her eyes seemed without expression.

"Yes. You are wrong," she said, her voice muted. "I do not have feelings for you. It is impossible. You are the brother of my friend and you are my tenant who will be leaving soon. That is all you are to me, Wyatt. I… You must not kiss me again. Ever. Do you understand this? No matter what, you must not."

She turned and hurried for the house, leaving him staring after her, hurt and confusion and rejection tumbling through him.

She sounded so very certain that he could not question her conviction. Apparently he had misunderstood everything. All this time, he had been falling for her, but the feeling apparently was not mutual.

She had told him they should stay away from each other. Why had he not listened?

He knew the answer to that. His feelings were growing so strong that he couldn't believe they could possibly be one-sided.

Lord, he was an idiot. No different than Jenna's cop, who couldn't accept rejection even after it slapped him in the face.

He should have kept his mouth shut. She had told him over and over that she was not interested in a relationship with him, but he'd been too stubborn to listen.

Now he just had to figure out how he was going to go on without her.

Rosa sat in her darkened apartment a short time later, window open to the ocean and Fiona at her feet. Usually she found solace in the sound of the waves but not now.

This night, it seemed to echo through Brambleberry House, accentuating how very alone she felt.

What had she done? With all her heart, she wished she could go downstairs, knock on his door and tell Wyatt *she* was the one lying now.

I do not have feelings for you. It is impossible. You are the brother of my friend and you are my tenant who will be leaving soon. That is all you are to me, Wyatt.

None of those words were true, of course. Or at least not the whole truth. She cared about Wyatt, more than any man she had ever known. She was falling in love with him. Here in the quiet solitude of her apartment, she could admit the truth.

She realized now that she had started to fall for him the first time she met Carrie's brother with the sad eyes and the adorable little boy.

How could she not love him? He was everything good and kind she admired in a man. He was a loving father, a loyal brother, a dedicated detective. An honorable man.

That was the very reason she had no choice but to push him away. Wyatt deserved a woman with no demons. Someone courageous and good.

If he knew the truth about her and her choices, he would quickly see how wrong he was about her.

The walls of the house did not embrace her with comfort, as they usually did.

Somehow, it felt cold and even sad. For some ridiculous reason, Rosa felt as if she had faced some sort of test and she had failed spectacularly.

It was a silly feeling, she knew. Houses could not be sad.

Fiona lifted her head suddenly and gazed off at nothing, then whimpered for no reason. Rosa frowned. There was no such thing as ghosts, either. And absolutely no reason for her to feel guilty, as if she had failed Abigail somehow.

"I had to push him away," she said aloud, though she wasn't sure just who she was trying to convince. Fiona, Abigail or herself. "Someday he will see that I was right. He will be glad I at least could see that we cannot be together."

Fiona huffed out a breath while Abigail said nothing, of course.

As for Rosa, her heart felt as if it was going to crack apart. She knew it would not. She had been through hard things before—she would figure out a way to survive this.

In a short time, he and his son would be moving out of Brambleberry House and back to their own home. As before, she would only see them occasionally. Maybe on the street, maybe at some town celebration. Maybe even at a party with Joe and Carrie. She could be polite and even friendly.

Wyatt did not ever need to know about these cracks in her heart, or how hard she found it to think about moving forward with her life without him, and without Logan.

CHAPTER FOURTEEN

Somehow, she wasn't sure exactly how, Rosa made it through most of the next week without seeing either Logan or Wyatt.

They seemed to leave early in the morning and come back late at night. She could only guess they were hard at work on the part of renovations Wyatt was handling on their house and getting it ready for their move back.

This guess was confirmed when she came home for lunch one day and found a note tucked into her door.

Repairs to the house are done, the note said in bold, scrawling handwriting. *We will be moving out tomorrow. Wyatt.*

Rosa had to catch her breath as pain sliced through her at the brusque, clipped note and at the message it contained.

Tomorrow. A week earlier than he had planned. He must have spent every available moment trying to finish things in his eagerness to get out of her house and her life.

She returned to the store with a heavy heart but a sense of relief, as well. She could not begin to put back together the pieces of her life when he was living two floors below her.

Even when she did not see him or Logan, she was still constantly aware they were both so close and yet completely out of her reach.

When she walked into the store, she found Jen laughing at something with a customer. The change in her friend was remarkable. She looked bright and pretty and happy, a far cry from the withdrawn, frightened woman she had been when she first came to Cannon Beach.

Jen finished ringing up the customer with a genuine smile Rosa once had feared she would not see again.

"You are in a good mood," she said.

"Yes. I heard from the online graduate program I've been in touch with. I've been accepted for fall semester and they're offering a financial-aid package that will cover almost the whole tuition."

"That's terrific! Oh, Jen. I'm so happy for you. How will you juggle teaching, graduate school and Addie at the same time?"

"It's going to be tricky but I think I can handle it, especially now that she's starting first grade. I can do the coursework at night after she's in bed. It will take me a few years, but when I'm done, it will open up other career doors for me."

"Oh, I am so happy for you."

Jen beamed at her. "It's all because of you. I never would have had the courage to even apply if you hadn't been in my corner, pushing me out of my comfort zone."

Rosa might not have a happily-ever-after with the man she was falling in love with. But she had good friends and wanted to think she was making a difference in their lives, a little bit at a time.

"We should celebrate tonight," Rosa said.

"You don't have a hot date?"

She made a face. "Not me. I have no date, hot or otherwise."

"What about our sexy neighbor?" Jen teased.

That terse note of his flashed through her mind again and her chest gave a sharp spasm.

"He will not be our neighbor long. Wyatt and Logan are moving out in the morning."

Jen's smile slid away. "Oh, no! Addie will miss having them around. She has really enjoyed playing with Logan in the evenings. I thought they wouldn't be moving for a few more weeks."

"Apparently, their house is finished. Wyatt left me a note on the door when I went home for lunch and to bring back Fiona."

Jen gave her a sharp look that Rosa pretended not to see.

"My evening is totally free," she said, "and I would love nothing more than to celebrate with you. Do you want to go somewhere?"

Jen gazed out the window. "It looks like it's going to be another beautiful night. I would be just as happy taking Fiona for a walk on the beach and then grabbing dinner at the taco truck. I think Addie would be all over that, too."

Rosa was not sure she would ever be able to eat at

the taco truck without remembering that delightful evening with Logan and Wyatt, but for the sake of her friend, she would do her best.

"Done."

The store was busy with customers the rest of the afternoon. Rosa preferred it that way. Having something to do gave her less time to think.

Jen's shift was supposed to end at five, but during a lull in the hectic pace about a half hour before that, Rosa pulled her aside. "Your shift is almost over and Paula and Juan will be here soon for the evening shift. Why don't you go pick up Addie from her day care and I will meet you at home?"

"Sounds great."

Jen took off her apron, then hung it on the hook in the back room and quickly left.

Rosa was going to miss having her around when school started, not just because she was a good worker, but Rosa enjoyed her company. They made a good team.

She finished ringing up two more customers, then spent a few more moments talking to the married older couple who helped her out a few nights a week during busy summer months.

Finally, she and Fiona walked out into a lovely July evening. The dog was eager for a walk and Rosa was, too. She was looking forward to the evening with Addie and Jen. Tacos and good friends. What was not to enjoy?

When she neared the house, she didn't see Wyatt's SUV. Rosa told herself she was glad.

Perhaps she wouldn't have to see him at all before he moved out the next day.

Fiona went immediately to the backyard. When Rosa followed her, she found Jen and Addie on the tree swing. Addie's legs were stretched out as she tried to pump and she looked so filled with joy, Rosa had to smile.

"Look at me!" Addie called. "I'm flying!"

"You are doing so well at swinging," Rosa exclaimed.

"I know. I never went so high before."

She almost told her to be careful but caught herself. She wanted all little girls to soar as high as they dared.

"We got home about a half hour ago and haven't even been inside yet," Jen said with a laugh. "Addie insisted she had to swing first."

"It is very fun," Rosa agreed. Addie's excitement and Jen's good mood went a long way to cheering her up.

She might not have everything she wanted but her life could still be rich and beautiful. She had to remember that.

"I noticed the handsome detective isn't home yet. I was going to see if he wanted to come with us to the taco truck."

Jen spoke so casually that Rosa almost missed the mischievous look in her eyes.

Rosa avoided her gaze. "He is probably at his house making sure things are ready for him and Logan to return home tomorrow."

"I'll miss them."

Rosa wasn't sure she liked that pensive note in her friend's voice. Was Jen interested in Wyatt, as well?

Why wouldn't she be? He was a wonderful man and Jen was exactly the sort of woman who could make him happy. The two of them would be very good together, even though the idea of it made Rosa's chest hurt.

"When you are ready to date again, maybe you should think about dating Wyatt. You both have a lot in common."

Jen gave her a shocked, rather appalled look that Rosa thought was out of proportion to her mild suggestion. "Besides being single parents, I don't think so."

"He's a widower, you're a widow," she pointed out.

"True. And that's the only thing we have in common. Don't get me wrong. I like Wyatt a lot. He seems very nice. But I don't think he would be interested in me. His interests appear to lie…elsewhere."

Jen gave her such a significant look that Rosa could feel her face heat.

I care about you, Rosa. Very much. For the first time since Tori died, I want to spend time with a woman. And I might be crazy but I suspect you wouldn't kiss me if you didn't have similar feelings for me.

Wyatt would soon forget her and any wild idea he had that he might have feelings for her.

Before she could answer, she heard a noise and saw someone walk around the side of the house to where they were.

For a moment, with the setting sun shining on his face, she thought it might be Wyatt. Her heart skipped a beat and she felt foolish, hoping he hadn't heard their conversation.

Jen suddenly gasped, her features going instantly pale, and Rosa realized her mistake.

This was not Wyatt. It was a man she didn't recognize.

This man was big, solid, with wide shoulders and a rather thick neck. He had close-cropped brown hair and blue eyes that should have been attractive but were somehow cold.

Fiona, at her feet, instantly rose and growled a little, moving protectively in front of the two of them. That didn't seem to stop the man, who continued walking until he was only a few feet away.

"Jenna," he said, gazing at her friend with an odd, intense, almost possessive look. "Here you are. It is you. It took me forever to track you down."

Rosa knew instantly who this was. Who else could it be? Aaron Barker, the police officer who was stalking Jen and had driven her from her Utah home to Cannon Beach. She should have realized it the moment the color leached away from Jen's features.

Jenna stood frozen for a moment as if she couldn't remember how to move, then she quickly moved to the side and stopped the swing, pulling Addie off and into her arms.

"Hey!" the girl exclaimed. "I'm not done swinging."

Addie started to complain but something of her mother's tension seemed to trickle to the girl. She fell silent, eying the adults around her with sudden wariness.

"What do you want?" Jen asked. Her voice shook slightly.

"I've missed you so much, baby. Aren't you happy to see me?" He took another step forward as if to embrace her. Jen quickly stepped back.

Rosa didn't know what to do. They were on the side of the house without an entrance. The only way to get inside to safety was through the front door. To get there, they would have to go around this man.

Aaron Barker was dangerous. She recognized the fierce, violent look in his eyes. She had seen that before…

Old, long-suppressed panic started to bubble up inside her, those demons she thought she had vanquished long ago.

Rosa drew in a harsh breath and then another, suddenly desperate to escape.

No. She had to protect her friend. She wouldn't let her be hurt again.

"What do you want?" Jen asked again. She took a sideways step, Addie in her arms, and Rosa realized she was edging closer to the front door.

"Just to talk. That's all."

Jenna shuffled to the side another step and Rosa moved, as well, hoping he hadn't noticed.

"I don't want to talk to you. I tried that before and you wouldn't listen. Please. Just leave me alone."

He moved as if to come closer but Fiona growled. She wasn't particularly fierce-looking with her long, soft fur and her sweet eyes, but she did have sharp teeth.

The dog's show of courage gave Rosa strength to draw upon her own.

"You heard her."

Jen took another sideways step and Rosa did, too. The front porch was still so very far away.

"This is private property," she went on. "You are trespassing. Please leave."

"I'm not leaving without talking to Jenna." When he spoke, she caught a definite whiff of alcohol on his breath. He had been drinking and he already had to be unstable to put Jenna through long months of torture. Rosa knew this was not a good combination.

"She clearly does not want to talk to you."

"She has to."

"No. She does not." Hoping to distract him further from realizing she and Jenna had maneuvered so that they were now closer to the door than he was, Rosa reached into her pocket for her cell phone. "I must ask you again to leave or I will have to call nine-one-one."

"You think that worries me? I'm a police officer."

"Not here," she said firmly. "The police here do not stand by while someone hurts a woman, even if he is also a police officer."

She had to hope that was true of all officers in the Cannon Beach Police Department and not only Wyatt.

"Now. I am asking you for the final time to leave or I will call the police."

Now Jenna was backing toward the door and Rosa did the same, with Fiona still standing protectively in front of them.

He frowned. "I'm not leaving without Jenna. We love each other."

He took another step closer and from behind Rosa, Jen made a small sound of panic.

"Jenna. Go inside. Call nine-one-one."

She must have made a move toward the house because several things happened at once. Aaron Barker growled out a sound of frustration and lunged for her. Fiona jumped into protective mode and latched on to his leg and he kicked out at the dog, who whimpered and fell to the ground.

"No! Fi!" Rosa cried out. The coward pulled his leg back as if to kick again and Rosa instantly dropped to the ground, her body over the dog's.

Seconds later, she felt crushing pain in her back and realized he had kicked *her* instead of the dog.

This was the first time in fifteen years someone had struck out at her in anger. Instantly, she was transported to another time, another place. The past broke free of the prison where she kept it, the memories pouring over her like acid.

Other boots. Other fists. Again and again until she was in agony as vicious words in Spanish called her horrible names and told her she was going to die.

Something whimpered beneath her and the past suddenly receded—she was back in the present with her back throbbing and her dog wriggling beneath her.

Fiona was alive, and was just winded like Rosa. Thank God.

She could not just lie here trying to catch her breath. She had to protect her friend. Already, the man was making his way past Rosa and the dog toward the porch, where Jenna was desperately trying to punch in the code to unlock the door.

"I'm sorry, baby," Rosa said to Fi, then rose shakily to her feet. Her amazing dog was right behind her and she realized Fi had been whimpering for her to get up so they could both keep fighting.

Rosa ignored her pain as she limped after him.

"Stop. Right now," she said. He had almost reached the porch and Rosa did the only thing she could think of to slow him down. Though her back groaned with pain, she jumped on him, her arms around his neck as she had been taught in the self-defense classes Daniel had insisted she take.

He cried out in frustration and swung his elbows back, trying to get her off. One elbow caught her mouth and she tasted blood but still she clung tightly.

"Stupid dog!" he cried out again and she realized Fiona must have bitten him again to protect them.

She was so busy hanging on for dear life, she almost missed the sound of the door opening as Jenna finally managed to unlock it. She could see the other woman looked undecided whether to go inside to safety or come to Rosa's aid.

"Go," she yelled to Jenna. "Call nine-one-one."

An instant later, she heard the sound of the dead bolt. She was so relieved, she relaxed her hold slightly, but it was enough for him to shake her off as Fiona would with a sand fly.

She fell to the grass, barely missing the walkway, and rolled out of the way of his kicking boots. Fiona was still growling but had retreated also, and now came to stand in front of her.

"You bitch," he growled. "You stupid bitch. This is none of your damn business."

She could hardly breathe, but she managed to squeeze out a few words. "My friend. My house. My business."

He started for the door and she grabbed the closest weapon she could find, a rock from the flower garden. Rosa stood up and held it tightly.

"I will not let you hurt her," she gasped out.

He appeared genuinely shocked by that. "I would never hurt Jenna. Never. I love her and she loves me."

He ran a hand through his hair. The man was definitely unhinged, whether from his obsession or from alcohol, she did not know. What did it matter? She only knew there was no point in arguing with him. She longed for the safety of the house, but didn't know how she could get inside without him following her and having access to Jenna.

"How can you say you love her? She ran away from you."

"I've been out of my head, worried about her. She disappeared in the middle of the night and no one would tell me where she went."

He sounded so plaintive that she would have felt sorry for him if she didn't know the torture he had put Jenna through these past few months.

"How did you…find her?" She was so afraid and in pain, she could barely breathe enough to get the question out, but had some wild thought that if she could keep him talking, perhaps the police would arrive before he killed her.

"Luck," he growled. "Sheer luck. A friend who knew how broke up I was about her leaving said he thought he saw someone who looked like her working in a gift shop when he was here on vacation with his family."

Rosa closed her eyes, remembering that day Jen had thought she saw someone she recognized. She had been right. Completely right.

"How did you know it was Jenna?"

He shrugged. "I'm a cop. I've got connections. I traced her Social Security number and found an employment record here at some shop in town. I figured they wouldn't tell me where she lived so I asked at the shop next door."

All their efforts to protect her hadn't been enough. Rosa had never thought of putting their neighboring stores on alert. She felt stupid for not thinking of it.

"As soon as I heard she might be here, I had to see if it was her." His face darkened. "I have to talk to her. Make sure she's okay."

"You have seen her. Jenna is fine. She wants you now to leave her alone."

"I'm not going to do that. We love each other. She's just being stubborn."

Rosa stood in front of him on the porch, Fiona growling at her side. "You cannot see her now."

She could see his talkative mood shift to anger again.

"Get out of my way," he said slowly and deliberately, and moved a step closer.

"No," she said, gripping the rock more tightly.

"You think I'm going to let some stupid little bitch keep me away from the woman I love after I've come all this way?"

Always, it was about him. Not about the woman or the child he had displaced from their home, forced to flee his unwanted obsession.

Rosa was shaking and she realized it was a combination of fear, pain and anger.

"Get out of my way. If you think I'm leaving, you don't know a damn thing about me."

Rosa lifted her chin. "I know all I need to know about you, Aaron Barker. I know you are a coward, a bully, a despicable human being. You have terrorized Jenna, one of the kindest women I know, who has already been through enough, because you refuse to believe a woman is not interested in you."

"Shut up. Jenna loves me."

"Then why did she move eight hundred miles to get away from you?"

His face turned red with anger. "Move. Last warning."

"I am not going anywhere."

He reached to shove her aside and Fiona lunged again. He kicked out at the dog, but she would not let her sweet canine protector be hurt again.

Rosa lifted the rock with both hands and, with every ounce of strength she had left, she slammed it into the side of his head. He stared at her in shock, dazed, then staggered backward, stumbling off the porch.

Rosa stared at him for only a second before she rushed to the door. She was fumbling to punch in the code when she heard sirens and a door slam, then a voice yelled out, "Don't move!"

Wyatt!

He had come.

Vast relief poured over her and Rosa, shaking violently now, sagged to the ground, her back pressed against the door and her arms wrapped around her brave, wonderful dog.

CHAPTER FIFTEEN

WYATT RESTRAINED THE son of a bitch, who seemed groggy and incoherent, and was mumbling about how much he loved Jen and how she had to talk to him.

It took every ounce of control he had not to bash the man's head against the porch steps, especially when he saw blood trickling out of Rosa's mouth.

This man had hurt Rosa. And not just physically. She looked…shattered. He wanted to go to her, but he needed to secure the scene first before he could comfort her.

"Where are Jen and Addie?" he asked. He had been at his sister's house when Jen had called, her voice frantic. He hadn't been able to understand her at first, but had quickly surmised through her distress that her stalker was there and he was hurting Rosa and Fiona.

She had hung up before he could ask any questions and he had assumed she was calling 911 as he heard the call go out of an assault while he was en route, screaming through town with lights and sirens blazing.

The door opened. "I'm here," Jenna said. "I sent Addie into our apartment. Oh, Rosa. You saved us."

She wrapped her arms around her friend and Wyatt didn't miss the way Rosa winced. She had more aches and pains than just the bloody lip he could see.

The bastard was bleeding, too, from what looked like a nasty contusion. Wyatt looked around and found a large rock with blood on it. Had Rosa hit him with that? Good for her.

He finished handcuffing Barker and read him his rights, all while the man kept babbling about being a police officer and how this was all a big mistake.

"Tell them, Jenna. Tell them you love me."

The woman looked down at the man who had so tormented her, driving her away from her home with his obsession.

"I despise you," she said clearly. "I hope you rot in hell."

Barker made a move toward her but Wyatt yanked the restraint.

"We can straighten everything out down at the station," Wyatt said, just as backup officers arrived to help him secure the scene.

Only after they had taken custody of the man and another officer started taking Jenna's statement about the incident and the months of torment preceding it could Wyatt finally go to Rosa, who was now sitting on the porch steps.

She forced a smile when he approached and he saw her lip was cracked and swollen.

"He hurt you." He reached a hand out and tenderly caressed her face.

She let out a little sob and sagged into his arms. He

held her, burying his face in her hair as he tried not to think about what might have happened to her.

How would he have endured it? He had already lost one woman he loved. He couldn't stand the idea of losing another.

"I am all right," she murmured. "Jenna is safe. That is the important thing. But I have to take Fiona to the vet. That man kicked her. She was so brave."

They both were incredibly brave. He looked over her shoulder, where Fiona's tail was wagging. She almost looked like she was smiling as the two of them embraced. "She seems okay to me."

Rosa drew away a little and he instantly wanted to pull her back into his arms.

"I would still like to have her checked out. The veterinarian is my friend. I will call her."

An ambulance pulled up, followed by a fire truck. The whole town was coming to her rescue, which was only proof about how well-regarded Rosa was in town.

Right behind them, a couple he recognized came racing up the driveway.

"Rosa!" Melissa Sanderson exclaimed. "What happened? We saw all the police racing past and hurried right over."

"I am fine," Rosa said. "A man came to hurt Jen but she and Addie were able to get to safety."

"Because of you," Jenna said as she approached with her daughter in her arms. "You saved us."

She hugged her friend again and Wyatt could see Rosa was trying not to wince.

"You look like you've gone a few rounds with a

heavyweight champion." Melissa's husband, Eli, a physician in town, looked concerned. "You should let me have a look."

Rosa, his battered warrior, glowered at them all. "This is all too much fuss for a sore lip."

"He kicked her in the back, too," Jenna said. "At least once. Maybe more. I don't know. I was so scared."

"You need to go to the ER," Wyatt said.

She shook her head. "Not until Fiona sees the veterinarian."

"You can at least let Eli and the paramedics check you out while I call the veterinarian," Wyatt said.

She gave him a grateful look. "Yes. I will do that. Thank you."

CHAPTER SIXTEEN

To his deep regret, that was the last chance he had to talk to her for the next few hours. He didn't want to leave, but as the on-scene arresting officer, he had paperwork and an investigation to deal with.

He had tried to interrogate Barker but the man was sleeping off what appeared to be a large quantity of alcohol, as well as a concussion delivered by Rosa and her trusty rock and several dog bites from Fiona.

By the time he left the station, the sun was beginning to set.

He knew from the other officers on scene that Rosa had refused transport to the hospital, though she had allowed Eli to clean and bandage her cuts.

Stubborn woman.

Only now, as he walked up the front steps to the house hours later, did Wyatt feel his own adrenaline crash.

He had never been so scared as the moment when Jenna had called him, her voice thready with panic. All he had registered were her words that Rosa was being hurt.

It seemed odd to be here without either Hank or Logan, but Carrie had offered to keep both of them overnight.

"You do what you need to for Jen and Rosa," she had told him when he called from the station. She had been half out of her mind with worry for her friend and only his repeated assurances that Rosa's injuries appeared to be minor had kept Carrie from rushing to the house herself.

He half expected to find Rosa in the flower gardens around Brambleberry House, seeking peace and solace amid the blossoms and the birds, as she so often did. But from what he could see, the gardens were empty except for a few hummingbirds at the bright red feeder. They immediately flitted away.

The big house also seemed quiet when he let himself inside. He walked to the third floor and knocked, but Rosa didn't answer. He couldn't hear Fiona inside, either.

He frowned, not sure what to do.

As he headed back down the stairs, the door on the second-floor landing opened. Jenna peeked out. "I thought I heard you come in."

"Yeah. How are you?"

"I've had better days."

"It has to help to know that Barker is in custody, doesn't it?"

She shrugged and he could see she wasn't entirely convinced her nightmare was over. He couldn't blame her for the doubt after the way the system had already treated her, but Wyatt was quick to reassure her.

"You should know that Barker won't be going anywhere for a long time. He's facing extensive state and federal charges. And we haven't even started on the stalking charges. That will only add to his sentence. He won't bother you again."

"I hope not."

He knew it would probably take time for that reality to sink in.

"Is Rosa with you?"

"No. I heard her take Fiona out about a half hour ago."

She paused. "I never wanted her to get hurt. I hope you know that. I thought we would be safe here. If I had for a moment dreamed he would find me and would come here and hurt Rosa and Fiona, I never would have come."

"I know that and I'm sure Rosa doesn't blame you for a second."

Jenna didn't look convinced about this, either. "She was amazing. I wish you could have seen her. She was so fierce. Aaron was twice as big, but that didn't stop her. She's an incredible woman."

"Agreed," he said, his voice gruff.

"She risked her life to protect me and Addie." Jenna's voice took on an edge and she gave him a hard stare. "For the record, I will do the same for her. Anybody who hurts her in any possible way will live to regret it."

Was that a threat? It certainly sounded like one. He couldn't decide whether to be offended that she could ever think he would hurt Rosa, or touched at her loyalty to her friend. He settled on the latter.

"You and I are the same in that sentiment, then," he said quietly.

She studied his features for a moment, then nodded. "I saw her from my window as I was putting Addie to bed. She and Fiona appeared to be heading for the beach."

He smiled and on impulse reached out and hugged her. After a surprised moment, Jenna hugged him back.

He headed for the beach gate, his heart pounding. As he went, he carried on a fierce debate with himself.

Rosa had basically ordered him to keep his distance and told him she wasn't interested in a relationship. He had tried his best. For a week, he had worked long hours at his house so that he and Logan could move out as soon as possible. The whole time, he had done his best to push her out of his head and his heart.

It hadn't worked.

The moment Jenna had called him in a panic, the moment he knew they were in danger, Wyatt had realized nothing had changed. He was in love with Rosa and would move heaven and earth to keep her safe.

He pushed open the beach gate and found her there, just beyond the house. She was sitting on a blanket on the sand, her arm around Fiona and her back to him as she watched the sun slipping down into the water in a blaze of color.

She didn't hear him come out at first. Fiona did. The dog turned to look at him, but apparently decided he was no threat because she nestled closer to her human.

He moved across the sand, still not sure what he would say to her, only knowing he had to be close to her, too.

He saw the moment she registered his presence. Her spine stiffened and she turned her head. He couldn't see her expression behind her sunglasses.

"Oh. Hello."

"Here you are. I was worried about you."

"Yes. We are here. The sunset seems especially beautiful tonight."

He had to agree. Streaks of pink and purple and orange spilled out in glorious Technicolor. "May I join you?"

She hesitated. He could see her jaw flex, as if she wanted to say no, but she finally gestured to the empty spot on the blanket, which happened to be on the other side of her dog.

He would have liked to be next to Rosa, but this would do, he supposed.

"Where are Logan and Hank?"

"They were both with Carrie when Jenna called me. After Carrie heard what happened to you and found out I was part of the investigation, she insisted they stay the night with her."

"Ah."

He reached out and rubbed her brave, amazing dog behind the ear. His hand brushed against Rosa's and it hurt a little when she pulled her hand away.

"How's Fiona?"

"Fine. Dr. Williams said she might be a little bruised, but nothing appears to be broken. I am to watch her appetite and her energy over the next few days and tell her if I see anything unusual."

"You're a good, brave girl, aren't you?" He scratched Fi under the chin and the dog rested her head on his leg.

All the emotions he had put away in the heat of the moment as he did his duty and stood for justice seemed to come rushing over him again, all at once.

"What you did—protecting your friend. It was incredibly brave."

She gave a short laugh. "I think you mean to say stupid."

"I would never say that. Never. You were amazing."

He reached for her hand, unable to help himself. He thought she would pull away again, but she didn't. Her fingers were cool and seemed to be trembling a little, but he couldn't say whether that was from the cool coastal air or from the trauma of earlier.

She drew in a breath that sounded ragged, and before he quite realized it, she let out a sob and then another.

Oh, Rosa.

His poor, fierce Rosa.

Fiona, blessed Fiona, moved out of the way so that Wyatt could pull Rosa into his arms. He held her while she cried silently against his chest, not making a sound except the occasional whimper.

His heart ached for her, both for the fear she must have felt and for everything else she had endured.

"I am sorry," she finally said, sounding mortified. "I think I have been holding that in all afternoon."

"Or longer."

She shifted her face to meet his gaze. Somehow, she had lost her sunglasses and he could see her now, her eyes dark and shadowed in her lovely face. Instead of answering his unspoken question, she focused on the events of the day.

"I was so frightened. I thought this man, he was going to kill me, then get to Jenna and Addie. I could not let him."

"He won't get to Jenna now. He is in custody and will be charged with assault, trespassing, drunk driving, driving across state lines with the intent to commit a felony and a whole host of other charges related to whatever stalking charges we can prove. He's not going to get out for a long time."

"I hope that is the case."

"It is," he promised. He would do whatever necessary to make sure of it.

"I suppose I should be relieved I did not kill him with that rock."

"You were pretty fierce."

"I could not help it. I could only think about protecting Jenna and Addie from someone who wanted to hurt them. Something seemed to take over me. Maybe some part of my brain that was fifteen years old again, focused only on surviving another day."

As soon as she said the words, she looked as if she wished she hadn't. She closed her eyes. He thought she would pull away from him but she didn't. She continued to nestle against him as if he was providing safe shelter in a sandstorm.

With his thumb, he brushed away a tear that trickled down her cheek, his heart a heavy ache. "Tell me what happened when you were fifteen."

"I have already told you too much. I don't talk about that time in my life, Wyatt. It is the past and has nothing to do with who I am now."

"You don't have to tell me. I understand if you prefer to keep it to yourself. But I hope you know you can trust me, if you ever change your mind."

She eased away from him and sat once more on the blanket beside him. Fiona moved to her other side and plopped next to her. Rosa wrapped her arms around her knees and gazed out at the water, a pale blue in the twilight.

She was silent for a long time, so long that he thought she wasn't going to answer. But then she looked at him out of the corner of her gaze and he fell in love with her all over again.

"Sometimes it feels like it all happened to someone else. Something I read about in a terribly tragic novel."

He did not want to hear what was coming next, but somehow Wyatt sensed it was important to both of them that she tell him. This was the reason she had pushed him away. He was suddenly certain of it.

That moment when he had rushed onto the porch earlier, he had seen raw emotion in her expression. That was the image he couldn't get out of his head. She had looked at him with relief, with gratitude and with something else, too.

She thought her past was a barrier between them. If he could show her it wasn't, that together they could face whatever demons she fought, perhaps she would stop pushing him away.

"I told you about the men who offered me a job in this country and who…brought me here."

"Yes."

"It was not a factory job they were bringing me to, as I thought. I was so stupid."

"I didn't think it was."

She closed her eyes. "You are a detective. I am sure you can guess what happened next."

"I've imagined a few possible scenarios since the night you told me."

"Pick the worst one and you might be close enough."

He gripped her hand tightly, not wanting to ever let go. "Human trafficking."

She made a small sound. "Yes. That is a polite phrase for it. I was brought here to work in the sex trade. Me, an innocent girl from a small town who had never even kissed a boy. I barely knew what sex was."

Everything inside him went cold as he thought about what she must have endured. "Oh, sweetheart. I'm so sorry."

"I refused at first. The men who brought me here, they did not care whether I was willing or not."

How was it possible for his heart to break again and again?

"You were raped."

She looked at him, stark pain in her eyes. "Now you know why I don't like thinking about the past. Yes. I was raped. At first by the men who wanted to use me to make money for them. Then by some of their customers.

I did not cooperate. Not one single time. They threatened me, hurt me, tried to make me take drugs like the other girls, so I would be quiet and do what they said. I would not. I only cried. All the time."

"That couldn't have been good for business."

She gave a short, humorless laugh. "No. Not at all. Finally, they left me alone. I still do not know why they did not kill me. It would have been easy for them. But then one of the girls died of too much drugs. She was... not well, so they had let her do all the cooking and cleaning for the other girls. They let me take her place. At least I no longer had to let strangers touch me."

He squeezed her fingers. How had she possibly emerged from that hell still able to smile and laugh and find joy in the world, with a gentle spirit and a kind heart? Most people would have curled up and withered away in the midst of so much trauma.

"This went on for a few months and then I made a mistake. I knew I had to do something to change my situation. I could not stay. I tried to escape but they... caught me. They would have killed me that night. They knew I could tell the police who they were. I expected to die. I thought I would. But somehow, I did not. I do not know why. I only knew I had to do all I could to survive. Mine was not the only life at risk that night."

"One of your friends?"

She gave a tiny shake of her head and gazed out at the undulating waves. He waited for her to explain. When she did not, suddenly all his suspicions came together and he knew. He didn't know how. He just did.

"You were pregnant."

She met his gaze, her expression filled with sadness and pain. "No one else knew. I did not even know myself until I was too far along to—to do anything. I told you I was innocent."

"How did you get away?"

She shrugged. "A miracle from God. That is the only thing it could have been."

He had never heard her being particularly religious but the conviction in her voice seemed unswerving. He would take her word for it, since he hadn't been there.

"We were kept above a restaurant in a tourist town in Utah. They left me to die in a room there, but I did not. I had only pretended. After they left, I saw they had not locked the door, like usual. They thought I was dead. Why should they?"

How badly had she been hurt? Wyatt didn't even want to contemplate. And she'd only been a child. Not much older than his niece. How had she endured it?

"Somehow, I found strength to stand and managed to go out, stumbling down the back stairs. I still cannot believe they did not hear me. Once I was out, I did not know what to do. Where to go. I knew no one. I was certain I only had moments before they found me and finished what they had started, so I… I somehow climbed into the back of a truck."

"With a stranger?"

He thought of all the things that could have happened to her by putting her trust in someone she did not know. On the other hand, she was escaping certain death so she probably thought anything was better than the place she was leaving.

"I was lucky. There was a blanket there for the horses and I was able to pull it over me so I did not freeze. The man was a rancher. He did not spot me until we were away from town, when he had a flat tire and found me sleeping."

"What did he do?" Wyatt was again almost afraid to ask.

"He called the police and a kind sheriff and a doctor came to my rescue. Daniel and Lauren. My parents."

CHAPTER SEVENTEEN

ROSA COULD FEEL herself trembling, though the night was pleasant. She knew it was probably a delayed re-action from the attack earlier and from the emotional trauma of reliving the darkest time in her life.

When Wyatt wrapped his arm around her and pulled her close to his heat, she wanted to sink into him. He was big, safe and comforting, and offered immeasur-able strength.

She could not tell by his expression what he thought about what she had told him. She thought maybe that wasn't such a bad thing. Did she want to know what he was thinking about her?

"They took you in."

"They were not married at the time. Not even to-gether. I like to think I helped them find each other. But, yes. Lauren took me home with her. I was still in danger. I had information about the men who took me. I knew who they were, where they were, so I—I stayed with Lauren until all the men were caught."

"All of them?" Wyatt's voice had a hard note she had

not heard before, as if he wanted to go to Utah right now and find justice for her.

Oh, he was a dear man. A little more warmth seeped into her heart. How was she supposed to resist him?

"Yes. Some were deported. Others are still in jail here in this country. Daniel made sure all the girls were rescued and the men were punished."

"I would like to meet Sheriff Galvez," he said gruffly.

"You two are similar. I think you would be friends. That is one reason why I…" Her voice trailed off and she felt her face heat, as she was unable to complete the sentence. *Why I fell in love with you.*

"Why you what?"

"Nothing," she said quickly. "I only wanted to tell you, after Daniel and Lauren married, they gave me a home and then legally adopted me."

"They sound wonderful."

"The best. Though they can be too protective of me."

"That's understandable, don't you think?"

She nodded. "Yes. I do understand but this is one reason I think I had to move somewhere else. Somewhere I would not be poor Rosa Galvez."

"What about your baby?" he asked.

Ah. Here was the most difficult part. The other things that had happened—the abuse, the beatings. Even the rapes. Those scars had healed. She hardly thought of them anymore.

Her child. That was a wound that would never close completely.

She chose her words carefully, wishing she did not

have to tell him this part. "I had a baby girl ten weeks later and...she was adopted."

There. The words still burned her throat.

He was quiet for a long time. Was he recoiling now from her? She could not blame him. It had been a terrible choice for someone who had been little more than a child to have to make.

"It's Bella, isn't it? Your daughter?"

That was the last thing she expected him to say. In horror, she jerked away and scrambled to her feet. Fiona immediately moved to her side, as if sensing more danger.

"No! Bella? How ridiculous! Do not say this. You are crazy."

He rose, as well, gazing at her across the sand. The rising moon lit up one side of his face, leaving the other in shadow. "I'm not crazy though, am I?" he said quietly. "I'm right."

She didn't know what to say. How could she convince him he had made a terrible mistake? She had no words to undo this.

"No. This is not true," she said, but even she could hear her words lacked conviction. "I do not know how... Why did you think of this?"

"The time frame lines up. Bella is the right age and she was adopted through your aunt Anna. You're her birth mother." If her own words lacked conviction, his did not. He spoke with a growing confidence she had no way to combat.

"I don't know why I didn't see the resemblance before. Maybe I didn't want to see it. Does she know?"

Rosa stared at him, not sure what to say. All of her instincts were shouting at her to go inside the safety of the house, but she couldn't leave. She had started this by telling him her history. It was her fault. He was a police detective. How could she blame him for connecting all the pieces of the jigsaw and coming up with the correct picture?

This was the part of the story she did not want him to know. The part she had been trying to protect him from. What must he think of her now? She had abandoned his niece, a girl he loved. She had given birth and handed her over to another woman to be her mother, then went on with her life. Learning English. Finishing school. Dating boys. Going to college.

Why did he not seem angry? Why was he looking at her like that, with a tender light in his eyes? Did he not understand what she had done?

She could not think about that now. For this moment, she had to focus on controlling the damage she had done. She should not have told him anything. Since she had, now she had to make sure he did not ruin all the care she had taken during the years she had lived in Cannon Beach, so close to her daughter but still far enough away.

"No. She does not know," she finally said. "And you cannot tell her. Oh, please. Do not tell her."

"I would never, if you don't want me to."

"You must promise me. Swear it."

He seemed to blink at her vehemence, but then nodded. "I swear. I won't tell her. This is not my secret to tell, Rosa. Again, please trust me enough to know I would never betray you."

Oh, she wanted to trust him. The urge to step back into his arms was so overpowering, she had to wrap her own arms around herself to keep from doing it. "I thank you. She might have come from an ugly time in my life but none of that was her fault. She is the most beautiful, precious girl. From the moment I felt her move inside me, I loved her. I wanted so much to keep her but it was… It was impossible."

"You were only a child yourself."

"Yes. What would I do with a baby? I had no way to take care of her myself, though I wanted to."

"It's obvious you love her. Whether she knows the truth or not, there is a bond between you."

"How could anyone not love her? Bella is wonderful. Smart and pretty, always kind. She reminds me of my mother."

"That's funny. She reminds me of *her* mother, now that I know who she is."

She blushed at the intensity in her voice. "Carrie is her mother. She has loved her and cared for her far better than I ever could."

"Do Joe and Carrie know?"

"Yes. Of course. I would not have come here without telling them. When Anna asked me to come to help her with the store, I knew I must tell Carrie and Joe first. I called them to see how they might feel if I moved to town. I did not want to cause them any tension or discomfort."

"What did they say?"

"They welcomed me. They have always been so kind to me. Always. From the day we met in the hospital. They never once made me feel as if I had...done something wrong."

"Because you hadn't!"

She sighed. It was easy for others to say that. They had not lived her journey. "I know that most of the time but sometimes I do wonder. I made foolish choices. Dangerous choices. And because of that, an innocent child was born."

He reached for her hands again and curled his fingers around hers. To Rosa's shock, he lifted her hands and pressed first one hand to his mouth and then the other.

"You did nothing wrong, Rosa. *Nothing.* You were an innocent child yourself, looking for a brighter future. You couldn't have known what would happen to you."

Tears spilled out again at his words and the healing balm they offered. He was not disgusted by her story. She did not know why. It seemed the second miracle of her life.

He pulled her back into his arms. She knew she should try to be strong but she couldn't. Not right now. She would try to find the strength later to restore distance between them but right now she needed the heat and comfort of him. She wrapped her arms around his waist and rested her head against his chest again, wishing she could stay here forever.

"If Carrie and Joe know the truth, why doesn't Bella?"

Thinking about it made her stomach hurt. This was her greatest fear. Every day, she worried Bella would learn the truth and would come to hate her.

"They wanted to tell her but I—I begged them not to. I thought it would be better for her if I could be in her life only as a friend. Maybe like a sort of...older sister or cousin."

"Why would that be better?"

She shrugged against him. "How do I tell her that she was created through an act of violence at a time in my life I wish I could forget?"

"You wouldn't have to tell her that part."

"What do I say when she asks me about her father? I did not know how I could answer that. I still do not know. How can I tell her I do not even know his name? No. It is better that she not know the truth."

His silence told her he didn't agree.

"When I came here, I did not want to intrude in her life," she said. "Carrie and Joe are her parents in every way that matters and they have been wonderful to her. I only wanted to...see her. Make sure she was happy. Healthy. I thought I would only be here a short time but then I came to love her and to love Cannon Beach and Brambleberry House. Anna offered me a partnership in the store and it became harder to think about leaving."

"I am glad you stayed. So glad," he said. And before she realized what he intended, he lowered his mouth and kissed her with a sweetness and gentleness that took her breath.

Her mouth still burned where she had been hit, but

she ignored it, lost in the peace and wonder of kissing the man she loved on a moonswept beach.

He still wanted to kiss her, after everything she told him. All this time, she had been so afraid for him to learn the truth. He now knew the ugliest part of her past and yet he kissed her anyway with a tenderness that made her feel...cherished.

"Thank you for coming to my rescue." She realized in that moment she had not really told him that yet. And while she was speaking about earlier, with Aaron Barker, her words held layers of meaning.

He smiled against her mouth. "I don't think you needed help from me. You were doing just fine. You're pretty ferocious, Rosita."

The endearment—Little Rosa—made her smile, too. Her mother had always called her that and Daniel still did.

"Ow. Smiling still hurts."

"Oh. I forgot about your mouth. I shouldn't have kissed you. I'm sorry."

"I am glad you did." To prove it, she pressed her mouth, sore lip and all, to his.

All of the emotions she could not say were contained in that kiss. All the love and yearning she had been fighting for so long.

When he lifted his head, Wyatt was breathing hard and Rosa realized they were once more on the sand, sitting on the blanket she had brought.

"I have to tell you something," Wyatt said after a long moment. He gripped her hands again, and even through the darkness, she could see the intense light in his eyes.

"I was scared to death when Jenna called me and said you were in trouble. I made all kinds of deals with God on my way to Brambleberry House, begging Him to keep you safe until I could get here."

"You…did?" She didn't know what to say, shaken to her core by the emotion in his voice. Her heart, already beating hard from the kiss, seemed to race even faster.

"Yes. Though I suppose I should have known you could take care of yourself," he said with a little smile. "You're amazing, Rosa. One of the most amazing women I have ever met."

She could not seem to wrap her mind around this man speaking such tender, wonderful words.

"I do not understand," she finally asked. "How can you say that after—after everything I have told you about my past? About what I had to do? About…about giving my baby to someone else?"

"All of those things only make me love you more."

She thought she must have misheard him.

"Love me. You cannot love me." She stared through the darkness, wishing she could see him better. She wanted to drag him back to the house so she could look at him in the light to read the truth.

"Yet I do," he said, his voice ringing with so much truth she had to believe him. "What you did was re-markable. Even more so because of what you have been through. You were scared to death but you still risked your life to protect your friend. You make me ashamed of myself."

"Ashamed? Why? You came as soon as you heard we were in danger."

"I don't have your kind of courage. I have been fighting falling in love with you for a long time. I think long before I moved to Brambleberry House."

"Why?" She was still not sure she could believe it but she wanted to. Oh, she wanted to.

"I loved my wife," he said simply. "When she died, I thought I had nothing else to give. I did not want to love someone else. Love brought too much pain and sadness and it was easier, safer, to keep my heart locked away."

He kissed her gently, on the side of her mouth that had not been hurt. "I am not brave like a certain woman I know who has endured horrible things but still manages to be kind and cheerful and loving."

His words soaked through her, more comforting than she could ever tell him.

"This woman. She sounds very annoying. Too good to be true."

He laughed. "She isn't. She's amazing. Did I tell you that she also reaches out to those in need and is willing to protect them with every fierce ounce of her being?"

She was not the perfect woman he was describing. But hearing how he saw her made her want to be.

Wasn't that what love should be? A window that allowed you to discover the best in yourself because someone else saw you that way?

She didn't know. She only knew she loved Wyatt with all her heart and wanted a future with him, as she had never wanted anything in her life.

"I know something about this woman that you might not," she said.

"What's that?"

The words seemed to catch in her throat as those demons of self-doubt whispered in her ear. No. She would not listen to them. This was too important.

"This woman. She very much loves a certain police detective. She has loved him for a long time, too. Probably since he moved to town with his sad eyes and his beautiful little boy."

He gazed down at her, those eyes no longer sad but blazing with light, joy and wonder. "Well. That works out then, doesn't it?"

He kissed her again, his arms wrapped tightly around her. Her entire journey had been leading her to this moment, she realized. This moment and this man who knew all her secrets and loved her despite them. Or maybe a little because of them.

She loved Wyatt. She wanted a future with him and with Logan. Thinking about that boy who already held such a big part of her heart only added to her happiness.

She could clearly picture that future together, filled with laughter and joy. Kisses and Spanish lessons and walks along the beach with their dogs.

She had no doubt that it would be rich and beautiful, full and joyous and rewarding. The scent of freesia drifted across the sand and Rosa smiled, happy to know that Abigail approved.

EPILOGUE

One year later

WHAT A GLORIOUS day for a wedding.

Rosa woke just as the sun was beginning to creep over the horizon in her third-floor apartment of Brambleberry House.

She stayed in bed for a moment, anticipation shivering through her. For a few disoriented moments, she wasn't sure why, then she caught sight of Fiona's head on the bed, the dog watching her intently, and she remembered.

Today was the day. This day, she was marrying Wyatt and becoming Logan's stepmother.

In a few short hours, they would stand in the gardens of Brambleberry House and exchange their vows.

Everyone was in town. Her parents, Anna and Harry, Sonia Elizabeth and her husband, Luke.

Fiona made the little sound she did when she wanted to go for a walk and Rosa had to smile.

"I am not even out of bed yet. You really want a walk now?"

The dog continued to give her a steady look she could not ignore.

With a sigh, she slipped out of bed, threw on sweats and a baseball cap and then put on Fiona's leash. A moment later, they headed down the stairs of Brambleberry House.

This was her last morning in this apartment and her last morning as Rosa Vallejo Galvez. Tonight she would be Rosa Vallejo Galvez Townsend.

A wife and a mother.

After their honeymoon, she and Wyatt would be returning to the ground-floor apartment of Brambleberry House. They had decided to stay here for now.

He was going to rent out his small bungalow and they would move to the larger apartment, with its sunroom and extra bedroom. It was larger than his house, plus had extensive grounds where Logan could play, as well as his best friend, Addie, living upstairs.

She knew it wouldn't last. At some point, they would probably want to find a house of their own. For now, she was glad she did not have to leave the house completely.

She knew it was silly but Rosa felt like Brambleberry House was excited about the upcoming wedding and all the coming changes. She seemed to smell flowers all the time and wondered if Abigail was flitting through the house, watching all the preparations.

The summer morning was beautiful, with wisps of sea mist curling up through the trees. It was cool now but she knew the afternoon would be perfect for a garden wedding overlooking the sea.

The decorations were already in place and she admired them as she walked through with Fi toward the beach gate.

Fiona, usually well-behaved, was tugging on the leash as Rosa walked onto the sand. She lunged toward a few other early-morning beach walkers, which was completely not like her.

It looked like a man and a child walking a little dog, but they were too far away for her to see them clearly. Suddenly Fiona broke free of Rosa's hold and raced toward them, dragging her leash behind her.

The boy, who Rosa was now close enough to recognize as a nearly eight-year-old boy with a blond cowlick and his father's blue eyes, caught Fiona's leash and came hurrying toward Rosa.

"Rosa! *Buenos*, Rosa!"

"Buenos, mijo." When he reached her, he hugged her hard and Rosa's simmering joy seemed to bubble over.

A few more hours and they would be a family.

A year ago, she never could have imagined this day for herself. She expected she would be content going to other people's weddings. She would dance, laugh, enjoy the refreshments and then go home trying to ignore the pang of loneliness.

Destined to be alone. That is what she had always thought.

She could not have been happier to be so very wrong.

"I don't think I'm supposed to see you today. Isn't it bad luck?" Wyatt's voice was gruff but his eyes blazed with so much tenderness and love, she felt tears of happiness gather in hers. He always made her feel so cherished.

"I think you are not supposed to see me in the wedding dress. I do not think the superstition means you cannot see me in my old sweatpants, when I have barely combed my hair and look terrible. Anyway, I do not care about such things. We make our own luck, right?"

He laughed and reached for her. "Yes. I guess we do. To be safe, I won't tell Carrie and Bella we bumped in to you on our walk. They *do* care about that kind of thing."

Rosa smiled and her heart seemed to sigh when he kissed her, his mouth warm and firm against the morning chill.

"You do not have to tell me. I have heard every superstition about weddings from them since the day we became engaged."

"I don't know how it's possible, but I think Bella is even more excited about this wedding than we are."

Rosa smiled, adding even more happiness to her overflowing cup when she thought of his niece. Her niece, after today.

And her daughter.

After talking with Joe and Carrie several months earlier, she had decided she must tell Bella the truth.

They had all sat down together and, gathering her courage and without giving all the grim details, Rosa had told Bella she was her birth mother.

To her shock, Bella had simply shrugged. "And?" she had said. "I've only known that, like, forever."

"You have not!" Rosa had said, shocked nearly speechless. "How?"

"It wasn't exactly hard to figure out. You just have to look at a selfie of us together. We look enough alike to be sisters."

"Why didn't you say anything?" Carrie had looked and sounded as shocked as Rosa.

"I figured you all would say something eventually when you wanted me to know. What's the big deal? You're like one of my best friends, anyway."

Rosa had burst into tears at that and so had Carrie.

Nothing seemed to have changed between them. Bella still confided in her about boys she liked, and Rosa still tried to be like a wise older sister.

In that time, Bella had never asked about her father. Maybe some day, when she was older, Rosa would figure out a way to tell her something. For now, she was grateful every day for the bright, beautiful daughter who seemed happy to let her into her life.

"She has done a great job of helping me plan the wedding. I would have been lost without her," she said now to Wyatt.

Bella was one of her bridesmaids and could not have been more excited to help her work out every detail of the wedding, from the cake to the dresses to the food at the reception. In fact, Rosa thought she might have a good future as a wedding planner, if she wanted.

"I'm sure she's done a great job," he said. "It's going to be a beautiful day. But not nearly as gorgeous as you."

She smiled as he kissed her again. A loud sigh finally distracted them both. "Can we be done kissing now? You guys are gross."

"Sorry, kid." Wyatt smiled down at his son but made no move to release her. "We both kind of like it."

That was an understatement. They were magic together. She loved his kiss, his touch, and could not wait until she could wake up each morning in his arms.

"Fiona and Hank want to take a walk," Logan informed them. "So do I."

Wyatt kissed Rosa firmly one more time then drew away. "Fine," he said. "But you'd better get used to the kissing, kid."

He reached for Rosa's hand and the three of them and their dogs walked down the beach while gulls cried and the waves washed against the shore.

The perfect day and the perfect life seemed to stretch out ahead of them and Rosa knew she had everything she could ever need, right here.

* * * * *

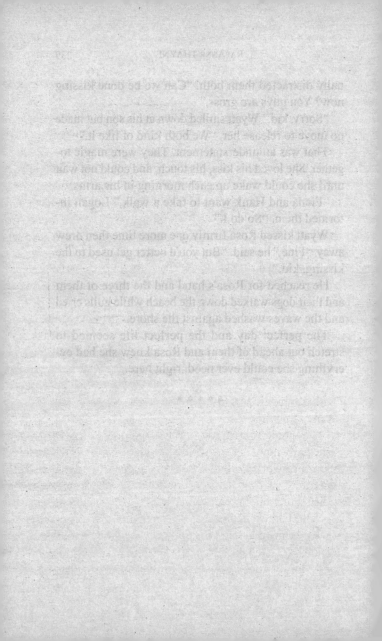

nally distracted them both. "Can we be done kissing now? You guys are gross."

"Sorry, bud," Wyatt smiled down at his son but made no move to release her. *The Book End of like life.*

That was a tender experience. They were at ric to gether. She felt his kiss, his touch, and could not wait until she could wake up each morning in his arms.

Dahls and Hank went to take a walk. "I begin informed them "to do it."

Wyatt kissed Rosa firmly one more time then drew away. "Fine," he said. "But you'd better get used to the kissing [...]."

He reached for Rosa's hand and the three of them [...] and their dogs walked down the beach while scollo crat [...] and the waves washed against the shore.

The perfect day and the perfect life seemed to stretch out ahead of them and Rosa knew she had ex [...] everything she could ever need, right here.

THE RANCHER'S
SUMMER SECRET

CHRISTINE RIMMER

For MSR, always.

CHAPTER ONE

Last New Year's Eve

JAMESON JOHN FULLY intended to ring in the New Year in style.

He wanted to hear some good music, play a little eight ball and, if the stars aligned, take someone sweet and willing home. To make all that happen, he'd jumped in his quad cab and headed straight for Wild Willa's Saloon.

Perched on Center Street, with the entrance in Bronco Valley and the dance floor in tony Bronco Heights, Wild Willa's was the most popular bar in Bronco, Montana. At Wild Willa's, things got loud and rowdy pretty much every night. On New Year's Eve, however, the fun reached a whole new level.

As midnight approached, the very air seemed charged with anticipation. The sound of boots stomping on hardwood competed with the wail of the fiddle, the beat of the drums and the driving rhythm from the bass guitar.

Tonight, every man wore his best boots and a snap-front dress shirt. Every woman had on her tightest

jeans or her shortest flirty skirt. Many wore light-up,
sequined cowboy hats. They blew party horns and
shouted encouragements at the band. The place smelled
of beer, perfume, saddle soap and sweat.

"Hey, cowboy, let's dance."

Jameson turned to the pretty blonde who'd just
tapped him on the shoulder. She had lipstick on her
straight white teeth and a woozy look in those big blue
eyes. Like just about everyone else in Wild Willa's tonight, she'd had one too many.

As for Jameson, in the two hours since he'd walked
through the wide, rustic double doors, he'd had a whiskey, neat, and a single beer. He wanted to be sharp, on
his best game, just in case he met someone interesting.
So far, that hadn't happened. It wouldn't be happening
with this cowgirl, either.

But the woozy blonde looked sweet and hopeful.
He gave her a smile and led her out on the packed
dance floor.

When the song ended, another cowboy stepped up.
Jameson thanked the blonde and left the floor. He tried
not to feel discouraged, but at this rate, he'd have nobody to kiss when the clock struck twelve. Maybe it
just wasn't his night.

With a shrug, he decided he needed a second whiskey and a seat at Wild Willa's famous Get-Lucky Bar,
which formed four loops of stools in a four leaf clover
configuration.

Too bad every stool had an occupant. Jameson considered heading for the pool tables. He could order a
drink there.

But then, in the split second before he turned for the tables, a guy at one end of the clover got up. Jameson moved in to claim the seat.

"Good luck, buddy," muttered the other man as he went by. He looked kind of glum, like maybe he'd just been shut down.

Jameson slid onto the vacant stool, with the wall on one side and a curvy brunette on the other.

He signaled the nearest bartender and ordered, "Knob Creek, straight up."

The brunette turned a pair of velvet brown eyes his way—and he almost felt sorry for that other guy. But then her wide, plump lips stretched in a devilish smile.

The rich, musical sound of her laughter had him forgetting all about that other guy. "Well, if it isn't the one and only Jameson John." She raised her glass as the bartender set his drink down. "Hot and handsome as ever, I see."

Suddenly, his evening looked a whole lot more promising. Apparently, this gorgeous woman knew him. He studied her more closely.

She did look a little familiar. He raised his whiskey and tapped the glass to hers.

"Wait—don't tell me," he said. "I know that I know you…"

She laughed again, tossing her head, her thick, wavy hair tumbling down her back, gleaming like polished mahogany. He found himself staring at the smooth olive skin of her throat. "I'm Vanessa," she said. "Vanessa Cruise."

"Wow." He never would have guessed. Tipping

his hat to her, he said with frank admiration, "Evan Cruise's little sister grew up."

Vanessa had always been cute and smart, but somewhere along the line she'd turned into a beauty—the natural kind, in a silky white shirt and a pair of snug jeans that hugged every gorgeous, generous curve. She had that thick dark hair, those fine eyes to match and freckles, too. Everything about her appealed to him.

She shook a finger at him. "You are staring, Jameson John."

"Sorry, can't help it. I like your freckles."

"Now, there's an interesting compliment."

"Freckles seem surprising, somehow, with your skin color."

"It's a fallacy that only redheads have them. You know that, right?"

He liked her voice—kind of low, husky. "Tell me more."

She laughed. "It's just a reaction to UV exposure. A result of the overproduction of melanin."

"Well, I like them on you. If I remember correctly, everyone used to call you Van, right?"

"Van or Vanessa, either way."

"Just checking. I really like Vanessa. It suits you better, somehow. Didn't you move away?"

She gave a slow nod. "I live in Billings now."

"A teacher, right?"

"You remembered."

"English?"

"Science—chemistry and biology."

"That's right. Always a brainy one."

"You'd better believe it." Her thick, dark eyelashes swept down and up again.

"Home for the holidays, huh?"

She leaned closer. "It's my last night in town. Tomorrow I head back to Billings." Her shoulder brushed his arm, and his breath caught. She smelled sweet and fresh, like the roses his mother grew beside the steps of the main house out at the family ranch, the Double J.

"Vanessa." He touched the brim of his hat, a salute meant to signal he held her in the highest regard. "You mind if I ask you a personal question?"

"Go for it."

"Got a guy in Billings—someone who can't wait for you to come home?"

She sipped her drink. "Not now, I don't."

Something in her tone alerted him. "Did I just hit a nerve? I didn't mean to—"

"Not your fault." She waved his apology away with a shapely hand, the nails cut short, businesslike. No-nonsense. Her full, tempting breasts rose and fell as she sighed. "I confess. There was someone, yes. I was *trying*, you know?"

"I don't quite follow. Trying to…?"

"What can I tell you? This someone I just mentioned wasn't my type, but my type kept messing me over. I go for the players and that never goes well. Trevor—that's his name—was no player. I met him at a science fair. He was so nice. Nerdy and shy, you know? I felt zero chemistry with him. But chemistry isn't everything, am I right?"

He stifled a chuckle. "Vanessa, I'm not touching that with a ten-foot cattle prod."

She let out another soft sigh. "I thought I could draw him out, get him to relax and have fun. I thought that he would be true to me and I would slowly come to care for him deeply, to be grateful for his steady ways."

"I have to say it. Trevor sounds dead boring—and let me guess. You finally had to face the fact that Trevor wasn't the guy for you?"

She seemed faintly amused. "Not exactly."

"Then what?"

"Just before I came home for Christmas, Trevor dumped me."

He couldn't believe it. "No way."

"Oh yeah."

"Trevor is a damn fool."

She leaned close again. The scent of roses beckoned him as she whispered, "He said he couldn't be with me anymore because he didn't find me sexually attractive."

Jameson knew he must have heard wrong. "What man with a pulse wouldn't be attracted to you?"

She grinned. "Yeah, well. You win some, you lose some, I guess."

From over by the pool tables, some guy let out a whoop and someone else whistled. Applause followed. The band struck up another song, this one loud and fast.

When the noise died down a little, she asked, "You here with a date?"

"Nope. Just having a drink with a fascinating woman."

She studied his face for a long count of five before declaring, "You're playing me, aren't you?"

He sat up a little straighter. "No, I am not. Trevor blew it, and I'm grateful to that clown. Because if he hadn't, you wouldn't be sitting here next to me on New Year's Eve."

Slowly, she turned her glass on its Wild Willa's coaster, the one that showed a sexy cowgirl in a short skirt riding a bucking bronc and waving her red hat above her head.

"What?" he asked low. "Say it."

"You are bad," she observed. "So. Very. Bad—and I like that about you far too much."

"Being bad is good, then?" he asked hopefully.

"Oh yes, it is. In the context of this moment, of you and me side by side on New Year's Eve at the Get-Lucky Bar, being bad is very, very good."

As the band struck up another fast one, they gazed at each other, eye to eye. Time passed, but neither of them looked away. He saw no reason to speak. He could just sit here beside her, staring into those sultry eyes of hers until next year came around.

Except he really did like the sound of her voice, especially when she kept those eyes on him and spoke to him alone.

He asked about her family.

And she brought him up to speed on the Cruises. Her brother, Evan, owner and operator of Bronco Ghost Tours, had just gotten engaged earlier that night to Daphne Taylor, estranged daughter of the richest rancher in the county. Vanessa's mother had a boyfriend now, and Vanessa's grandmother Dorothea, whom the

Cruise family called Grandma Daisy, had recently found out that *her* mother was not her birth mother.

"That is some big news," he observed.

"And there's more."

He couldn't wait another second to touch her. Prepared to apologize profusely if she slapped his hand away, he guided a thick curl of hair behind the perfect shell of her ear. She didn't object. Instead, a tiny smile pulled at one corner of that mouth he hoped he might get to kiss when midnight rolled around.

"Tell me everything," he commanded.

"Well, I'll tell you this. Grandma Daisy's birth mother—*my* great-grandmother—is *the* Winona Cobbs."

"Wait. You mean Winona Cobbs who wrote the famous 'Wisdom by Winona' syndicated column?" He used to read that column every week. Winona Cobbs gave good advice.

"The one and only."

"Lots going on with you Cruises." Things never got that exciting on the Double J.

Lowering her voice and leaning closer to him once more, Vanessa confessed, "I feel a little bit guilty. I ran out on tonight's family New Year's Eve party at Daphne's Happy Hearts Animal Sanctuary." Daphne Taylor was somewhat famous locally—not only for being the only daughter of cattle baron Cornelius Taylor, but also for not eating meat in the middle of cow country *and* for her rescue farm, where she took in every brokedown horse and runaway goat that wandered by.

"Please don't get me wrong," said Vanessa. "I'm glad Daphne and Evan found each other. And my mother, who's in love with her boss, is happier than she's ever been before."

"But?"

"It's just that seeing the people I love all cozily coupled up only makes me more depressed about my own romantic future—plus, well, the family doesn't exactly know that it all blew up with Trevor."

He pretended to look stern. "Holding out on the family. That's just not right."

"Maybe not." She drew her shoulders back. "But I don't feel up to dealing with their loving concern at the moment, if you know what I mean." She looked sad.

And he felt bad for teasing her. "I was just yanking your chain. Honestly, I hear you. Sometimes the people you love are the last ones you want in your business."

She braced her elbow on the bar and propped her pretty chin on the heel of her hand. "Thank you." She seemed to mean it.

He nodded in acknowledgment. "And I want you to know that your secret is safe with me."

"Good." Her expression changed, and he had no idea what she might be thinking as she warned, "And *you'd* better watch out."

"Why is that?"

A slow grin curved that mouth, which was so damn inviting it probably ought to come with a warning. "I'm in a mood to forget all my troubles, and I have a weakness for players like you."

Wait, he thought. *Players?*

He was no player—yeah, okay, maybe he'd come

here tonight in hopes of meeting someone like her. And maybe, back in the day, he'd dated a lot of different women.

But since then, he'd grown up. He'd been married and divorced. He was older and wiser now, a man who'd learned enough about what mattered in life to want more from a woman than a one-night stand.

However…

Apparently, Vanessa Cruise *liked* players. He didn't want to mess with the program if she might be considering making his night.

"Vanessa, Vanessa," he chanted under his breath.

"Hmm?"

"You're so direct."

She frowned. "Is it too much?"

"I like it."

Her frown smoothed out. She signaled the bartender.

How many had she had? It mattered. No self-respecting man took advantage of a woman under the influence.

The bartender stepped close. Vanessa said, "Another club soda with lemon." Jameson felt relief—and Vanessa must have seen something in his face. "What?"

"You're not drinking."

She gave him a half shrug. "I'm my own designated driver—and if I do get lucky here at the Get-Lucky Bar, I don't want my senses dulled by alcohol. I want to be wide-awake and fully functional when things get thrilling, you hear what I'm saying?"

Did he ever.

She nodded her thanks at the bartender as he set her

club soda in front of her. After that, she stared down into the drink for a second too long.

"Hey," he said gently, and brushed a hand down her arm. "Where'd you go?"

Her soft shoulders slumped as she blew out a breath. "Just tell me the truth. Am I ridiculous?"

"Hell, no." He said it with feeling. "Whatever gave you that idea?"

She looked at him sideways, kind of pooching out her lower lip, looking a little bit pouty and so damn cute. "It's hard on the ego, being dumped for a complete lack of sex appeal."

Jameson felt nothing but outrage on her behalf. "Don't talk like that. Your ex was the one with the problem."

"As in, it's not me, it's *him*?"

He stuck to his guns. "That's right. You're way too much woman for Trevor."

She sipped her drink. "Just hypothetically…"

"Hypothetically, what?"

"Well, say we went home together…"

"I'm liking the sound of this."

She bit the corner of her ripe lower lip before asking sheepishly, "Would you tell me if I was bad in bed?"

Where the hell did that Trevor guy get off, making her doubt her desirability? Mr. Nice Guy was nothing but a jerk. "It's not an issue. You aren't bad in bed."

"Jameson. Get real. You have no way of knowing that."

They were leaning into each other again, close enough that his sleeve touched hers. It was a simple matter to lean in the necessary fraction closer.

Their lips met.

Her mouth was even softer than it looked, and the scent of her was driving him a little bit crazy. He kissed her slowly, his body heating with sexual need, though he exercised care not to take it too deep. "That proves it," he whispered, his lips still brushing hers. "You are amazing in bed."

Her slow-blooming smile foreshadowed really good things. "Tell me you live alone."

"I'll go you one better. I'll show you." He signaled the bartender for the check.

Van's butterflies had butterflies as Jameson settled the bill, helped her into her fleece-lined coat and led her outside, where a light snow was falling.

Wrapping a strong arm across her shoulders, he pulled her in close to him. "Ride with me."

No way. Tonight would be her first—and most likely only—one-night stand. She intended to do it right. And that meant sober, with her own vehicle to get her there and, when the night was over, back to her brother's house, where she was staying alone while Evan stayed at Daphne's.

"I've got snow tires on my SUV," she said. "I'll follow you."

Jameson didn't argue. He walked her to her Subaru, opened her door for her and closed it with care. She watched as he jogged through the thin layer of snow to a black quad cab. Starting her engine, she waited for him to take the lead.

He led her out of the parking lot and down Center

Street to the intersection with the state highway, where dirty snow had piled up on the shoulder, but the road itself was clear. The snow came down sparsely, not really sticking.

After maybe ten miles, he took a side road. A few minutes later, they turned onto a wide, well-tended gravel driveway and passed under a rough-hewn sign for the John family ranch, the Double J. In the distance, she could make out the shadows of barns and outbuildings and a big log house. Jameson led her past the turnoff to that house.

The long driveway curved up the gentle slope of a hill and then down to another house, one not quite as large as the log home they'd passed earlier. Of gorgeous, weathered wood and stone, the house had lots of windows and a more modern style than the usual sprawling log homes that most of the wealthy local ranchers favored.

Two of the four garage doors rumbled up and Jameson drove in the first stall, jumping out and signaling her to take the next stall over.

She rolled down her window. "I'll just park out here." When it came time to leave, she wanted a clean getaway, one that did not include asking him to please shut the garage door behind her.

He went in through the garage, and she parked in the driveway, meeting him at the front door.

Inside, he took her coat and hung it in the entry closet. "Drink?" he asked, leading her down a wide hallway with a skylight overhead. The hallway opened onto a sprawling, gorgeous combination kitchen and great room. The kitchen end had a stone floor, counters of black granite and warm wood, the appliances the kind any top chef might envy. A wall of windows looked out on the dark, shadowed peaks of the mountains in the distance.

"Nothing for me, thanks," she said, setting her leather shoulder bag on one of the stools at the granite island.

He pulled her over to the rough-hewn trestle table and moved in close. Really, he was such a gorgeous man. She'd always admired his thick, dark gold hair and celestial blue eyes. He smelled so good, like saddle soap and clean leather—a healthy male in his prime, the kind that lured a woman to mate.

And that reminded her. "I'm on the pill," she announced, "and really hoping that you have condoms."

Had that come out sounding painfully abrupt? Maybe. But it had to be said. A woman needed to take responsibility for her safety and reproductive health. No surprise pregnancies—and no STDs, either.

"Yes, I do." He took her hand. His was warm and thrillingly rough from ranch work. Her heart skipped a beat with anticipation. "This way," he said in a low rumble.

He led her out of the kitchen area to the open great room, which had a high, peaked ceiling and more gorgeous skylights. Large, comfortable-looking sofas and chairs formed two conversation groups on either side of the plain, modern fireplace.

Across from the fireplace, a staircase with metal railings led down to other rooms below.

"This way." He led her along the short hallway next

to the staircase, where a door opened on the master suite, with its own large bathroom and private deck. The room had a peaked ceiling, too. It was all warm, rough-textured woods, the linens in soothing, soft grays.

She hesitated at the door. He stopped and turned to her.

Before he could wrap her in those big arms, she stepped back. "I have something I need to say."

He lifted a hand and touched the side of her face. The simple caress thrilled her, sent a tingle rushing through her just from that small, brushing contact. "Tell me, then."

She suddenly felt awkward and silly and…too young. But she said her piece anyway. "I just need to lay out the ground rules, so we both know where we stand."

One side of his sinfully sexy mouth quirked up in amusement. "There are ground rules?"

She gave him a firm nod. "Yes, there are. This, to-night, is a special circumstance."

"Very special," he agreed, those beautiful eyes gleaming at her, promising all manner of heavenly delights.

"Well, that may be. But I meant special as in a one-time deal. Tomorrow, I head home to Billings."

"You mentioned that already."

"And it bears repeating. I live in Billings, and your life is here. And in future, when I come back again to visit my family and you and I happen to see each other somehow in passing, we will not stop. We will not give each other more than a nod and a simple hello. We will never discuss what happened here tonight. No digits will be exchanged. Neither of us will try to contact the

other. This is 'The Night That Never Happened'—"
Yes, she actually air-quoted it for emphasis. "—and
we need to agree that it is."

His burnished eyebrows drew together in a doubtful sort of frown.

She barreled on. "Which, er, won't be a problem for
you because you don't do relationships."

"Vanessa, I never said—"

"Wait." She put up a hand. "I won't get in touch
again because that would make you think I want a relationship, which I don't. As for you, well, you won't
contact me because, um, you're Jameson John and you
don't do commitment."

His frown had deepened. "Hey, now. Hold on a minute. I do plan to have a relationship that lasts. I want a
family, children."

"Sure you do," she teased. "Someday, right?"

"That's not fair." He really seemed troubled, somehow, by this subject.

"I'm sorry," she said, and meant it. "Sometimes I
get a little carried away trying to make a point. I didn't
mean to insult you, Jameson."

"You didn't. It's just, well, yeah. Maybe I was that
guy you're describing. But I'm not anymore. You like
players and, back at Wild Willa's, I wanted to be whatever you needed tonight. But I'm not that guy, Vanessa, not the thoughtless boy you remember from high
school. I've been married and divorced. I'm settled
down now, a grown-ass man. I'm ready for something
more than just one night."

Her heart kind of melted—but come on. She'd just

been dumped. A new relationship wasn't even on the table right now and she needed to make that crystal clear. She gazed up at him defiantly. "Well, I'm not ready for anything but tonight."

He stared down at her long and hard. Was this it, then? Would he walk her back out to her car and say good-night? She braced herself for that.

But then he shook his head. "I do want you, Vanessa. A lot. And if tonight is all I'm getting, so be it."

She drilled her point home. "After this, there will be no contact. You and me, we won't be happening again."

He caught her hand and pulled her close. "Fair enough."

"Jameson," she whispered, pressing her palms to his hard chest as his mouth touched hers.

Oh, he was perfect. Exactly what she needed. This beautiful man to ring in a whole new year, to make her feel gorgeous and wanted for one perfect night. She slid her hungry hands up to encircle his neck.

When he lifted his head, she opened her eyes. They gazed at each other. "Agreed?" she asked again.

His eyes spoke of reluctance to go along with her terms. She shouldn't allow herself to feel thrilled at the idea that he might hope for more. Yet she did feel thrilled. Just a little.

Finally, he acquiesced. "I agree. Tonight and that's all."

Gathering her close again, he shut the door to the hallway with the heel of his boot.

Much later, when Vanessa woke beside Jameson in his big, comfy bed, it was still dark out. The bedside clock showed ten past three.

A whole new year had begun—and boy, did Jameson John know how to give a girl a really good time. For several dreamy seconds, Van stared at him through the shadows. He lay on his back, sound asleep. Looking at his chiseled profile, she could almost wish that she didn't have to go.

But they had an agreement. And she intended to keep it.

Carefully, so as not to wake him, she slid out from under the thick down comforter and tiptoed around the room gathering up her clothes. In the bathroom, she dressed and finger-combed her tangled hair.

Then, carrying her boots in order not to make a sound, she crept along the short hallway and across the great room to get her purse from where she'd left it on the kitchen stool.

Her contacts were extended wear, but still her eyes felt gritty and tired. She switched to her glasses—the ones with the large, black frames.

At the bottom of her bag, she found the small notebook and a blue Flair pen she always carried with her. Tearing out a page, she wrote a brief note.

Leaving the note on the island, she headed for the entry, where she paused long enough to put on her warm coat. The front door opened silently on well-oiled hinges when she carefully pulled it wide.

Outside, the sky had cleared, and a light rime of snow made the ground glitter as though scattered with tiny diamonds. She paused on the step to breathe in the fresh, icy air.

And then, with a secret smile on her face and a lightness in her step, she turned for her Subaru.

Jameson woke alone to pale sunlight—a clear winter morning.

When he reached out a hand, the other side of the bed felt cold to the touch. He stared up through the skylight at the pale, cloudless sky and hated that Vanessa had already left him.

Rising, he pulled on last night's jeans and went out to the kitchen area to brew some coffee. He found her note waiting on the counter.

> *Jameson,*
> *I just want to say that you are incredible. Thank you for a perfect New Year's.*
> *Yours,*
> *Vanessa*

Two sentences bracketed with his name and hers. That's all he got.

As he crumpled the scrap of paper in his fist, he weighed the pros and cons of breaking her damn rules—right now, today. She wouldn't have left town yet. He could probably track her down at Evan's house or her mother's place on the Bronco Valley side of town.

But he'd given his word not to go after her. He'd promised to walk on by any time he happened to see her again. Plus, she lived in Billings, while he loved Bronco and the Double J. He never planned to live anywhere else.

Beyond all that, maybe she was right. She'd insisted she wasn't in the market for a relationship. And the last thing he needed was to fall for another woman who couldn't honestly, openly give him her heart—even a woman as surprising and sexy and smart and charming as Vanessa Cruise.

Jameson drank his coffee, fried bacon and scrambled some eggs. After breakfast, he went out to meet his brothers, Maddox and Dawson. Together, they rounded up some frisky heifers who'd busted through a fence and wandered out onto the state highway. That evening, he had dinner with the family at the main house.

And New Year's night, in bed alone, he stared up into the darkness and tried to picture Vanessa at home in Billings, lying in her own bed, maybe smiling a little, remembering the night before. Faintly, he smelled roses. He grabbed her pillow and pressed it to his face. Breathing in the scent of her like some sappy lovesick fool, he reconsidered the idea of going after her.

But he did no such thing. She didn't want to see him again and he'd given her his word he wouldn't track her down. Jameson John always kept his word.

Eventually, he promised himself, the desire to go after her would fade.

CHAPTER TWO

Present day

THE NIGHT THAT Never Happened turned out to have a day of reckoning, and that day was July 2.

By then, due to her inability to say no to Daphne, Vanessa had been in town for a month. Her brother's fiancée had mad skills when it came to coaxing people to do things they would ordinarily have no trouble politely turning down. Things like spending the summer in the hometown Van never visited for longer than a week or two at a stretch. Somehow, Daphne had convinced her that she needed to teach science to tweens and early teens out at Happy Hearts Animal Sanctuary.

Daphne's day camp, Young Adventurers, kept a lot of kids busy in the summer while their parents worked. In the mornings, Young Adventurers offered a fun and absorbing curriculum, an opportunity to learn cool stuff about chemistry, math, technology and biology. After lunch, the younger kids could pet the animals and learn about animal behavior while the older ones pitched in on the farm. They all seemed to love summer day camp at Happy Hearts.

And truth to tell, Van loved it, too. She loved it enough that she might not even have minded spending a whole summer in the town she'd left behind—except for the niggling little issue of a guy called Jameson John.

Every day for the past month, Van had wondered and worried, dreaded and anticipated the moment when she would finally come face-to-face with Jameson again.

Yet somehow, one day had followed another and she'd seen no sign of him. She'd even started imagining that she never would.

Wrong.

That gorgeous, sunny, early July day just happened to be the opening day of Red, White and Bronco—because in Bronco, people took their patriotism seriously. Every year, the town leaders and merchants pooled their resources to put on a four-day festival in celebration of Independence Day.

Van and Callie Sheldrick, Van's summer roommate, had arrived at Bronco Park early to make sure they got a picnic table. A down-to-earth sort of person, both perceptive and warmhearted, Callie worked for Evan at Bronco Ghost Tours. She and Van had quickly become BFFs. In fact, during a girls' night, just the two of them, a month ago, Van had shared her hardest secrets with Callie.

Today, Bronco Park looked nothing short of festive, with red, white and blue paper cloths on the tables, Old Glory waving from every tree and a whole marketplace of booths selling fireworks and patriotic hats, horns, dishware and souvenirs—along with just about every kind of picnic food and drink known to man. The smells of barbecue, popcorn and cotton candy filled the air.

Maybe twenty minutes after Van and Callie claimed their table, Evan and Daphne joined them, followed by three bright young girls who attended Vanessa's morning workshops at Young Adventurers. More girls arrived—too many to fit at the table. But one of the girls had brought a blanket. They spread it out between the tables and sat on the grass.

Red, white and blue bunting graced the front of the outdoor stage set up in full view of all the picnic tables. The festival committee had also put out rows of white folding chairs so that everyone would have a place to sit and enjoy today's main event—the Miss Bronco beauty pageant, held every year on the second of July, right here in Bronco Park.

This year, the contest had sparked controversy, thanks to several of Van's students at Young Adventurers—the ones sitting at the table with her and nearby on the grass, as a matter of fact. The girls had spearheaded a successful campaign to rewrite the pageant rules. Some people weren't happy with the changes.

Van thought it was great, and she'd shown up today to support her girls. She'd always made it a point to encourage her pupils to think outside the box. She urged them to transform what they found unfair or even downright wrong about their world and the way it was run. To that end, at Young Adventurers, she held discussion time each morning before everyone got down to work on current projects.

Back in early June, during discussion time, one of the girls had brought up the Miss Bronco pageant. She'd complained that girls from the same families almost always seemed to win, and that didn't seem fair. A lively chat ensued.

And after that, the girls had done more than talk. They'd created a petition to change the rules and then gone door to door collecting the signatures to make that happen.

Van beamed with pride as the pageant began and Earl Tillson, this year's host, kicked things off by explaining the new contest rules.

"This year," announced Earl, "Miss Bronco will be chosen *not* by the usual panel of pillars of our community, but by an open vote to be held right here, today, as soon as the competition is concluded. Anyone in town can cast a vote as long as they fill out a ballot. Also this year, as a nod to all the single ladies you admire and want to recognize, you'll find a space on your ballot for a write-in. Any and all unmarried females sixteen years of age or older are eligible."

"Sixteen years or *older*?" A skinny cowboy in a purple shirt jumped up from one of the picnic tables. "How *much* older?"

"Well," replied Earl, "she would need to still be breathin', I'll tell you that." A ripple of laughter passed through the crowd.

That same cowboy argued, "That means any woman,

no matter how old, can enter—long as she ain't got a ring on her finger."

"Young man," growled Earl, "that is exactly what it means. As long as any single female person is sixteen, which we all agree is old enough to carry out the duties of the position, that person is welcome to claim her chance at the crown."

"Well, that is plain wrong, Earl Tillson. We'll end up with somebody's single grandma wearing the sash and crown."

Thirteen-year-old Cleo Davidson, one of Vanessa's brightest summer students and an organizer in the campaign to make the Miss Bronco contest less biased and more inclusive, put her hands to either side of her mouth and shouted, "It is fair, and it is right!" Several spectators, including the girls seated around Van, cheered in support.

The cowboy bellowed, "No, it's not!"

"Yes, it is!" Cleo shouted back. "Your grandma should have the right to enter."

"Like hell she should!" yelled the cowboy. "Some old lady can't be Miss Bronco. It's a beauty pageant. I love my grandma, but she's no Miss Bronco."

Snickers and titters followed that pronouncement.

"Young man, curb your tongue!" Earl, who did a brisk side business as an auctioneer at local livestock shows and estate sales, knew how to take control of an iffy situation. He stared that cowboy down.

Muttering under his breath and shaking his head, the cowboy sank back to his seat.

"Now. Where was I?" Earl straightened his bolo

tie. "Ahem. There will be no swimsuit competition."
That brought some serious booing. Earl waited for the
yahoos to take a breath before shouting out, "The categories of competition are talent, evening wear, an interview centering around the contestants' dreams and
goals—and a platform for a social cause that has special meaning for each candidate."

Van felt so proud. Her girls had done well. She
beamed at the three across the table from her and
turned to give a big thumbs-up to the five sitting on
the grass.

And it was right then, as she shifted her focus to
the girls on the blanket, that the moment of reckoning found her.

She spotted Jameson. He sat at a picnic table on the
other side of the rows of folding chairs. At the table
with him, she recognized his dad, his mom and his
two younger brothers.

Her mouth went dry, and her face felt too hot. She
couldn't stop herself from drinking in the sight of him.
He looked so good, all strong and broad and big and
manly.

It seemed almost impossible that she'd actually seen
him naked. But she had. And their night together had
been beautiful. Perfect. Spectacular.

Yeah. All those things and then some.

But what she needed to remember, the most important thing now…

That night was Over. Capital *O*.

Just one night, she reminded herself. One night,
months ago. Little more than a blip on the radar of

eternity. The mere sight of him shouldn't affect her so strongly.

She was supposed to be over him—no. Wait. She had no need to get over him. There was nothing to get over. They'd had a good time and gone their separate ways.

Except, well…

For her, their one night had been the best night ever.

The sheer sexual excellence of it couldn't quite be forgotten. Her body remembered and wanted more.

And that meant that her face had flushed with heat and her mind had gone blank as a fresh-washed chalkboard. All of a sudden, a hive full of bees seemed to buzz beneath the surface of her skin.

And he'd spotted her, too.

Their gazes collided—and locked. They stared at each other across the rows of spectators as Earl Tillson droned on up on the stage. Everyone else—Callie, Evan, Daphne, the girls—they all just faded away. Her brain had only one thing in it: a tall, broad-shouldered, blue-eyed, golden-haired cowboy.

He gave her that slow smile, and she felt summoned.

She had to actively resist the desire to rise from the picnic bench and go to him, take his hand, lead him away from the crowd to someplace private where they could get up close and very personal all over again.

Not that she would do any such thing.

Uh-uh. Van stayed right there at the picnic table next to Callie.

It was just, well, she'd daydreamed about him way too often—about him and The Night That Never

Happened—so much so, in fact, that she'd come to think of that night simply by its initials: TNTNH.

Van shut her eyes. Closing out the very sight of him, she ordered the bees to stop buzzing and her face to stop burning. With a slow, deep breath, she made herself look at him again. With a dignified nod and a reserved little smile, she turned away.

"So you've met Jameson?" said a soft voice in her ear.

She turned to aim a bright smile at Callie, who was watching her much too closely. "I did grow up here," she reminded her friend, who had no idea what Van had been up to last New Year's Eve. She and Callie hadn't been that close back then. And now, well, what did it matter? Yeah, she'd shared her hardest secrets with Callie, but Jameson?

He was a *good* memory, a happy secret. She didn't need to cry on her friend's shoulder over him. Plus, Jameson was one night and nothing more.

"Of course I've met him," she said to Callie. "Everybody in town knows Jameson John."

Was that a smirk on Callie's face?

If so, Vanessa refused to acknowledge it.

When the slender, pretty blonde stepped forward from the pack of ten contestants up on the stage, Jameson tore his gaze from the hot brunette across the way. After all, that pretty blonde was his baby sister. Her name was Charity. Along with his brothers and his parents and a lot of other people in the park that day, Jameson clapped and cheered wildly as Earl introduced her.

Charity looked beautiful, as always, in a pretty summer dress, her shining hair loose on her shoulders. Jameson had shown up with the rest of the family to support her in her current bid for the Miss Bronco crown. They all knew she had it nailed this year.

Nineteen now, Charity had been working toward the Miss Bronco title every year since she turned sixteen. Each of those years she'd come closer to winning. She'd taken, respectively, fourth place, third place and runner-up. This year would bring her the crown.

She smiled her brilliant smile and gave a short speech about how she loved her hometown, had graduated with honors from Bronco High and had finished her first year at Valley College. The John family and her other supporters clapped louder than ever when Earl thanked her and she stepped back for the next contestant to take her turn.

As for Jameson, his gaze strayed once more to the unforgettable brunette at the table on the opposite side of the stage. The sight of her had decided him. He might have come today to support his sister, but now he had a second goal—finding an opportunity to reconnect with Vanessa.

Word traveled fast in Bronco. He'd known for a month that she'd moved to town for the summer. Within a week, he'd found out that she was rooming with Callie Sheldrick. He'd ached to head straight for Callie's place. He wanted to get up close and personal, to intimately welcome Vanessa back to town. He hungered to find out if the sparks between them burned as bright and hot as they had last New Year's Eve.

But he'd stopped himself from going after her. He'd reminded himself that he'd given his word not to seek her out, that he needed to stick with the promise he'd made New Year's Eve.

However, seeing her again in the flesh changed everything. To hell with her rules. He wanted to get closer to her.

And one way or another, he would.

For the next hour, he tried his damnedest to sit tight with his family, to keep his mind on the pageant. He got through the interviews, snapping to attention when his sister stepped up. Charity spoke of her dreams and goals with warmth and feeling. She went first in the talent portion and stole the show. Charity played the piano like a virtuoso and she sang like Carrie Underwood—kind of looked like her, too.

Yeah, he might be a tad prejudiced in his little sister's favor, but objectively, everyone could see that she deserved the crown. People clapped louder and with greater enthusiasm for her than the other nine contestants. Even with the new rules in place, Jameson knew she would win.

As he cheered his sister on, he kept one eye on the woman across the way. He was biding his time, waiting for the right moment. Eventually, Vanessa would get up to say hi to a friend at another table, maybe check out the rows of marketplace booths, buy herself a cold drink or some patriotic trinket. When she did, he would make his move and find a way to get a few words with her.

An hour and a half crawled by after that exhilarating moment when he'd looked over and spotted her sitting with her brother and the others. Now and then, he would slide her a glance, kind of keeping an eye on her. Once or twice, he caught her looking his way.

But she didn't hold his gaze. And that one measly, cool little smile she'd given him that first time their eyes locked together, well, that was all the smiles he got.

One way or another, he intended to get more.

Finally, she made her move, rising from the table, hovering there a minute to say something to Callie. And then she took off, headed for the two rows of marketplace booths set up facing each other farther into the park, on her side of the stage.

In order not to be too obvious, he waited until she'd made it forty yards or so from her table, before whispering to his brother Maddox, "Be right back," and setting out after her.

Up on the stage, wearing a determined expression and dressed in a sequined bodysuit, Hermione Sanchez tap-danced to "I'm a Yankee Doodle Dandy" as Jameson circled around the last row of folding chairs. By the time he made it beyond the far group of picnic tables, Vanessa had disappeared from his line of sight. He walked faster until he entered the marketplace area, after which he slowed a little to check out each booth as he passed it.

Where the hell had she wandered off to?

Not that it mattered. If it took him all afternoon, he would find her. He'd made up his mind to get a word with her, and he wouldn't give up until he got what he wanted.

* * *

Pie.

Van loved it. And she needed it. Jameson had started to get under her skin, the way he kept glancing over at her—the way she couldn't seem to make herself stop glancing back. He was a blue-eyed devil and her hopelessly hungry libido required a serious distraction from the temptation he posed.

If you asked Van, no finer distraction existed in the material world than pie.

She followed her nose to the booth where the Bronco Ladies Auxiliary sold just about every sort of baked treat known to man. One of the Abernathy ladies, Angela, gave her a tiny sample slice of cherry pie to help her choose between it and the apple raspberry.

Van got right to work on that sample, groaning aloud at the sweet, tangy taste and the perfectly flaky crust. "So good…"

"One of those Dalton boys baked it," said Angela with a big grin. "He brought us six of them. We cut one up for samples, and four have sold already. We've only got one left."

"I want it."

"Twelve dollars," Angela smiled at her tauntingly.

"A bargain at the price."

Angela beamed. "Vanessa, it is yours." She started folding a pink bakery box as Van tried to make the sample last.

"Looks good," said the smooth, deep voice that haunted far too many of her dreams. It came from right behind her.

Carefully, she swallowed her bite of pie before slowly turning to face him. The sight of him so close kind of weakened her knees. In new jeans and a crisp black shirt, he looked yummier than her sliver of pie. "Jameson." Somehow, she kept her voice casual, friendly—but not *too* friendly. "How've you been?"

"Can't complain." He leaned in a little. She got a whiff of soap and leather, and she wanted to reach out and yank him in close just to smell him better. And then he smiled. "I didn't know you wore glasses."

Today, she wore the ones with the big tortoiseshell frames. Nervously, she adjusted them. "Sometimes it's just easier than contacts, you know? Not to mention more comfortable."

"I get that. You look good in them."

Too bad she felt so awkward and so completely unprepared to deal with him. "Thank you."

He nodded. "I'm thinking you look good in whatever you wear." He was still smiling.

And she couldn't stop herself from smiling right back—a real smile this time. He had that look in his eye, that teasing, tempting look she remembered with such pleasure from TNTNH, like she was the prettiest girl he'd ever seen and he couldn't take his eyes off her.

"You've got a dab of cherry filling," he said low, for her ears alone. And then, right there in front of God and everyone, he lifted a lean, tanned hand dusted with gleaming gold hairs and rubbed his thumb at the corner of her lower lip. Tingles shivered along every nerve ending she possessed.

Oh, she really shouldn't have let him do that.

And it got worse. He brought that thumb to his beautiful mouth and gave it a lick. Something low in her belly went liquid. Was Angela Abernathy watching?

Somehow, at this point, Van couldn't bring herself to care.

She stared at his mouth, admiring his close-trimmed dark gold beard and mustache—a Vandyke, they called it. Like Custer at the Little Big Horn, like David Beckham and Viggo Mortensen. A Vandyke only looked good on a certain type of man.

The rugged, confident type.

"There's a pie contest on the Fourth," he said in a low, lazy drawl.

"I remember the pie contest." She dropped her used paper plate and plastic fork into the trash basket by the pie table. "It's held right here in Bronco Park at the town barbecue, am I right?" She might not live here anymore, but she knew her Red, White and Bronco events as well as any Bronco native. She sent a glance over her shoulder at Angela, just to see if the older woman had her eye on them. She didn't. Angela had already packed up Van's pie and moved on to filling a box with cookies for a good-looking fortyish woman Van didn't recognize.

"Are you planning on baking a pie to enter in the contest?" asked Jameson.

She faced him again. Had he moved in even closer— or was that merely wishful thinking on her part? "I don't bake, but I promise you, I will be eating."

He gave her a slow once-over, sending more tingles spreading through her traitorous body. Some men made her uncomfortable when they looked her up and down. Not Jameson. He just made her yearn.

"A girl who likes her pie," he said quietly.

"I'll take that is a compliment."

"Good. It was meant as one."

"As I recall, Miss Bronco always judges the pie contest," she said. At his nod, she added, "I'm betting on Charity to take the crown. She's talented and so pretty—and she has a way with words, too."

His eyes gleamed with pride as he said mildly, "I think she's doing well. And she's got her heart set on it, that's for sure."

"Tell her we're all rooting for her."

"That I will…" His voice wandered off into silence. He stared at her, and she stared back. Nobody else existed right then. She knew she should break the sudden spell that mutual attraction and scorching-hot memories had conjured between them.

But it just felt so good, standing there in dappled sunlight, the smell of pie on the air, staring at this beautiful man and almost wishing—

"Here you go, Vanessa." Angela Abernathy cut off Van's dangerous thoughts. She held out a pink bakery box. The cherry pie sat inside it. "How's it look?"

"Too delicious for words."

Angela tucked in the lid. "That's twelve dollars even."

Van traded her the money for the box. "Thanks."

"You are so welcome, dear."

"Hey, aren't you Vanessa Cruise, the one who teaches the summer camp kids out at Daphne Taylor's animal sanctuary?" The good-looking fortyish woman Van had noticed talking to Angela a moment ago moved closer just as Angela stepped away to wait on another customer. The woman had another pink bakery box in her hands.

"I'm Vanessa, yes."

"Lurline DuBois." The woman shifted the bakery box to her left hand and offered her right. Van gave it a shake. "I'm just off my second divorce and ready for a fresh start, if you take my meaning." Lurline slanted a smirk at Jameson. "How 'bout you, handsome? Got a name?"

Van introduced them. "Lurline, this is Jameson John."

Jameson, looking wary now, accepted the woman's hand and let go of it quickly. Lurline gave a loud laugh. "My, my. They do grow you boys up tall and strong here in Montana."

Was she making a move on Jameson?

For a moment, it looked that way—but then she surprised Van and turned to her again. "I heard about your students, how they got the Miss Bronco rules changed."

"Yes, they did." Van spoke with pride.

"I love that. I mean, why are beauty queens always barely more than babies? A real woman ought to toss her hat in the ring, show 'em how it should be done. I'm thinking next summer, I might just enter the contest myself." Lurline's eyes twinkled as she tossed her crow-black hair. "That is, if I'm still single."

"Go for it, Lurline." Van patted her shoulder—and remembered that cowboy in the purple shirt. He just might have a coronary if Lurline entered next year. So be it. Van's Young Adventurers hadn't fought for change so that everything could stay the same.

"Catch you two later." With a flirty smile and a jaunty wave, Lurline moved along, leaving the two of them staring after her.

"Lurline's a pistol," Jameson remarked wryly.

Van met his gaze. They both started laughing.

When the mirth faded to silence and they were left gazing too long into each other's eyes, he took her arm. She allowed him to pull her out of the Ladies Auxiliary booth, and into a space between that booth and the next one.

Carefully, she eased her arm free of his hold. "I should go."

"Wait." He had such gorgeous eyes, so clear, so vivid. So impossibly blue. Those eyes held her captive to memories she shouldn't allow herself—memories of his rough palm skating down her bare back, of his breath in her ear, his mouth doing incredible things to all her most secret places… "Just a phone number, Vanessa. That's all I'm asking for."

Her throat felt tight. She forced the words through it anyway. "It's a bad idea."

"No. It's a good idea. The *best* idea. I missed you. I can't stop thinking about you. Tell me to my face right now that since that night, you've never thought of me, never wondered what I might be doing, never considered looking me up. Just tell me you'd forgotten all about me. Just say it right to my face."

"I never thought of you." It came out flat, completely unconvincing.

He shook his head slowly. "Lying's beneath you."

She felt breathless and so sad, both at the same time. "We had an agreement."

He said nothing for an endless count of five. "Why? That's what I want to know. Why is it necessary that we can't get some coffee or maybe get dinner somewhere quiet, you and me?"

"It's a long story, one I don't care to share."

He glared at her. "I'm not giving up." And then, without another word, he turned on his boot heel and walked away.

She almost ran after him, to argue with him, insist at least one more time that TNTNH was never going to happen again.

Somehow, she kept her feet rooted in place. Clutching her pie, she drew slow, even breaths as she counted to a hundred at a measured pace. Only after her pulse had settled down a little and her stomach felt at least marginally less fluttery did she head back to rejoin her family.

An hour after Van got back to her table, the Miss Bronco competition came to an end and the voting began.

Volunteers passed out the ballots, along with short pencils for anyone who needed one. Van voted for Charity and felt sure that just about everyone else in the park had, too. Jameson's sister stood out among the ten pretty young contestants, most of whom, as happened every year, were daughters of the influential families in town. Charity had that special something every beauty queen required. Not only was she gorgeous, she had a megawatt smile and a good head on her shoulders, and she came across as kind and thoughtful, too.

The volunteers moved through the crowd again, gathering the ballots and then disappearing into a tent set up specially for the purpose of tallying the votes.

As they waited for the results, Van got out the paper plates and plastic forks she'd bought on her way back to the table. Carefully, she took her pie from the pink box and proudly held it up for everyone to admire. "Who wants cherry pie? Baked by one of the Dalton boys and it is amazing."

Evan wanted a slice, and Callie had one, too.

Daphne, a strict vegetarian, voiced her suspicion that the Dalton boy who'd baked that pie had used lard rather than vegetable shortening. "And lard is made from animal fat. I guess I'll have to pass," she concluded regretfully.

Van put on a sad face. "I feel so bad for you." And then she grinned. "But hey. More for me." Both she and Daphne laughed.

Surprisingly, Van's students all claimed they weren't hungry. She found that a bit odd. Her students were *always* hungry.

And yet, the girls turned down the amazing pie and huddled together on the blanket, whispering to each other. Vanessa wondered vaguely what they might be up to. They giggled and nudged each other and whispered some more.

Whatever secrets they kept snickering over, they seemed to be having a terrific time. Well, more power to them, Vanessa thought as she cut an extra-large, mouthwatering slice for herself. Grabbing a plastic fork, she swung her legs to the other side of the bench.

With her back to the table, she could see the stage better, even if that position made it all too easy to let her gaze stray toward the John family table across the way. Uh-uh. Not going to happen. She kept her eyes trained on the stage.

The volunteers emerged from the tent. One carried an envelope up to the stage and passed it to Earl Tillson, who passed it to the mayor as another volunteer wheeled out a stand bearing two crowns on blue velvet pillows, one larger and more ornate than the other.

Earl called all ten contestants out from behind the curtain at the back of the stage. Last year's winner, an Abernathy cousin, stood at the mayor's side holding an enormous bouquet of red roses. The contestants lined up in their evening gowns wearing big smiles, their heads high and their shoulders back.

The mayor announced that Hermione Sanchez had taken fifth place. Her smile all the wider, Hermione stepped forward. To enthusiastic applause, last year's Miss Bronco handed her a single rose as Earl helped her into her green satin fifth-place sash. Fourth place went to one of the Taylors and third to another Abernathy. Van couldn't help thinking that the new rules hadn't changed much of anything, after all. Girls from

Bronco's prominent families seemed to be winning, same as before.

However, she reminded herself, change didn't happen overnight. She remembered Lurline DuBois and grinned. Next year, the rules her Young Adventurers had pushed for might inspire a whole new group of girls and women to compete.

The mayor announced, "And now we come to the first runner-up. Second only to Miss Bronco herself, the first runner-up is ever at the ready to assist Miss Bronco whenever she's called to help—and even to step in for Miss Bronco should scheduling conflicts occur. This year, our first runner-up is once again Miss Charity John!"

A slight silence elapsed before everyone started clapping. In that silence, Van felt sure she hadn't heard right. None of the others had compared to Charity. Of course she should have taken the crown.

But no. Van stared in disbelief as Charity, her beautiful smile a little bit wobbly, stepped forward to accept her single rose, the runner-up sash and the smaller of the two crowns.

"What's going on?" whispered a woman at the next table.

"Not a clue," replied another as murmurs of confusion and disapproval rose from the crowd.

Clearly, most everyone thought that Charity should have the big crown.

With a heavy sigh, Van forked up a giant bite of delicious pie. Sometimes the right person lost, but at least there was pie to ease the pain of life's disappointments.

She stuck that hunk of sweet, tart, saucy cherries and perfect, flaky crust into her mouth just as the mayor announced, "And this year's Miss Bronco, on a first-time ever write-in triumph, is Miss Vanessa Cruise!"

A gasp went up from half the spectators. Van choked on her pie so hard she sprayed cherries and crust all over her ripped jeans and soft, well-worn T-shirt.

This could not be happening.

Oh, but it was. "Get on up here, Vanessa!" shouted the mayor. "Join us on the stage and claim your crown!"

CHAPTER THREE

As Van brushed bits of crust and cherry filling off her jeans, her Young Adventurer girls jumped up to surround her. Like a flock of birds at a feeding station, they all twittered at once as they clapped and high-fived each other.

Cleo Davidson, wearing a wide, proud smile, grabbed Van's hand and pulled her upright. "Come on! You need to get up there. They're waiting for you."

"Yes!" crowed eleven-year-old Emma Bledsoe. "We did it! We got you written in. You won, Miss Cruise. You will be the best Miss Bronco ever!" She and Cleo high-fived each other yet again.

"Girl power!" shouted twelve-year-old Mandy Highwalker and held up her hand.

"Girl power!" the others hollered in unison, each reaching up to slap Mandy's palm, one after the other.

Loudly congratulating each other, they herded Van toward the stage. A frantic glance back at the table revealed Evan, Daphne and Callie, staring after her, looking bemused.

Van mouthed, "Help!" at her roomie and Callie gave

her a determined smile and a big thumbs-up—whatever that meant.

Numbly, she mounted the side steps leading up the stage.

Last year's Miss Bronco came to meet her halfway. "Congratulations, Vanessa," the girl said in a sweet and silky voice. Gently, she took Van's hand. "This way…" And she led Van to center stage.

Dumbfounded, Van tried to pull herself together, but she felt pretty much immobilized at what had just happened. She ended up staring blankly out at the crowd, registering random facial expressions—everything from glee to fury to total bewilderment.

The former Miss Bronco handed her the winner's massive armful of roses and then helped her juggle them in order to settle the victory sash across Van's cherry-stained Science Is Like Magic—but Real T-shirt.

Carefully, after last year's winner set the crown on her head, Van reached up and straightened her glasses. As she did that, her gaze slid to the John family's table, where Jameson looked troubled. He probably didn't know how to feel about his beautiful, talented sister losing to his one-night stand from New Year's Eve.

His mother looked crushed, and his father shouted angrily, "What's the damn point, I ask you? This is ridiculous. We don't need a Miss Bronco who didn't even bother to compete. How can this be happening when several talented young ladies gave their all for the crown today? And come on, just look at her. Old jeans and a baggy shirt? Look at the expression on her face. She doesn't even want to be up there!"

Vanessa's head spun and her stomach roiled. She drowned in a sea of conflicting emotions. She felt pride at what Cleo, Emma, Mandy and the rest of the girls had accomplished. Yet at the same time, she couldn't help mostly agreeing with Jameson's dad. The write-in rule sucked. Why hadn't she realized that earlier and convinced her Young Adventurers that it had to go?

It wasn't fair. She hadn't competed. She'd never *wanted* to compete. And now she wore the crown that Charity John truly deserved.

Random voices called out, demanding a recount.

Earl tried to shout them down, but they wouldn't be silenced until the volunteers counted every ballot for a second time right there on the stage. As they re-tallied every vote, Van, the ten actual contestants, the mayor, Earl and the former Miss Bronco stood up there and waited.

That process seemed to last forever and a day. Vanessa spent most of the recount clutching her roses while secretly rooting for the agonizing process to end her unexpected reign before it could really begin.

She did not get her wish. Somehow, her Young Adventurers had convinced a clear majority of voters to write in her name—all without anyone telling Van what they were up to.

When the mayor declared Van the winner—again—most of the crowd applauded with enthusiasm, after which the mayor invited her to say a few words.

A speech? He had to be kidding her.

But he wasn't.

She pulled it together, praising the skill and heart

of the ten real contestants and thanking the people of Bronco, especially her brilliant, resourceful Young Adventurers. Almost all the spectators actually applauded when she finished, so she supposed her impromptu acceptance speech hadn't been *that* bad.

At last, Earl Tillson took over again. He thanked everyone for coming and reminded them to get their tickets for the rodeo tomorrow and not to miss the big barbecue on Independence Day or the Favorite Pet Contest July fifth out at Happy Hearts Animal Sanctuary.

He added with enthusiasm, "As all of you are probably aware, our lovely Miss Bronco will be hosting all three events. Be sure to attend, folks. Red, White and Bronco is an important and meaningful town tradition, one none of us can afford to miss."

A last burst of applause followed and finally, the crowd began to disperse.

Van remembered her manners and thanked Earl, the previous Miss Bronco and the other contestants. Before she could make her escape, a woman slipped out from between the curtains at the rear of the stage, marched straight to Van and introduced herself as Maureen Kelly, pageant coordinator. She took Van's email address and phone number so that she could get in touch with her when necessary.

Maureen promised, "As soon as I finish up here, I'll email you the list of events at which you'll be expected to appear. The list includes your duties at each event, what time you'll need to be there and with whom you should check in when you arrive."

Though Van longed to rip off her crown, tear the

victory sash from her chest, toss the roses over her shoulder and sprint away screaming, she answered politely, "Thank you so much, Maureen."

When Van finally escaped the stage, Callie, Evan, Daphne and the still-excited Young Adventurers met Van at the foot of the steps. They surrounded her with hugs and congratulations. Evan suggested pizza for all, his treat. Not all the girls could come, but the ringleaders' parents gave permission. They went to Bronco Brick Oven Pizza and claimed a big table.

The girls were still flying high with the success of their campaign to transform the Miss Bronco beauty pageant. They kept offering toasts, raising their draft root beers high. Van tried to keep a positive attitude in order not to bring her day campers down.

She waited until she and Callie got home alone to let her true feelings show.

"This is awful," she moaned, bracing her elbows on the kitchen table and burying her face in her hands.

Callie scooted her chair closer, wrapped an arm around Van's shoulders and gave her a side hug. "It will be fine," she soothed.

"Fine? There are *events*," Van cried. "Starting tomorrow with the big rodeo out at the fairgrounds. I'm supposed to greet people and make introductions and walk around the arena smiling till my face breaks, doing the fancy pageant wave." She pulled out her phone and checked her email, opening the big file from the pageant director. "Fifty pages here on where I need to be—*appropriately* dressed, wearing my sash and crown or a flashy hat—for every event I'll be hosting and/or attending within the next year. I'm even cutting the ribbon at the end of the month when they open the remodeled convention center. They want me to give a speech for that, to talk about change and growth and the power of working together in our community."

Callie side hugged her a little tighter. "How about if you just breathe deep and take it one step at a time?"

"One step? But there are so many steps. How am I going to be Miss Bronco all year from Billings? Not to mention, being a beauty queen is completely not me. I just keep thinking I need to resign and let Charity take the crown. No one can argue that she wants and deserves to win."

Callie rubbed Van's back and asked gently, "You really think you can do that to your girls at Young Adventurers?"

Van groaned. "Oh God, no. But why didn't they warn me? Why didn't they at least give me a chance to explain all the reasons that writing me in was a bad, bad idea?"

"Well, because they wanted you to win and they weren't taking any chances you might say no, that's why. But you're right that they shouldn't have added the write-in rule. It's not fair that someone who didn't even enter can beat out contestants who got up there and gave their all for a chance to win."

"Exactly."

"The good news is I'm betting we can find a way to change that rule for next year."

"Next year? What about right now? I'm not beauty queen material. Never have been, never *wanted* to be."

"Van. You're beautiful and smart and not the least bit shy. You're a teacher. You know how to get up in front of people and make yourself heard."

"It's not the same."

"Yeah, it kind of is. You're just not giving yourself enough credit."

"Oh, trust me. When it comes to the beauty queen thing, I don't *want* any credit. It's not who I—" A knock at the door cut her off before she could really get her rant on. "What now? Are we expecting someone?"

With a shrug, Callie pushed back her chair and went down the entry hallway to the door. She must have peered through the peephole. A moment later, she darted back into sight. "It's Charity," she whispered. "And her hot brother Jameson is with her."

Jameson. Van's silly heart pounded too fast. She did not need more time around her annoyingly unforgettable one-night stand. As for Charity, Van wouldn't mind a word or two with Jameson's sister. She could smooth things over, at least, confess how crappy she felt about the way things had turned out today.

"Up to you," Callie said.

"Go ahead. Let them in."

"Good choice," Callie said with a nod. She turned and disappeared down the hall again. Van heard her open the door. "Charity." Callie's voice was warm, welcoming. "Jameson. Hello. Come on in, you two."

Van jumped to her feet as Charity and her brother emerged from the narrow hallway. "Hey."

Charity, so pretty and pulled together in dressy jeans and a lavender top, shifted the giant pink binder she carried to her right hand and took hold of Jameson's arm with her left. "I had to come. I had to see how you're doing." She glanced up at her big brother. "I dragged Jameson along for moral support."

Jameson patted his sister's hand and then removed his hat. "Happy to help any way I can."

Oh, I'll just bet you are. Van kept her expression calm as she met his gleaming blue eyes. "How thoughtful of you." She kind of wanted to scream. But she didn't.

Callie gestured at the table. "Sit down, everyone. Please."

Charity sat on Van's left. Jameson hooked his hat on the back of the chair to Van's right and sat there. Callie took the last seat, the one across from Van.

Charity set her huge pink binder in front of her and gave it a little push toward the center of the table. Then she leaned closer to Van. "I just needed to see if you're all right. You looked so shocked today—I mean, you handled yourself really well, but still. I could see that you'd been taken completely by surprise."

Van looked in those blue eyes so much like Jameson's and felt humbled. "Wait. You're worried about *me*?"

Charity put her slim hand over Van's. "Of course. It's a big job being Miss Bronco, and it's not as if you applied for the position."

"I, well, you're right about that. And I…" Okay, so maybe Charity had an ulterior motive here. She'd come to suggest that Van step down, leaving Charity to accept the crown she should have had in the first place.

Nothing wrong with that. In fact, it sounded like the perfect outcome for Van, too. "Okay, here's the deal. I had no idea that this would happen, and I can't help thinking my best move now is to step down and let you claim the crown you so completely deserve."

Across the table, Callie stiffened. Van knew her friend worried how the Young Adventurers would react to such a decision, but Callie also knew it wasn't her choice to make. She kept her mouth shut.

Too bad Charity didn't. "No! Vanessa, you can't."

Van blinked. "Huh? But I thought—"

Charity shook her head. Her thick, golden curls shifted and shimmered like a river of silk. "I mean it. You can't. True, it didn't go the way we expected it would. I was shocked, too. I really thought it was finally my year."

"Because you deserve to win."

"No." Charity sat up straighter. "That's just not so. A lot of people wrote your name on their ballots. You are the chosen Miss Bronco, and the truth is I'm just…not." She grabbed Vanessa's hand and stared deep in her eyes. "It's your job, your *duty* to rise to the occasion."

"But I don't even live here anymore."

"You're a Bronco girl and everyone knows it—and it's okay, Vanessa." She added, with feeling, "I promise you it's all going to work out. Because I'm going to help you—and I know, I know. Jameson mentioned that you live in Billings now. But really, Billings is not *that* far away."

"Jameson mentioned that, did he?" She slanted a

dark glance at the maddeningly hot man on her other side. In return, he gave her a slow, knowing smile. Across the table, Callie watched them much too closely.

Charity demanded, "Did you get your schedule from Maureen?"

Confused, Van turned to Charity again. "Uh, Maureen?"

"The pageant coordinator."

"Oh. Yes. I did." She tried not to scowl. "All fifty pages of it."

"Have you had a chance to look it over yet?"

"Well, I…"

"When you do, you'll notice that the Miss Bronco events after summertime are few and far between. It's all going to be workable. You'll see. I know what I'm talking about. I've been doing this every year since I was sixteen. And I'm going to teach you everything you need to know."

Wait! No! she wanted to shout.

But she knew she couldn't. Charity was right, damn it. And the pretty blonde's passion and enthusiasm for the tradition of Miss Bronco made Van want to grab her in a great big hug—so she did.

Charity hugged her right back.

And then Callie broke out the snacks and cold drinks. Charity opened her giant pink binder, which turned out to be her own personal planner, a blueprint for Miss Bronco success.

For the next two hours, the four of them munched Cheez-Its and trail mix as Charity guided Van through everything from what to wear for her upcoming appearances to the main points she should hit when speaking at various gatherings. Van kept her focus on the job at hand—mostly.

Yet she couldn't forget who sat on her other side. More than once, she got distracted by his low, sexy chuckle. She would shoot him a furtive glance and then have trouble looking away again. When Charity asked for her phone number, she gave it and then couldn't stop herself from sliding another look at her top-secret lover from TNTNH. That steady gaze of his was as compelling as ever. And those lips she'd loved kissing way too much twitched at the corners with a hint of a grin. She knew his thoughts exactly—she'd insisted no numbers would ever be exchanged but he'd gotten her digits, after all.

"Come on." Charity took her hand. "Take me to your room. Let's decide what you're wearing tomorrow."

It felt weird, to leave Jameson and Callie alone. Callie had a look like she might go a little bit rogue and press for answers to questions Van didn't want her asking.

But Charity gave a tug and Van found herself up out of her chair, following Jameson's sister down the hall to the second bedroom. They weren't in there long. She showed Charity a pair of red jeans, her best boots and couple of dressy Western shirts she'd brought with her from Billings. Charity chose the blue one with the white trim and silver stitching, declaring that the silver thread would really pop with her rhinestone crown.

"Me, in a crown." Van shook her head, readjusted

her glasses and grinned. "Never thought I'd see the day."

Charity beamed. "You're going to look fantastic. You need to be at the fairgrounds at 1:00 p.m., right? I'll be here at noon to do a final wardrobe and hair check, and then we'll ride to the fairgrounds together."

Tomorrow was Saturday. Weekends Daphne welcomed any and all Young Adventurers to Happy Hearts. Van didn't teach classes on weekends. But on Saturday, as a rule, she dropped by for morning coffee with Daphne and Evan, after which she would stay and help out if Daphne needed her.

"Noon works," she said. She could easily stop in at Happy Hearts, work for an hour or two at whatever chores needed doing, and still have time to pull herself together for her "wardrobe check."

As she led Charity back to the main room, she could hear Callie talking about her job with Evan at Bronco Ghost Tours. "He's a taskmaster, Van's brother. But in a good way. I like the work. Never a dull moment when ghosts are involved." Callie laughed. "And did you hear? Van and Evan's great-grandmother, Winona, has opened a shop right there with us on the premises. She's billing herself as sort of a cross been a life coach and a psychic. If you need guidance or advice, Winona can help."

"You're telling me that *the* Winona Cobbs has a psychic shop at Bronco Ghost Tours?"

"Essentially, yes," Callie replied, as Van and Charity rejoined them at the table. "She moved to Bronco from up in Rust Creek Falls after meeting Van and her family down here. Did you hear that it turned out Van's grandma Dorothea is Winona's long-lost daughter?"

"Wow," said Charity.

Jameson slid Van a knowing look. "I did hear that, yes."

"Anyway, Winona is very wise," Callie said. "She really does give great advice." She asked Jameson, "You've heard of 'Wisdom by Winona'?"

"Of course. That column was syndicated. I was a fan back in the day."

"You should come by, check it out."

"I just might." He looked straight at Van then, a lazy sort of look, intimate and smoldering. "Never hurts to get some good advice about all the important things. Money. Love. Whether or not all my secret dreams will ever come true…"

Charity, completely oblivious to her brother's real agenda, picked up her pink binder and chirped brightly, "Okay, then. Tomorrow. Right here at noon."

"I'll be here," Van promised.

Charity aimed her dazzling smile at her brother. "Jameson, you ready?"

"You bet." He unfolded his long, strong frame from the kitchen chair, grabbed his hat and followed his sister to the door. "Nice to see you, Callie," he said as they went out. "Vanessa." He gave her another one of those scorching-hot looks. Her hormones cried out at all the months of unfulfilled longing. "It's been a pleasure."

She pasted on a smile, muttered, "'Bye, now," and quickly shut the door.

* * *

The next morning, Van found Daphne alone at the kitchen table in the Happy Hearts farmhouse, her sweet yellow Lab, Barkley, snoozing at her feet.

"Where's Evan?" Van headed straight for the coffee maker. Though Daphne usually drank tea, she had coffee ready for anyone who wanted it.

Daphne worked a bit of hay out of her haphazard ponytail. She always rose before the crack of dawn and went out to look after the animals first. Tea and breakfast came later. "Winona summoned him. She needed some help moving things around out at her shop. It seems the spirits have their own specific requirements concerning what has to go where."

"Feng shui matters, in this world or the next."

Daphne nodded. "Apparently so."

Van smiled at the idea of her often-gruff big brother rushing to do Winona's bidding. "He can be such a tough guy, that fiancé of yours, but he's good to his great-grandma."

"Yes, he is. Hungry?"

"I ate with Callie, thanks." Van took her usual chair at the table. Barkley got up, came over for a scratch behind the ear and then settled back down next to Daphne. "So what's going on at Happy Hearts today?"

"You know, I'm almost afraid to say it out loud, but we're actually pretty much on top of things—for the moment, anyway. As we speak, there are ten young, hardworking volunteers outside mucking stalls, feeding the goats and cleaning out the cat barn." Yep. Happy

Hearts had a whole barn where the cats and kittens lived.

Van felt relieved. "Glad to hear everything's under control. I can't stay that long today. I have to head back to Callie's by ten thirty or so to get ready for the rodeo this afternoon."

"That's right." Daphne set down her mug. "Miss Bronco will be making an appearance."

"Oh yes, she will—and is it weird that we're talking about her in the third person?"

Daphne snickered, "You mean, given that she's you?"

"Exactly. Who knew *that* would happen? Oh, guess who came to see me yesterday evening."

"Not a clue."

"Charity John." Van brought her future sister-in-law up to speed on her visit from Charity and Jameson, taking care to mention Jameson only as an afterthought, keeping the focus strictly on Charity's kindness and generosity. "I really like her," Van added. "She's not only a truly good person who's willing to help me get Miss Bronco right, but she's also given me a whole new appreciation for the, er, Miss Bronco tradition."

"More people should be like Charity." Daphne frowned into her empty mug. When she glanced up again, Van saw shadows in her blue eyes. Daphne had something weighing on her mind. "I think I need one more cup," she said. "You?"

"Please." Van waited until Daphne had fixed herself more tea and refilled Van's mug to ask, "What is it? What's wrong?"

Daphne puffed out her cheeks with a heavy breath. "I wish more people were like Charity John. But they're not. Some get so set in their ways they can't accept any kind of change at all. And some are just so entitled. Yesterday, when you won the crown, there was some grumbling about how you hadn't even entered, and you didn't deserve to be Miss Bronco."

"I heard some of that. Randall John shouted it right out." She shrugged. "You have to admit, he kind of has a point."

Daphne gave her a sideways look. "So you're not upset about that stuff?"

"No, I'm not. I *didn't* enter. It's completely logical that some people would be pissed off about that. For a half second or so, I even considered stepping down."

Daphne gasped. "What? No! Don't do that."

"Don't worry, I'm not. All the Bronco old guard will have to get over themselves. I've got Charity on my side, and all my Young Adventurers are looking to me to stand up and be counted for fairness and change."

"Excellent. That's what I needed to hear." Somehow, as Daphne spoke, she visibly deflated until, once again, she stared down into her fresh cup of tea. "I do love your attitude. I love it a lot." She sounded downright sad.

Van reached over and squeezed Daphne's arm. "What has gotten you down?"

"You don't need to hear it." Daphne stared into the cup some more, her expression glum.

"If you need to say it, I need to hear it. This isn't really about the pageant, is it?"

Daphne glanced up. She wrinkled her pretty nose. "It's just my dad. It never ends with him."

"Wait a minute. Your dad? I thought everything had worked out between you and him."

Daphne pushed her cup away. "Not exactly…" Cornelius Taylor did not in any way approve of her vegetarianism *or* that she'd created Happy Hearts, where, her father claimed, she made "pets out of livestock."

"Daphne, are you trying to tell me that you and your dad didn't reconcile, after all?"

"Back at Christmas, I felt we were doing better with each other, kind of easing our way onto the same page. But the good feelings didn't last. He just doesn't approve of me and it shows. Things have really been going downhill between us again lately."

"What happened, exactly?"

"Well, for instance, last night, after the pageant, Evan and I went out to the ranch for a family barbecue. My dad got all over me for not eating the ribs and started in about what a laughingstock I've made of him with Happy Hearts."

Van wrapped a comforting arm across Daphne's shoulders. "That's just wrong. What is the matter with him?"

"I don't know. The down stroke is we're right back where we started, as far as I'm concerned. I'm not giving up Happy Hearts, and I'm never eating animal flesh."

"Of course you're not."

"Yeah, well, my dad just refuses to accept that. At this point, I'm not even sure he's going to come to our wedding." She and Evan were getting married in October.

Van took Daphne's hand and wrapped both of hers around it. "Hey. He's your dad and he loves you. One way or another, he's going to be there to walk you down the aisle."

Daphne's smile didn't reach her eyes. "That's pretty much what Evan said."

"Because it's true."

"Yeah, it's true to you and Evan because of how you grew up. Things were different for me."

"What are you talking about? We had problems with our father, too. Big ones. Our dad deserted us. He walked out and never looked back." He'd also taken every cent the family owned right along with him.

"It was awful, what your dad did. But I'm not talking about him. I'm talking about your mom and your grandmother. They would walk through fire for you. And now you have Winona, and she is amazing, too. On the other hand, my mother's remarried."

"And lives in Billings, right?"

"That's right. I hardly see her anymore. My first stepmother is long gone. As for my current stepmother, well, at least Jessica tries. We get along well enough, though I wouldn't say we're close. I love my brothers, but they can be as bullheaded as my dad. Sometimes I feel like a cuckoo hatched in a nest of eagles."

Van couldn't bear the pain on Daphne's face. "No. Uh-uh. Come here." She reached out again. Daphne kind of fell toward her. They hugged between their chairs. Down on the floor, Barkley whined at them in doggy sympathy.

As Van rubbed Daphne's back and whispered words of comfort and understanding, she found herself thinking how right Daphne was about Van's family. Life hadn't always been easy in the small house on West Street where her mom had been forced to move after her dad ran off with all their savings. Yet somehow, they'd scraped by. Never once in all the years in that little house had Van lacked for love or understanding.

Too bad her mom and Grandma Daisy disagreed with her decision to make her life in Billings. They both wanted her to find happiness in Bronco. As for Great-Grandmother Winona, she'd made it more than clear that she agreed with them.

Well, too bad. Not going to happen. Nine years ago, when Van left for college with her heart shattered and her pride in tatters, she'd made herself a promise never to move back. She'd had enough of her hometown, of mean girls who mocked her, of the boy who'd once said he would love her forever—and then made her into an object of ridicule, hatred and derision at Bronco High. She would return to visit the people she loved, but never to stay.

Then again, though her mom and grandmother—and now, her newly found great-grandmother, too—disagreed with her choices, they loved her unconditionally anyway. They would never treat her callously, the way Cornelius did Daphne. As she held Daphne and whispered reassurances that everything would work out with her dad in the end, Van felt gratitude welling toward the two strong women who had raised her, the grandfather she missed every day and the big brother who could be gruff and bossy but always had her back.

And toward Winona, with her generous heart, her ingrained kindness, and the weird and wonderful wisdom she was only too eager to share with everyone she met.

A half an hour later, as Van drove back to the apartment, she tried really hard not to wonder if Jameson would show up with Charity. "He'd better not," she muttered under her breath to no one in particular. Scowling out the windshield at the bright, sunny day, she staunchly ignored the anticipation in her heart and the silly, fluttery sensation in her belly.

CHAPTER FOUR

CHARITY, LOOKING GORGEOUS in dark-wash jeans and a blue shirt with rhinestones glittering on the collar, arrived at Callie's right on time. She'd pinned her blond hair into a perfectly tousled updo, carried a small suitcase under her arm—and had Jameson in tow.

"Gotta support my little sis." Faking an innocent expression, he looked right at Van.

Charity patted his sculpted jaw with its perfectly trimmed short beard. "You are my favorite big brother."

He grinned down at her. "I've heard you say the same thing to both Dawson and Maddox."

Charity let out a peal of happy laughter. "Busted." She turned to Van and Callie. "I got super lucky in the big-brother department. Now let's get to work. Callie and Jameson, make yourselves comfortable out here. Vanessa, lead me to your makeup area."

Van had her own bathroom right next to her bedroom. She took Charity in there. The dinky counter had just enough space for Charity's small suitcase, which turned out to be a professional makeup kit, the kind that opened out, accordion-style, into tiers. The kit contained over a hundred different eye shadow choices, a wide array of makeup brushes and foundation colors to match any skin tone.

Once Charity had her kit arranged to her liking, she whipped out a white cloth and draped it over Van's shirt. "Don't look so horrified. This isn't a makeover."

Van glanced heavenward. "Thank you, Lord, for small favors."

"As your personal Miss Bronco coach, I'm all about you doing you, Vanessa."

"And I like that. A lot."

"I'm only going to enhance your natural beauty." Charity frowned and accused, "You've covered your freckles—or most of them, anyway."

"Sometimes I like them, and sometimes they annoy me."

"And this is one of those days when you're annoyed with them?"

"Pretty much, yeah."

Charity peered closer. "Are you wearing contacts?"

"I am." Van pointed her thumb at her chest. "Beauty queen here—not that I don't love my glasses. I do. But they're one accessory too many once I add my crown."

"Yes, I think you're right." Humming under her breath, Charity went to work with her fancy brushes and endless pots of blush, lip color and eye shadow. Not ten minutes later, she took a step back. "There. Perfect."

Van peered at her reflection. She didn't look made up, but her eyes appeared larger and her skin had a new glow. "It's great."

"And so simple." Charity ran down a quick makeup tutorial tailored to Van's coloring, skin type and the shape of her face. She insisted that Van keep the brushes and makeup she'd used. "Tomorrow, you can do it yourself. I'll stop by again before the big barbecue just to give you my seal of approval."

"Charity, you're a wonder."

Charity's glowing smile shone all the brighter. "Why, thank you, Vanessa." Next, she primped Van's hair. "Where's your crown and sash?"

Van gave her a slow look from under her eyelashes. "You know, the more I think about it, the more I think I'll just pass on those today."

Charity wasn't having that. "We both know you can't do that—well, maybe you can skip the crown. That's more for formal occasions. And as it happens, I brought over a few pretty hats just in case. You can wear one of them."

"Do you always come prepared for any eventuality?"

"I try." Charity put on a stern expression. "But you're wearing your sash. Don't try to get out of it."

Van fluttered her eyelashes. "I wouldn't dream of it."

Jameson whistled in appreciation when Charity led Van back out to the main room. "Miss Bronco," he said, "you're even more beautiful than before."

Was he wearing her down with the hot looks, the flattery and the teasing?

Well, maybe a little. He was always so charming,

the very definition of irresistible. No matter how often she reminded herself that she needed distance from the man, a certain rebellious streak deep in her heart couldn't help looking forward to the next time she might see him.

She desperately wished she could actually forget The Night That Never Happened.

"Your sister knows her way around a makeup kit," Van said.

Charity seemed pleased. "A few enhancements never hurt. Now let's get going."

"Plenty of room in my truck," Jameson said. "We can all ride together."

Forbidden images of their night together dancing in her head, Van nipped his suggestion firmly in the bud. "Callie and I will follow you two."

Charity grabbed her hand. "First, we need to choose your hat." The four of them left the apartment and gathered around Jameson's big, black quad cab, from which Charity produced three gorgeous spangled hats. She tossed two of them back onto the rear seat and held up the third. It was snowy white with an actual tiara sewn on above the brim.

"This one," she declared. "It's a crown and a hat at the same time." She placed it at a jaunty angle on Van's head. "Perfect." Charity primped a couple of Van's loose, dark curls in a proprietary manner. Really, Van thought, Jameson's sister was a sheer delight. "You have your sash?" Charity demanded.

Nodding resignedly, Van held it up.

"All right, then," said Charity. "We're ready to go."

* * *

Jameson felt more than a little disappointed that Vanessa gave him zero chance to persuade her to ride with him. Instead, he had to watch her follow Callie past her silver Subaru to an olive-green Jeep. Vanessa took the passenger side and Callie slid in behind the wheel.

"Well?" asked his bossy little sister. "Are we standing here in the parking lot all day for some reason?"

He turned and chucked her under the chin. "Get in and let's go."

The Bronco fairgrounds consisted of a giant, open, graded field on rolling land not far outside town. Both Jameson and Callie found spots in the main parking lot, but he knew that by the end of the day, trucks and SUVs would fill the overflow lot farther out.

Jameson had planned ahead and bought plenty of tickets two weeks before, enough for his whole family and then some. He gave Vanessa and Callie two of the extras so none of them had to wait in line to get them. Once they were through the gate, Charity led Vanessa off to take care of Miss Bronco business. He and Callie climbed the stands to claim enough space for four in one of the rows of benches.

"There they are." Callie pointed into the arena, where Vanessa was shaking hands with a tall, powerfully built cowboy. Even from up on the stands, that cowboy looked a whole lot like the guy who played the lead role in the *Creed* movies. "That's Geoff Burris, isn't it?" Callie asked.

"The one and only." Burris, Bronco born and raised, was currently setting the rodeo circuit on fire. Women loved the guy. Jameson sat forward. He watched Vanessa closely for any sign that she found Geoff as fascinating as everyone else did. He relaxed a little when he saw her smile. It was friendly and easy, that smile—with none of the heat he felt when she looked at *him*. Now, if he could just get her to admit that their one night had not been anywhere close to enough...

Callie said, "I heard we might get the Mistletoe Rodeo right here in Bronco, at the convention center in November. I also heard that Geoff is a big part of why that might happen."

Jameson nodded, his eyes on the action down below. A couple of the clowns led out a white mare with a thick white mane and tail to match. They gave Van a boost into the saddle. "It never hurts," Jameson said, "when a homegrown cowboy grows up to be a rodeo champion. Hey, I didn't know Vanessa could ride."

Callie shrugged. "Looks that way to me."

Earl Tillson, apparently the official announcer for all the Red, White and Bronco events this year, introduced the new Miss Bronco. Waving and flashing her pearly whites, Vanessa rode the mare around the arena. God, she was gorgeous—and already coming into her own as a special kind of beauty queen, one with attitude and sass and her own personal style.

By then, the stands were full. The roar of applause, whistles and stomping feet filled the air. One or two yahoos booed. Jameson stiffened and started to rise.

Callie reached across the two spaces they were saving and grabbed his arm. "Easy, cowboy. Some people are still upset about Van's surprise win. Let them blow off a little steam."

Scowling, he stayed in his seat and muttered, "They kick up much more sand, I'm dealing with them."

"So…" Callie drew out the word. "What's really happening between you two?"

He grunted. "Me and Geoff Burris? Not a thing."

"Har-har. You and Van. She claims there's nothing, but she and I have gotten real close the last month or so. I can read her, and I see the way you look at her. There's something."

"No clue what you're talkin' about, Callie."

"You know you're fooling no one, right?"

He pretended not to hear that and kept his focus on Vanessa as she finished her circle of the arena and dismounted. One of the clowns led the mare away. His sister joined Vanessa. Charity had already spotted him and Callie. She said something to Vanessa, who nodded. They left the arena.

A few minutes later, they sidled their way along the row toward Jameson and Callie, Charity in the lead, which worked out great. Charity stepped past him and took the seat next to Callie, leaving an empty space with Charity on one side and Jameson on the other. He scooted close to his sister, which left Vanessa the empty space on his other side.

She sat. The rhinestones on her hat caught the afternoon sun and glittered. He wanted to grab her and kiss her.

Of course, he did no such thing. But he did lean her way until his arm brushed hers and the scent of her tempted him. "You looked great out there. Didn't know you could ride."

"You'd be surprised at the things I know."

"I have no doubt of that."

She met his eyes then, a hint of a smile curving those lush lips of hers. "It's true I grew up in a split-level on West Street. But back in my teens, I used to work summers out at the Ambling A, saving up for college and to earn spending money. I mucked stalls and fed pigs. That old guy, the cook, Malone?"

Everybody knew Malone. And Malone seemed to know everyone's secrets. "I know Malone."

"Well, Malone said it was a damn crime, a Bronco girl who didn't ride. He kind of made it his mission to teach me."

Charity bumped his arm. He frowned at her. "What?"

"Callie has to go."

Vanessa's roommate held up her phone. "Guys, sorry. Text from Evan. He needs me immediately to make a few emergency tweaks to the tour route for tonight."

"He *always* needs you immediately," Vanessa grumbled.

"What can I say? I'm indispensable." Callie was smiling. If Evan Cruise made her work too hard, at least she seemed to enjoy the job.

"I've made my appearance," said Vanessa. "I'll go with—"

"You can't!" Charity cut her off before Jameson could do it. "Miss Bronco never walks out on the Red,

White and Bronco rodeo. We'll take you home—right, Jameson?"

He hid his satisfied smile. "Of course."

"Well, I—"

"Stay." Charity reached across Jameson to pat Vanessa's knee as Callie said goodbye and headed off down the row away from them.

Jameson leaned into his favorite brunette again. "Hungry?"

Of course, his sister answered before Vanessa could say a word. "Yes! I'm dying for a Coke. Get us both a pop and a hot dog, won't you, Jameson—and popcorn, too?"

He asked Vanessa, "That sound all right to you?"

She looked at him, her gaze straying to his mouth, then snapping back up again. "Thank you."

"Anytime." He would fetch and carry a thousand hot dogs, bring her kegs full of pop just to get her to look at him the way she was right now—like she couldn't help wanting to kiss him again.

She fished some bills from a pocket and held them out.

He slowly shook his head.

"I like to pay my own way," she said.

"I've got it, no problem." He held her dark gaze, thinking how good it felt every time he stared into her big brown eyes.

Finally, she gave in and stuck the bills back in her pocket.

Only then did he rise. "'Scuse me." She slanted her

knees to the side, and he headed off toward the nearest concession booth.

It took a while. When he returned, Vanessa and Charity were whispering together, leaning over the empty seat they'd saved for him. As soon as he reached them, Vanessa scooted closer to Charity, as though his little sister might save her from his bad self.

Hiding a grin, he dropped down beside her and passed out the treats. On the dirt down below, bareback riding and steer wrestling had come and gone. And just after Earl Tillson announced team roping, some smart-ass a few rows back spoke too loudly for his own damn good. "Hey, look. That's the fake Miss Bronco right there."

"Yeah," said some other fool, as Jameson slid his hot dog and root beer under his seat. "Where does she get off, stealing the crown like she thinks she's got a right?"

Charity, Coke in one hand, hot dog in the other, started to stand to confront them.

Jameson reached behind Vanessa to clasp her shoulder. "I'll take care of them," he said quietly. "Be right back."

"Wait—" Vanessa tried to stop him. Too bad she had both hands full.

And he was already on his feet, mounting the benches, striding straight up between seated spectators, scattering "'Scuse mes" as he went.

The two troublemakers, both of whom Jameson recognized as local kids a year or two younger than Charity, snickered as he reached their row. One of them sneered, "What's your problem, man?"

"Gentlemen," Jameson replied in an even tone. "The way I see it, we have two options at this point. You apologize to the rightfully chosen Miss Bronco here and now. Or you and me head on out to the parking lot where we can avoid blocking anyone's view of the hardworking cowboys down in the dirt and discuss this unfortunate situation at length." By then, both trouble-makers were looking a tad worried.

"Apologize, you fools," growled a middle-aged man down the row.

The skinnier of the two kids sent a glare at the older man and jumped to his feet. Sticking out his scrawny chest, he blustered, "Bring it!"

The other kid frowned, but he did get up.

Jameson led them out to the aisle and down to the ground. He was halfway to one of the side exits when he heard frantic whispering behind him. Counting silently to himself, he kept walking.

Five seconds elapsed before he heard two sets of boots take off at a run. Jameson turned to watch them flee—through the nearby exit and into the parking lot. He considered giving chase but figured the two had embarrassed themselves enough for one day. He headed back up into the stands again.

"Everything okay?" Charity asked when he sat down.

"Just fine. I think those two boys must've left the gas on at home. They ran off before we had a chance to communicate."

Charity chuckled. "I remember them from high school. All hat, no cattle."

Down below, a roper flanked and tied—smooth, clean and fast. The stands erupted in applause, the two troublemaking young fools long forgotten.

By everyone but Vanessa. She leaned close. "I am a schoolteacher, you know. I could've handled those two kids."

That gave him another perfect opportunity to look into those deep, dark eyes again. "I know you could. But I see no reason why you have to fight every battle all on your own."

The next hour and a half passed too quickly. To no one's surprise, Geoff Burris triumphed, taking home a fine purse and the coveted Red, White and Bronco belt buckle. As they got up to go, Jameson had his mind on how to somehow get rid of his sister and then convince Vanessa to come to dinner with him.

A couple of Charity's girlfriends came bouncing up just as the three of them were almost to the aisle. "Charity, party tonight out at the Kingston Ranch. You've got to come."

Well, didn't that just play right into his hand? Charity beamed him her sweetest smile. "I can get a ride home."

One of the girls batted her eyelashes at him. "I'm driving, Jameson."

"Fine with me. Vanessa and I will manage."

Charity gave Vanessa a sheepish look. "Will you hate me for running off like this?"

Vanessa laughed. "Of course not. You've more than

done your duty as my Miss Bronco coach. Go have some fun. I remember those bonfires. Best time ever."

Charity grabbed Vanessa in a hug, then took her by the shoulders. "Okay, tomorrow's the big barbecue. You need to be there by two. I'll be over at one with extra hats. We can double-check your makeup and wardrobe and I'll answer any last-minute questions you might have. And then we'll ride to the park together."

Vanessa suggested, "I think I can manage on my own if you just want to—"

"Nope." Charity put up a hand to punctuate the word. She brought that hand to her chest. "I'm there. You can count on me."

Vanessa grabbed her in a final hug, and then Charity headed off down the row behind her friends.

"Ready, then?" Jameson asked. Vanessa wore a look he couldn't quite read. Did she plan to insist on hitching a ride with someone else—or maybe calling an Uber? The Uber would take a while. Uber drivers in Bronco were thin on the ground.

Not that it mattered. "We've already been through this. You're riding with me." Was that too damn caveman? He softened the command with, "Please?"

The smile she gave him then had him almost believing he might finally be getting somewhere with her. "I was just thinking about how smoothly you defused the situation with those boys. I should be more appreciative. Thank you for doing that." She said it softly, with what sounded like real admiration.

He tipped his hat to her. "It was my pleasure." He wanted to try his luck, take her hand.

But no. They should talk first. He needed her agreement to change the rules she'd laid down on The Night That Really Did Happen, no matter how hard she tried to pretend it hadn't.

"After you." He gestured for her to go ahead of him to the aisle.

It was a scramble, getting out of the parking lot, with everybody leaving the arena at once. They got in line with all the other vehicles.

Once they were out of the lot, she took off her hat and turned to set it on the back seat with the other ones Charity had brought for her to choose from. They'd turned onto the highway into town when she said, "Is there someplace private we could talk?"

Talk? That sounded promising. Maybe they were finally on the same page. "How about a beer?"

She shot him a glance. "At a bar, you mean?"

"I was thinking maybe DJ's Deluxe." The bar there was gorgeous, and they could move to the main restaurant for a nice dinner after he got her to agree to go out with him, to see where this attraction might take them.

Another quick sideways glance from her. Then, "I was thinking someplace quiet, just you and me. The turnoff to Bushwhacker Creek's coming up. Let's go there."

He had a blanket in back and he knew a couple of pretty spots along that creek. "All right."

A few minutes later, he turned onto a dirt road. Not long after that, at a wide bend in the road, he pulled over and parked.

She didn't wait for him to see to her door but got out

on her own. He refused to take that as a bad sign. Vanessa Cruise was an independent woman, and he liked that about her almost as much as he wished she would give in and let him treat her the way a man ought to treat his woman.

He took the blanket from the toolbox in back. They set out along the road until they came to the trail that descended to creek side. After a nice stroll along the bank, they came to a tree-shaded spot he particularly liked.

"This looks good," he said.

They spread the blanket and sat down. "It's nice here," she said, her gaze on the clear, rushing water.

He studied her profile, admired the graceful slope of her nose and the inviting fullness of those lips of hers. He loved her freckles, the darker ones visible even today, with the sexy Miss Bronco makeup masking them. One rode the apple of her right cheek. He couldn't see that one at the moment, but he knew it was there, waiting to tempt him when she turned her head his way. As for the small constellation of them closer to her mouth on the left side, those he could touch right now with a brush of his fingers—or better yet, the press of his lips, the swipe of his tongue.

If she would let him.

At this point, he couldn't be sure she would, and that had him hesitating to make his move.

She turned to him. There it was, that lone visible freckle on the apple of her cheek. "I can't help thinking that there's still a lot of summer left." Not near enough, if you asked him. "I'm here till the end of August."

He actively held himself back from touching her. It took serious effort, but somehow, he managed it. So far, at least. "A lot can happen in two months."

"Well, I, um…"

"Yeah?"

"Jameson, I think I need to face facts."

"About…?"

"Well, I keep knocking myself out, trying to make myself forget our one night together…"

Hope burned hot in his chest, but he kept his tone light. "And how's that working out for you?"

She blew out her cheeks with a hard breath. "Not well. Today, at the rodeo, it all kind of came clear to me—that you are a good guy and I enjoy your company and…" She seemed to run out of steam.

He leaned in a fraction closer to her and her scent of roses taunted him. "Say it."

"It's just that I think about you." Her thick, dark brows drew together. Was that longing he saw in her eyes?

He gave her words back to her, meaning every one. "I think about *you*. A lot."

And she smiled with a relieved little sigh. "I kind of thought so."

He couldn't resist teasing her. "Did you think I was trying to hide that I can't stop thinking of you?"

"Um, no."

"Good."

"So then…" She gave a tiny cough into her hand, a stall, really, as she braced herself for whatever she'd been working up to saying. "I was thinking today that, if we were to agree to keep things just between us, why shouldn't we have a little fun together until I leave at the end of August?"

He would have pulled her close right then, except for that last line. "Just between us, you said?"

"Yes. I'm not comfortable with taking it public, but I do want to be with you. I want that a lot. So if you're willing to keep the time we spend together private, not let anyone else know we're seeing each other, I would love to go back to your place with you right now."

"You're saying nobody can know that we're spending time together."

"What?" Her low voice had a definite edge to it now. "I didn't make that clear?"

He needed some distance. Jumping to his feet, he swept off his hat, beat it once on his thigh, put it back on and stared out at the creek until he felt he could speak without yelling at her. "Vanessa, what is up with you?"

"I told you at New Year's. I'm not staying in town, and whatever goes on between us is just for fun and just for now."

He turned to look down at her. "Fine. It's only till the end of August. That doesn't mean we can't have dinner together at a decent restaurant like any other single man and woman who are attracted to each other might do."

She got up, too. They faced each other across the empty blanket. Somewhere in the bushes on the far side of the creek, a meadowlark loosed its high, plaintive song.

"I just don't want my family in my business," she

said. "You know how it is around town. If we go out to dinner, people will notice. Word will get back to my mother and my grandmother—and now Winona, too."

"So what?"

"They want me here, at home and happily married. I just don't want them to get their hopes up, that's all."

He'd had enough of the careful distance between them. Stepping onto the blanket, he reached for her hand.

She didn't resist. On the contrary, she came into his arms with a soft, willing sigh. "Vanessa," he whispered into her upturned face, his voice like a growl to his own ears. "You've made me wait too damn long."

She had her soft hands on his chest and her head tipped back at just the right angle. Those beautiful freckles were on full display. "And what am I trying to tell you? I'm saying that you don't have to wait any longer."

He swooped down and took her mouth.

She tasted so good, like all the best things—sweetness and heat, laughter and tenderness. For too long, he'd wondered if those things would ever really be his.

Her right hand strayed upward and wrapped around his neck. He felt her fingers sliding into the hair at his nape, and he took the kiss deeper, gathering her body closer, sense memory firing—the way she felt naked in his arms, strong and so soft, more than enough to grab onto, to *hold* on to. He wanted to take her to the blanket, peel off every stitch of clothing and have her right here, by Bushwhacker Creek, under the late-afternoon sky.

But they still had things to settle between them. He broke the kiss, taking dark satisfaction in her groan of protest as he lifted his mouth from hers. "You don't want your family to get their hopes up about what?"

She gazed at him, her mouth swollen from his kiss, her eyes dreamy and soft. "That I might, um, fall for a local man and, you know, move back home."

He couldn't seem to stop touching her. With the tips of his fingers, he combed the hair back from her temple and asked gently, "I can't believe that they're going to get their hopes up because I take you out to dinner. We all have to eat. Sometimes men and women eat together in a restaurant. It doesn't have to be life changing. It's only dinner. And your mom and your grandma and wise old Winona, they all seem like pretty sharp women to me. They're not going to start planning the wedding just because you're seen around town with me."

She let out a little groan and rested her forehead against his chest. "You're right. I know it." And then she looked up to meet his eyes again. "But I'm not ready to go public with you."

He dropped his arms from around her and stepped back off the blanket. "When, then? When *will* you be ready?"

"I can't answer that. I…" She seemed to catch herself. And then she bit the corner of her lower lip and confessed, "Okay. That's not so. I'm not *ever* going to be ready. I can't do that again. Not now, anyway. Maybe eventually…" She might have used the word *eventually*, but he heard her real meaning in her voice. In this case, *eventually* meant *never going to happen*.

"You can't do what again?"

"Get stars in my eyes. Start thinking that…" Her voice trailed off. She sucked in a deep breath and said, "Jameson, I want to be with you, but it's really not going anywhere beyond the end of August. I don't want to have to talk to my family about how I like you a lot, but it's only for now. I just want you. I want you and I think you want me and I'm willing to be with you for the summer—discreetly."

"Discreetly. You mean in secret, sneaking around so no one will know."

"Fine. Yes. If you want to put it that way."

He wanted to agree to her terms. He wanted that so bad.

But he also wanted a chance for more.

How could he get more if she wouldn't even say yes to dinner at DJ's Deluxe? "No. That's not good enough." Dropping to a crouch, he swiftly rolled up the blanket. "Come on." He rose and tucked the blanket under his arm. "I'll take you home."

CHAPTER FIVE

AFTER JAMESON DROPPED her off at the apartment and drove away without once glancing back, Van found Callie inside at the stove. She'd cued up her favorite country-and-western playlist and she bounced around to Haley Mae Campbell singing "Highway Honey."

"Spaghetti and Italian sausage, anyone?" she asked between verses.

Van longed to grab her and hug her and cry on her shoulder. Instead, she put on a bright face and replied, "Let me wash my hands. I'll cut up the salad."

"I bought a bottle of red."

"We are so livin' large."

"Do the honors and screw off the top? I like my wine to have a chance to breathe."

Twenty minutes later, they sat down to eat.

Callie held up her juice glass of red. "A toast. To you and me and this elegant meal." Van tapped her roomie's glass with hers, and they both drank, after which Callie said, "Whatever it is, you should just tell me. We'll eat our dinner and drink more wine and I will share with you all the wisdom of my twenty-five years."

Van should have known her friend would sense her need to talk. She set down her glass. "It's Jameson."

Callie made a show of widening her big brown eyes. "Shocker."

"As in you're *not* shocked at all?"

"As in when he looks at you—fireworks. And when you look at him? Same. I'm just not getting why you don't follow up on that."

"Long story."

"I understand." Callie's teasing tone had gentled. "A story of three players who broke your heart. And the boring guy you decided to settle for, who ended up dumping you, too."

"Even when you say it kindly, that hurts."

"Am I wrong?"

"No—and that's why it hurts. And just for the record, Donnie Bell really wasn't a player. At least, he didn't start out as one." Somehow, that had made his screwing her over in front of everyone at Bronco High all the worse.

Really, Donnie *was* the worst. He'd hurt her so deeply, cut her right to the core. Because she had loved him with her whole young, naive heart and soul.

A Bronco Valley native who lived down the street from her growing up, Donnie Bell was the love of Van's life—or so she honestly believed at the time. They were BFFs from early childhood. At thirteen, Van realized she loved him as more than a friend. They shared their first kiss that year, in eighth grade. In ninth grade, they declared their undying love for each other. He asked her to marry him sophomore year. She said yes and he slipped a sterling silver promise ring on her trembling finger. They planned a simple ceremony for right after they graduated from Bronco High.

Handsome and kind, Donnie was all hers. He'd always been all hers. At sixteen, she'd believed in his love absolutely. Donnie Bell would be true until death.

But as he grew up, Donnie's body filled out with muscle, and his smooth face became square-jawed and manly. More than just handsome by then, he was a real heartthrob.

Donnie not only proposed to Van sophomore year, he also joined the football team. He became a Friday night hero. Still, he had eyes only for Van.

Until senior year.

By then, more than one of the rich girls from Bronco Heights had set her sights on him. Donnie ignored those girls—at first.

But Maura Flannigan wouldn't give up. She was pretty and popular, and her dad had plenty of money. She went after Donnie with single-minded, unwavering determination. In the end, Donnie let her catch him.

He shattered Van's trust as well as her heart and her love for her hometown. By the time he and Maura and her posse of popular girls were through with her, Van couldn't wait to get out. When she left for college, she'd felt nothing but gladness to be moving on, leaving Bronco behind for good.

Callie brushed her shoulder, a fond touch. "I get it. I do. But after Donnie, you didn't give up, did you? You kept trying."

Oh yes, she had. Through David and Chaz and Trevor.

Callie spun pasta on her fork. "I mean it. You can't give up now. You need to give love a fighting chance." She ate the bite of pasta before concluding, "That's what life's all about."

"Ugh."

"That sound?" Callie put on a reproachful glare. "That sound is not the least encouraging."

Van and Callie had spent more than one evening sharing grisly tales of life in the trenches, romance-wise. What Van hadn't said a word about to her summer roomie–turned–BFF was what had transpired on TNTNH. "I have a confession…"

"I love those." Callie picked up the wine and refilled their glasses. "Continue."

Van told her friend everything—about TNTNH as well as all that had gone down by Bushwhacker Creek earlier that evening.

When she finished, Callie said, "You wild thing, you. There we all were at New Year's, hanging out at Happy Hearts eating vegetarian finger food, toasting Evan and Daphne and their forever love, while you were at Wild Willa's hooking up with Jameson John." She offered a high five and they slapped palms. "Way to go, Cruise. That's how you ring in the New Year, if you hear what I'm sayin'."

"You're right. It was wonderful. And he and I both agreed it was just that one night."

"Please. He likes you. You like him. Step outside your comfort zone and give the man a chance."

"A chance? Didn't I just explain that I offered to be with him for the summer and he turned me down?"

"Because you said you want to sneak around."

"Yes, well, I said I wanted to keep it private, but whatever. He said no. So it's over without ever really even getting started. No way he's going to be coming around looking to try again."

"And yet here you are, missing him already. Because you really like him. And when you really like someone, you reach out and try again. I'll say it one more time. Give the man a chance."

Charity breezed in the door at one the next afternoon looking absolutely beautiful, wearing her usual glowing smile. "It's gorgeous out today. The perfect Independence Day—and, Vanessa, you look fabulous. I like that shirt as much as the one yesterday."

"Thank you." Van tried to ignore the elephant missing from the room. But she couldn't quite do it. "Where's Jameson?"

Charity set her makeup kit on the table. "Oh, one of the fences went down out at the Double J, and a couple of steers got out. He'll deal with that and be along later."

"I see. Well, I hope it all, um, works out."

Charity shrugged. "It's a ranch. Fences are bound to go down now and then."

Van took care not to lock eyes with Callie. Her friend knew way too much now. And Van had no doubt they would be discussing the Jameson situation again at some point.

Just not this afternoon, with his sister in the room. Besides, what more was there to say? Her fantasy of a hot, secret summer romance had ended without ever getting started.

End of story. Nothing to see here. Time to move on.

Charity picked up her makeup kit again. "Let's get to it. This won't take long."

Charity, Van and Callie caravanned to the day's Red, White and Bronco festivities.

At Bronco Park, the barbecue experts from all the local ranching families had their smokers and charcoal grills going. The rich, tempting smells of hickory smoke and seared meat filled the air.

Three of Charity's girlfriends came running up. They wanted her to head over to the row of carnival-style booths on the other side of the barbecue area. The girls couldn't wait to dunk last year's high school football hero off his perch and into a giant tub of icy water.

"Go," Van instructed. "I'm on this. Have fun."

"But I should take you to the pie tables." Charity grabbed her hand. "Come on. I'll introduce you to Mrs. Abernathy and Mrs. Brandt. They're heading up the pie contest committee this year."

"I can see the pie tables from here, and I know both Angela and Mallory. Don't worry. You have taught me well, and I love pie. There is no problem here. Go with your girls. Win a carnival glass bowl or a stuffed giraffe."

Charity hugged her—carefully, so as not to mess up her perfectly arranged hair or knock her red spangled cowboy hat askew. "I'll be back to check on you, just in case you need me…" She was still offering aid and suggestions as her girlfriends dragged her toward the game booths.

"Vanessa! Callie! Over here!" Van glanced toward the sound of her mother's voice. Wanda Cruise waved at them from a picnic table about twenty yards away.

Callie took her arm. "Let's go say hi to your folks."

At the table, Wanda sat with Grandma Daisy and Great-Grandmother Winona. Sean Donohue, Wanda's boyfriend, had come, too. They'd worked together for years, Sean and Van's mom. Shortly before last Christmas, they'd finally come out to the family as a couple. Before that, they'd kept their romantic relationship a secret—which people did now and then for any number of reasons, damn it. Too bad a certain thickheaded rancher refused to see it that way.

"Sit with us," Winona commanded.

Well into her nineties, Winona Cobbs was slender, almost birdlike, with a halo of snow-white hair. She looked frail, and she'd been ill a lot last year when she still lived up north in Rust Creek Falls. Since reuniting with her family, though, Winona had not only miraculously regained perfect health, but she'd also developed a flashy personal style. Today, she wore an electric-green silk shirt and jeans, along with a crystal-bedecked cowboy hat to match.

"You look beautiful, G-G." Van used the pet name she'd chosen a few months before in order not to have to say "Great-Grandmother" all the time. She took the seat next to Winona.

"Thank you, sweetheart." Winona patted Van's knee with her spider-thin, wrinkled hand. "Where's that handsome fella of yours?"

Callie snickered as she slid in on Van's other side. Van shot her a warning glare and turned back to Winona. "G-G, I don't have a fella." Van kept her smile easy and her tone gentle. "I'm a happy single woman, and you know that."

Winona leaned closer, bringing the faint scent of sandalwood and patchouli. Since she'd opened her little fortune-telling enterprise, Winona had switched from light floral perfumes to more earthy essential oils. "Sometimes, sweetheart, you have to lose in order to win."

Van decided not to ask what, exactly, that might mean. A quick change of subject seemed the best way to go. "Where are Evan and Daphne?"

Across the table, her mom shook her head. It was answer enough. From over in the large, open area where the men had the smokers and grills going, Cornelius Taylor let out a loud bray of laughter. Beef was the order of the day, with all the local ranchers competing to win the blue ribbon for Best of Bronco Barbecue. Daphne's dad tended to rule the roost at the Independence Day cook-off—and right now, he and Daphne weren't getting along. Not surprising she'd chosen to sit this one out.

Van's mom had set the table with dishes and flatware she'd brought from home. She'd also brought Tupperware containers full of sides, including fresh, oven-baked rolls. As for the savory main course, barbecue, the family would buy that right here at the park. Wanda, Sean and Grandma Daisy got up together to head for the booths that sold the perfectly cooked meat straight from the smokers.

"Hmm," said Callie. "I think I need to check out the choices while they're still on the grill. Be right back."

Van didn't want to leave Winona all on her own, so she stayed put. G-G regaled her with an update on her new psychic business venture and then sent a meaningful glance toward the barbecue area. "Callie is such a lovely girl…"

"Yes, she is," Van replied with a nod. Over by the smokers and grills, Van's roomie had struck up a conversation with one of the Abernathy men—Tyler, if Van remembered correctly. He'd been a year or two ahead of Van in school. As Van watched, Callie laughed at something Tyler said, her gaze shifting shyly away and then back, her cheeks a little flushed. Cutest thing ever. With Van, Callie was always frank and straightforward. Sometimes Van forgot that her friend had a shy side.

Winona remarked, "Don't those two look good together?"

Van was just about to agree when Tyler's mom, Hannah, appeared at his side. She had a baby in her arms. With a quick nod at Callie, Hannah passed the baby to Tyler. A moment later, Callie turned to go. Tyler stared after her, but Callie didn't look back.

"She really ought to just ask him," Winona said quietly.

Van frowned at her great-grandmother. "Ask him what, G-G?"

But Winona only jumped lightly to her feet. She started taking the covers off the side dishes. A few minutes later, the others, Callie included, returned with clamshell containers of hot, fragrant barbecue.

Van waited for everyone to settle into the meal and start chatting together before asking her friend in a whisper, "So…? Tyler Abernathy, huh?"

Callie leaned in close and answered for Van's ears alone, "I didn't see his wedding ring until his mom handed him his baby girl—whose name is Maeve, by the way. Maeve is nine months old and, as you might have noticed, completely adorable. Just like her mother, I have no doubt."

Van made a sad face. "Sorry, honey."

Callie grabbed another rib from one of the containers in the middle of the table. "At least the food is the best ever."

Earl Tillson jumped to the stage where the band would play later. He stepped up to the mike there. "May I have your attention, ladies and gentlemen. Once again, Red, White and Bronco is giving you the best barbecue in Montana, courtesy of our local ranchers. The entries have been judged and the competition was fierce, and I'm up here right now to give you your winners."

A wave of applause followed.

Earl announced, "In third place, the Double J!" Everybody clapped as Randall John got up to accept the white ribbon. Taylor Beef came in second. Cornelius strutted to the stage to claim the red, his second-born son, Brandon, at his side.

"And in first place, let's have a giant round of applause for…" Earl drew out the moment before shoving a fist in the air and shouting, "Abernathy Meats!"

It wasn't much of a surprise. For as long as Van could remember, the Taylors and the Abernathys inevitably won the top two ribbons. Still, the applause level rose higher than before as Tyler and his handsome brothers broke out in cheers. Their father, Hutch, stepped up to take the blue ribbon.

But not everyone approved of the Abernathy win. At the next table over, Van heard a man mutter, "Right. Once again, it's the Abernathys and Taylors taking first and second place…"

"Surprising exactly no one," groused the woman beside him.

The complaint was picked up and echoed here and there through the park. One of the Dalton boys, Boone, said right out loud it wasn't fair. A distant Abernathy relation shouted at him to pipe down.

Earl Tillson put an end to the barbecue controversy by announcing, "And now, I want to introduce you all again to our one and only Miss Bronco. Vanessa Cruise, get on up here and say hi to the folks!"

"Yippee," she muttered under her breath as she cleaned the barbecue off her hands with a wet wipe. Rising, Van executed a fancy pageant wave at all and sundry. Everyone applauded as she headed for the stage—which was good. Wonderful, even. At least today no one had questioned her claim to the crown or called her "the fake Miss Bronco."

Not so far, anyway.

Up on the stage, Earl stuck the mike in her face, and she said a few words about the superior quality of barbecue produced by Bronco ranchers and how great it was to see everyone out having a fine time on this gorgeous Independence Day.

"Vanessa," Earl spoke into the mike again. "It's my job to ask you the all-important question…"

"Hit me with it, Earl."

"Are you ready to judge twelve tasty pies created with love and skill and tender care by the best bakers in Bronco?"

"Earl, when it comes to pie, I'm always ready."

"And ain't that what we needed to hear, ladies and gentlemen?"

The park erupted in applause, whistles and catcalls.

Earl waited till the ruckus died down a bit to instruct, "Right this way, Vanessa." He led her to the three pushed-together folding tables decked with patriotic bunting, accented with vases of red, white and blue mums, and crowned with a row of absolutely beautiful pies.

Sometimes the duties of a beauty queen sucked. But judging the Red, White and Bronco Fourth of July pie contest almost made it all worthwhile.

Right then, Charity, carrying her own folding chair, appeared on Van's left.

Van sat in the chair Earl held for her and beamed up

at Charity. "Come on, sit right here beside me. Let's get to work."

Such a challenging task, but someone had to do it. Van and Charity took their time tasting each and every pie—some more than once. Just to be sure. They had a great time, laughing together, making a big deal of each offering so that no baker would feel slighted.

A crowd gathered around them, including all the contest entrants and several of Van's Young Adventurers. Everyone laughed and offered suggestions and encouragements as Van and Charity consulted and argued the merits of each pie, with Van always eager to dig right in and take another bite. Charity held her back, reminding her that they had to respect the "physical integrity" of every pie.

"It's important," Charity insisted, "that we don't eat too much of any one pie, in order that enough of every pie remains to take an attractive picture of at least one large and appetizing slice when the winners are declared. You know we'll make the front page of the *Bronco Bulletin*, right?"

Van slung an arm across her favorite runner-up's slim shoulders and leaned close to whisper, "You're not only gorgeous and talented and smart, but you also have way too much integrity, even about pie. I mean, *nobody* has integrity about pie. It's too delicious. We all just want to gobble it right up."

Charity giggled. "I love pie, too." She drew in a big breath and tipped her head at a determined slant. "But we have a job to do here."

And do the job they did, posing with the winners

when Earl announced them. First and second place, a lemon meringue and a spiced apple, respectively, went to women who lived in Bronco Valley. One of the Dalton boys claimed third with a perfectly tart strawberry rhubarb. Each winner got enthusiastic applause, and Van heard not a single muttered complaint about the fairness of the judging.

Was it possible that her detractors were getting used to a girl from Bronco Valley wearing the Miss Bronco crown?

"I think that went well," Charity declared with an approving nod once Earl mounted the stage again to remind everyone of all the fun still to come, including music and dancing and fireworks after dark.

Van grabbed Charity in a hug. "Couldn't have done it without you."

"Yes, you could." Charity hugged her back. "But we sure are a great team."

"Let's face it. We rock."

Right then, Charity's friends ran up to sweep her away.

"Coming," Charity promised them, then turned to Van again. "So. You have the Favorite Pet Contest tomorrow at Happy Hearts. I'll be at your apartment at, say, eleven?"

"Just meet me at Happy Hearts, okay? I have Young Adventurers in the morning. So I'm thinking if you could be there by noonish?" The contest started at one.

"See you at noon, then." With a last quick hug, Charity went off to join her friends.

Van watched Jameson's little sister go, her thoughts

turning bittersweet. She hadn't spotted Jameson once all day. Had he skipped the barbecue because of her?

Though he'd only turned her offer down yesterday, somehow it felt like she'd been missing him for a long time—missing his sexy smile and that devilish look in his eyes, the look that promised things she shouldn't even let herself think about.

Because where could it go, anyway? Yes, she wanted to spend her summer nights with him. But really, wasn't a secret summer fling just asking for trouble? She'd never been any good at casual relationships. Consider TNTNH as an example. She'd finally indulged in a one-night stand—and then spent way too much time afterward trying not to think about the man she'd shared it with.

What made her imagine she'd suddenly become the kind of woman who wouldn't end up getting attached?

One way or another, she always did. And so far, getting attached had only brought her heartbreak in the end.

"Hello, Nessa." The familiar voice came from behind her—and no, it wasn't Jameson's voice, but the voice of the boy she'd once loved to distraction. The voice she'd once thought she would never grow tired of hearing.

How sad, really, that love could turn into ashes, into nothing but an echo of remembered pain. She didn't even want to look at him.

In the nine years since Donnie Bell decimated her heart, she'd come face-to-face with him twice. Both times, just the sight of him had cut her to the core.

The first time, seven years ago, he'd given her a big, phony smile. He'd behaved as though she was just some girl he knew once and hardly remembered anymore. The second time, four years later, he'd bragged to her about how his father-in-law, who owned two car dealerships, had put him in charge of the larger one in Bronco Heights, where they sold the luxury cars.

That second time she'd run into him, he'd worn a fake smile, too. And that time was even worse. That time, the fake smile seemed sleazy and he'd had a certain unacceptable look in his eye. She'd felt sick to her stomach thinking he might try to make a pass or something.

If he'd tried that, she would have kneed him in the family jewels without a second thought. In high school, she'd been a lot more trusting. He'd annihilated her heart and then come back for more. She'd believed him when he said he was sorry, that he'd been so wrong, that he loved *her*, that he couldn't live without her and that he and Maura Flannigan were finished.

Van had forgiven him.

And then he'd betrayed her all over again.

Now, she just wanted not to have to deal with him. She considered her next move—walk away without looking back? Or face him for the third time in all these years?

"I just thought I'd say hi," he said.

Her pride won out. Drawing her shoulders up tall, she turned and met the hazel eyes of the boy she'd once trusted completely, the one who was supposed to be her forever.

Not a boy anymore, Donnie still looked good. A little tired, maybe, but strong and tall and handsome. "Donnie. How are you?"

"Fine." His gaze wandered—down over her body and slowly back up again. "You look beautiful."

She didn't know what to say to that. "What do you want, Donnie?"

A chasm of silence yawned between them. Apparently, he couldn't decide how to answer her question.

Strange how life goes. This time the sight of him brought none of the anguish the mere thought of him used to cause her. And the complete lack of pain she felt at this moment had her realizing that the impossible had finally happened.

She was completely over Donnie Bell. Only an echo of sadness remained.

And that echo? Mostly from the loss of the friendship they'd shared as kids—the two of them a team, a couple of awkward poor kids from Bronco Valley. Kings of West Street, they used to call themselves. They would race their battered secondhand bikes up and down the block, flying so fast they swore no one could catch them.

Down by the narrow creek that ran behind Donnie's house, they'd built a fort of willow branches tied together with strips of bark. In their fort, they would whisper to each other of the things they wanted most. A trip to Disney World and a new bike for him. And for her, a good dad, one who didn't disappear from her life without warning, never to return.

"Just wanted to congratulate you on becoming Miss

Bronco," Donnie said at last, drawing her out of the lost world of memory, plopping her down in the here and now.

"Thanks. It's an all-new experience for me, and I'm pretty much playing it by ear."

"Donnie!" a slender, pretty, harried-looking blonde shouted from maybe thirty feet away. Pushing a toddler in a stroller, with a baby in a sling attached to the front of her and a little girl of maybe seven or so running along beside her, Donnie's wife, Maura, came rushing toward them.

The little girl kept tugging on Maura's arm. "Mommy, pink popcorn. I want the pink popcorn."

Maura shushed her and kept on coming. The toddler in the stroller had started to fuss. As Maura pulled the stroller to a stop next to her husband, the toddler squawked louder.

The little girl turned to her father. "Daddy, can you *please* buy me the pink popcorn!"

"Sure, princess," said Donnie. He stroked a big hand down her fine blond hair. "Just give us a minute here."

"Vanessa," said Maura, bending to stick a binky in the toddler's mouth and then straightening up with a tight little smile. "Congratulations—on the Miss Bronco thing?"

"Thank you."

"A lot of people were beyond stunned when Earl called your name the other day. I mean, you didn't even enter the contest, and you never were exactly the beauty queen type, now were you? But you look great. Have you lost weight?"

Vanessa managed not to roll her eyes. "Maura, *you* haven't changed a bit."

"Yes, well, I try to keep fit—and with these three little broncos, what choice do I have? Being a mom's a big job." She frowned. "But you never even got married, did you?"

"Nope. Still single. Somebody has to have all the fun, right?"

Maura narrowed her sharp eyes, most likely trying to decide whether Van had just insulted her. In the end, she simply scoffed and turned to her husband. "Come on, now. We can't stand here forever. My parents are waiting."

Donnie sent Van the strangest look—a little sad. And way too weary for a man of only twenty-seven. "Good to see you, Nessa."

"'Bye, Donnie." Van watched them walk away, the toddler starting to fuss again, the little girl still demanding pink popcorn. Yeah, she really had loved Donnie once. It was young love, fierce and passionate, the kind of love that feels destined to last forever.

But it hadn't lasted. Donnie had betrayed her. Twice.

And now, for the first time in the years since it all blew apart with him, she found she really wanted to let all the hurt go, get past the memory of the mean girls whispering behind their hands, pointing at her, laughing at first—and later writing rotten things on her locker with red nail polish, calling her the worst sorts of names, tormenting her, putting her through the high school version of hell.

Today, for the first time, she felt she could almost

forgive Donnie's initial betrayal—the one where he showed up one Wednesday morning for advanced biology with his arm around Maura Flannigan after whispering words of love to Van on Tuesday night.

As for his second, more brutal act of treachery, that one still got to her when she let herself think about it. After that second betrayal, she'd stopped being a laughingstock and become the object of outright scorn and hatred. Forgiveness came harder for that.

But it had all happened so long ago. Better to let the hurt go, wish the man well—maybe not for his sake, but for the sake of those three little kids of his. Innocent children needed a loving dad they could count on.

And who was she kidding? No, Van couldn't completely forgive Donnie yet. But she liked to think she was getting there.

For the next few hours, Van sat with her family, enjoying the brownies and coffee she and Callie had bought from one of the booths. Afternoon faded to early evening, and the first star appeared in the clear Montana sky.

Winona leaned close to her. "Make a wish upon a star, sweetheart."

"G-G, haven't you heard? If wishes were rocket ships, we would have settled the far reaches of the galaxy by now."

Winona chuckled, a dry sound, like leaves rustling together high on a mountaintop where few ever go. "Wishes matter. They shape our dreams. And without dreams, how can we foresee what we need to make happen?"

Van leaned close enough to kiss her soft, wrinkled cheek. "That's beautiful, G-G."

"So then, make your wish."

Van gave in. She closed her eyes and let her wish take form. She did it in gratitude for all she had already—her teaching career, which she adored, a family she treasured, who cherished her right back, and good friends like Callie and Charity—and a couple of her girlfriends in Billings, too.

Dear first star, please send me someone to count on, someone I can trust, someone who will never cheat or walk away. Send me a forever sort of man—and yeah, I know it's a lot ask, but it's about time, don't you think?

So shoot her. Her greatest hope had not died completely. Somewhere deep down, she still nurtured the dream that she might find the right man for her.

"There now," said Winona. "Didn't that feel good?"

Van leaned her head on her great-grandmother's thin shoulder. "Oh, maybe a little bit."

Winona gave another dry-leaf chuckle. "You're a tough nut to crack, sweetheart. Oh, look. Here comes that dear girl, Charity, with one of her good-looking big brothers."

Did Van's silly heart leap? It might've. It definitely skipped a beat when she turned and met Jameson's sin-blue eyes.

"See, Vanessa," announced Charity, slipping her arm into the crook of Jameson's elbow. "He did come."

"I see that."

"Welcome, you two," said Winona. "Sit with us," she commanded, "for a few moments, at least."

Charity took the empty space next to Wanda.

Wanda offered her the paper plate with the last three brownies on it. "Help yourself."

"Thank you." Charity chose a brownie and took a bite. "Yummy."

As for the blue-eyed devil named Jameson, he sat next to Van. "Looks like this is the only spot left."

Van dared to look straight at him. Wouldn't you know? She'd wished for a good, steady man who would love her forever, and what did she get? Sheer temptation. Did he *have* to be so hot? "I heard you had some fences down over at the Double J."

That wonderful mouth tipped up at the corners. "A couple of pesky heifers knocked out some posts."

"Wait. Charity told me steers were the problem."

Across the table, Charity chimed in, "I said the steers got loose."

"And they did," Jameson agreed. "But those heifers, *they* were the problem. Dawson saw them headbutting fence posts, like they thought they had horns or something. They're a temperamental pair. We should have culled them early on."

"Don't even think about it." Charity glared at him—but then she grinned. "They're funny, those two. They've got personality."

"If that's what you want to call it," Jameson muttered.

"That is exactly what I call it," Charity replied. "And I do have a say about what happens to them. Wasn't I the one who fed them by hand when both their mamas died in that freak April blizzard?"

Jameson wore an obstinate expression. His eyes, though? They sparkled with humor. They also stayed focused on Van. "Charity calls them Frilly and Dilly."

"That's cute," said Van's mom.

"Thank you, Wanda." Charity's smile was both sweet and smug.

Jameson grunted. "Please. Personality is the last thing a breeder wants in a heifer. A good heifer is docile. Calm. A docile heifer eats better than a skittish animal. They put up with handling. They produce better meat and calmer-natured offspring. Breeding only docile heifers can dramatically improve the general temperament of a herd within just a few years."

Van ventured, "Should I even ask what's going to happen to Frilly and Dilly?"

"Well, I had to put my foot down." Charity scowled at her brother. "Nobody is eating my babies, and that's that."

"They'll be moving to Happy Hearts," said Jameson resignedly. "I called Daphne about it today. First thing tomorrow morning, I'll be trucking them over there."

"I'll miss them," said Charity. "But I'm really grateful to Daphne that she's made a place where heifers with personality can find a loving home."

The talk turned to other subjects. Winona invited everyone out to see her at Wisdom by Winona. She promised support and advice for anything that might be troubling them—no issue too large or too small—at a reasonable fee. Grandma Daisy, an artist who'd once illustrated a famous series of children's stories, shared a couple of funny anecdotes about her favorite students in the art class she taught now at the local senior center.

Jameson sat right there beside Van for a good half hour. She took way too much pleasure in his nearness and tried not to act at all interested in him. That would only get the family on her case. They would start in about how she ought to move home. She didn't need that.

But the clear, cool evening seemed even more beautiful since Charity's big brother had claimed the space at Van's side.

As for Jameson, he seemed happy just hanging out, joining in the easy conversation at the table. And each time Van met his eyes, she felt that secret little thrill shimmer through her.

Too often, love had disappointed her. But attraction? That always felt great. There was nothing so sweet as wanting a guy and knowing that whatever did or didn't happen, he felt the pull, too.

Had he reconsidered the offer she'd made last night?

She couldn't help but hope so.

The shadows lengthened, and nighttime approached. A six-piece local band took the stage over by the portable dance floor erected in the park every year for the barbecue.

Jameson glanced up at the darkening sky. "Time I checked on the folks. Maddox and Dawson can always use another hand loading the cookers."

Charity added, "And there's all the picnic gear to pack up." The two rose to go.

"Thanks for everything." Van gave Charity back her spangled hat.

"Tomorrow," said Charity, settling the hat on her flowing blond curls. "Noon. Happy Hearts."

"Perfect." As Van watched them go, she couldn't help hoping she might see Jameson again that evening.

Meanwhile, Van's mom and grandmother started putting the lids on the Tupperware. Everyone over fifty seemed to think it was time to head home.

Grandma Daisy spoke of watching the fireworks later from the front yard. "I like to head straight to my bed once the last rocket shoots skyward," she said with a tired little smile.

After hugs all around, the older folks went on their way.

Van and Callie sat at the table, enjoying the evening together, until one of the Sanchez boys asked Callie to dance. Van got up, too. She stood on the edge of the dance floor, watching, loving the sound of boots tapping rhythm in time to the music.

Some cowboy she'd never met before moved close. "Dance?"

"I would love to."

They joined the crowded floor for "Boot Scootin' Boogie." When that one was over, another cowboy stepped up. They danced to an old Kenny Chesney song. As that song ended, she thanked him and turned—right into the arms of the man she'd been waiting for.

The band launched into a cover of "Beautiful Crazy."

Talk about a glorious moment. Van closed her eyes

and gave herself up to the clear night, the glow of the party lights strung overhead, that first star keeping watch far above and the perfect feel of Jameson's strong arms around her.

"We should talk." His breath was warm in her ear.

"Hmm." She brushed the close-cut hair at the back of his neck, reveled in the feel of his skin under her fingers. So what if love never worked out for her? Heat and magic, passion and tenderness—on a night like tonight, those felt like more than enough. "Talk? That's what you want from me?"

"To start, yeah."

She pressed her body closer to his. It felt so right when he held her in his arms. All through the long winter, into spring and early summer, she'd missed this.

Missed *him*.

Just one night. That's all they'd had. And yet, she couldn't get the man out of her thoughts.

It's only for now, she reminded herself. *This, between us, it's for the summer and that's all.*

Did her heart listen?

Never mind about that.

She wrapped her hand around the nape of his neck, stroked her middle finger in that tender place behind his ear. "You know I'm interested. I thought I made that clear *last* night."

He nuzzled the hair at her temple. "I love how you smell. Like roses—and something else. Something woodsy, a little sharp."

"Juniper."

"That's it." He breathed deep. "I like it. A lot."

"So you wanted to talk about what shampoo I use?"

He chuckled. The sound vibrated from his body into hers. "I wanted to talk about doing things your way."

Her hopeless heart beat a faster rhythm. "Yeah?"

"Yeah, Vanessa. You still open to that?"

She looked up into those eyes that were deep and dark now, night-blue. "I am, absolutely. I'm open, Jameson. To you."

CHAPTER SIX

Now that he had Vanessa in his arms, Jameson knew he'd made the right decision. He'd lain awake half the night last night, staring at the shadows lurking up near the vaulted ceiling, trying to tell himself that *he* was right and she was wrong, that he'd had enough of trying to get through to her.

But then, a few hours before dawn, he'd finally faced the truth. He wanted to get close to her. And with a skittish woman like Vanessa, a man only had a chance of getting close if he agreed to do so on her terms.

The irony of the situation did not escape him. He'd spent a lot of years having nothing but a real good time when it came to the fairer sex. When a woman got too clingy or started talking marriage and babies, he couldn't get the hell out fast enough.

And then he finally grew up. He'd started hungering for a family—with the right woman. He'd met Maybelle. They'd married. And from her, he'd learned a painful lesson. In the immortal words of Jon Pardi, "It ain't always the cowboy that rides away."

Would Vanessa have him humming the same tune in the end?

It sure did look that way. But a man could never win if he refused to play the game.

So for now, forget the future. He had Vanessa in his arms, and the way she looked up at him, dark eyes soft and hopeful, promised a great night ahead and, just maybe, if he played his cards right, more nights to come.

Whatever happened, at least he'd have a good time while she remained in town. It wasn't near enough for him. But to have a prayer of more, he needed to stay in the damn game—and keep a check on himself.

She'd made it painfully clear that she had no interest in getting serious. He needed to remember that, needed *not* to get too attached.

And who could say? Maybe they'd grow closer. Close enough that she'd learn to trust him. Close enough that she'd be willing to change her rules.

Right now, though, he needed not to push her when she refused to budge.

"You want to stay for the fireworks?" Jameson asked as the song ended and another slow one began.

Van pulled back enough to meet his waiting eyes. "Nope. I was kind of thinking I might follow you to your place."

The way he smiled at her made her stomach hollow out and hot shivers race up and down her spine. "Get our own fireworks going?"

She returned his smile. "You just read my mind."

"Damn, woman. I do like the way your mind works."

She wanted to lift up and fit her mouth to his. But there were too many people around who didn't need to know that she and Jameson had plans for the evening—intimate plans.

Apparently, his thoughts followed the same track as hers, because he quirked a dark gold eyebrow and said, "I really want to kiss you now."

She gave him her sternest schoolteacher glare. "But you won't."

A low, rough chuckle escaped him. "Just checking. I want to be sure I'm clear on the rules."

"Simple. Nobody else needs to know, and nobody else *gets* to know."

Something happened in his eyes. He glanced away for a fraction of a second. But then he nodded. "Got it."

"So, I'm thinking you go first. I'll say good-night to Callie and then I'll be along."

"You remember the way, then?"

"Oh yes, I do."

He pulled her close again. With a contented sigh, she tucked her head under his chin. As they swayed together, he suggested, "Let's just finish out this song."

They held each other close—but not too close—until the song ended.

He whispered, "If you get lost, you call me." And then he was gone.

One of the Dalton boys asked for a dance. It was a fast one. As soon as the fiddle hit the last note, Van went looking for Callie.

She spotted her roomie by the picnic tables and hurried over to say good-night.

When Van reached Callie's side, her friend leaned in close and teased, "So? Nice dance with Jameson?"

Van couldn't hide her grin. "Very nice, thank you."

They shared a long look, and Callie said, "Let me guess. Things aren't exactly over between you two, after all."

"You are sworn to secrecy. I really don't want anyone in my family to know."

"Haven't you heard? Secrecy is overrated. You're a grown woman. Your family really can't tell you what choices to make."

"I know. But I don't want them hoping and dropping hints and, well, all up in my business in their sweet and loving way."

"I'll say it again. They can't make your choices for you."

"I mean it. Not a word to anyone." She crooked her little finger and held it out to Callie. "Pinkie swear."

Callie groaned, but she hooked pinkies with Van. "Happy now?"

"Very."

"You have a certain look about you. You're meeting him, aren't you?"

"I will say this much. Don't wait up."

When Van pulled her Forester into the driveway at Jameson's house, he was waiting on the front step, his tall frame silhouetted by the inside lights behind him.

Van grabbed her shoulder bag and got out. Shoving

the door shut, she ran around the front of the car, eager to get to him. He held out his arms and she jumped into them, laughing, wrapping her arms and legs around him.

Laughing along with her, he spun her in a circle.

In the distance, she heard whistling sounds and a series of loud pops. She pointed skyward, where a streak of red shot high and bloomed into a giant flower of light. "The fireworks have started."

"You'd better believe it." His lips met hers. She opened for him, tasting him, her mind a hot, eager whirl of joy and desire.

His big hands cradling her bottom, he carried her inside, not once breaking their kiss as he crossed the great room, finally letting her slide to her feet when he reached the kitchen. She dropped her purse on the counter chair and grinned up at him.

"I'm so glad you're here." He bent to take her mouth again.

It was another one of those kisses, the endless kind. But he didn't pull her close, and she somehow kept herself from swaying into him. Their bodies a few inches apart, their mouths fused together, they kissed for the longest time.

When he lifted his head, she opened her eyes and gazed up at him, feeling dazed and maybe a little bit delirious.

Then something batted against her boot. She looked down. A skinny, white-spotted brown dog stared up at her. "I didn't know you had a dog."

"Meet Slim. He's a German shorthair—mostly, anyway. Slim's about a third Weimaraner."

She bent to take Slim's long face between her hands. "Hey, buddy." Slim gazed at her through soulful brown eyes and gave a low, happy whine. His tail slapped the floor as she scratched under his chin and around the back of his ears. "Where were you last New Year's Eve?"

"At the vet's, as I recall. Little run-in with a coyote. Slim won the match, but the coyote got in a lick or two."

She gave Slim a last scratch. Jameson put down a hand, and she took it. A sweet shiver coursed through her as she rose. "I can't believe I'm really here again."

He touched her hair—a careful touch, his palm resting lightly against the curve of her skull. "You want something to drink? A snack, maybe?"

She reached up and brushed her fingers along the sculpted line of his jaw, enjoying the feel of his short beard against her fingertips. "Just you."

He caught her hand. Pausing only to give Slim the command to stay, he led her down the short hall to his room—and kicked the door shut behind him, rousing a memory of that night last winter, of the sheer glory of it. He'd kicked the door shut that night, too.

And she'd promised herself that the wonder she'd shared with him would never happen again. Some promises, apparently, just begged to be broken.

They stood by the turned-back bed in the light of a single lamp. He unbuttoned her shirt and took it away, dropping it on the bedside chair. Quickly, he got rid of the rest of her clothes—or most of them, anyway.

He pushed her down to sit on the side of the bed, knelt at her feet and removed her boots and her socks. Taking her hand, pulling her upright again, he took down her jeans and her panties, spinning them on a finger before tossing them on the bedside chair.

"Lie down," he commanded.

Without a stitch on, she stretched out on the cool sheet. "Your turn."

Took him about a minute and a half. Boy, did he look good naked. Since last New Year's, her memories of him without his clothes had filled her fantasies and carried her to her happy place a whole bunch of times. But her memories had nothing on the reality of him—so beautifully manly, everything broad and hard and cut.

As he came down to her, she reached up and put her hand flat against his chest. He felt so good—the silky heat of his flesh and beneath that, the strong, steady beat of his heart.

"I missed you," he whispered, as his mouth came down to capture hers.

He settled his body over hers, and her need became frantic—to get her hands all over him, to kiss him long and deep and thoroughly, to give herself up to each thrilling sensation.

She needed to get her hands all over him, and he seemed equally eager to touch her everywhere. They laughed together, rolling from one side of the big bed to the other, hands stroking, grabbing, holding, her long hair tangling all around them.

He cupped her full breast in a big hand, position-ing it for his mouth, and then he claimed it, sucking, nibbling—biting, too. She moaned and gathered him tight against her as his other hand strayed down. Out-side, far in the distance, she heard fireworks exploding.

"So wet, so ready..." He lifted his head from her breast and took her mouth again.

"Condom," she commanded against his parted lips. "More foreplay later. Right now, I can't wait."

He didn't hesitate. Sticking out a muscular arm, he caught the knob of the bedside drawer and pulled it open. She helped, taking the pouch from his hand, quickly peeling it open, then pushing him onto his back and straddling him.

"You're so beautiful." He stared up at her, eyes glit-tering, face intent, his fine mouth slightly parted, big chest expanding with each ragged breath. "Like that painting of Venus by that Italian guy."

"Botticelli?"

"Yeah, that one. So soft and full and gorgeous."

She bent for a quick kiss before rolling the condom down over his hard, thick length. "There."

He took over. Big hands clasping her hips, he rolled her under him. She watched his face, loving the heat in his eyes, the strong set of his jaw. He eased his thick, powerful thighs between her soft ones, nudging her legs wider, making room, reaching down to line him-self up with her.

"Eyes up here, on me, Vanessa." He growled the words.

She obeyed, lifting her chin and meeting his un-wavering gaze.

He thrust in.

She let out a deep groan of pure pleasure as he filled her. "It's been too long."

"Tell me about it."

And then she was grabbing for him, pulling him down to her, wrapping her legs around him, meeting each stroke, her body quickly rising, heat racing down her spine, blooming outward in a sudden, powerful climax.

"So fast," she moaned. "I'm going over..."

"Right there with you." He surged in deep and she felt him, pulsing inside the condom, joining her in a free fall off the edge of the world.

For a few minutes, they simply lay there, panting, holding on to each other.

When he got up to dispose of the condom, he commanded, "Don't even move. I'll be right back."

He wasn't kidding. Two minutes later, he rejoined her on the bed. "Come here." Pulling her good and close, he settled his mouth over hers.

The ecstasy started all over again.

Much later, he tugged the covers up around them.

"It's after midnight," she said. "I should go."

Canting up on an elbow, he smoothed her tangled hair out onto the pillow. "Stay for just a little while."

She reached up, traced the straight lines of his eyebrows, skated a finger down the bridge of his commanding nose. "Not for long."

He dropped a kiss on her chin. "What time do you have to be at Happy Hearts in the morning?"

"Eight at the latest. I run my science workshops from nine to noon."

"If you just stayed here with me, you could—"

She silenced him with the tips of two fingers. "Can't. I have to pull it together in the morning, full-on hair and makeup, all that, because I need to be Miss Bronco in the afternoon. Your sister will be there, checking my look. She's the best, and I refuse to let her down."

"You won't let her down. You couldn't." He kissed her fingertips, caught a thick lock of hair and guided it tenderly behind her ear. "You're beautiful just the way you are."

She let out a low, happy laugh. "Flatterer."

"God's honest truth." He gazed at her so intently.

Sometimes, when he looked at her, she felt…unte-thered, somehow. Free of all the everyday limitations that held her anchored to the earth. She felt she could sprout wings and fly, go anywhere—even come back home. That she could shed all her doubts and fears, forget the pain she'd suffered in this town, put aside the hard lessons she'd learned in her life. Sometimes he made her feel that she could safely give herself up to him, trust that he wouldn't hurt her, see where this magic they shared might take them.

But no. She wouldn't do that. Donnie and David and Chaz and Trevor had schooled her but good. The fifth time would not be the charm—not now, anyway, and definitely not with a man who lived in Bronco. She accepted that.

Maybe someday she would follow through when

she wished on the night's first star. Not any time soon, though.

This, with Jameson, was just for the summer. She would love every minute with him and go back to her real life in Billings when summer ended.

"Hey," she whispered.

He bent close, rubbed his nose against hers, pressed a featherlight kiss between her eyebrows. "Yeah?"

"I have to go in an hour. Kiss me like you mean it. Let's not waste a minute."

"My pleasure." He claimed her mouth.

She twined her arms around his neck and gave herself up to the moment.

Much to Jameson's satisfaction, Vanessa stayed later than she planned. Like their night last winter, they fell asleep in each other's arms. But unlike that last time, this time he woke when she left the bed.

He turned on the light and watched her get dressed, watched her cover that curvy, beautiful body he would never get tired of looking at. "Don't forget your other sock, now."

She picked it up off the rug, waved it at him and sat on the bed to pull it on. Her boots came last. She stood. "See you."

"I'll walk you out."

She protested that it wasn't necessary, but then she lingered, watching him through heavy-lidded eyes as he grabbed last night's Wranglers and put them on.

Slim was waiting just outside the door.

"Hey, boy." Vanessa knelt to give the mutt a last scratch behind the ears.

And then she headed for the kitchen where she'd left her shoulder bag. Pausing there at the counter, she took out her contacts and put on a pair of tortoiseshell glasses, turning to wink at him as she grabbed up her bag. "I'm out of here."

He stepped in close, blocking her way to the door. "I like those glasses."

She gave him a look, like he'd better not try keeping her here too long. "Um, thank you?"

"They make you look seriously sexy. And also like a really good teacher who won't let her students get away with anything."

"That's me—but with wiggle room. In my class, everybody gets second chances."

He took a lock of her hair and tugged on it. "I'll be at Happy Hearts early to drop off Charity's heifers."

"Maybe I'll see you."

He couldn't stop wanting to touch her. Lowering his mouth to hers, he brushed a slow kiss across her soft lips. "Oh, you'll see me. I think I'll just hang around, help Daphne out with whatever needs doing. I think I should be there for the pet adoption. After all, it's the final Red, White and Bronco event for this year. Wouldn't want to miss that."

"I would like it if you were there."

"That settles it, then."

Her dark eyes had that gleam in them. They made him think of her, in his bed, without a stitch of clothing separating them.

He kissed her again. He just couldn't get enough of kissing her. "Tomorrow night…"

"Jameson, it's already tomorrow."

"Tonight, then. Be with me tonight."

She hesitated. He dared to breathe again when she decided in his favor. "All right. Tonight, then."

"I'll grill us some steaks."

"Sounds good."

"Be here at six?"

"Works for me."

He shouldn't push his luck. But he did it anyway. "I want every night, all through July and August. Every night you'll give me—maybe some days, too. If you're not teaching your workshops, if I don't have fences down, if you've got time to spare."

She laughed. He drank in the sound. "The whole idea is it's just for the summer. And we play it by ear."

"I'm aware." *Two months.* It wasn't enough. Now he just needed to make her see that. He tugged on the pointy collar of her fancy Western shirt. "Can't blame a man for trying."

She laid her hand on his chest and lifted up to kiss him again. "I really do need to go."

Reluctantly, he stepped aside. He and Slim followed her out. Slim at his feet, he stood on the porch waving as she backed out and drove off.

When he looked down at Slim, the dog whined, a questioning sound. "All right. Go on. Take care of your business and let's get some sleep."

* * *

Callie, all dressed and ready for work, was sitting at the table sipping coffee and reading the *Bronco Bulletin* when Van finished showering, putting on her makeup, getting dressed and fixing her hair just so. Being a beauty queen entailed way too much grooming, in her humble opinion. She'd run through her limited wardrobe of Miss Bronco–worthy Western shirts, so she'd recycled the shirt she'd worn to the rodeo.

"There's coffee," Callie said. "And you're going to need some more sparkly shirts."

"Yeah." Van poured herself a mug. "Lucky for me, this is the last event I've got to attend in my official capacity till the end of the month. I'll make time before then to go shopping, maybe go hog wild and get some showy hats and cool boots, too." She sipped coffee and lifted the cover off the plate Callie had left on the counter. "Yum. French toast."

"Figured you might be hungry."

"Have I told you lately that I love you?"

"Love you, too. Eat your breakfast. Don't be late."

"Yes, Mother." She joined her roomie at the table and dug in. "So good. Thank you."

"Mmm-hmm. Have a nice time last night?"

"I had a wonderful time."

"Good." Callie turned the newspaper around so Van could see the front-page news. The headline read, A Miss Bronco Like No Other.

The picture showed Van onstage Friday in her old jeans and T-shirt, her hair in a messy bun, wearing her winner's banner, looking faintly bewildered as last year's Miss Bronco placed the crown on her head. "Like no other, indeed."

"Face it. You're a star."

Van loved teaching high school science. But this summer, she had tweens and early teens in her science, technology, engineering and mathematics workshop—and they were a whole lot of fun.

DIY bottle rockets thrilled them. She'd had the kids collecting two-liter plastic pop bottles since day one. Last week, they'd made the launch pads, which consisted of small sections of two-by-four with a cork nailed to the center of each one.

In the barnlike shed that Daphne had provided for their summer classroom, Van gave a short recap lecture on the chemical interaction between vinegar and bicarbonate of soda.

"Bakers often mix the two in their recipes," she said. "Vinegar and soda are also useful in homemade cleaning products. In both cases, you have other, neutral substances to contain the interaction. Substances like…?"

The kids shouted out answers. "Flour!"

"Soap!"

"Correct. Last week we mixed vinegar and baking soda and poured the result into a wide open container surrounded by a small mountain of sand. We watched how carbon dioxide rose to the top of the mixture, creating bubbles and foam that looked like…"

"A volcano!"

"That's right! Today, we make our bottle rockets.

With a bottle rocket, you're confining the chemical reaction in the restricted space of the bottle with only a small opening for possible escape, causing the chemical interaction to do what?"

Several of the boys made exploding sounds, while Emma Bledsoe called out, "Vinegar and baking soda make carbonic acid, which decomposes into carbon dioxide gas. The tight space and small opening are what blows the bottle off the cork." Not only a fighter for equal rights in the Miss Bronco beauty pageant, Emma was also a budding scientist.

"Exactly," said Van. "And that makes…"

"The rocket!" crowed more than one of the boys.

They all filed outside to the cleared area in front of the classroom shed and went to work setting up the rocket assembly stations—including the empty bottles with colored tape and markers to decorate them, water and vinegar in measured amounts, baking soda that had to be carefully rolled up in sections of paper towel. And finally, the launching pads with their nailed-on corks.

More than one of the kids had made DIY bottle rockets at home as a family project. Van put one of those students in charge of each station, with Emma running the launching pad station, where the final step had to be done quickly, inserting the nail-mounted cork in the prepped bottle, turning it over to set the launch pad on the cleared space designated for takeoff—and then stepping back fast.

A few of the bottles failed to launch. But most of them soared skyward, sixty feet on average, a few as high as a hundred. It was quite the show. They quickly acquired an audience that broke into applause and whistles each time one of the homemade rockets took off into the sky.

Van spotted Charity in the group of spectators, with Jameson right behind her. She gave them each a big smile, lingering maybe just a little too long on the handsome cowboy with the killer blue eyes and close-cropped, dark gold beard. He actually winked at her, and she tried to ignore the thrill that surged through her in response. She longed to run to him, breathe in the manly scent of him, offer up her mouth for a long, sweet kiss.

Pheromones, she reminded herself. Sexual attraction. No. Big. Deal.

She laughed. He was such a charmer and, really, she couldn't wait for tonight, just the two of them at his place, sharing dinner followed by a whole other kind of sharing, naked in his bed…

And, oops. She needed *not* to stare at him with her tongue hanging out when surrounded by a crowd. The two of them having sex with their eyes in public had to stop or more people were bound to figure out that they'd agreed to make the most of their summer nights—together.

She dragged her gaze back to the cleared space as another bottle rocket achieved liftoff. Too bad she couldn't keep herself from glancing his way again a few minutes later. That time, her gaze snagged on Charity. Jameson's sister was staring right at her, a pensive expression on her pretty face.

No way, Van decided. Charity knew nothing. And

from now on, Van would be more careful about where she let her gaze linger.

Clapping her hands to get her Young Adventurers' attention, she praised their creativity, growing knowledge and hard work, thanked their impromptu audience—and instructed the class to get going on cleanup.

Half an hour later, Van sat on a stool in Daphne's small spare bathroom as Charity primped Van for the fast-approaching Bronco's Favorite Pet Contest.

Daphne stuck her head in the door. "Half an hour to showtime."

Charity replied, "We'll be ready, no worries."

"Missed you yesterday," Van said.

Daphne gave a tiny, resigned shrug. "Maybe next year."

"Hope so." Van gave her friend and future sis-in-law a warm smile.

Daphne tapped her knuckles on the door frame. "Well, I'd better get out there, see how it's going." She left them.

"She okay?" Charity asked.

"She's amazing. But, you know, family problems…"

Charity nodded and didn't probe further.

Van asked, "So how did it work out with Frilly and Dilly?"

"Daphne had us put them in a pasture out beyond the hay barn with a bunch of ancient cows that Daphne said are rescues, too. I warned her that my heifers can be troublesome. She said not to worry. The cows and the heifers would work it out. When we left them, Dilly and Frilly were grazing side by side with the elderly cows, looking perfectly content in their new home."

"Glad to hear it."

Charity smoothed Van's eyebrows with a brow gel wand—and asked the big question. "So, you and Jameson…?"

Busted. Van didn't want to lie—not to anyone, really. But especially not to this sweet and generous girl.

She evaded instead, with a vague wave of her hand and a nebulous question. "What do you mean?"

Charity tipped Van's chin up with a finger and brushed on cheek color. "Not going to talk about it, huh?"

Rather than lie again, she said, "Well, it's complicated."

And Charity put down her blusher brush. "I *am* nineteen, you know. I've been to college—yeah, only freshman year so far, but that counts. I've been in love and I've had my heart broken. I like you, and I love my big brother…" Her smooth brow crinkled with a thoughtful little frown. "And what am I getting at here? That I do know a little about what goes on between women and men. For instance, I know that when people say, 'It's complicated,' they're in some kind of semirelationship that they don't want to talk about."

Now Van felt like a complete jerk. She moaned and dropped her head to the little counter next to the sink.

Charity yelped, "No smearing!"

Van popped back up straight. She'd left a smudge of powder foundation on the edge of the counter. "Sorry."

"It's all right." Charity grabbed the kabuki brush

she'd been using earlier and dabbed at Van's forehead. "There we go. Good as new."

"Listen…"

"Hmm?"

"It's just, well, I *do* like your brother." She liked Charity, as well—liked her too much to keep lying to her by omission. "I like Jameson a lot and I'm going to spend time with him over the summer."

That radiant smile of Charity's bloomed wide. "Ha. I knew it."

I just…" She fumbled for the right words and settled for, "Okay, I'll be honest with you. I don't want my family to know that I'm seeing Jameson."

Charity put the brush down. "Do I get to ask why?"

"Of course." Van explained what she'd already explained to Jameson and Callie—that her family wanted her married to a local guy and living in town, and that wasn't going to happen. "I don't want them getting ideas that I might move back to Bronco."

"So what if they do get ideas? Isn't that their problem?"

Van almost face-planted on the counter again. "Sometimes I can't believe you're only nineteen."

"Because I'm right. Am I right?"

"Yes, if they can't accept that I get to make my own life decisions, it *is* their problem. But I don't want to disappoint them. At the same time, I feel awful that I resent them a little. They try so lovingly to run my life."

Van hovered on the brink of saying more, about what had happened in high school, about how she'd hurt her mother and Grandma Daisy and Evan, too, when things went from bad to worse—hurt them with worry for her. She'd kept her suffering to herself. But they'd known there was more going on with her than she ever told them about. And when they'd tried to get her to open up about the awful things she was keeping from them, she'd lied and said there was nothing.

She'd held on to her pride. It had felt like all she had left. She'd wanted to handle the problem all by herself. And she had.

But Charity didn't need to hear that old horror story. And Van didn't want to go there, anyway.

"Let me ask you this," said Charity. "What if, say, things go really well between you and Jameson this summer and he decides that he might be willing to move to Billings?"

"That's not going to happen. He's a Bronco rancher, through and through."

"But just say theoretically—"

"Stop. It's for the summer and that's it."

"Because you like Jameson, but you don't like him *that* much?"

"Your brother is wonderful, he really is."

"Then what's the problem?"

She thought of Donnie and the awfulness of the way he'd dumped her—twice. Of what Maura and her girlfriends had put her through.

Maybe she'd developed something of a neurosis around the whole idea of ever moving home. Or maybe it was simply that, as much as she longed for love, right now she needed to protect her heart. Keeping the thing with Jameson a secret and putting a time limit on it had the effect of constantly reminding her that it was just for now. It kept her from getting serious.

She met Charity's gaze. "I like my life the way it is, you know?"

"Relax your lips. Good." Charity set to work with a lip brush. "So, being single in Billings, that's a big thrill?"

Van couldn't suppress a snort of laughter at that one.

"Smeared it—and that was my bad. I shouldn't have asked you a question while trying to apply your lip color." Charity dabbed at the corner of Van's mouth with a round cosmetic pad. "And as for my question itself, sorry."

"For what?"

"I kind of insulted Billings, and I get that you like it there."

"Uh-uh. Don't be sorry. We're friends. You get to say to me what you really think."

"Okay, let's try this again." Charity commanded, "Hold still, lips parted—I mean it this time. Don't move." Neither of them spoke as Charity stroked on Van's lip color. "Perfect." She stepped back an inch or two in the limited space. "Jameson really likes you. I can tell."

Van answered honestly. "And I really like *him*."

Charity blew out her cheeks with a hard breath—a very un-Charity-like action. "Well, okay. I just want you to know. He's a good guy, and I would love it if you two got together in a permanent way, and I—"

"Charity, honestly. How many ways can I say that's not going to happen?"

Charity showed her the hand. "Excuse me, Miss Bronco. I was not finished speaking."

"You're right. Sorry. Please continue."

"Thank you, I will. I just want you to know that Jameson is someone you can count on. Someone you can trust."

Van almost scoffed at that one. But then she thought twice.

True, Van used to have a certain idea of him, an idea based on what she'd heard of him years ago. Back then, they all said that he liked a good time, but he didn't get serious with any girl. Really, though, those had only been rumors. She hadn't *known* him then. He'd been three or four years ahead of her in school, a popular, good-looking older boy from a well-to-do family, someone all the girls her age crushed on.

She needed to stop judging him by what she'd heard about him growing up. If everyone judged Van by old rumors, they would probably view her the way Maura seemed to—as someone trashy and dangerous, someone who wouldn't hesitate to try to steal her man.

"Vanessa," said Charity sternly. "Stop scrunching your forehead. You'll get wrinkles."

Van laughed. "A few wrinkles never hurt anyone."

"Maybe not. But as rule, Miss Bronco is never wrinkled. Her wardrobe *and* her skin are always pristine."

"It's a whole new Miss Bronco nowadays, and don't you forget it. She could be anyone, a regular girl—even someone's single grandma."

"Of course she could be anyone. But this year, she's you. And a smooth brow is prettier. Given a choice, you might as well be pretty." Charity closed up her makeup kit. From the hook on the back of the bathroom door, she took the gorgeous, spangled hat she'd brought from home. "Here, now. Hold your hat and let me fix your hair." Van sat up straight, cradling the hat on her knees, keeping still as Charity fussed with her hair. "Okay, hat, please."

Van handed it over, and Charity set it just so on her head.

"There." Charity studied the final effect. "Perfect. My work here is done. You're ready to wow them."

Van spun on her stool and grinned at herself in the mirror. "Bronco's Favorite Pet Contest, here I come."

CHAPTER SEVEN

VAN AND CHARITY walked out together to join the day's festivities. Held in a pretty, rolling pasture dotted with alder and burr oak trees, Bronco's Favorite Pet Contest had drawn a good crowd.

"It looks great," said Charity, and then she went to join Jameson, who'd saved her a seat.

Van agreed with Charity's assessment. Daphne had gathered her minions—kids of all ages who volunteered at the pet sanctuary, as well as any spectators who happened to show up early. They'd all pitched in to set up folding chairs in rows. They'd hung flags and red, white and blue bunting from every available tree, booth or bit of outdoor furniture, including the judges' table, the trophy display, the refreshment area and around the podium. Now, they'd all taken their seats, many with pets of their own.

Van took the front-row seat reserved for her and watched as Daphne's many young helpers, more than half of them summer camp Young Adventurers, emerged from the nearest barn with pets on leashes and leads, in carriers and cages. Everyone applauded as the kids brought out cats and dogs, several pigs, a few goats, more than one exotic bird, and various small, furry creatures, too. Van spotted a ferret, a family of hamsters and a large number of rabbits. The helpers and their charges formed a wide arc behind the podium and the trophy display.

Daphne stepped up to the podium. She thanked everyone for coming and reminded them that all Happy Hearts pets were either rescues or animals born right there at the sanctuary.

"Each of these loving fur babies is available to you and your family. I hope you'll consider giving one or more of them a caring, forever home." She swept out a hand to a couple of teenagers seated at the table with the big sign that read Adoption Center. "Toby and Allison are ready to help you adopt the favorite pet of your choice—and now let's get the contest underway."

Daphne went on to introduce the five judges, after which she grinned at Van. "I'm going to need a little help handing out the trophies and ribbons, so I want to introduce you all to my dear friend and soon-to-be sister-in-in-law. Ladies and gentlemen, youngsters and pets, let's give a big welcome to our own Miss Bronco! Show her some love with a round of applause!"

Everyone clapped some more, and one or two whistled as Van got up, waved to the crowd and went to join Daphne at the podium.

For the next three hours, Daphne introduced each category and Van passed out the trophies. Spectators brought their pets forward to compete, and the helpers did the same with the Happy Hearts animals.

The categories of competition changed depending on the species. Cats got points for qualities like dignity and mesmerizing eyes. Dogs were judged on friendliness, best bark and willingness to chase and fetch a ball. The usual animal-competition traits of obedience and conformation didn't even get a nod. Furry friends at Happy Hearts tended to march to their own individual drums, and few of them had pedigrees. Prizes were plentiful—for the pets brought from home and the Happy Hearts rescues.

A white mutt named Maggie became the star of the day. A border collie/Australian shepherd mix with a brown spot on one eye that reminded Van of a pirate's eye patch, Maggie barked with the best of them and wagged her tail a lot. She perked her floppy ears and tipped her head sideways when spoken to, as though amused by the humans who surrounded her. She chased a ball when her helper threw it, returning it—not to the helper, but to a little boy and girl in the second row.

"Mommy, Maggie loves us!" cried the little girl as she knelt in front of her chair to give the mutt a hug.

"Daddy, she wants to be with us," said the little boy, gazing up at his father, hopeful and so sweetly serious.

The parents put their heads together, and Maggie found her home. Rising, the mom headed for the adoption table. Everyone clapped and shouted encouragements as she filled out the papers.

More rescued pets found homes as the contest continued. No one was surprised when the grand prize went to Maggie. When Van tied a big blue ribbon around Maggie's neck, spectators, helpers and judges alike burst into boisterous applause.

After that, Daphne encouraged them to stroll around the farm where more loving animals waited to find a good home. She offered coupons for discounts on pet supplies available at the Happy Hearts store and a discount card for microchipping at any local vet.

More spectators lined up at the adoption table, checkbooks and credit cards ready. Happy Hearts Animal Sanctuary didn't charge for adoptions, but new owners paid for the veterinary care already provided to the animals they chose. Many made generous donations to the sanctuary, as well.

"Bronco's Favorite Pet Contest is a hit," Van said to Daphne in a quiet moment when it was only the two of them not far from the podium.

Daphne nodded. "I'm pleased. So many of our residents have found new homes today—and everyone does seem to be having a really good time."

"A fabulous time," Van agreed. She heard a musical trill of laughter. It was Charity, flirting with one of the college boys who volunteered to help out a few hours a day in the summer.

"Charity John's a sweetheart. And her big brother Jameson set out half the folding chairs and helped assemble my new trophy display." Daphne gave a dip of her head toward the now-empty display, where Jameson and Evan stood with their heads together.

Talking about what, exactly? Van couldn't help wondering.

Innocuous man things, no doubt, she reassured herself. After all, Jameson had given her his word not to tell anyone that they were seeing each other. He knew she didn't want her family to know. No way he would tell her brother that they couldn't keep their hands off each other.

Van asked, "When did Evan get here?"

Daphne gave a half shrug. "Around eleven. He pitched in setting up, too."

Again, Van reminded herself that Jameson wouldn't say a word to her brother about the two of them. Still, her palms felt sweaty and her pulse raced. She was about to march over there and see what the two of them were talking about when a cry went up from near the refreshment tables.

"Maggie!" cried the little boy who'd adopted the white dog. "Come back!"

"Don't run away!" the little girl pleaded. "We love you! We want you to come home with us!"

Van glanced toward the shouting in time to spot the grand prize winner racing off, headed for a stand of cottonwood trees and the hills beyond them.

Evan yelled, "We'll get her!" He and Jameson took off at a run. They jumped in Jameson's truck and kicked up a cloud of dust heading down the dirt road that cut through the cottonwoods.

Over by the tables, the two little kids had tears running down their cheeks. Their parents knelt beside them, trying to comfort them.

"I'll go see what I can do," Van volunteered.

"I'll come with you." Daphne fell in step beside her,

but two teenage boys came running up with a whole new emergency.

"That mare with the bad attitude stepped on Brian's foot," one of the boys said. Van remembered Brian—a lanky high schooler, sweet-natured and prone to daydreaming.

"I've got the Maggie crisis," Van offered.

"I'll be right there," Daphne promised the boys. "Let me get the first aid kit."

Van ran toward the group of people gathered around the young family with the two sobbing kids. She worked her way into the center of the crowd.

"Miss Bronco, our Maggie ran away." The little girl sniffled and rubbed at her wet eyes with a soggy-looking tissue.

"Don't worry. The search party has already mobilized." Did Evan and Jameson qualify as a search party? Well, there were two of them and they were searching, so why not?

The little boy mumbled, "Wh-what's *mobilize* mean?"

"It means the search party is out looking for Maggie. I'm sure they'll be back with her before you know it."

"I miss her already!" cried the little boy.

"Me, too," the girl chimed in. "I miss her so much!"

Distraction seemed the best option at this point. Van suggested, "While we wait, why don't we visit the kitten barn?"

Both kids stopped sobbing. They blinked up at her through wide, wet eyes. The little girl sniffled. "Are there a *lot* of kittens?"

"Yes, I believe that there are."

Van led the kids and their parents to the cat barn. After a half hour in the kitten enclosure, the parents decided to adopt a sweet twelve-week-old gray tabby. By then, the children had stopped sobbing, at least. They were still worried about Maggie but smiling through their tears at the idea of bringing a new kitten home.

One of Daphne's helpers provided a cardboard cat carrier, and the family set off for the adoption table once again. Van stood watching just outside the cat barn as Jameson and Evan met them halfway. Maggie the dog was nowhere to be seen. Both men shook their heads sadly as they spoke to the young family. Even from several feet away, Van could hear the regret in their voices.

The little boy opened the top of the carrier so that the men could admire the kitten.

When the family set out again toward the adoption table, Jameson and Evan came toward her.

"No Maggie, huh?" she asked them.

"Sorry," said Jameson.

Evan gestured toward the stand of trees where Maggie had disappeared from sight. "We thought we might catch up with her in those cottonwoods."

"But she was long gone when we got there." Jameson took off his hat and slid it back on again.

"That dog can run." Evan put his arm around Van and gave her shoulders a squeeze. "But the parents are talking about getting flyers out around town. I doubt Daphne can scare up a picture of Maggie, but a description on the flyer might work."

Van couldn't stop looking at Jameson. The warmth in his eyes tempted her. She wanted to go to him, feel his strong arms gather her close in a hug.

But that couldn't happen. She needed to watch herself, not give herself away.

Fun, she reminded herself. *We're just having fun.*

"Where's my girl?" asked Evan.

Van explained about the injury at the horse pasture, and Evan left to find Daphne.

"You okay?" Jameson asked. He took off his hat again and hit it on his thigh.

"Yeah, just… I hope that dog is all right."

"I'm sure she is. She'll either wander back here to Happy Hearts or someone will find her. A lot of people will remember her after today. One way or another, those kids will get their dog back." He put his hat on again.

They stared at each other. She wondered if he wanted to touch her as much as she wanted to throw herself into his arms.

Finally, he seemed to shake himself. "I need to head back to the Double J. I'll say goodbye to Daphne and get a move on. See you at six?"

Her heart lifted a little. Tonight it would be just the two of them. She could touch him at will. "I'll be there."

Once he disappeared behind the next barn over, Van straightened her shoulders and went looking for Charity, but one of the helpers said Jameson's sister had left with a couple of her girlfriends as soon as the contest ended.

In the ranch house, Van found her brother and Daphne canoodling in the kitchen. "Okay, you two. Get a room."

Daphne laughed and turned in Evan's arms. He kept those arms firmly around her, linking his hands at her waist. "This is my house," she said, "so technically we've got *all* the rooms."

Van scoffed. "A likely excuse. What happened at the horse pasture?"

"Brian wasn't paying close attention and the mare, Prudence, decided to mess with him. What can I say about Prudence? She's a troublemaker. But she always causes problems in a conscientious kind of way. Today, she didn't really stomp on Brian's foot so much as put her hoof on it and press down."

"Yikes!"

"He's okay, bruised but otherwise unharmed. I sent him home with instructions to keep it elevated. He'll use an ice pack on it and take it easy for a few days."

Evan bent and nuzzled Daphne on the side of her neck. She giggled like a giddy schoolgirl.

Sometimes Van wanted to ask Daphne what she'd done with her *real* brother. Evan used to be a lot harder to get along with. He had trouble keeping assistants at Bronco Ghost Tours, he was so tough on them. Not anymore. He got along great with Callie now and he catered to Winona, giving her whatever she wanted for her fortune-telling project, always ready to help her change this or move that.

"Clearly you two could use some alone time," she said to the lovebirds. "I'm out of here."

"See you tomorrow," Daphne called after her.

Van waved without looking back.

"Your mom's marinating tri-tips," coaxed Jameson's dad.

It was ten minutes of six and Jameson hoped to get rid of the old man before Vanessa drove up. "Thanks, Dad. I've got steaks of my own to grill."

"They'll keep for a day or two. Come on over, have a beer with me and the boys."

"Not tonight."

Randall opened his mouth to keep trying, but the sound of tires crunching gravel had him turning to see who had just driven up.

Vanessa's silver Forester sailed toward them. Jameson half expected her to drive right on by once she spotted his dad, but she turned into the driveway, after all.

Randall said, "Why, that's Vanessa Cruise," as she got out of the car, circled the front of it and approached the steps. She'd traded her studded snap-front shirt and dress boots for sandals and a silky purple top. In her hand she carried the hat she'd borrowed from Charity that day.

At Jameson's feet, Slim wagged his tail and whined in eager greeting. "Stay," Jameson commanded. The dog dropped to his haunches with another hopeful whimper.

"Hello, Mr. John," said Vanessa. She looked a little worried. Jameson couldn't blame her. His dad could so easily put it together that they had something going on.

And not only that—the old man had spoken out against her when she won the Miss Bronco crown.

His dad whipped off his hat. "You call me Randall, you hear?" Even Jameson blinked in surprise when his dad said that. Randall sounded downright friendly. And then he glanced at Jameson and muttered, "Shut your mouth before the flies get in, son." He turned to Vanessa again. Fiddling nervously with his hat brim, he said, "My daughter gave me a talking-to about your win last Friday. She says you are the chosen Miss Bronco and I need to respect that. After giving it some thought, I have realized that my little girl is right. I want to apologize for my rude behavior at the pageant and to congratulate you on winning that crown. Also, since the day you won, I've seen you in action—at the barbecue and the rodeo—and you are doing our town proud."

Vanessa actually looked flustered. "Your daughter is very special."

"She is indeed."

"And thank you, Randall."

He donned his hat again. "Are you looking for Charity?"

"Well, yes." She gave the old man a big smile with maybe a touch of relief in it. After all, if his dad assumed that she'd come to see Charity, then she wouldn't have to answer any uncomfortable questions about what else she might be doing here. "Charity's been so great, helping me out, showing me the ropes. She lent me this hat to wear for the pet contest out at Happy Hearts, and I didn't get it back to her before she left."

"Truth is, my little girl is growing up. She's always out with her friends these days. I'm guessing she won't be home till later tonight—but I will be more than happy to give her that hat."

"Would you? Thanks."

Randall took the hat and wiggled his thick eyebrows at Jameson. "Tri-tips?"

"Thanks, Dad. Some other time."

"How about you, young lady?" Randall offered. "Care to join the John family for the best tri-tips in the county? We're also serving grilled corn on the cob and a fat baked potato slathered in butter and sour cream."

"It sounds so good and I appreciate the invitation, but I already have a date tonight."

"Ah. Another time, then?"

"I would love that."

With a quick salute, Jameson's dad turned for his pickup. He waved at them as he drove away.

"That went pretty well," said Vanessa with a careful smile. She knelt to greet Slim. "Hello, handsome. How're you doing?" Slim whimpered with happiness as she scratched his ears. "I like your dad," she said as she looked up and their eyes met.

He gave her a slow smile. "Surprised?"

"A little. I mean, he didn't seem too crazy about me last Friday."

"He can be hotheaded sometimes, but he owns up when he blows it—and was it wishful thinking on my part, or did you call tonight a date?"

She rose. "You're cooking me dinner. Kind of feels like a date to me."

"So, we've moved on from hookup, then? We're past one-night stand?"

She gave a little snort of laughter. "How about summer romance?"

"That'll do." He wrapped an arm around her waist and pulled her close. She felt so good in his arms. "For now." Yeah, he was testing her a little. He wanted to see if she'd jump to denials and insist again that they had an agreement, that she was leaving at the end of August no matter what.

She didn't. Instead, she said, "I brought wine and brookies."

"What's a brookie?"

"Half brownie, half cookie."

"Did you bake them yourself?"

"Nope. Callie did. Trust me, you're glad about that. I burn everything I bake."

He ran a finger down the side of her throat, just to feel the texture of her soft skin. Teasingly, he asked, "But isn't baking just chemistry—and isn't science your best subject?"

She gave him an eye roll. "Hypothetically, yes. In practice, I'm thinking there's a baking gene and I don't have it. That's my excuse and let's leave it at that."

He kissed her. She tasted so good, and he let his hands stray a little, into the dip of her lower back and then out over the soft, gorgeous twin curves of her bottom. "Where are you hiding these brookies you brought?"

"Well, it's like this. I kind of freaked when I saw your dad and I left them and the wine in the car."

"You were scared he would figure out that we're a thing, you and me?"

"Yeah—and then I went and made that remark about having a date. What was I thinking? He'll say something to someone and it'll get back to my mom and grandmother."

"No worries there, and I mean that. My dad knows how to mind his own business."

"Well, good, then. I'm glad." She glanced away and then back.

"Whatever it is, just say it."

"I feel guilty, that's all. I made you promise not to tell anyone about you and me…"

"What? You think I said something to my dad? I didn't."

"No. Did you hear me? I said *I* feel guilty. Ergo, the problem is not with you."

He took both her hands and pressed them against his chest. "Vanessa. Why do you feel guilty?"

"I swore you to secrecy about you and me—and then I told Charity that you and I will be seeing each other this summer. Callie knows, too."

"Wait. You're saying we don't have to be a secret, after all?"

Before he even had a chance to feel happy about that, she shook her head. "I'm saying I told them because they'd already pretty much figured out what was going on. Then I made them both promise to keep the information to themselves."

He tried to look on the bright side. At least he didn't have to be a secret to every single soul in Bronco—

though really, he didn't get her continued insistence that no one could know. It made no sense that a strong, smart woman like her couldn't simply tell her family to back off.

But he wanted her. A lot. He'd spent all of last winter and right on through spring missing her. Something about her really got to him. She made him want to try again. And after the complete disappointment of his marriage to Maybelle, he'd had his doubts that he'd ever want to try again.

He took her hand. "Come on. Let's get the goodies from your car and I'll put the steaks on."

She pulled him back. "What's your hurry?" Her lush mouth was right there, tempting him.

What could he do but take it? He covered those soft lips with his and drank in her sweet, pleasured sigh.

Really, he could stand here on the front step kissing her forever.

But he made himself pull away. "Wine," he reminded her. "And those brownie things. We need to get those. I have to feed you."

She went up on tiptoe and stole another quick kiss. "You seem so determined."

"I am. You'll need your energy for the night to come."

CHAPTER EIGHT

VAN FOUND BEING with Jameson downright addictive. He said he felt the same.

They easily fell into a rhythm of spending their evenings together. That first night, Monday, she did pretty well. She climbed from his bed at two on Tuesday morning and went home to Callie's. But Tuesday night, she slept straight through until seven thirty Wednesday morning and ended up scrambling to get back to the apartment, shower and change and not end up late for Young Adventurers.

Tuesday night, she went against her own rules, taking toiletries and a change of clothes to Jameson's with her. "Just in case," she explained when she walked in his door.

He grabbed her hand, led her down the short hall to his room, and into the walk-in closet, where he'd cleared off hanger space and emptied three drawers. "Bring more stuff. Bring all your stuff. I have plenty of room."

She hung the clothes she'd brought on the empty rod and shook her head. "That's a slippery slope."

He hooked a big arm around her waist and pulled her close. After a long, steamy kiss, he nuzzled the side of her neck and argued, "When it comes to you, slippery slopes are my favorite kind. I told you. I want your nights. I want *all* the nights. All summer long." He kissed her again.

They didn't leave the closet for another hour. He had two condoms in his pocket, and to her that seemed altogether too convenient—not that she complained while he had his hands on her.

After the second go-round, when the two of them were lying on the floor of the closet on a makeshift bed of his coats, with a rolled-up pair of overalls for a pillow, she asked him about that. "Did you plan to have your way with me in this closet?"

He gave her a slow, shameless grin. "Yes, I did. In this closet—and anywhere else we happen to be. I'm not fussy. You, me and proper protection. The way I see it, that's a recipe for lasting happiness."

Before dinner, he took her out to see his prize breeding bulls and explained that he'd developed the Double J's artificial insemination program. When she wanted to know more, he led her into the office on the lower level of the house, sat her down at the PC there and gave her a virtual tour of DoubleJGenetics.com.

"We train ranchers in artificial insemination," he explained. "And the Double J provides AI services to breeders who don't want to perform the process themselves. We also sell semen. Finding the right sire is the key to the long-term health of any herd. And using semen from new bulls on a regular basis means genetic diversity and that helps keep a herd strong."

The scientist in her found the whole process spell-binding. She asked a lot of questions, each of which he answered patiently, in satisfying detail, finally teasing her, "Only you would find artificial insemination fascinating."

He started kissing her, which led to a mutually satisfying interval right there on his desk. Both of their stomachs were growling by the time he put the chicken on the grill.

After dinner, they watched a movie and then went to bed about eleven—but not to sleep. One time was never enough for either of them. And two just seemed like another reason to make love again.

Thursday morning, she was really glad she'd brought a change of clothes. She showered at Jameson's. He jumped in with her, and not really to get clean. When she finally got dressed and ready to go, it was a little after eight. She drove too fast to Happy Hearts, watching for state troopers. Her luck held. She didn't get a ticket, and she made it to Happy Hearts on time.

When she got back to the apartment that afternoon, she found Callie making herself a sandwich in the kitchen.

Callie held up a butter knife coated in mayonnaise and faked a look of alarm. "Who are you and what are you doing in my apartment?"

"Very funny."

"Don't get defensive." Callie gave her a coaxing smile. "I'm only kidding. I'm glad you're having a wonderful summer—and yes, I do consider it my job to give you a hard time."

"I get that. I mean, what are friends for?"

"Exactly. How about a chicken salad sandwich?"

"I had lunch, thanks. And you're home early."

"Evan gave me a few hours off."

"Wait. Let me guess. You have to work tonight."

"A couple of rich out-of-towners have booked a large group. And what fun is a ghost tour in daylight? I'll be lucky to get home by midnight." She grabbed a banana from the fruit bowl, peeled it and had a bite. "So, I take it things are going well with you and Jameson?" As Van tried to decide how to respond to that, Callie teased, "Can't do without him, huh?"

"No. Yes. Maybe."

Callie pointed her bitten-off banana at Van. "I like that you always give me definitive answers."

Van scoffed at her friend's teasing and then made a sad face. "I do miss hanging out."

"Me, too."

"We need a girls' night."

"We do, yes." Callie finished off her banana and turned to dispose of the peel. "But I have to work and you're going to the Double J."

"Yeah. There is that. I just came by to grab a change of clothes. For some reason I seem incapable of getting out of Jameson's bed when my alarm goes off in the morning."

"Just take a suitcase. Stop making it so hard on yourself."

"I should be more…" Van let her voice trail off as

she sought the right word. "Disciplined, I guess. Last New Year's, I made him promise that it was only that one night and no more. And now, here we are, having *more* because I want to be with him, and he wants to be with me. This time, I made him agree that it's only for the summer and nobody else gets to know. And then you figured out that we're seeing each other and so did Charity."

"Van. Don't. It's not wrong to be with someone you really like."

"Yeah, but I need *not* to get carried away."

"That's not true." Callie regarded her so steadily. "You're *afraid* to get carried away."

Van wanted to go straight to denial. But there was no point. Callie would see right through her. Van trusted Callie and had told her all the painful things she'd never felt ready to share with her own family. Callie knew exactly why she would never return to Bronco to live. "You're right. I *am* afraid. I feel out of control over him."

"And that scares you, to be out of control?"

"Yeah. When I really fall for someone, it never goes well. I don't seem to know how to do casual. I get all wrapped up in the guy—and then he messes me over."

"But that doesn't mean it will never go well. What's that old saying? You have to kiss a lot of frogs? I'm thinking that it's possible you've finally met your prince."

"Ugh! Don't you even." Van laughed, but it came out sounding nervous and strange. "I'm a grown woman. I don't believe in princes anymore."

"Liar."

"It's the truth, I promise you."

"Tell that to someone who doesn't know you better." Callie picked up her sandwich and took a bite.

"I can't stand here and argue the point with you. I have to get going." She turned for the hallway to the bedrooms.

"Pack a suitcase!" Callie called after her.

"You brought a suitcase." Jameson looked far too happy about that.

Just inside his door, she set the suitcase down in order to properly greet Slim, who kissed her with way too much wet, floppy tongue. "Ew. You're such an eager guy—but I'm glad to see you, too." She petted him and scratched his ears and then grabbed the suitcase and rose to her feet. "Callie insisted. What could I do?"

He pulled her close. She dropped the suitcase again as they indulged in a toe-curling, bone-melting kiss.

When he finally lifted his head, he said, "Come on. I'll help you unpack."

"Down, boy." She flattened a hand on his hard chest. "You stay out here. If you go in that walk-in closet with me, we might never come back out."

"And that's somehow a bad thing?"

She bent and grabbed the suitcase again. "I'll be quick." He had that look, like he intended to follow her. She pointed a finger at him. "You be good." And she headed for the master bedroom.

When she emerged a few minutes later, he had a

glass of wine waiting on the kitchen island for her. She cut up a salad, and he served the meatball stew he had ready on the stove.

The food was delicious. "You're a good cook," she said as she spooned up another yummy bite.

He shrugged. "My ex-wife didn't cook. One of us had to do it."

She wanted to ask about the ex. But it seemed like a bad idea to go down that road. Too serious. Too much the kind of thing people talked about when they were building a real relationship. She and Jameson weren't building anything. Uh-uh. They had fun together and it was just for the summer and she needed to keep it light. So she teased, "And here you are, spending your nights with another woman who can barely boil water."

"Lucky for you I know my way around a kitchen. It's a long drive into town just to pick up a pizza."

"Where's Grubhub when you need it, huh?"

"Exactly. I did have a cook for a while, but that didn't last. So I do it myself. And I eat at the main house a lot. It all works out."

She enjoyed a spoonful of stew and felt a little bit guilty. "I'm monopolizing you the past few days."

His boot touched hers under the table. Even through two separate layers of rawhide and their socks, she felt that contact acutely. "It's not considered monopolizing when I want you here."

"Yeah, it is. You may be happy about it, but I'm still monopolizing you."

He toasted her with his longneck. "I'm so glad we cleared that up."

She probably shouldn't ask, but somehow the question got out anyway. "Your parents, your brothers? Have they noticed that my Subaru has been parked in front of your house every night this week?"

"I have no idea. They haven't mentioned it."

The doorbell chimed.

Now what? It occurred to her that she hadn't thought this thing through.

Spend every night with Jameson?

Yes, please! But nobody can know that we're having a thing.

All righty, then. What happens when the doorbell rings?

She had no idea, because the thought of the doorbell ringing had never so much as crossed her mind.

Jameson chuckled as he stood. "You aren't going to run and hide under my bed, are you?"

"Am I being ridiculous?"

He'd started toward the door but stopped and turned back to her with a tender, questioning look. "You know, you—" The doorbell chimed again, cutting him off. "On my way!" he shouted, then said gently to her, "I'll be right back."

She watched him cross the great room and disappear around a corner into the front hall. A moment later, she heard him talking to someone, the answering voice as deep and masculine as Jameson's own. And then she heard the door close.

Jameson reappeared—alone—and came back to her. He took his chair again. "Just Dawson dropping off a load of mineral barrels for me to fill in the morning."

Grinning, he added, "And no, he didn't ask about your car in the driveway." He picked up his fork.

She groaned. "It's official. I *am* ridiculous."

Jameson set his fork down without taking a bite.

Ridiculous. The word rubbed him the wrong way, had him wondering who had made her doubt herself, made her feel less than the beautiful, brilliant, tender-hearted woman she actually was.

"No, you are not ridiculous," he answered firmly, eyes locked on hers.

She forced a laugh. "It was just an offhand remark."

He didn't think so. "You asked me if I thought you were ridiculous the night we met, the night you said would be our only night, the one that 'never happened.'" He air-quoted those last two aggravating words.

Her gaze slid away, and the corners of that lush mouth of hers turned down. "I did?"

"You did. That night, I thought it was sexy, that someone so gorgeous and smart and strong would let me have a glimpse of her shyness, her insecurity."

Again, she tried to pretend it was nothing. "This conversation has become altogether too serious."

"Vanessa. Please don't blow me off. One time *was* sexy and so damn cute. But now you've called yourself ridiculous again. I'm starting to believe that someone has made you doubt yourself."

He could see the pulse beating—too fast—beneath the silky olive skin of her throat. She gave a half shrug. "Okay, yeah. As you said, I do have insecurities. Some-times I let them show. We struggled when I was a growing up. Money was always tight. I didn't have a lot of friends, and sometimes the richer kids made fun of me for not being thin, not having the right clothes, not looking just so."

"And that's why you don't want to live in Bronco ever again? Bad memories from when you were a kid?"

"Essentially, yes."

He wanted to press her, to get her to tell him more about those memories, about who had made her feel less than beautiful and desirable, smart and bighearted. But he respected her reluctance. He could see that she wasn't ready to give him her secrets.

Maybe she never would be. And that hurt. The woman had gotten so far under his skin in such a short period of time. It amazed him.

It scared him, too. With Maybelle, he'd been ready to find love and settle down.

With Vanessa, it was so much more than just readiness. He wanted to be the man she needed, the man she wanted to move on to the next step with. The man she turned to in the night, *every* night. The man she stood with proudly in the bright light of day.

He wasn't that man. Yet.

But at least for now, he did own her nights. He intended to make the most of whatever time she gave him.

Rising, he rounded the end of the table and held out his hand. Warmth and hope spread through him when she displayed no hesitation to take it. And when he pulled her up, she came happily into his waiting arms.

He lowered his mouth to hers, and she opened to

him. She tasted of wine, of desire and, just maybe, the promise of more. All good things—the things that came to a man willing to practice patience when the right woman finally came along.

As he lifted his head, her long, dark lashes fluttered open. He waited for her to meet his gaze directly before making his request. "Give me one thing…"

"Hmm?"

"The Night That Never Happened?"

Those dark eyes went dreamy. "It was a great night."

"Yes, it was. And I'm hoping we can agree to give that night the appreciation and respect it deserves."

"And how will we do that, exactly?"

"For starters, let's give that night a better name."

She tipped her head to the side, a tiny smile flirting at the edges of her mouth. "Such as?"

He had nothing, really. But he took a stab at it anyway. "The Night That *Did* Happen?"

"Ugh."

"Okay, fine," he admitted. "That's not my best work."

"True." She fiddled with the top snap on his shirt. "How about Best One-Night Stand in the History of All the One-Night Stands Forever and Ever?"

"I love it. But it might be a tad long. Also, it's seven months later and here you are in my arms. Our first night is disqualified as a one-night stand."

"A Hookup to Remember?"

He scoffed. "Now you're insulting the wonder that is us."

"Best New Year's Eve Ever?" She popped that top snap. "Our First Night?" The second snap gave way.

She pressed her lips to the slice of bare chest she'd revealed. "The Night We Could Never Forget?" She popped two more snaps as she rattled that off.

He tipped up her chin and kissed her again—a deeper, hungrier kiss than the one before.

When she dropped back to her heels, she pretended to sulk. "You are ruining my concentration. My brain doesn't work when you kiss me like that."

He bent just long enough to scoop her high in his arms. "It's okay. Right now, let's skip the thinking and get down to the action."

She laughed and grabbed him around the neck. "Wait a minute. We should clear the table first. I'll do it—after all, you cooked."

He eased her feet to the floor. "Let me help." He swept out an arm. Dishes, spoons and glassware crashed to the floor. Slim, snoozing by the fireplace, let out a whine of surprise, followed by a giant yawn.

"Jameson!" Vanessa shrieked as he scooped her up again. "I can't believe you just did that."

"Yeah?" He growled the words against the velvety skin of her throat as he lowered her to the just cleared table. "Wait'll you see what I do next."

She sighed as he kissed her. And then she moaned. And before he finished making dessert of her, she screamed his name over and over again.

That weekend, he took her away—not too far. Just to a family-owned cabin in the mountains a few miles from town. They picnicked in the wildflowers of his favorite secluded meadow and swam buck naked in the icy creek formed by a hidden underground spring.

Saturday night in bed after a couple of satisfying bouts of enthusiastic lovemaking, she stacked her hands on his bare chest and closed her eyes. "I could lie here like this forever."

He combed her hair back from her temples with his fingers, catching a random swatch of the thick, silky stuff and slowly wrapping it around his hand. "Don't get too comfortable. I'm edging up on feeling frisky again."

With a big, fake groan, she rolled off him and snuggled up to his side. "You are insatiable."

"Are you complaining?"

"No way."

"That's what I wanted to hear." He ran his palm up the velvety skin of her back and fiddled with her gorgeous, wildly tangled hair some more. "One more time with you always seems like a great idea. But a gentleman never wears out his welcome."

She reached up, touched the side of his face in a tender, slow caress. Her fingertips skimmed his short beard, skated higher to brush his bare cheek.

He pulled her close enough to kiss the end of her nose. "You seem thoughtful."

"Well, I want to ask you something, but maybe it's too personal…"

He caught those fingers, brought them to his lips and bit the tips, lightly. "Nothing you could ask would be too personal. Go for it."

"You said you were married…?"

Damn. Finally.

He'd been waiting for her to ask about Maybelle. Not so much because he looked forward to telling her what a fool he'd been, but because he wanted to get closer to her. And he'd learned enough from past experience to know that to get closer, a guy had to open up. He had to show a woman the things he was proud of—and the stuff he could have handled a whole lot better.

"Her name was Maybelle. Maybelle Butler."

Vanessa frowned. "Her name's familiar. Should I know of her?"

"Most likely. She's a rodeo queen, a champion barrel racer."

Vanessa drew in a sharp breath. "Petite, right? Acres of red hair? And really pretty?"

"That's Maybelle. Beyond being a star, she's also a fine horse trainer. Six years ago, at the end of the rodeo season, she showed up at the Double J looking for a winter job to tide her over. My dad hired her on the spot to work with the horses. He liked her. Maybelle's a charmer. And he was a little starstruck, that *the* Maybelle Butler had come to work for us. At his insistence, she took the foreman's cottage not far from the main house. It was empty at the time. My mom liked her, too, and extended an open invitation to dinner with the family."

"And what about you?" Vanessa asked that with a playful smile. "Let me guess. After Maybelle started working here, you spent a lot of time at the stables?"

"I did. And I went to dinner at the main house just about every night, because Maybelle did, too. What

I didn't know at the time was that Maybelle had had enough of eating dust. She wanted a rancher with a decent-size bank account. She wanted a chance to take things easy, live the good life. She admitted later, when it all fell apart with her and me, that she'd set her sights on me before she showed up on the Double J asking for work."

"Wait. She went looking for a rich husband and decided you were it?"

"Yeah, but you make it sound so pretty calculated."

"Jameson," she chided. "It *is* pretty calculated."

He gave it up. "You're right. But you'd have to know Maybelle. She hadn't had an easy time of it. She'd been raised in the Bronco area, on a few acres of dry grass and scrub brush ten miles from town—what some would generously call a ranchette."

"So then, she knew all about you and she'd shown up looking for a job in order to get close to you, in particular. You're saying that it wasn't just any rich guy she wanted. She'd set her sights on you."

"That's right. She was open about that with me from the start. She said she'd had a crush on me back in high school."

"You were flattered."

"You bet I was."

"Did you remember her from high school?"

"No."

"Because you hung out with the Taylors and the Abernathys and the other rich kids on the big ranches and in Bronco Heights."

He tugged on the lock of hair he'd wrapped around his finger. "Is that an accusation?"

"Maybe. A little. I was a poor girl, too. I sympathize with a girl like Maybelle. And please continue with the story. I'm through busting your chops just because you're a rich guy—for now, anyway. Tell me more about Maybelle."

"When she was seventeen, she ran away from home in the middle of the night driving the ancient pickup she'd bought from a junkyard and sweet-talked her mechanic boyfriend into fixing up. From her hard-drinking daddy, she stole a horse trailer and the only thing at that run-down ranchette that she loved, a pretty little paint named Fancy Lady."

"She ran away to ride the rodeo circuit?"

"Yes, she did."

Vanessa made a sound of approval low in her throat. "Maybelle sounds like a fighter. I like that."

And I like you, he thought. *So much. Maybe more than is good for me.*

Twin lines formed between Vanessa's smooth, dark brows. "Jameson, you look worried suddenly. What's the matter?"

He shook his head and lied. "Not a thing—and yeah. Maybelle's a fighter, and I liked that, too."

Vanessa watched his face so closely. "You fell hard."

"I did. Looking back, I can see all the ways she and I weren't a good fit. At the time though, I wanted her enough to tell myself it was true. Essentially, I was ready to settle down, get married, raise a family. Maybelle said she wanted a family, too. So we tied the knot. I thought I had it all."

"What went wrong?"

"She'd lied about what she really wanted, but not maliciously. I think, first and foremost, she'd lied to herself. Looking back now, I think that pretty soon after the wedding, she began to realize that being a rancher's wife didn't work for her, after all."

"She told you this?"

"Not till much later. Not till the end. She'd thought she wanted a settled-down life, but then she missed the action, the variety of the rodeo circuit. She craved excitement, and she wasn't getting it living with me on the Double J."

"Then why didn't she just start entering rodeos again? Why couldn't she be a rodeo star and your wife, too?"

"It's a good question. If she'd faced the problem early on and told me about it, maybe we could have worked it out. But in hindsight, I would say her pride wouldn't let her do that. She'd really come on strong about hating the rodeo life, being sick and tired of living from one win to the next, wanting to make a home, have a family. Before we got married, she insisted that she wanted to start trying for a baby right away."

"And you…?"

"I agreed."

"Because of what you said at New Year's, right? That you want kids, the whole family thing."

"Right. But somehow, time went by and Maybelle never got pregnant."

"How much time?"

"Three years."

"Did you guys see a doctor, find out what the problem might be?"

"After we were married a year and a half or so, I suggested that. She put me off. She said everything would be fine. We just needed more time, she would get pregnant eventually, we would have the family we'd planned for. I didn't push. I'm not sure why. I think I was also having second thoughts about our marriage, second thoughts I didn't want to admit to, not even to myself. I should have been more focused on what was really going on between the two of us. That should've come first. But instead, I was all about 'making a family,' as though having kids is how you build a relationship.

"It wasn't really working between Maybelle and me and I think, somewhere in the back of my mind, I did finally start realizing that having a baby when everything felt so up in the air wouldn't be a solution to anything. Maybelle and me, we weren't big on communication. We were drifting apart, and I knew it and I let it happen."

Vanessa laid her hand on the side of his face. "I'm so sorry, Jameson."

He turned his mouth into her hand, breathed a kiss in the heart of her palm. "I didn't fight for her, for what we had. Somehow, by the time a couple of years had passed, whatever connection we'd shared at first was pretty much gone—and then, near the end of the third year, I found the discarded packaging from her birth control pills."

Vanessa's eyes got extra wide. "Wow."

"Yeah. That's when I finally decided to talk to her about it."

"Well, that's good, that you two started talking, right?"

"It should've been, but I was pissed—more than pissed. I was furious. I demanded to know how long she'd been on the pill. She gave my attitude right back to me, said a better question would be when had she ever been *off* the pill, because she hadn't."

"Omigod."

"Yeah. It was bad. I was mad enough to spit nails, and even though I'd also had second thoughts about her and me, about rushing toward parenthood rather than figuring out how to live and work together as a couple, I didn't admit any of that. I made no effort to try to talk to her honestly about it. I went straight to an ultimatum. I ordered her to throw her pills away immediately, or it was over between us. And she said, 'Fine. Have it your way, then. I want a divorce.'"

"Oh, Jameson…" Vanessa cuddled in close. Tucking her head under his chin, she pressed her lips to the side of his throat. "How awful. I truly am so, so sorry…" The words were warm and comforting, like her breath against his skin.

He stroked her hair, then caught her earlobe between his thumb and finger and rubbed it gently. "Yeah, it was a bad moment. I was an ass. Maybelle was scrappy as ever." Looking back now, after the anger and the emp-

tiness that followed, after the divorce and the slow real-
ization that he and Maybelle never really had a chance,
he could almost smile at the memory. "She said it was
just as well I found out that she'd never stopped taking her pills. Said she couldn't go on living this boring
life, said that yeah, she was still kind of crazy about
me, but being a ranch wife? Not for her. She told me
straight out, 'Jameson, I need this marriage to be over
or I will start to hate you, and there's no good in that.'"

"So…?"

"So, it was more than apparent to both of us by then
that the marriage *was* over—that it was pretty much
doomed right out of the gate. She'd lied to me. Looking back, I get why she wasn't real big on open, honest communication. She'd spent her whole life fighting
to make her own way and she had no communication
skills whatsoever. Frankly, I was no better. I was a bad
husband to her, a guy who never made the effort to find
out what was going on with her until it was way too
late. I gave her the divorce. We agreed on a onetime
settlement. I paid her off, and that was that."

"How long ago did all this happen?"

"She moved out two years ago. Haven't seen her
since."

Vanessa tipped her head back. Those dark eyes
gleamed at him. Sometimes when she looked at him,
he felt she could see inside his head.

Finally, she spoke again. "You don't seem bitter."

"I'm past all that, but I was plenty bitter at first. I
told myself I hated her. I thought she'd played me good
and proper. And she did. But over time, I started to

admit to myself that it takes two to make a marriage—a good one *or* one that fails."

"Hmm." Vanessa held his gaze. "I don't know that she played you, really. It sounds like Maybelle played herself. You were collateral damage."

"Ouch."

"What? You'd prefer to think that she played you on purpose, that she used you and took advantage of your trust?"

He laughed then. "Yeah, I would."

She tucked her head down again and muttered something about men under her breath. He decided not to ask what.

"Hey." He curled a finger under her chin, lifting her face up so that she looked at him. Once she focused those fine eyes on him, he rubbed his thumb back and forth across her pillowy mouth. "You're tough on a guy, you know that, Miss Bronco?"

"Just calling it the way I see it."

He rolled to his back and pulled her with him, so all that lush softness ended up on top of him, tempting him. He wanted her again. But then, he always did.

She asked, "You really think I'm too tough on you?"

Gruffly, he commanded, "Kiss me," and lifted his head to capture her lips.

She pulled back to grin down at him. "You didn't answer my question."

"All right. You're a *little* too tough on me, maybe."

"Aww. Poor baby."

"No guy likes to think of himself as collateral

damage, like he's just an incidental bad result from a woman working through her problems."

"I hear you. But, Jameson, isn't it always that way when love doesn't work out? For both people, really? They've been writing songs about collateral damage forever. From 'You Always Hurt the One You Love' and onward. People hurt each other because they're too busy struggling through their own crap to be careful of the other person's heart. To me, that seems better somehow, than to mess someone over on purpose. At the end, Maybelle said she was still 'kind of crazy' about you. That means she really did love you. She just wasn't very good at loving."

"Maybelle being 'kind of crazy' about me is not anything that I would call love."

"I only mean she still cared about you. The way you just told it to me, even at the end she seemed to have real affection for you. That's something, isn't it? That matters."

"Yeah, I guess so."

"But you're not sure?"

"Who can say? Whether she played me or I was just random damage of her acting out her own personal drama, it didn't work out. I felt really bad for a while. But I'm over it now." He eased his fingers up under the heavy fall of her hair and wrapped them around her nape. "Right now, I want you to kiss me. A kiss would make everything so much better."

"How, exactly, is a kiss going to fix anything?"

"Trust me. It will."

"A woman knows not to trust a guy who says, 'trust me.'"

"Do it anyway." He guided her head down so that their lips almost touched. "Make my night. Your kiss is the solution to all the world's problems."

"Oh, you are a silver-tongued devil, Jameson John."

"Kiss me, Vanessa."

On a sweet little sigh, she covered his waiting mouth with hers. He wrapped his arms tighter around her and wished for things he would probably never have.

CHAPTER NINE

AFTER THAT NIGHT at the cabin, the night Jameson opened up to her about his marriage to Maybelle Butler, Van stopped trying to tell herself she needed to pull away. She gave up feeling guilty for not maintaining a certain emotional distance from him.

His honesty about what had happened in his marriage had gotten to her, weakened her resolve not to let him too close. She fully accepted now that, if he'd once been a player, those days were gone. Though she continued to insist that they not go public in Bronco, she gave herself up to spending every moment she could with him.

The next weekend, they made the two-and-a-half-hour drive to Bozeman and stayed at the Armory Hotel in a beautiful, restful suite with a king-size bed and sheets so soft she hated to get out of bed in the morning. In Bozeman, they did all the touristy things. They hiked the Bridger Foothills National Scenic Trail, visited the Museum of the Rockies and the American Computer and Robotics Museum.

Hand in hand, they strolled Main Street downtown,

stopping to window-shop and so she could pick up a couple of souvenirs. It was so good, just to be with him out in the open without worrying that someone might see them together and say something to her mom or Grandma Daisy.

Getting away alone, just the two of them, had her giving more thought to her own insistence on secrecy. Van started to see that her fear didn't really center on her family. She would never move home just because they pressured her to.

The problem lay in her own vulnerable, hopeful heart. Once she outed her relationship with Jameson in her hometown, she would become so much more likely to let herself go further, to start imagining a future with him, to long for a real, lasting bond with him.

That way lay trouble. Tempting, lovely trouble—but trouble, nonetheless.

To give her trust again, take a chance on love again… *No.*

The risk still felt greater than the possible rewards. To give in, let herself fall and believe that he would be there to catch her…

It was asking too much of her battered heart.

As the second week of July became the third and she spent every moment she could steal at Jameson's side, Van somehow managed to cling to their original agreement—that it was only for the summer, that at the end of August she *would* walk away.

So what that the pull between them only seemed to get stronger? So what that she loved being with him, in bed and out?

So what that sometimes she could almost picture a life with him, right here in Bronco, close to her family?

She had her life all worked out, and love would not mess with it. Not this time. She'd been hurt once too often. No way was she headed for heartbreak again.

The weekend after their Bozeman getaway, Van and Jameson decided to stick close to the ranch. Saturday morning, she woke with his arms around her and knew she wouldn't be heading for Happy Hearts to have coffee with Daphne and Evan, wouldn't be there later to help with whatever chores needed doing.

She felt a little bit guilty about that…

But not guilty enough to leave the warm shelter of Jameson's arms.

"Mornin'." His voice was sleep-rough and arousing, as was the feel of his warm palm skating over the curve of her hip and easing inward in search of all her womanly secrets.

She gave them all up to him. Twice. Once with his face buried between her thighs as he coaxed a powerful orgasm from her using his clever mouth and thrillingly rough, hardworking hands. And then, a few minutes later, she surrendered again, this time with him buried deep inside her, rising with her to the top of the world, soaring over the edge into free fall only seconds after she did.

For a while, as the sun rose and sent fingers of golden light easing in around the edges of the blinds, they just lay there together. She felt so close to him, happy and unguarded, completely content.

Which might have been the reason why, later, after

breakfast, when they sat at the long table in his kitchen together, relaxing over that second cup of coffee, she failed to evade when he said, "Sometimes lately, like this morning, I get the feeling you're learning to trust me at least a little."

"I do trust you," she answered softly with a smile to match. "You're a good man, Jameson, you really are."

He gazed at her so steadily as he offered his hand. She took it. They wove their fingers together across the tabletop.

"What is it, then?" he asked. "What happened to you? I know you joke about the players who did you wrong. And I'm sorry for all that. But there's something else, something deeper, I think. Something that happened right here, in Bronco. Something that you can never quite get past, never completely forgive."

She didn't look away. "You're right. My worst heartbreak happened here."

"Will you tell me about it?" He said it so gently, not expecting her to give him her hardest truth, but asking her to share if she might be willing.

That he'd asked so quietly, so hopefully—it mattered. She couldn't deny those deep blue eyes, couldn't refuse him the answer he sought.

She did pull her hand from his, though. She retreated to her side of the table, withdrawing from him, surrendering to her instinct for self-protection. "You would have to promise not to do anything about what I tell you—not to try to track down the people involved. I need your word that you will just leave it alone."

"The people involved?" He kept his voice carefully

controlled—but not carefully enough. "What the hell happened, Vanessa?"

"That." She pointed at him. "Right there. You can't do that. You can't protect me from something that happened years ago, something I've dealt with in my own way. If I tell you this story, you have to let it be."

"I can't promise you—"

"If you can't agree to let it go after I tell you, then I won't tell you." He just glared at her until she prompted, "Yes or no, Jameson? Will you keep my confidence about this or not?"

"Damn it, Vanessa."

"Yes or no?"

He blew out a hard breath. "All right. Yes, I'll keep your confidence. You have my word."

She rose and poured herself yet another cup of coffee. When she held out the pot, he nodded. Once she'd topped him off and put the pot back, she took her seat again.

How to even begin? "When I was thirteen, I fell in love with my best friend…"

Taking care not to use any names, she told him about her love for Donnie Bell. Jameson sat there, barely moving, his gaze holding hers, as she spoke.

"I believed," she said, "I really did, that he and I were forever. That nothing could rip us apart…"

Jameson listened, eyes locked on her, never once glancing away, as she told him everything, how the boy she loved betrayed her for a prettier, more popular girl, a girl with a rich dad who could offer him a better future. She told how Donnie came back to her—

for one night—and then betrayed her all over again the next day.

"The new girlfriend and *her* friends, they were brutal. They called me a lot of ugly names, said I was a cheat and a man stealer, a lowlife, a loser and, well, you know—all the awful words they use on girls sometimes. They tripped me in the halls, scrawled really disgusting things on my locker, even broke into it, tore up my stuff and then lit it all on fire."

He asked why the school hadn't done something.

"Nobody talked and nobody got caught. I knew who did what—they made sure that I knew—but that doesn't mean I could prove anything."

"What about the guy?" demanded Jameson, his eyes hard now, angry, a muscle ticking in his jaw. "Seems to me like he was the lowlife."

"Jameson." She adjusted her black-framed glasses on the bridge of her nose. "It was high school. I was an idiot to go back for more with him, to believe him when he swore he'd made a big mistake and he would never, ever hurt me again. I should have learned my lesson about him when he dumped me the first time."

"Just give me that douchebag's name."

Had she known that was coming? Yeah. "Not going to happen. You gave me your word that you would stay out of it."

"Who else knows about this?"

"A few of my closest girlfriends, a therapist I saw a few years later—and now you. Other than that, no one."

"What about your mother, your grandmother, your brother?"

"No way. Evan would have hit the roof and gone after my old boyfriend just the same as you want to do right now."

"A man needs to protect the people he—"

"Stop. Look, my family knew it hadn't worked out with that boy and that I was heartbroken over it. But that's all they knew. It was my battle. I fought it. And it's long over now."

"It's not over if you won't ever even consider living in Bronco again because of what happened back then."

"Stop. I mean it. You're just proving to me why I never should have told you a thing."

Silence. A bleak one. They scowled at each other across the suddenly yawning span of the tabletop.

Finally, his expression softened. He asked gently, with care, with respect, "Tell me the rest?"

"Not if you're going to go all caveman on me."

"You're right. I gave my word, and I will stick by it. I'll keep my shit together."

She probably shouldn't tell him. What good would it do, really, to share her ultimate teenage humiliation with him?

But she really did care for him so much now. She wanted him to understand why she was who she was, why she could only go so far with him. "You know Digger's Trail?" In densely wooded wilderness a few miles from town, Digger's Trail wound upward into the mountains.

"Yeah, I know it."

"I used to go there to get away by myself, when things were rough, when I needed to be alone. Before we broke up, I would go with the boy who dumped me. Anyway, a few weeks before high school graduation, those girls who were bullying me, they followed me up there…"

Even nine years later, it made her heart beat a lurching rhythm in her chest, caused sweat to break out on her upper lip, to remember it, the way they'd surrounded her, slapped at her, mocked her, called her all the usual hideous, cruel names.

"They had a rope. They overpowered me and tied me to a tree. They put a burlap sack over my head and left me there."

"My God. For how long?"

"A few hours. Eventually, a couple of tourists found me."

"Tell me you went to the sheriff."

"No, I did not. The tourists tried to talk me into reporting the incident. I refused. I thanked them. I said I was fine, and I went home."

"Fine? You weren't fine."

"No, I wasn't. But that's what I did, the choice that I made at the time. I was eighteen and I had my pride, and I decided to handle it myself."

"How badly were you injured?"

"Not at all—not physically, anyway. All they did was slap me around and back me into the tree so that one of them could throw the rope around me and they could tie me up."

"It was still an assault."

"Yeah. But I'll say it again. I did what I did, and it was a long time ago."

"But you did retaliate?"

She nodded. "That night, I broke into the school, jimmied open their lockers, tore up what was inside them and poured pancake syrup on what I'd already ripped to pieces. Nobody caught me, and I felt vindicated."

"And then what?"

"And that's all. Believe it or not, after that, it was over. Those girls never bothered me again and the boy stayed clear of me. Looking back, I think maybe those girls actually scared themselves with what they did to me on Digger's Trail."

"You could have been attacked by a cougar or a bear. You could've—"

"I know. And after that, I was angry for a long time. Nobody messed with me. Everyone left me alone, and I was fine with that. I was through with Bronco High and the boy who broke my heart and those mean girls and everything else about this town. I left for college in the fall, and I moved to Billings as soon as I graduated. I've lived there ever since."

He got up, circled the table and went to stand above her. "Come up here. Please." He held out his hand.

She eyed it cautiously, but then finally put her fingers in his. He pulled her up and into his arms. With a sigh, she leaned into his solid strength. "I did get therapy. I worked through it. I really am okay."

He held her a little closer. She felt his lips brush the crown of her head. "You're a fighter, that's for sure."

She looked up at him then. "And believe it or not, the experience has helped me as a teacher. I'm pretty sensitive to what goes on with my students. If someone's being bullied, I usually pick up on it and I take the necessary steps to make it stop. I make sure the offender is dealt with and the victim gets help."

"That's good."

"I think so."

"That old boyfriend of yours still needs his ass whupped, though."

"Not by you, he doesn't."

"I need to ask…"

Something in his voice sent a shiver racing down her spine. "What?"

"The guy who messed you over. Was that Don Bell?"

She gaped up at him, feeling panicked and also immobilized.

And he *knew*. "All right, then. Don was the guy and his wife, Maura, she was the ringleader of those girls who attacked you on Digger's Trail."

Van managed one word. "How…?"

He gazed down at her for the longest time before he answered. "At the barbecue on the Fourth of July, I saw you talking to them. You looked like you couldn't wait to get away."

She held his gaze, and she drilled her point home. "I mean it, Jameson. You gave me your word. Do not go after Donnie—or Maura, for that matter."

"You don't have to worry. I keep my promises. Besides…"

She wasn't sure she liked the look in his eyes. "Besides what?"

"I wouldn't have a clue what to do about Maura. I don't beat up women, and I'm guessing the statute of limitations has run out on what she did to you. As for Don Bell, I saw his face when he looked at you. He knows what he lost. I'm thinking that's payback enough for that sucker."

She was the one gaping now.

Because she believed him.

And not only about what he *wouldn't* do to Donnie Bell.

She believed in his good heart and his kind ways. She believed that he cared for her, that his word meant something to him, and he would always keep it, that he would never thoughtlessly hurt her.

She loved being with him, in bed and out. Lately, when she didn't keep a good rein on herself, she could almost picture a life with him, right here in Bronco, close to her family.

But she had to remember that was only a fantasy and fantasies ended in pain when things went bad. She just wasn't ready go there again. One way or another, it never worked out.

She only needed to hold on to reality. To enjoy this time they had together. And, when the end of summer came, to do what she'd promised to do—walk away.

CHAPTER TEN

GENTLY, JAMESON EASED Vanessa's glasses off and set them on the table. Then he kissed her.

The kiss heated up fast. They ended up in the bedroom once more, naked on the tangled sheets of his bed, holding on tight to each other in a bright pool of morning sun.

After the lovemaking, she closed her eyes.

He held her in his arms as she slept. She looked so peaceful. He stared down at her beautiful, freckled face, and the truth hit him like a damn wrecking ball, square in the chest.

He was in big trouble with her. He loved her.

And she'd been hurt one too many times.

She'd made it way too clear. No matter what he did to try to get through to her, she wouldn't let it happen for them. She would leave as she'd always said she would, head back to Billings at summer's end.

Maybe if he moved to Billings…

He couldn't believe he'd actually let himself consider such a thing. He'd always been a Bronco man through and through.

But sometimes a man had to prioritize, be willing to make changes to get what he wanted most. He could buy good land up there. It was only a couple of hours away from Bronco, and he could come home often, help out here when needed—and run the family AI business from the new place.

A cynical voice in his head mocked, *It doesn't matter what you do. She's not up for forever, fool.*

He knew it in his heart. She liked what they had right now, liked getting close, but with a definite end date.

Lovewise, in her life, the hits had just kept coming. She didn't have it in her to give love another chance.

He knew it. He *got* it. And still, he couldn't stop himself from hoping that somehow the two of them might make love work.

Through the layers of sleep, Van heard her cell ring.

She blinked and opened her eyes to see Jameson smiling down at her. "Sorry. I drifted off."

"No problem. That's what weekends are for." He grabbed her phone off the nightstand and gave it her.

"Thanks." The display, a little blurry without her glasses, said Mom. She put the phone to her ear. "Hey."

"Hello, honey. You sound sleepy. Did I wake you?"

"I stretched out just for a minute. Guess I must've dropped off."

"You're always on the go. You deserve a nap now and then."

Still canted up on an elbow above her, Jameson gave her a teasing smile.

With a playful nudge, she pushed him back to his own pillow. He settled on his side facing her and shut his eyes—apparently stealing a catnap while she talked to her mom.

Wanda asked about Happy Hearts and how the summer camp was going.

"Really well. We're on the reptile unit now. Everyone loves the snakes and lizards."

"Oh, I'm sure they do," said her mom. "You're a marvel with those kids."

"I do have fun with them. Most of them are still at that age where the natural world is fascinating and new. Chemical reactions give them a big thrill, and they get all excited just spotting a lizard sunning on a rock. How's everything at home?"

"All good."

"G-G?"

"Amazing as usual."

"And her new fortune-telling business?"

"Bite your tongue," Wanda chided. "Your great-grandmother does not tell fortunes. She dispenses wisdom. She claims her connections to the paranormal world are real and based on solid science and that her knowledge of human nature goes much deeper than mere fortune telling."

Van laughed. "G-G will always defend her pseudoscience to the death."

"Do *not* use the word *pseudoscience* in your great-grandmother's presence."

"Yes, Mother."

"And, honey, I was wondering…"

"Hmm?"

"The summer is flying by. I know you're busy, but we don't see you enough."

Guilt took a serious poke at her. She hadn't seen her mom, Grandma Daisy or G-G since the barbecue on the Fourth. How was that possible? Almost three weeks had slipped by during which she'd spent every spare moment with Jameson.

She needed to get a grip on herself. Half the reason she'd let Daphne talk her into teaching the Young Adventurers for the summer was the opportunity it would give her to spend more time with her family.

Sitting up, Van pulled the sheet with her to cover her breasts as Jameson sat up and poked a thumb back over his shoulder, indicating that he would leave her to her conversation. She gave him a nod. He rolled off the bed and reached for his jeans.

"You're right, Mom. I miss you guys."

"Come to dinner tonight."

She slid a glance at Jameson. He was watching her, frowning a little as he zipped up his Wranglers. He mouthed the words, "Everything okay?"

Was it? Not really. She'd been ignoring her family to spend all her time with him. That had to stop. But she gave him another nod anyway. He turned to go. When he opened the bedroom door, Slim sat waiting on the other side. The dog gave a loud whine.

"That sounds like a dog," said her mother, as Jameson went out, silently pulling the door shut behind him. "Are you at Callie's?"

Van lied by sidestepping the question. "Dinner, huh? Sure. What time?"

"Oh, honey. That's great. Six?"

"I will be there."

"Bring Callie..." Wanda's voice trailed off and then she added kind of coyly, "Or *another* friend, if you'd like."

Van cringed. Bringing Jameson to dinner on West Street? Not going to happen. That would mean way too many questions she didn't feel like answering. Plus, it would give Jameson the wrong sort of signal—the kind of signal that didn't fit their agreement to spend time together privately, with no one else the wiser. "Thanks, Mom. I'll see you then."

"Wonderful."

They said goodbye.

For a minute or two, Van just sat there, clutching her phone against her chest, staring blindly out the slider that led to a sunlit deck. She felt out of sorts, apprehensive—but why?

Because she couldn't just lie around in Jameson's bed forever, she decided. She needed to stop gazing at nothing and get moving.

Tossing back the covers, she put on her clothes and straightened the bed.

In the kitchen, she found Jameson shutting the dishwasher door after loading in the breakfast dishes. She grabbed her glasses off the freshly wiped table, put them on and then knelt to give Slim a little love.

When she rose, Jameson came to her. He framed her face in his big hands and brushed a kiss on her forehead, just above the bridge of her glasses. "How's your mom?"

"Good, thanks."

"Everything okay with the family?"

"Fine, yes."

He guided a thick swatch of her hair back over her shoulder. "It's a warm day. How about we tack up a couple of horses? I'll show you a pretty, private spot I know right here on the Double J. It's up in the foothills, a little swimming hole. Deep enough for diving with a nice, grassy bank at water's edge to spread a blanket on."

She thought of her real life, of the family she'd essentially been ignoring, of all the ways she'd grown too attached to this beautiful man, of what she'd just revealed to him back there in his bed.

Her family didn't even know about all that. The ones who did know were women—women she trust. She'd never told anyone else. Especially not the men she'd believed herself in love with—not David or Chaz or even open-minded, mild-tempered Trevor.

Only Jameson…

Really, she needed to put a check on herself. She'd said she would go to dinner at her Mom's tonight. And she wasn't about to bring a date.

She needed to pull back a bit, get herself some space, stop neglecting the people she cared about—the ones who would be there for her at the end of the summer when this thing with him came to its natural end.

Jameson asked gently, "What is it? What's wrong?"

"Well, I was just thinking that I've got a million

things to do at Callie's. And then my mom asked me over for dinner tonight. I haven't seen the family for weeks, so of course I said yes. I would love to see that swimming hole. But really, I think I ought to pull myself together and get going."

He seemed to be studying her, but when he spoke, his tone was mild. "Of course. It's important to spend time with the family."

"Exactly."

"I'll get some work done around here today and take my own advice, join the folks for dinner at the main house."

"They probably wonder where you've been the past three weeks."

He had that thoughtful look again as he asked, "Later tonight, then?"

She felt this tug, like a hungry little ache in the vicinity of her heart, as though a strong, secret thread held her bound to him, a thread that pulled her toward him. She wanted tonight with him. She wanted *all* the nights with him. "Yes—I mean, if that's okay?"

"It's more than okay." He touched her cheek, a slow, light caress. Her nerve endings heated and fired in response. "What time?"

"Nineish?"

"I'll be here."

"Okay, then. I'll just grab my stuff and get going."

Fifteen minutes later, Vanessa came out of the bedroom with her suitcase.

Jameson played it easy and cool, though he had a

bad feeling about this. She seemed withdrawn. He worried that she'd find some reason not to keep her date with him tonight.

But then he reminded himself that they both needed to pay attention to the other people in their lives. He had work he'd been putting off in order to spend more time with her.

Today, he'd get stuff done, burn ditches, check fence lines, move ornery cattle to fresh pastures. And tonight—unless she freaked and didn't show—he would find his reward in her arms.

He kissed her at the door, took comfort in the way her body pressed, warm and willing, against him. After her SUV disappeared down the ranch road, he went back inside to change into work clothes.

In the closet, he saw that she'd taken all her clothes with her.

Not a good sign.

They needed to talk—about changing the rules. About taking the next step.

Too bad he had no idea how to broach that loaded subject with her. At least he still had weeks left of summer to find a way to convince her that they could have it all if she'd only give them a half a chance.

When Van let herself into the apartment, Callie wasn't there. She gave her roomie a call.

"Honey, I'm home," she teased when Callie answered.

"Who is this?" Callie razzed her back. "How did you get this number?"

They laughed together and Van said, "I tore myself away from my sexy secret cowboy lover." She put on a sad voice. "But you're not here and I'm all alone."

"Yeah, I'm working till four."

"What about dinner? I'm going to Mom's and you're invited."

"I would love that."

By four thirty, when Callie got home, Van had done laundry, cleaned the apartment top to bottom, showered and changed.

Callie took one look at her and asked, "What's wrong?"

"It's just…" She hardly knew where to start.

"When your voice trails off like that, there's only one thing to do. Have a glass of wine with me and tell me everything."

Callie poured the wine. They sat on the sofa and Van cried on her friend's shoulder because her fun summer romance had grown way too important to her.

When she finally fell silent, Callie asked, "What exactly are you telling me? Does he want to break it off?"

"No. Not at all. He'd have me there with him 24/7 if possible."

"So then, this is a problem, because…?"

"I'm getting way too attached. It's dangerous for me to get attached. When I get attached, something always goes wrong."

Callie made prayer hands. "This could be the time it *doesn't* go wrong. Have you thought about that?"

Van tipped her head back with a groan. "You shouldn't put up with me. You're the best friend ever, way too wonderful and patient with me. I know you're right. I do." She tapped at her temple. "In here. It's just, well…"

"Love has not been kind to you. I get that. Come here." Callie reached out.

Van sank into a much-needed hug. "Thank you," she said when they broke apart.

"For what? I didn't do anything."

"For being here, being my friend."

"I just wish I could convince you that sometimes things actually do work out."

"I hear you." A change of subject was definitely in order. "Let's talk about you. How are things at Bronco Ghost Tours?"

They spent a half hour catching up and left for the house on West Street early.

The whole family was there—including Evan and Daphne. Van took pleasure in watching her mom and Sean together. Her mom seemed genuinely happy with Sean—as happy as Evan was with Daphne. Grandma Daisy talked about the series of watercolors she was working on, and G-G demanded that they all pay her a visit at Wisdom by Winona.

Van loved them all a lot, and she enjoyed the evening.

Except…

Thoughts of Jameson kept intruding. A day away from him and she couldn't wait to throw herself into his arms again. She needed to get a grip on herself, chill a little when it came to him. She needed to give more time to her real life.

For instance, tomorrow. She ought to head over to Happy Hearts early, have coffee with Daphne and Evan, hang around to help muck out some stalls, gather and prep the necessary materials for upcoming projects at Young Adventurers.

Really, she needed to leave the Double J in time to sleep in her own bed for a change. Using Jameson's house as her home base had to stop.

When he heard Vanessa's SUV pull up to the house at nine that evening, relief washed over Jameson, cool and soothing as a dip in a cold creek on a blistering summer day. He'd started to worry she wouldn't show.

But he opened the door, and she ran to his arms. He kissed her hard and deep—and took her straight to bed.

Later, he got them each a longneck and they drank them right there in bed. She laughed at his story about Slim tangling with a garter snake that bit him on the nose and wouldn't let go. He asked about her family, and she said everyone was fine.

They started kissing again and that led to more lovemaking. Around midnight, she fell asleep in his arms.

He woke sometime later, alone in the bed. "Vanessa?"

No answer. The bathroom door was wide open, with nothing but darkness inside. He got up and pulled on his Wranglers. With Slim at his heels, he went out into the main room.

No sign of Vanessa. He didn't really have to check the driveway for her Forester to know she was gone. But he checked it anyway.

He stood on the front step staring at the empty driveway. At his feet, Slim gave a sad little whine. He looked down into those big, soulful brown eyes. "It appears she took off, buddy."

Back in his room, he sent Slim to his bed in the corner and picked up his phone. No voice mail, no text. He started to call her. But come on, what would he say? Would he end up begging?

Vanessa, please. Talk to me. Tell me what's wrong. No.

He needed to wait for the right moment to get into it with her. Two o'clock on Sunday morning wasn't it. He let it go, though he had no idea when he would see her again, if at all.

The next day was pretty bad. More than once, he had to quell the powerful impulse to whip out his phone and call her—or worse, to jump in his pickup and go looking for her.

He didn't do it.

A man had his pride, after all.

Van knew she needed to put up or shut up—to actually talk to Jameson, try to work it out with him, however that might end up going. Or to leave him alone.

Working it out, though? The thought simply paralyzed her.

Because she'd tried to work it out so many times in her life before. And every time, she ended up messed over and left behind. Maybe for once, she should try a different way.

They'd agreed where this was going when they

started in together. She'd wanted it to last until the end of August.

But she needed to face facts here. The longer she let it go on, the more she would suffer when it ended.

All that day, she waffled between letting last night be their final night and simply staying away—or going to him, trying to talk to him, to explain to him, to somehow get him to see that she needed to walk away now, that sticking through another month would only make it harder to say goodbye.

Explaining herself to him—or just disappearing. Both options seemed weak and wrong and selfish. Probably because both options were all three of those things.

Around five, alone in the apartment with Callie still at work, Van made her decision. She would stay away. He deserved better than to have to deal with her baggage and excuses.

Ten minutes later, she grabbed her keys and ran out the door.

Feeling pretty damn low, Jameson sat on the front step with Slim. As he watched the cottony clouds roll by in the wide, blue sky, he kept thinking he ought to drag himself inside, find something for dinner.

So far, he hadn't budged an inch.

"Come on, boy. Let's rustle up some grub."

He was just about to get up and go inside when Vanessa's Subaru came flying over the last ridge on the access road from the highway. Kicking up dust devils, the silver SUV raced right for him. When she turned into his driveway, she hit the brakes hard, spun the wheel and sent a wild spray of dirt and pebbles flying in the air behind her.

Slamming to a stop inches from the garage door, she jumped from the car and ran around the back end of the vehicle as he rose to his height from his perch on the step. Beside him, Slim let out a whine that might have been a greeting but sounded more like pure apprehension.

"Stay, boy," he said low. "It's okay."

Slim plunked his haunches back down as she strode up the front walk.

Stopping a few feet from him and the dog, she dragged in a big breath, swiped a wild curl of hair out of her eyes and announced, "All right. I get that we really do have to talk."

"Come on inside." He spoke softly, soothingly, the way he would to a nervous filly. Turning, he pulled open the door for her.

She marched past him into the foyer. He ushered Slim in behind her and took up the rear. She only got as far as the grouping of oversize sofas and easy chairs around the fireplace. Halting beside the low, long coffee table, she knelt to greet Slim, who dropped to his butt and sat looking up at her hopefully as she stroked his forehead and rubbed his skinny back.

"Right here is fine." She gave Slim one last pat on the head and then rose.

With a low whine, his tail dragging a little, Slim headed for his water bowl. Even the dog knew something bad was happening.

As Slim lapped up water by the counter in the kitchen, Jameson gestured toward a chair. "Let's sit down."

"No, thanks." She stuck her hands in her pockets, her eyes not quite meeting his. "I'll stand."

Judging by the frantic look of misery on her face and the rigid set of her shoulders, he didn't hold out a lot of hope for whatever she planned to say—and that made his gut twist in a knot. She hadn't even dumped him yet, and already he was feeling the pain.

Desperate to make the moment go in a better direction, he said, "I've got an idea…"

She blinked. Apparently, she hadn't banked on him making suggestions before she finished telling him goodbye. "I, um, what?"

"Let's go out, you and me. Right now. We'll have dinner at DJ's Deluxe or that great French place, Coeur de l'Ouest. If you're in the mood for casual, we can get pizza or stop in at Bronco Burgers. It doesn't matter where we go, just that we do it. Let's walk out of here together and go where we want to go and not hide away here like we're some dirty secret."

Those frantic eyes looked as if they might bug right out of her head. "What are you talking about? We've been through this. You said you understood."

"No. I never said that. I don't understand. I want to be with you, so I did things your way. But your way isn't working. It's time we changed things up. Time you got past whatever's holding you back. You're not eighteen, with a cheating ex-boyfriend and a bunch of mean girls on your ass. You're not dealing with Don or

David or Chaz or Trevor. You're with me, and I want to be with you. You are a brilliant, beautiful, grown-up woman, and I think, if you would just get out of your own damn way, you would see that you want to be with me, too."

"No. You're not listening. You refuse to see. I'm not going out openly with you in this town. I can't do that, and you know I can't."

He answered with a sad shake of his head. "Come on, Vanessa. We both know you damn well *can* go out with me tonight. You just *won't*, and that's the plain truth."

Now she looked a little less frantic and a lot more miserable. Her rigid shoulders slumped. "Okay. You're right. I *won't*. That's what I came here to tell you. I considered just staying away, but that felt all wrong."

"And this, what you're doing now—that's somehow *right*?"

"It is right. It's the right choice for me."

"Wrong."

She pressed her lips together and glared at him. "Will you let me finish?"

He returned her glare. "You go right ahead."

"I just… I realized I needed to say it straight to your face, Jameson. Because this isn't anything against you, it really isn't. You are the most amazing man and it's not—"

"Wait. Are you about to hit me with some tired phrase that women always use when they show a guy the door? Are you about to say that it's not me, it's you? If you are, save it. I don't need to hear that crap. I know it without your saying it. Because it *is* you. If we don't work this out, that's on you. I'm knocking myself out here to get through to you, and you're giving me nothing but arguments that don't hold water and a bunch of lame excuses."

"I just… I can't…" She caught herself. "I mean, I *won't*. I won't go there again. I won't take that chance again. I just need to face reality here. It never goes well. It's always a disaster. *I'm* a disaster, romantically speaking." Her wonderful face was a portrait in pain.

His growing exasperation melted away. He wanted to comfort her, but he knew she wouldn't allow him to get one step closer than where he stood now, ten feet from her, at the end of a long gray sofa.

Again, he tried to get her to reason it out. "It's what life is, Vanessa. You fail and fail and every time you fail, you have to pick yourself up and try again. You can't give up—or you'll never succeed."

"It's just not the same for you. You failed once. I just keep doing it over and over. It always has a bad ending for me, and I have to learn to protect myself at least a little. The way I see it, if we walk away now, at least we have a great memory of how good it was for a while."

He hardly knew where to go with that. "But why walk away when we're just getting started? Why walk away when we could have so much more? I've got no intention of messing this up. I want to be with you. I'm open to you. I want it all with you. I want to take this thing between us wherever it goes. I love—"

"Stop. Right there." Her face had paled, her freckles standing out in sharp relief.

How could he get through to her if she refused to hear the words? "You're not even going to let me say it?"

"No, I am not. There's no point in saying it. It won't change anything. You know where it goes. We've been through this. In August, I go back to Billings and we both get on with our lives."

"Just, please, give it a chance between us, Vanessa." Damn. He'd descended to begging. This was bad. Really bad. Still, he gave it one more shot. "Just say yes to dinner at DJ's. That's all I'm asking for. One step at a time."

She made a strangled sound, a sound full of pain. Behind her black-framed glasses, her eyes gleamed with moisture. A tear got away from her and dribbled down the curve of her cheek. Angrily, she swiped at it. "I can't. I'm sorry. No."

No.

And where did that leave him?

Screwed, that's where. "So I guess that makes me collateral damage once again, huh? You said it and I agreed with you. This really *isn't* about me. This is on you, Vanessa. And I'm tired. I'm done. I don't want to give up on you. But what else can I do? A man needs to know when to call it quits."

"Yes." Her voice was so small, so lonely. "You're right. It's not going to work, and it's good that you can see that."

They stared at each other.

There was nothing more to say.

He walked away from her, to the kitchen area and the wide window with a view of the mountains, their craggy peaks reaching into the sky. "Just go," he said over his shoulder.

"Goodbye, Jameson." The words came out ragged but way too damned determined. He heard her footsteps retreating. The front door opened and clicked shut.

He refused to turn from the window until he knew she'd gone. His soul ached at the sound of her car starting up, the engine revving as she shifted and backed out. Finally, she must have put it in Drive. He heard the faint sounds of tires crunching gravel. He stared at the faraway mountains as the sound of her engine faded away.

Behind him, Slim whined. To Jameson, that whine—forlorn, bewildered—said it all.

He turned and met Slim's worried eyes. "It's okay, boy," he lied. It was not in any way okay. "We did what we could."

Slim followed him over to the long gray sofa. The dog sat and stared up at him through sad, soulful eyes. Dropping to the cushions, Jameson put his head in his hands. With another mournful whine, Slim rested his head on Jameson's knees.

CHAPTER ELEVEN

VAN GOT HOME before Callie. She went straight to her room and threw herself across her bed.

She cried for over an hour, stopping now and then to blot her streaming eyes and blow her nose—only to start sobbing all over again.

Finally, Callie tapped on her door and asked apprehensively, "Van?"

She considered trying to tell her friend she was fine. But it would be a flat out lie, a lie that Callie wouldn't buy, anyway. And Van desperately needed the comfort her friend would give her—comfort she knew she didn't really deserve.

She grabbed the tissue box again. Too bad it was empty. With a low moan, she called, "It's not locked!"

Callie pushed open the door enough to poke her head through. Her pretty face fell. "Oh, honey. What's happened?"

Van cast a sad glance at the pile of used tissues in drifts all around her and held out the box. "I broke up with Jabesud, ad I'b all out of tissues."

"Oh, sweetie…" Callie came to her, swept a pile

of tissues off the bed, dropped down beside her and wrapped her in a hug.

Half an hour later, Callie coaxed her into the kitchen and pulled out a stool for her at the counter. "Sit. This calls for tomato soup and a grilled cheese sandwich."

Van blew her nose with a tissue from the fresh box Callie had found in the hall cupboard. "I'm not hungry."

"Too bad. Tomato soup and grilled cheese are what Dr. Sheldrick ordered. You will sit there and take your medicine, are we clear?"

"Ugh. Fine."

Callie whipped up the comfort food and served them both at the counter.

"Thank you," muttered Van after she'd savored the first gooey bite of grilled perfection.

Now Callie looked at her sternly. "I love you a lot. But you've made a giant mistake breaking up with that man."

Van sipped a spoonful of soup. "Noted. Can we talk about something else now?"

Callie changed the subject, and Van loved her all the more for letting it go. Later, they streamed a movie and shared a giant bowl of popcorn.

In the morning, Van got up and went to Happy Hearts. She kept it together, getting through the day's workshop, hanging around afterward to muck stalls and groom horses, mostly sweet old nags who would no longer be breathing if Daphne hadn't provided them a loving place to live out their twilight years.

"Stay for dinner," Daphne urged when Van came in

from the stables. "The family is coming." She meant Wanda, Grandma Daisy and Winona, not the Taylors. The situation between Daphne and her dad had not improved.

Van started to decline the invitation, but why? It wasn't as though she had somewhere else to be. Callie didn't need to spend another evening babysitting her. This way, she would have a reason to keep a smile on her face—either that, or she would have to get honest with the people she loved.

No. Never mind honesty. They didn't need to hear how she'd gotten way too serious about a Bronco man. They wouldn't understand her original plan anyway, how it was all supposed to be fun and casual, something she could easily walk away from. And then she'd gone and let her heart get involved and so had he— which meant she'd had to end it a month early.

None of that would make a lick of sense to them.

Really, would it make any sense to anyone? When she laid it all out like that, she just felt like a fool on top of having a broken heart—one she'd inflicted upon herself.

No.

She would be cheerful and upbeat, and none of them would ever have to know.

It didn't go quite as Van planned. She tried to keep her attitude light and easy, but the family knew that something had gone wrong for her. They each found an opportunity to speak to her privately, to ask what she had on her mind and reassure her they were there for her any time she needed them.

In response, she hugged them and said that she loved them and lied through her teeth, promising she was totally fine.

She felt bad about the lying.

But then her mom took her aside last. It was just the two of them, at the kitchen table.

Wanda asked softly, "Are you happy, sweetheart?"

And it was too much. Van couldn't bring herself to tell one more lie. "I'm doing my best, okay? Just putting one foot in front of the other."

"Is that really enough for you?"

"Of course not. But it's where I am right now—and please don't start in about how I need to find a nice local guy and move back home. I like my life in Billings. It's a good life." And it was. Still, her heart ached to think of returning to her pretty little condo in August. Somehow now, after Jameson, the thought of going back to Billings felt hollow at the core.

Her mom took her hand, turned it over, and gently stroked her palm. "I know you've made a good life there. And, yes, I do wish that you would decide to move home. But that's your decision. I promise I'm not trying to live your life for you."

"Well, I just don't think you approve of my choices."

"That's not so, honey. I don't always agree with you, true. But I admire you. You're a terrific teacher. You have a big heart. You're generous with your time and talents and you've made a meaningful, productive life for yourself. I respect your right to do things your own way."

Van felt ashamed. "Thanks, Mom. I did really think you were judging me."

"I'm not. *We're* not."

Van sagged in her chair and said in a small voice, "I'm sorry if I jumped to conclusions. Over the years, though, you and Grandma Daisy *have* gotten on me now and then about how much happier I would be in Bronco."

"We love you. We want you close. And you're right, your grandma and I have made it painfully clear we wish you would move home. I promise you, though, we do get that it's your decision where you live, *how* you live. As long as you're happy with your choices, we're happy too."

Van told her mom the truth. "Well, I'm not all that happy right at the moment. Does that mean you're going to start in on me to move back here?"

Her mother's laugh was soft and knowing. "Not a chance. I am getting your message loud and clear and I will take it to heart, I promise you. Yes, I want you happy. But I do understand that I can't *give* you happiness. You have to claim it for yourself."

"So where does that leave us?"

"Hmm. That leaves me telling you again that I respect your choices. And that I'm here for you whenever you need me."

They gazed at each other for the longest time. Van was the one to scoot her chair closer to Wanda's. She laid her head on her mother's shoulder with a sigh. "I love you, Mom."

Her mother's arm was warm, comforting around her. "And I love you…"

* * *

Back at the apartment, Callie met her at the door. One look at her friend's determined expression and Van longed to spin on her heel and get out of there.

"This way," said Callie. She took Van by the arm, led her to the sofa in the living area and gently pushed her down. "I realize I didn't come on strong enough with you about the Jameson situation."

"Wait. What? Strong enough?" Where was shy, un-assuming Callie when Van needed her? Ordinarily, Van loved that her friend always told her the truth. Right now, though? No, thanks. "Callie, I told you, there *is* no Jameson situation."

Callie braced her hands on her hips. "Denial is not a good look on you."

"I really don't want to talk about this."

"Great. You don't have to talk. Just sit there and listen. Let me say what I need to say, and then we can leave it alone."

With a heart-heavy sigh, Van slumped into the couch cushions. "Get it over with, then."

"Thank you." Callie dropped down next to Van and shifted to face her. "I just want you think about it. Think about how Jameson treats you, how much he wants to be with you. I think, if you just push your fears aside and look at what he *does*, how he *communicates*, all the ways he treats you thoughtfully, with real care, you will see that he's nothing like the men who hurt you."

"Callie. Those guys were all good to me, too. At first."

"As good as Jameson?"

Van hated that question. It had her thinking of all

the ways Jameson treated her right. Cooking meals for both of them, rearranging his schedule to be with her, planning weekend getaways—to a secluded cabin with all the amenities, to a luxury hotel—getaways that followed her rules of no contact with anyone else in Bronco.

"Okay," she muttered darkly. "The man's a real prize. So far. But that doesn't mean he would stay that way if I hung around."

"What it means is that you need to give the guy a chance."

"You know how many times you've said I should give Jameson a chance?"

Callie scoffed. "Not enough times, apparently. Because you're still not hearing me."

"Oh, but I do hear you, loud and clear. I hear you and I simply refuse to go there. I will not give my heart again and end up getting it back in pieces."

Callie seemed to be running out of steam. She gave it one more valiant push. "Truly, Van, you know you have to keep trying. Not all men are like your dad and those other four losers whose names I don't even want mentioned ever again. You'll never get what matters if you give up now."

"Then I'll never get what matters."

Callie let out a dejected little moan. "You are just making me so sad."

Van took both her hands. "You are the best friend ever. I love that you're trying so hard to convince me to do what you think is right. It just, well, it isn't right for me. And I have to do what works for me."

Callie hung her head.

Van pulled her close in a hug. "Thank you. I mean that." She took her friend by the shoulders and held her away enough to capture her gaze. "Now, can we stop talking about this. Please?"

"All right." Callie gave a weary nod. "I've said what I needed to say and you're still dug in. I give up. Have it your way."

Callie kept her word. Over the next few days, she never once mentioned Jameson.

Too bad Van thought of him constantly. And she remembered everything Callie had said, damn it. She couldn't stop thinking of all the ways he'd shown her how much he cared. And she couldn't stop missing him, stop reaching for him in the middle of the night.

But she didn't take her friend's advice. She stayed away from him. Her fear of getting hurt again had more power than her longing to make things right.

On Wednesday, the third day after Vanessa dumped him, Jameson woke before dawn to the sound of the doorbell ringing. He almost pulled the covers over his head and went back to sleep, but it was time for him to get up and get to work, anyway.

The doorbell chimed again as he stuck his feet in his jeans, zipped up and pulled on an old Grizzlies sweatshirt. "I'm coming! Hold your horses!"

With Slim at his bare heels, he headed for the door.

It was his mom. "Hey." He put on a smile. "You're out and about early."

She folded her arms across her middle and tilted her

chin high. "Chicken-fried steak tonight. It's your all-time favorite, and I am frying it up for you. We never see you. Tonight you are coming for dinner. Be there. Six o'clock." She didn't wait for a reply, but turned on her boot heel, ran down the steps, jumped into the old pickup she often used around the property and drove off.

He didn't want to go. He just wanted to work and be left the hell alone. But once roused to action over one of her children, Mimi John wouldn't quit. If he didn't show up tonight, she would march back over here, Dawson and Maddox in tow. And when she ordered his brothers to drag him bodily to the main house right this instant, they would do it, no questions asked.

Bottom line on this issue: he would end up at dinner with the family whether he wanted to go or not.

He went. At least he got chicken-fried steak with country gravy and buttery, light-as-a-cloud mashed potatoes for his trouble.

All three of his siblings showed up. Charity sat next to him. When she thought no one was paying attention, she whispered, "Everything all right, big brother?"

"Sure. Yeah. Fine."

"I should talk to her…"

He looked at her dead-on. "Don't."

She gave him the sad eyes, but she left it alone after that.

A few minutes later, his dad said, "Jameson, we haven't seen that silver Subaru over at your place the past few days. Everything all right?"

Jameson gave his dad the same look he'd given

his sister—the one that said Randall should drop that subject now.

His dad pretended not to get the memo. "A man can't be sitting around waiting for what he wants to come to him. He's got to go out and go after what's his."

Jameson glared at the spot between his father's bushy gray eyebrows. "Dad. I mean it. Don't."

His family knew better than this—and no, he wasn't surprised they'd all noticed the absence of Vanessa's car in his driveway. Of course, they all knew that he'd been seeing Vanessa. Nothing got by any of them. But as a rule, they had the good sense not to butt in on his business.

His mother settled the matter by chiding mildly, "Randall, let it be." And then she changed the subject. "How's the gravy, Jameson?"

He gave his mom a slow nod. "The best. Thanks, Mom."

The rest of the dinner went by without incident in that no one else tried to bring up the sudden absence of Vanessa from his life. He really didn't want to talk about her.

Too bad not talking about her didn't stop him from thinking of her all the time. He conjured images of her at Happy Hearts leading her Young Adventurers in some new science experiment. He kept remembering her face at the moment she won the Miss Bronco crown, so horrified and absolutely adorable, spitting a giant bite of pie all over her old T-shirt and jeans. Even pissed off on behalf of his sister, he'd thought

Vanessa was about the cutest, most bewildered Miss Bronco he'd ever seen.

He loved the way she treated Slim, always taking time to greet the mutt properly, give him a good scratch around the neck as she let him lick her face. She asked Slim how he was feeling and then listened as if he actually answered her in English. Vanessa was the kind who always made sure Slim got plenty of kibble. She took him out to do his business any time he whined at the door.

Slim missed her. The sound of a vehicle driving by out front would have him racing to the door. Plunking his butt down, staring hopefully at that shut door, Slim would wait for her to come through it.

Since Sunday, she never did.

For Jameson, nights without her were the worst of all. He woke often with his hand stretched out into the cool expanse of sheet where her lush, soft body damn well belonged.

He needed to do something, change something, make a move.

But he couldn't think of any move that would get through to her, help her to see the light, get her to accept that he loved her and wanted to be with her. That she was the one for him, that he was all hers, the man different from all the others, the one who would never let her down.

Thursday morning, he remembered he hadn't picked up the mail in a while. He drove out to the mailbox and gathered the stack of bills and flyers and worthless junk. Back at the house, he tossed his keys on the kitchen table and went through the envelopes and advertising circulars, tossing most of it in a pile to discard.

At the bottom of the stack, he found a flyer for Winona Cobbs's new psychic enterprise. Printed on deep purple cardstock with bright yellow lettering, the flyer announced that Winona could be consulted at her new shop, Wisdom by Winona, located on the premises of Bronco Ghost Tours.

Life! Love! Happiness! the flyer proclaimed in giant shouty yellow caps. The flyer announced that consultations, consolation and excellent advice could all be attained in a visit with Winona.

Jameson stared at that flyer for a good five minutes. For half that time, he was shaking his head. He admired Winona, but that didn't mean he would ever waste good money on a visit to a fortune teller.

He tossed the flyer on top of the junk mail stack— and then snatched it right up again. Sticking it in a back pocket, he scooped up his keys from where he'd thrown them on the table and headed for the door.

At Bronco Ghost Tours, he found that Winona had her own separate building. The discovery brought relief that he wouldn't have to go near the office or the gift shop, where he might run into Vanessa's roommate or even her brother, Evan.

It was something of a shed really, Winona's shop— a very charming wooden shed. Painted turquoise, the rough plank siding had been decorated with stars and crescent moons. Wisdom by Winona, announced the sign above the heavy purple door. To either side of that door, thick curtains covered the old-fashioned double-hung windows. He couldn't see anything inside.

Jameson stood on the step for a few minutes, growing more and more unsure that he had any right to be here. Really, seeking out Vanessa's great-grandmother could end up being just as awkward as meeting up with Callie or Evan.

In fact, the more he considered going through that purple door, the more certain he became that showing up here was a bad idea. Better to just get out. He turned for his quad cab—and heard the door open behind him.

"Jameson John," said a husky voice with only the slightest quaver of age.

Slowly, he turned back to face her. "Winona. Hello."

Wizened and bright-eyed as ever, Winona wore an outfit worthy of his ex-wife, the rodeo queen, including purple jeans, boots to match and a jewel-bedecked purple shirt. On her head she wore a purple turban accented with an enormous gold brooch in the shape of a crescent moon.

"About time you came to see me." With a gleeful little laugh, Winona reached out her skinny, wrinkled hand and grabbed his arm. "Don't dally on the step, young man. Come in, come in. We need to get moving on this."

This, what? he would have asked, if only his throat hadn't suddenly locked up tight.

A moment later, he found himself on the other side of the door. Winona gave that door a push. It swung shut, and semidarkness descended. The only light came from dim bulbs in ancient-looking lamps. Jameson breathed in the heavy scent of incense. It burned in several brass containers set on small tables next to faded wing chairs.

Apparently, this was some kind of waiting room—a very purple waiting room almost completely enclosed in purple velvet curtains. Anchored in the center of the ceiling, the curtains draped outward to the top of the walls. From there, except for where they parted above the door, they hung straight to the floor.

"Winona." He had to pause to clear his throat. "This is very, er, atmospheric."

The old woman glanced around with a grin. "Designed it myself. The older I get, the more I love purple." Her grin flattened out. "Unfortunately, Evan is insisting that I'll have to move indoors. He says we can't possibly keep this sweet little shed warm through a Montana winter." Before he could sympathize with her, she brightened right up again. "All right, then. Let's get started, shall we?" She lifted a hidden split in the curtains, revealing another door that led to a second room. "This way." Ushering him over the threshold first, she followed him in, shutting the door behind them.

He breathed a little easier. No incense burned in this room. And there were no draperies back here, either, just clean walls of a pale, soothing robin's egg blue.

Winona signaled him to take one of the two chairs at a central table of simple bleached pine. "Sit, please."

He sat. Winona perched on the chair across from him.

Feeling nervous as a sinner in church, he coughed

into his hand again—and suddenly realized he hadn't taken off his hat. Swiping the thing from his head, he turned to hook it on the back of the chair.

When he faced Winona again, her piercing dark eyes watched him, seeming to see right to the center of him. Did she find him lacking somehow? "I, uh, always enjoyed that column of yours."

"Thank you." She reached across the table and took his wrist. "Down to business." Turning his hand palm up, she cradled it in her birdlike claw. Bending her turbaned head close, she hummed low in her throat. "Hmm…"

Alarm jangled through him. "What is it? What's wrong?"

She glanced up, sharp eyes pinning him again. And then her face softened. Her voice changed, became gentle, soothing. "Let's just sit quietly, shall we?"

He longed to leap up and run out, but he heard himself answer calmly, "Sure." As he said the word, his urge to run faded. A sort of peacefulness stole through him.

They sat. Minutes ticked by. He felt truly unconcerned, relaxed, certain now that something good would happen. He only needed to be patient, to let the truth unfold at its own chosen pace.

Gently, Winona touched the tips of his fingers one by one. She bent even closer and stared at his open palm.

Again, she made that humming sound.

"Hmm… It appears to me, Jameson, that you are the kind of man who likes to take charge. You don't care for ambiguity, and you do not like to wait." She glanced up, and their gazes locked. "Has there ever been a time when you didn't get what you wanted?"

He took a while to consider her question. "When I was younger, no. Things came easily to me back then."

She chuckled. The small, spare room seemed to fill with light. "You've led a charmed life?"

He glanced around, trying to figure out where the extra light had come from. There were windows on three of the walls, each with white lace curtains drawn shut, letting muted light in that didn't seem to have gotten brighter. And the two lamps on side tables gave about the same amount of light as before. Still, the room did seem brighter.

Winona shook a finger at him. "Pay attention, please, Jameson."

He blinked and sat up straighter. "Sorry, ma'am."

"Answer my question."

"About my so-called charmed life?"

Winona beamed. "That's the one."

"Ahem. Well, yeah. Looking back, I'd have to say that I've had it really good."

"Until...?"

"I got married. It didn't work out. We divorced. She moved away. I felt disappointed in myself, you know? That I never really understood her. And then, once she was gone, I didn't even miss her all that much. I started to wonder if there was something missing in *me*. If I would ever find someone to be my one. To be my only."

Winona held his gaze again. "There is nothing missing in you, Jameson."

Hope rose like a bubble in his chest. He swallowed. Hard. "There's not?"

"Nope." She popped the *p*, looking almost childlike at that moment. "You're on the right path. Patience is required, though. You can't have what you want until the one you want is ready."

"Before she left…" He realized he should clarify. "I mean the one I want. Not my ex-wife."

Winona's smile turned serene. "I know what you mean."

Did she? He really had no idea. But in this quiet, bright little room, just Winona and him, alone, well, it seemed like the right choice to take her at her word. "I started to tell her how I really feel for her. I wanted to let her know what's in my heart…"

Winona said nothing. She waited for him to finish.

He did. "Because I love her."

"But you *didn't* tell her?"

"No."

"You changed your mind?"

He shook his head. "She wouldn't let me say it— and I let her stop me. I shouldn't have let her do that. I should've said it anyway."

Winona touched his curled-up fingertips again, and he relaxed them until they opened as before. "Timing matters," she said. "That might seem wrong. It might even seem unfair. But sometimes, there's no point in saying your love out loud if the one you love can't hear you yet."

"I don't know about that."

Winona lifted one narrow shoulder in a tiny shrug. "Think on it."

"I will." He stared into the old woman's eyes. And the truth just popped out. "It's Vanessa. I'm in love with Vanessa." There. Finally. He'd said it. And it felt damn good to say it, so he said it again. "I love your great-granddaughter."

Winona granted him an angel's smile. "Yes. I know."

Huh? That made no sense at all. "I don't understand. Vanessa said she didn't want her family to know about us. I'm surprised that she told you."

"She didn't. Vanessa never said a word. But I have spent many years watching and learning. Sometimes the secrets of the heart are open to me. I simply *know* things—secret things, the things we all try to hide about ourselves. That first time I met you, at the barbecue on Independence Day, I knew then that you were already falling in love with my great-granddaughter. And the moment I looked in your blue eyes today, Jameson, I knew that it had happened, that you *are* in love with Vanessa."

He had no idea what to say to that. Maybe no words were necessary. After all, Winona clearly had him pegged.

She said, "Sometimes I know the deepest secrets, the ones in people's hearts, the ones they haven't even shared with themselves. For instance, Vanessa…"

He leaned in, eager for anything the old woman might share. "Yes, what? Tell me."

Winona lowered her voice to a whisper. "Vanessa's been hurt. Love hasn't been kind to her."

"I know that. She told me."

"She told you because, deep in her wounded heart, she *does* trust you. And she's hiding the truth from herself. But that doesn't make it any less true."

"Whoa. Slow down a second there. What truth are you talking about?"

"Why, that she's in love with you, too."

Should that news have surprised him? It didn't. He believed that Vanessa loved him—and that loving him scared the hell out of her. What he needed to do next to get through to her, that was the real question.

"And you must be patient," Winona said.

"Yeah," he replied glumly. "You mentioned that already."

"Patient and available, too."

"Oh, come on, Winona. How can I be available when she's already dumped me?"

"Find your opportunities. She misses you."

He shouldn't get his hopes up, but Winona could be so damn convincing. His pulse quickening, he sat up straighter. "You're sure about that?"

"Yes. She loves you and she misses you, she absolutely does. So show up. Let her see exactly what she's missing."

"Winona, even if I could get her to agree to be with me again, it wouldn't be for real, you know? She doesn't want anyone in town to know about us. And I went along with that for a while, I did. But enough is enough. I just don't want to be a secret anymore."

"Of course you don't. And you shouldn't have to be."

"So, how do I make *her* see that?"

"Patience. Don't stay away just because she insists

on terms you can't accept—but don't push, either. She has to come to you in her own time."

He let out a groan. "You don't ask much, do you?"

"Jameson, you have to lose in order to win."

"Winona, what does that even mean?"

For that he got her most beatific smile. "All will become clear. In time. Right now, you need to show up. Your very presence will serve to remind her of all that's at stake."

"Show up where? Are you saying I should stalk her?"

"Of course not. There will always be opportunities for you to be where she is."

"Right," he said bleakly.

"Don't descend into cynicism," Winona warned gently. "Love is on the line, Jameson. Above all, you mustn't give up the fight."

CHAPTER TWELVE

THE NEXT DAY, SATURDAY, Van and Callie were sitting at the kitchen counter sipping second cups of coffee at eight in the morning when the doorbell rang.

"I'll get it." Van got up and went to answer. A glance through the peephole showed her Charity John's smiling face. She pulled the door wide to find Jameson's sister, resplendent in dress jeans and a gorgeous Western shirt, clutching the handle of her makeup kit. "Just thought I'd drop by in case you could use a little extra primping for the ribbon cutting today." The newly remodeled Bronco Convention Center had its grand opening that morning at ten. Miss Bronco was slated to do the honors.

"It's so good to see you." Van stepped back. "Come in."

Charity entered the narrow entry hallway. Van shut the door and grabbed her in a quick hug, one made awkward by the case caught between them. "How 'bout some coffee?"

"Yes, please."

There were only two stools at the counter, so the

three of them sat at the table for a while. At eight thirty, Callie left to run errands, promising to see them both at the ribbon cutting.

"I bought some dressy shirts and hats," Van reported. She led Charity down the hall to her room, took her new Miss Bronco wardrobe from the closet and laid the various pieces out on the bed.

"I love them," the younger woman declared. She fingered the sleeve of one of the shirts. "I think this bronze color is amazing, and I love the gold beading. It's perfect for your skintone. You can wear the chocolate-brown studded jeans with it, the dark boots and dark hat with the gold-colored crystal beading."

Van put the other pieces back in the closet.

"Let me do your makeup, just like old times," said Charity.

Van laughed. "Old times meaning four weeks ago?"

Charity grabbed her in another hug. "I've missed you," she whispered.

"I've missed you, too." Van took her hand. "All right. Enough with the hugfest. Let's get to work."

In the bathroom, Charity plunked the makeup kit on the counter. She took off Van's glasses, tipped up her chin and studied her face. "Your eyes are a little red."

She hadn't been sleeping. Her bed just felt so empty without Jameson beside her. "The contacts have been bothering me," she lied.

"You have eye drops?"

"Of course."

"Use them. And I think you should wear glasses today."

"Miss Bronco in glasses?" Van put on a snooty voice. "Is that done?"

"*You* are Miss Bronco, and you wear glasses—so the answer is yes. It is most definitely done. I think those tortoiseshell ones will look best with that gorgeous shirt..." Charity's voice trailed off. She seemed to gather her courage.

"What is it?" Van demanded.

"I just need to say something. Please don't cut me off."

Van drew a long breath. "All right. Go ahead."

"You could have everything. You're so smart and you are loved, Vanessa." Tears filled her eyes. "I don't know what went wrong between you and my brother, but I do know that whatever it is, you can fix it. You can make it right. I know him. You can trust him. He will never, ever mess you over." Charity pulled a tissue from her pocket and dabbed gently at her eyes.

"Okay." She gave a delicate little sniffle. "That's it, all I needed to say to you—I mean, except that, no matter what happens, I really want us to still be friends."

"Always," Van vowed, as it came to her that her deepest hurts were truly healing, in no small part due to her friendship with Charity. "And I..."

Charity looked at her through hopeful, shining eyes. "Yes? Oh, Vanessa. Whatever it is, you can tell me."

Could she?

She went for it. "The truth is, I have been thinking about Jameson. Constantly. And Charity, you are so right. He's a good man, the best. And I do need to let my old hurts go."

Charity nodded hard. "You need to make room in your heart. Room for happiness."

"I do."

"But…" Charity's smooth brown crinkled. "What hurts are we talking about here, exactly?"

Van gave a tiny shrug. "Well, for starters, disappointments in love. There have been a lot of those in my life so far."

"Jameson won't be one of those guys. He knows how special you are. I meant what I said a minute ago. Jameson will not let you down."

"I know he won't." Van felt strangely breathless. She'd blown it with him. She really had. She'd been too busy protecting her wounded heart to let him in. "He's different. I know it. You're right about that, too."

Charity took both her hands. "I really think you two are meant to be together."

Van couldn't suppress a chuckle. "You're such a romantic."

Charity drew her slim shoulders back. "I am, and proud of it—and don't stop now. Tell me what other past hurts are bothering you."

Van confessed, "Well, in my life there have been some extremely mean girls."

Charity groaned. "Ugh. The mean girls. They're the worst. You have to stand up to them, show them they won't get you down."

"You're right. And I did. And it was a long, long time ago. Long enough that there's no excuse for me not to get past it. Luckily for me, now I have you and Callie and Daphne. Good women and wonderful friends with open minds and big hearts. I feel so grateful for you and for them."

"Oh, Vanessa!" Charity cried, grabbing her in another, tighter hug. "I feel grateful for you, too."

It all seemed so clear suddenly. She'd judged her hometown by the heartbreak she'd suffered in high school. She'd run away and refused to return except for short family visits—because of a boy she'd trusted with everything who then threw her away, because of a group of jealous, vindictive high school girls.

But already, from last Christmas through this summer, she'd forged some wonderful relationships with terrific women right here in Bronco. She'd met Jameson, a man she knew she could count on, even as she refused to let herself trust him. She needed to stop blaming her hometown for Donnie's betrayal and the vindictiveness of Maura and her crew.

She needed to be braver. Truer. To be more like the Bronco women she loved—open, authentic, full of love and understanding, proud to step up and live their convictions.

"What?" Charity took Van's face between her slender hands. "You look stunned. Are you okay? Did what I said upset you?"

"Upset me? No! I'm good. Really, I am. As a matter of fact, I feel better than I've felt in a long time." Even the ever-present ache of loss that had dragged at her since she'd walked out Jameson's door last Sunday had somehow lessened, at least a little. "And what you said about Jameson, I *was* listening. I really was. And

I know you're right. He's a fine man. The best. I promise to take what you said to heart."

Charity stroked Van's hair. "I'm glad." She hugged Van again. "Anytime you need someone to talk to, I'm here for you. I hope you know that."

"I do. And thank you. You know I'm here for you, too."

Charity beamed. "Yes, I do." She turned to her makeup case. "All right. Let's get you ready to wow them at the ribbon cutting."

Charity had plans with her friends for that afternoon, so she and Van drove separate vehicles to the convention center.

When they arrived, the parking lot was already more than half-full. Charity honked and waved Van into the first empty space.

Van parked, jumped out and ran to Charity's side window. "I'm good from here. I'll be watching for you in the crowd."

"I'll be whistling and waving."

Van reached in and squeezed her friend's shoulder. "Thank you. You're the best." She stood for a moment, watching the back end of Charity's cute little pickup until it disappeared down the next row.

Twenty minutes later, she sat in a row of folding chairs on a raised platform erected in front of the new convention center. The mayor and other dignitaries filled the chairs to either side of her. Below the stage, a brass band played a patriotic anthem, and beyond the band, the plaza that surrounded the center was packed with the citizens of Bronco.

All the flags and bunting from Red, White and Bronco had been repurposed to celebrate the dedication of the center. In the distance, the craggy peaks of the mountains pierced the wide blue bowl of the sky. A nice breeze stirred the flags to full, waving glory.

After three rousing Sousa marches, the band took a break, and the speeches began. Van spotted Charity and her parents in the crowd, but she didn't see Jameson. The ever-present ache in her heart intensified.

She needed to make things right with him. She'd messed everything up with her fears and her doubts. And oh, she did miss him so.

Was it too late for them? Had she finally found the right man for her and then destroyed their chance for happiness by walking away?

Right then, over at the podium, the mayor swept out his arm toward the row of folding chairs. "And now, let's give a big Bronco welcome to the little lady chosen to do the honors today. May I introduce our own Miss Bronco, Vanessa Cruise!" The crowd on the plaza erupted in cheers, whistles and excited applause. "Come on up here, Vanessa, and say a few words."

Vanessa played her part. Rising, she swept off her sparkly hat and gave the crowd a big, wholehearted Miss Bronco wave.

They clapped all the louder. She felt their acceptance. Some might have mocked her win at first. But she'd slowly won them over by simply being herself and putting her whole heart into the job.

Leaving her hat on the chair, she approached the podium. The mayor tipped his hat to her and stepped back.

She adjusted the mic and began, "Hello, Bronco!" Again, a surge of applause washed over her. She waited for it to die down a little and then parroted the few remarks she'd planned, all about fresh starts and the importance of community, of people supporting each other, working together. At that point, she was supposed to take the giant pair of scissors from the mayor, step to the ribbon and cut it in two.

But in that split second before she turned to accept the scissors, she realized she had more to say. "I've learned so much since becoming Miss Bronco."

She paused for a slow breath. Out on the plaza, you could have heard a feather float toward the ground. She frowned. "Yeah, okay. I admit it. I didn't enter the pageant to win this honor, and there were ten wonderful contestants who did enter, each of whom had every right to feel a little cheated that I ended up with the crown.

"But every one of those contestants has treated me kindly. Every one of them would have made a great Miss Bronco, I have no doubt. However, thanks to my wonderful, brilliant Young Adventurers out at Happy Hearts Animal Sanctuary, here I am." The whistles and shouting and wild clapping started up again, louder than ever.

The second the sound died down a little, she continued, "And I wear the Miss Bronco crown with pride, thanks in great part to the coaching and encouragement of my fabulous runner-up this year, Charity John. Thank you, Charity!" The crowd went wild.

Again, Van picked up as soon as the wave of sound leveled off. "I know I'm not a traditional beauty queen, but every woman has beauty within her, and none of us should be afraid to let the world see what we know and feel inside." Her voice died in her throat.

But her heart took wings.

Because right then, she saw him—saw Jameson, way back from the platform, working his way toward the front of the crowd. His eyes…they were only for her, locked on her so intently. He wore a look of great tenderness, one that seemed to speak straight to her heart, to say it was far from over between them, after all.

Her vision blurred. Careful of her makeup, she lifted her glasses enough to dash the tears away. And then, drawing her shoulders back, aiming her chin high, Van spoke her truth out loud and proud. "I have known heartbreak. Way too much heartbreak. And this summer, in Bronco, you all have taught me how to get over it—not by hiding what I feel, but by sharing it. I've been so afraid to lose my heart again…" She paused, half expecting the mayor to grab her arm and drag her away from the podium.

Nobody moved. The mayor made not a peep. Out on the plaza, the crowd that seemed to contain everyone in town watched her through wide, rapt eyes.

"However," she said, her gaze locked with Jameson's as he kept moving closer, "sometimes you have to lose in order to win." Another lightning bolt of understanding struck and she found herself remembering something she'd said to Jameson that day he revealed the sad secrets of his failed marriage. She repeated it now, slowly. Clearly. "And sometimes people hurt each other because they're too busy struggling through their own crap to be careful of the other person's heart. I have done that. Everyone messes up now and then. The real progress happens when we learn from our mistakes."

Again, she paused. She drew a deep breath and pictured G-G's beautiful, wrinkled face. Oh, she could feel it now, Winona's love and approval. Winona would be so proud that she'd finally found her own path.

"So I'm just going to say it, right here, right this minute in front of the whole town." She smiled at the man who'd almost reached the platform now. "I have lost my heart to Jameson John—and I'm finally seeing that loving him is the best thing that could ever have happened to me. Because this time, I've lost my heart to the right man, a man I can count on, a man worthy of my trust."

"Vanessa!" Jameson leaped onto the speaker's platform. "I love you!" he shouted, striding straight for her.

The crowd cheered louder than ever. They whistled and threw their hats in the air as the man she loved swept her into his arms.

"I love you," she said, and he swooped down to claim her mouth with his. They kissed for a long, sweet time, the crowd egging them on with more whistles and catcalls.

When they finally came up for air, she said "I love you so much, Jameson," in barely a whisper. Their kiss had knocked her glasses askew. He carefully settled them more firmly on the bridge of her nose.

Behind them, the mayor took matters into his own hands and cut the ribbon. Not that either Van or Jameson cared.

Holding her close, Jameson dipped his head even closer, close enough to speak directly into her ear. "And I want you to know that I honestly don't care where we live as long as I'm living with you. When you leave at the end of the summer, I'm going with you."

"No need!" She had to shout the words to be heard over the clapping and shouting from the plaza. "I'm ready, Jameson, ready to come home for good. I'm applying for a job at Bronco High. One way or another, I'm going to be living here in our hometown."

"With me." It was an outright demand. "Openly."

"Yes, absolutely. With you, for the whole town to see. I love you so much. I've missed you so terribly."

"Never leave me again." His eyes were blue fire.

"Never," she vowed. "I'm sorry I made you a secret. But your willingness to keep it just between us for a while did give us time, at least, to know that we're meant for each other."

"I agree."

She blinked. "You do?"

"Absolutely," he replied. "I thought it over, back the night of the rodeo, after I turned down your offer at Bushwhacker Creek. I figured out then that I would never get a chance with you if I didn't bend a little."

"So that was you, bending, when you showed up at our table during the barbecue on the Fourth?"

"Yes, it was—and dear God, I love you." He touched her cheek with a gentle hand, causing a riot of glorious sensation to flash like sparks across her skin.

"And I love you," she said yet again. "All my disappointments, all my bad boyfriends, my questionable romantic choices, they led me finally to you. Every time I lost at love, I was only getting closer to finding the real thing. Now, I can't wait to see where the future will take us."

"Together," he said in a rough rumble.

"Always," she promised as he pulled her close for another endless, tender kiss.

* * * * *

COMING SOON!

We really hope you enjoyed reading this book.
If you're looking for more romance, be sure to
head to the shops when new books are
available on

Thursday 8th
July

LET'S TALK
Romance

For exclusive extracts, competitions
and special offers, find us online:

 facebook.com/millsandboon

@MillsandBoon

@MillsandBoonUK

Get in touch on 01413 063232

For all the latest titles coming soon, visit
millsandboon.co.uk/nextmonth